Praise for Alan Dean Foster's Founding of the Commonwealth

PHYLOGENESIS
Book One

"Foster does a fine job with his misfit heroes and even with his minor characters (such as the reptilian Aann). He shows his usual mastery of narrative pacing and slips in a great deal of wry wit. The novel will be a treat for those who have followed Foster's tales of the Humanx Commonwealth."

—*Publishers Weekly*

DIRGE
Book Two

"Foster's mining of the human-Thranx affinity continues to yield compelling stories."

—*Booklist*

"Fast-paced action and likable human and alien protagonists."

—*Library Journal*

By Alan Dean Foster

Published by The Ballantine Publishing Group

THE BLACK HOLE
CACHALOT
DARK STAR
THE METROGNOME AND OTHER STORIES
MIDWORLD
NOR CRYSTAL TEARS
SENTENCED TO PRISM
SPLINTER OF THE MIND'S EYE
STAR TREK® LOGS ONE–TEN
VOYAGE TO THE CITY OF THE DEAD
. . . WHO NEEDS ENEMIES?
WITH FRIENDS LIKE THESE . . .
MAD AMOS
THE HOWLING STONES
PARALLELITIES

The Icerigger Trilogy:
ICERIGGER
MISSION TO MOULOKIN
THE DELUGE DRIVERS

The Adventures of Flinx of the Commonwealth:
FOR LOVE OF MOTHER-NOT
THE TAR-AIYM-KRANG
ORPHAN STAR
THE END OF THE MATTER
BLOODHYPE
FLINX IN FLUX
MID-FLINX

The Damned:
BOOK ONE: A CALL TO ARMS
BOOK TWO: THE FALSE MIRROR
BOOK THREE: THE SPOILS OF WAR

The Founding of the Commonwealth:
PHYLOGENESIS

DIRGE

BOOK TWO OF

The Founding of the Commonwealth

ALAN DEAN FOSTER

A Del Rey® Book
THE BALLANTINE PUBLISHING GROUP • NEW YORK

This book contains an excerpt from the forthcoming hardcover edition of *Reunion* by Alan Dean Foster. This excerpt has been set for this edition only and may not reflect the final content of the forthcoming edition.

A Del Rey® Book
Published by The Ballantine Publishing Group

www.randomhouse.com/BB/

Library of Congress Catalog Card Number: 2001116592

ISBN 0-345-41863-8

Manufactured in the United States of America

First Edition: June 2000
First Mass Market Edition: June 2001

10 9 8 7 6 5 4 3 2 1

To John Haynes
Web-site designer *par excellence*

1

Kairuna was kneeling beside a flattened blue-brown bush that rose no higher than his knee, watching half a dozen dull yellow slugs with legs combine their efforts to spin a mutual home out of what appeared to be cerise silk. The nature of the instinct that impelled them to effortlessly meld their minuscule exertions would have to be identified by the xenologists. Absolved by his work classification of the need to analyze or classify, he was free to marvel and wonder at the intricate beauty of the delicate alien phenomenon. He felt sorry for the techs who were required to stop, stand, and interpret. Sometimes it was a lot better just to be able to look.

Straightening, he let his gaze rove over the endless forest. Well, not literally endless. The Earthlike pseudo evergreens only occupied the broad temperate belt that followed the planet's equator. A traveler journeying to north or south would eventually run out of forest and into one of the great ice caps that dominated the surface of Argus V. But since preliminary surveys from orbit had indicated that the forest belt varied between two and three thousand miles in width, there was plenty of room left between the brooding ice for trees.

And for ambulatory life, not all of which was as inconspicuous as silk-spinning slugs. In the two months they had been exploring the planet the surveyors had encountered a number of interesting and exotic larger life-forms. The local carnivores were efficient but not especially impressive—nothing the team couldn't deal with. Their presence added to the ambience of what was proving to be a chilly but otherwise hospitable world.

"Norway." Idar came up behind Kairuna, puffing hard and lugging her tripod-mounted census taker with her. "Western Canada. Tasmania." Slapping her gloved hands together, she began to set up her instruments. Depending on how they were calibrated, they could take an image of a chosen section of ground together with an approximation of every kind and variety of life-form that dwelled therein.

"Kind of cold for me." Kairuna came from and preferred a warmer clime. The pristine atmosphere and the oxygen infused into it by the untouched forest helped to compensate for temperatures that, while remaining above freezing, precluded anyone but stoic fanatics from running around in short pants. He was glad of his insulated jacket and boots.

"Won't keep colonizers from coming." Idar squinted into an eyepiece, adjusted a readout, bent slightly to squint again. "Some folks would call this paradise."

"If so, it'll always be one with limited horizons." Kairuna gazed northward. They were working about a thousand miles south of the northern ice cap, but he still fancied he could see the glint from its leading edge sparkling on the sharp blue horizon.

"So it's not another New Riviera. What would be? But so far it looks as good or better than Proycon, and people are clamoring to settle there." Laboring behind her instrument, the census taker shrugged. "There's still plenty of room available for settlement. Oceans are small because so much of the planet's water is locked up in ice. People will like it here." Raising her head to look over the top of the eyepiece, she grinned. "Should be bonuses all around."

Kairuna contemplated the possibility and found it warming. The gruff voice that chose to dissent made him wince and smile at the same time.

"Bonuses! Ha! I wouldn't count on it!"

Both techs turned a rueful, knowing smile in the direction of the newcomer. Alwyn was a short, stocky, dyspeptic, highly experienced member of the survey mission's support team. Able to raise a shelter, arrange for purified water, or fix an enormous variety of instruments in the field with little more than a pocket repair kit, he was as valuable a member of the expedition as he was personally irritating. Nobody on board the *Chagos* liked him very much, not even his fellow corps members. In addition to recovery and repair, his other area of specialization seemed to be carping and bitching. He did not even have the good grace to shut up when he was working, forcing whichever tech or scientist whose gear he was rejuvenating to have to stand around and listen to his complaining.

He was, however, very good at what he did.

"Why shouldn't we?" The more argumentative Idar confronted the support specialist without hesitation. "It's been years since anybody found a world that was even remotely Earthlike." She gestured expansively at the forest. "Maybe it's only partly colonizable because of the ice caps, but the rest of it, the upper temperate forest lands like this, will draw settlers in droves. You know the rules: Everybody qualifies for a share in the primary finding and exploration benefits." She chuckled. "Even you, unless you want to sign over your presupposed nonexistent bonus to me."

"Thanks," the specialist muttered, "but I'll hang onto the designation, just in case I'm wrong and the government decides to play fair and honest with this one."

"With this one?" Kairuna's heavy black eyebrows arched. "How many primes for colonizable worlds have you been on?"

"Well, none, actually." The small, muscular form turned away. "This is my first."

"This is everybody's first." Kairuna mentioned the obvious while Idar adjusted her instrumentation slightly in order to take a new sighting. "There are a lot more ships out looking than there are habitable worlds being found."

"Right enough," Alwyn agreed. "And half of those seem to be full of giant bugs who've already laid claim to the place."

Idar looked up from the eyepiece of her taker. "The thranx are our friends."

"Yeah, sure," the tech groused. "The government keeps trying to convince us of that. Trying too hard, if you ask me. What about that covert colony they set up in the Reserva

Amazonia? If it hadn't been for that wandering street thug stumbling into the place the rest of us still wouldn't know about that!"

"It was part of a secret government project." Kairuna watched something slim and elegant soar across the clear blue sky. At this distance he could not tell if its wings were fashioned of feather, membrane, or some as yet unidentified organic substance.

Alwyn was nodding vigorously. "Sure was. It was such a secret government project even the government didn't know about it. You ever seen a thranx? I mean, in person?" he challenged the bigger man.

"No," Kairuna confessed. "Only tridees."

"They're ugly little bastards. Like big crickets or mantids with an extra set of limbs." He shuddered. "I don't care what the lovey-dovey we're-all-sapients-together-in-this-galactic-arm propagandists mew. You won't catch me cuddling up next to no goddamn giant bug. And there are plenty of people who feel even stronger about it than I do. Me, if I ran into one, I'd step on it."

"The thranx are a little big to step on," Kairuna reminded him. "Especially for someone your size."

"And they might step back," Idar added without looking up from her work.

Alwyn thrust his chin forward belligerently. "Exactly my point. The galaxy's a vast, unfriendly, dangerous place."

"The more reason to make friends with those who inhabit it alongside us," Kairuna argued.

Lively blue eyes stared back up at him. "The more reason to be careful just who we nestle up to."

The discussion was interrupted—not by the weather or the indigenous wildlife, not by the need to continue working, but by a reverberant, insistent howl. Standing on the little knoll debating interstellar relationships while taking the measure of the alien forest, they turned as one in the direction of the wailing, sonorous bellow. It was unfamiliar to all of them.

"What the hell is that?" Alwyn had walked quickly to the edge of the knoll to gaze with even more than his usual wariness in the direction of the landing transport. Idar's recording was forgotten. Kairuna stood behind the two of them, staring over their heads in the direction of the mournful, insistent howl.

It came not from the vicinity of the landing transport but from the vehicle itself. It was Kairuna who finally recognized it.

"That's the general alert."

"General alert?" The census taker frowned back at him. "What the hell's a 'general alert'? I know all sorts of situation-specific alarms, but I've never heard of a general alert. Especially not on surface." Her expression was bemused as she stared down the hill in the direction of the camp that had sprung up around the landing field that had been cleared to allow shuttle craft a safe place to set down.

"I told you!" Alwyn was irritatingly triumphant. "You can't trust a new world, no matter how benign a face it presents."

In reference to faces, Kairuna wished the annoying service specialist would take his elsewhere. It did not matter that he might be right: The botanist was tired of listening to the other man's ranting.

"Come on," he urged them. "We'd better go and see what's happening."

"General alert." Nodding smugly, Alwyn joined them in descending from the densely forested knob and retracing their steps. "I knew it."

Surrounded by members of the *Chagos*'s staff, Burgess was staring intently at the tridee. Magnification was visual, not schematic, so he was able to observe the craft that had just joined them in orbit in all its alien glory. It was an impressive ship, at least twice the size of the *Chagos*. While the prevalent configuration was similar to that of the *Chagos* and all other vessels equipped with the universal variant of the KK drive, its design and execution differed in a multitude of significant respects.

"Not ours," one of the techs seated nearby murmured unnecessarily.

"Not thranx, either," the first officer added. "Unless they've been hiding something from us. Could it be one of those AAnn ships the thranx are always trying to warn us about?"

Burgess looked doubtful. "I've seen the AAnn schematics the thranx have provided. This design is much too sleek. Could it be Quillp?" Burgess longed for expertise in an area his crew, through no fault of their own, did not possess.

"I don't think so, Captain." Though far from positive, the first officer felt secure in hazarding a guess. If he was proved wrong, he would be delighted to admit the mistake. He hoped he was wrong. The inherent pacificity of the Quillp was well known.

Looking sharply to his left, Burgess snapped a question. "Any response to our queries, Tambri?"

The diminutive communications officer glanced over at him and shook her head. Her dark eyes were very wide. "Nothing, sir. I'm trying everything, from Terranglo through High and Low Thranx to straight mathematical theorems. They're chattering noisily among themselves—I can pick up the wash—but they're not talking to us."

"They will. Keep trying." Burgess turned back to the three-dimensional image floating in the air of the ship's bridge. "Who are they and what the blazes do they want here?"

"Maybe they've already claimed this world." The observation no one had wanted to voice came from the back of the command section. "Maybe they're here to inform us of a claim of prior rights."

"If that's the case," the first officer declared, "they've been mighty subtle about advertising any prior presence here. There isn't so much as an artifact on the planet, much less an orbital transmitter. There's nothing on either of the two small moons, or anywhere else in the system."

"That we've found yet, you mean." Having stated a contention, the dissenter felt bound to defend it. "We've only been here a couple of months."

"Okay, okay," Burgess muttered. "Let's everybody keep calm. Whatever the situation, we'll deal with it. We didn't expect to encounter sapience here, much less evidence of another space-traversing species. They're probably taking our measure as carefully as we are theirs." *But I wish they'd respond to our communications,* he thought tensely.

"Look there!" Someone in the growing crowd pointed.

A second, much smaller vessel was emerging from the side of the first. Winged and ported, obviously designed for atmospheric travel, it began to recede swiftly from the flank of its parent vessel. Its immediate purpose was self-evident. Anything else those aboard might intend could not be divined from tracking its progress.

"Get on to Pranchavit and the rest of the landing party," Burgess barked at the communications officer. "Tell them they're probably going to have company."

Once again the officer looked up from her instrumentation. "They'll want to know what kind of company, sir."

Burgess glanced over at the tridee holo. "Maybe they can tell us."

By the time Kairuna and his companions arrived at the camp, it was alive with questions and concerns, anxiety and confusion. No one seemed to know what was going on, including those who had recognized the audible signal for what it was. Now they troubled themselves with unsupported inferences and paranoid suppositions. In such company, Alwyn was in his element.

Pushing and shoving their way into an already crowded mess hall, the three late arrivals found themselves confined to the narrow remaining open space next to the rear wall. Up by the service door that led to the main stockroom, Jalen Maroto was waving his arms for quiet. When that didn't work, he put a compact amplifier to his lips and simply shouted everybody down.

"Shut up! If you'll just shut up, I'll tell you what's going on." As the crowd noise subsided he added apologetically, "Or at least, what we know."

"I know!" Alwyn was not afraid to proclaim theories where others were hesitant to venture facts. "Something local's finally showed up to cause trouble. What is it?" he demanded to know. "A herd of predators? A fast-mutating plague?"

"There's a plague, all right," the team leader declared through the amplifier, "but it's one we brought along with us." Delighted to take advantage of the emotional release, a number of the assembled turned their laughter in the specialist's direction. Unrepentant but temporarily subdued, he tried to meet the ridicule of each and every one of them with a defiant glare of his own.

"A ship has gone into orbit near the *Chagos*," Maroto informed scientists and support personnel alike. "We don't know where it's from, what species built it, or what their intentions are. So far nobody on the *Chagos*, including the people who are supposed to know about such things, has been able to pull a fact out of a big basket of ignorance."

"They're not thranx?" someone in the crowd wondered loudly, referring to the intelligent insectoid race with whom humankind had been cautiously developing relations over the past thirty years.

"We don't know who or what they are," Maroto replied, "because they're not responding to the *Chagos*'s repeated queries to identify themselves. If they're thranx, they're being mighty close-mouthed about it."

"The bugs may be ugly, but I've never heard of them going mute," Idar murmured softly.

"I know what they are." When no one reacted to his latest assertion of certitude, Alwyn assumed a plaintive tone. "Well? Doesn't anyone want to know what I know?"

"Nobody wants to know what you know, Alwyn, because you never know half of what you claim to know." Unlike his companions Kairuna had the advantage of being able to see over the heads of just about everyone in the crowd.

"Go ahead and mock." Alwyn was confident as ever. "These are the hostile, rampaging, bloodthirsty aliens we've always feared encountering as we extend our sphere of influence."

"I thought the AAnn were supposed to be the hostile aliens," Idar pointed out.

"That's what the thranx claim, but so far we've only the bugs' word for AAnn hostility. No, these are something new.

New and hostile," he concluded with an assurance that regrettably was not born of proof.

"If they're hostile," a contrary Kairuna argued, "why are we still standing here talking? Why haven't they turned this site and all of us to dust?"

"Just you wait." Secure in his latent mistrust, the specialist glanced knowingly skyward.

Aside from the fact that scattering into the trees could be misinterpreted by those aboard the rapidly descending alien shuttle as a hostile gesture, there was—the feelings of a certain suspicious support specialist aside—no overwhelming reason to do so. The parent ship continued to swing in low orbit within viewing distance of the *Chagos*, moving neither toward nor away from the human vessel, its communicators silent, the identity of its occupants still a mystery. No one on board the *Chagos* was surprised when the alien shuttle braked atmosphere and began a swift, calculated curve that would put it on the surface directly in the midst of the survey team's encampment. Indeed, given the ongoing proximity of the two KK-drive craft, Burgess and his fellow staff officers would have been perplexed had the alien shuttle chosen to set down anywhere else.

"No component of the landing team is properly trained to handle a first contact," the *Chagos*'s second officer felt compelled to point out.

"Pranchavit has good people working for him," Burgess reminded the officer. "And Maroto's had offworld experience. Between our support personnel and the scientific complement I'm sure relations will develop in an orderly and prudent manner we can all be proud of."

"What if they can't communicate?" the first officer wondered. "Even the best intentions can go awry if misinterpreted."

"We don't have any choice." Burgess's expression was solemn. "I can't tell Pranchavit and Maroto to ignore the aliens. The rest of us will just have to maintain the alert and hope nothing untoward happens down below." Seeing the apprehension on the faces of his staff he added, "Look, there's nothing we can do from up here. Zdanko's contact team has been back on board for weeks because we didn't find any sentients on the surface in our first month here. Nobody could imagine that they'd show up later. It's never happened before."

"There must be something we can do," someone shouted wistfully from across the room.

"There is," the captain admitted. "Prayer would not be out of order. All of you please feel free to invoke whatever deities enjoin your affection." He turned back to the tridee. "Especially on behalf of those of us who are stuck down on the surface until this situation resolves itself."

Idar and Alwyn stood beside Kairuna as they had been instructed: assembled with the rest of the survey team between the cleared landing field and the trees ready to greet the arriving aliens. Argusian vertebrates soared high above the open grassland, scanning the surface for prey or seeds according to preference. A cool breeze kept the somber proceedings from becoming stiff, making it necessary for the anxious assembled to keep moving in order to stay warm.

"I don't get it." Both arms wrapped across her chest, Idar watched her breath congeal in the afternoon air. "What are we doing here? Not that I'm not as curious as the next person, but I don't see why our presence is necessary. We're not part of any formal first-contact squad."

"Neither is anyone else." Kairuna gestured skyward, once. "The official contact team is stuck up on the *Chagos*. So the job, and the burden, not to mention the responsibility, has been dumped on Pranchavit and Maroto." He gazed across the bobbing heads in the direction of the field, where the leaders of the survey team's scientific and support contingents stood side by side, watching the northern horizon and waiting for something to happen. "Better them than you or I."

"I could do a better job than any of 'em," Alwyn avowed. "At least I wouldn't be standing out there with my ass exposed to the four winds and no gun."

"You heard the appraisal from the experts on board the *Chagos*," Kairuna admonished him. "If these aliens intended hostilities they would already have attacked the ship."

"Not if they're still sizing us up and trying to gauge our strength," Alwyn shot back. "Or waiting to see if we're good to eat."

"What are you doing here, anyway?" Idar challenged him angrily. "If you're so worried about malicious aliens, what possessed you to apply for a position on a deep-space exploration run?"

"Let me guess." Kairuna responded before the other man could reply. "Money."

"Good guess." Alwyn tugged the brim of his warming cap down over his forehead, trying to shut out the wind. "But that's not the only reason. Earth was getting too dangerous. Too many people crammed into too many big cities. That's what the colonies are all about. Room to move around and keep clear of the crazies."

"So why didn't you apply to move to one of the Centaurus worlds, or New Riviera?" Idar wondered aloud. "With your technical qualifications you could have emigrated anywhere."

"It's the same there as on Earth," he responded without hesitation. "Too many lunatics. The only difference between Earth and the colonies is that the more adventurous nuts apply for emigration." He nodded skyward. "Deep space seemed the safer bet. At the time."

"It still is." Kairuna exuded quiet assurance. "I think you're going to be surprised. I think we're all going to be surprised."

"Yeah, we'll be surprised, all right," the specialist muttered. "That's why I'm standing back here, as far away from the designated greeting point as possible. Closer to the forest that way. At least in the woods we'll have a chance."

"You'll have a chance." Idar did not try to hide her distaste. "The rest of us aren't going anywhere. I've got work to do, and as soon as this formality is concluded, I'm going right back to it."

Not deigning to respond, Alwyn turned to his other companion. "What about you, Kai? You with me?"

"Only as far as dinner." The big man taunted him gently. "Why wait for disaster to strike, Alwyn? Why not make a break for the forest now, before the unspeakably horrid alien invaders arrive?"

"Because I'd have my pay docked for disobeying a general directive, and you know it. Go ahead and laugh. We'll see which one of us snickers last, and which of us is still able to do so."

"Hush!" Idar was staring to the north, where the first snow-covered mountains rose above miscolored alien trees. "I think it's coming."

At first nothing more than a distant point of light sifting down through an azure sky, the alien landing craft grew rapidly in size and dimension until its descending silhouette differentiated sharply from the framing clouds. Assembled between field and forest, fewer than a hundred human faces strained to make out the lines and design of the unknown vessel.

As it drew nearer still they saw that it boasted a peculiar arrangement of wheels instead of the familiar, all-purpose struts that extended from the underside of similar human and thranx craft. Half a dozen wings protruded from its flanks, running from the nose all the way back to the tail. This extravagance of lifting surfaces was counterbalanced by an absence of any visible antennae or weapons. Tinted bright yellow, the sides and undercarriage of the alien superstructure were flecked with unfamiliar and indecipherable mauve hieroglyphs.

The landing was smooth and almost silent, as if the pilots had been practicing on similar open fields for years. As the whine of multiple engines became tolerable, hands fell from ears to shade eyes as the craft turned to approach the crowd. There being no need for ceremony while engaged in survey, Pranchavit and Maroto were reduced to greeting the visitors in clean duty clothes. Kairuna smiled to himself. The prim head of the Argus scientific team, at least, was no doubt regretting the absence of his fancy dress uniform.

There was a stirring as the landing craft maintained speed during its turn, and a few of those gathered in front found themselves wondering if perhaps their desire for a good view of the proceedings might not be misplaced. But the many-winged alien lander pivoted neatly on its double set of nose wheels and lined up parallel to the crowd. Those in front relaxed. Nothing of an overtly offensive nature was in evidence. Kairuna knew of several researchers and techs who had armed themselves in defiance of directives. Pistols remained concealed by multiple layers of cold-weather clothing and bulky jackets.

Eagerness filled the air like a cool fog. What would the aliens look like? Would they be atavistically alarming like the thranx? Elegantly handsome and yet vaguely sinister like the AAnn? Or quaintly charming like the Quillp? Humankind had yet to voyage sufficiently far, had still to encounter enough intelligent species, to be blasé at the prospect of meeting still another.

Perhaps they would look like nothing the smooth-skinned simians in their glistening new KK-drive starships had yet met. They might be towering horrors or diminutive pacifists. Or diminutive horrors or towering pacifists. No one knew. The aliens had failed to respond to interrogatives from the *Chagos*, either verbally or visually. Kairuna and the rest of the survey team would be the first to gaze upon these new, previously unencountered alien countenances. He and his associates were acutely conscious of the singular privilege that was being accorded them.

Everyone had been thoroughly, if hastily, briefed. No matter what the aliens looked like, no matter how repulsive or absurd or disconcerting or surprising, all reaction was to be kept to a minimum. There was to be no cheering lest sudden loud noises upset the visitors. No wrinkling of faces, no distorted expressions that might be misinterpreted in the event the visitors communicated by similar means. No expansive gestures in case they asserted themselves in a manner akin to the highly gesticulatory thranx. Response to any overtures and all expressions of greeting would be made by Pranchavit and Maroto. Everyone else was welcome to watch, but in stillness and silence.

That did not prevent Idar from nudging Kairuna in the side as an opaque cylinder slowly and silently descended from the belly of the alien craft. It looked as if a particularly sleek bird was laying an oblong egg. Nearby, a grim-faced Alwyn patted his side.

"Not to worry. I'm carrying a regulation sideshot with a full clip."

"It won't be of much use to you in the brig," Idar hissed at him.

"Both of you, be quiet." Kairuna nodded. "They're coming out. Or something is." The possibility that the aliens might choose to make first contact through intermediaries such as mechanicals could not be discounted.

There were no mechanicals, however. The aliens had chosen to greet the tightly packed crowd of anxious bipeds in person. There were three of them. Nitrox breathers themselves, they were clad only in lightweight clothing of some unfamiliar fabric that shimmered in the bright, cold air, and no helmets or other headgear whatsoever.

The reaction to their appearance was a uniform gasp on the part of the assembled humans. Kairuna was unaware that his lower jaw dropped slightly, leaving him standing in full defiance of orders with a mock stupid expression on his face. Idar stood wide-eyed but with more presence of mind as well as person. Alwyn, whose left hand had been hovering in the vicinity of his concealed weapon, was moved to comment, but mindful of the general directive to keep quiet, he held his peace.

It was a good thing he had the forbearance to keep from drawing the gun. The aliens might not have reacted immediately to its emergence, but his fellow humans surely would have. It was not that his naturally suspicious nature was in any way mollified by the aliens' utterly unexpected and novel appearance, only that he was for once no less shocked than his companions.

2

The reaction on Earth to the announcement that yet another intelligent space-faring species had been discovered no longer dominated the news portion of the general media. People were more interested in the progress of the new settlements being opened in the Centaurus group, the results of the lottery to determine who would be granted emigration visas for New Riviera, the latest DNA-HGH gene splicing scandal involving the parents of would-be sports superstars, whether a new wholly artificial fat-free chocolate was safe for human consumption, and possible ballot fixing involving the two run-off candidates for world council representative from Oceania. As far as relations with nonhuman species were concerned, the vote on the possible expansion of the thranx colony in the Reserva Amazonia and a series of trade overtures from the AAnn Empire drew far more attention than anything that might have happened on far-distant Argus V.

Therefore officials were mildly surprised but hardly shocked when the *Chagos* materialized from the arcane torquing of space-plus into Mars orbit and commenced the far more gradual and easily monitored arc sunward toward Earth. On board was a contingent of officers from the survey and exploration party that had been exploring the Argus system. A sufficiently large, self-sustaining team had been left on the fifth planet of that benign, inviting sun, now named Treetrunk by its investigators, to continue the work of preparing it for an expanded series of studies and the possibility of eventual colonization.

The principal concern of Earth-based authority had been allayed when it was learned that the representatives of the

Pitar, as their name for themselves was transcribed, were not native to Argus V but came from another nearby system entirely. Nor did they, according to admittedly preliminary discussions, have any claim on that particular world, nor any other in the Argus system. Out exploring on their own, they had picked up quantified radiation from the vicinity of Argus V only to discover that it emanated from another ship. Contact had been made, initiated by the Pitar themselves. In this instance of interspecies coming together it was humankind that had been discovered, and not humans who had done the discovering.

Shrouded in procedure and safe from the glare of sensation-seeking publicity, the appropriate personnel were designated and gathered to prepare for the arrival of the representatives of the latest in a series of recently encountered nonhuman species. By now a routine had been developed, rehearsed, and refined. Formal greetings and processing would take place on the island of Bali, a sufficiently isolated yet well-developed site that had been used for such purposes several times previously. In addition to its physical beauty, the island and its man-made shuttle landing strip were situated near the equator, thus allowing for the easiest and most economical lift-offs into orbit. Facilities for the elaboration of contact were already in place, and government operatives who knew how to best facilitate relations would be ready and waiting for the arrival of the incoming visitors.

Those on board the *Chagos* had yet to transmit pictures of the newly contacted creatures, but no one in the government contact offices on Bali or the reception facility that had been established on the nearby island of Lombok nor anyone else on Earth was in any particular hurry. The media could wait to image tridees in person—provided it was a slow newsday. The physical appearance of intelligent aliens had ceased to be an especially newsworthy event nearly a hundred years ago.

So while interested but far from agitated staff waited on Bali and Lombok for the arrival of the new aliens, the *Chagos* was directed into a parking orbit that would keep it isolated from other ships, shuttles, and orbiting stations until the appropriate authorities informed those on board that it was time for the representatives of the Pitar to be received. Quarantine and related biomedical canvassing had already been performed on the ship while it was traveling through space-plus and prior to orbit insertion. If such procedures had not been carried out in the safety of deep space, the *Chagos* would not have been permitted to take up orbit around Earth, much less disembark its esteemed passengers. As a craft equipped with the latest technology for carrying out survey and exploration, the facilities on board were the qualitative if not quantitative equal of anything available at any Earth-based medical agency. Had the tiniest indication of a possibly dangerous bacterium, virus, or other potentially infectious element been detected abiding on or within the Pitar, the *Chagos* would have been stopped in lunar instead of terran orbit, where additional, more intensive tests could have been performed in perfect safety.

According to the exploration vessel's accomplished and experienced medical staff, the Pitar on board carried nothing harmful to humans individually or as a group. The aliens had been completely cooperative with their human hosts, readily acceding to any and all requests for blood, tissue samples, or scans by assorted instrumentation. In fact, they were as interested in the results of such procedures as the men and women who carried them out. To the irritation of their landed colleagues, the *Chagos*'s techs had chosen not to release any information via relay. Like their appearance, the biology of the Pitar remained confined to the storage facilities of the ship. Only enough information was transmitted to reassure the relevant departments in Zurich, Gauteng, and elsewhere that these dozen representatives of a new intelligence posed no medical threat to humankind.

Not only had they been cooperative where biological testing was concerned, the twelve Pitar who had been delegated to represent their civilization had shown no hesitation at leaving their friends and shipmates behind while entrusting their lives and futures to their new human acquaintances. Following a succession of polite, formal farewells, their own craft had departed for home to announce the mutual discovery. Though there had been plenty of volunteers from among the *Chagos*'s crew to travel with them, as the dozen chosen Pitar had elected to do in the company of their human counterparts, the Pitar preferred to proceed in a different fashion, according to their own traditions. Human travelers and ambassadors would be more than welcome in the very near future, Pranchavit and his superiors on the *Chagos* had been assured. The Pitar they were conveying to Earth would establish formal relations and commence arrangements for the exchange of diplomatic personnel.

Events were proceeding so smoothly and the declarations from the *Chagos* were so reassuring that after its first day in orbit no one thought it necessary to further monitor the newly arrived KK-drive craft. So it was that the release of a shuttlecraft from the starship's hold was not noticed until it was skimming the upper levels of the atmosphere, and was not remarked upon until an insecure watcher aboard one of the two nearby orbiting stations tentatively brought the matter of the unscheduled and unannounced trajectory to a superior. That individual regarded the confirming readout in puzzled and then stunned silence before demanding re-reconfirmation. When this was provided, a controlled state of all-hell-breaking-loose promptly went into effect on both stations.

When the situation was communicated to the surface, the relevant authorities had more than a little difficulty accepting the evidence. Ground-based instrumentation confirmed not only the existence of the unauthorized shuttle descent but its path and velocity. No one panicked—no matter what was on board the vessel, it could not be terribly threatening. The shuttle was not large, was not disrupting normal atmospheric traffic patterns, and had promptly put itself in touch with and under the guidance of Denpasar authority. It had begun an unannounced descent but had subsequently taken time to carefully clear its final approach with ground control.

The contact personnel who were hastily summoned from downtime and off-duty to configure an appropriate reception team were bemused and in certain cases angry, but none of them were fearful. The shuttle was approaching openly, if irregularly. There was as yet no evidence of malice on the part of its crew: only a kind of ceremonious irreverence.

By the time the shuttle appeared beneath the low-hanging, moisture-heavy clouds, a proper if irritated greeting party had managed to assemble in the reception foyer that had been specifically designed to put first-time arrivals to Earth at ease. Several high-level executives were frantically checking each other's uniforms while lower-level functionaries busied themselves with more mundane preparations. Behind them, facilities for the unobtrusive scanning and recording of the visitors' shape, habits, and actions were being activated. Everyone wanted another hour, another half day, to ensure that everything was in order. As that was obviously not to be forthcoming, many of them substituted grumbling and muttering for the time they were not to be granted.

Guided in by both land-based and onboard instrumentation, the shuttle performed a near-perfect final approach and touchdown. As it did so, the morning cloud layer began to clear, dropping the humidity level somewhat and alleviating the discomfort the diplomatic staff felt in their hastily donned dress uniforms. After slowing, the shuttle turned at the far end of the artificial runway and taxied slowly over to the reception hall, bypassing the main terminal.

As soon as it stopped, several of the senior diplomats strode forward to await disembarkation. They were dressed neatly but not flashily, having no wish to overpower the traditionally disoriented visitors with an overabundance of personal color and light. They wore no arms, nor was any sort of formal military color guard in evidence. Everything about the ceremony had been designed to put cautious, hesitant visitors at ease while impressing upon them the friendliness as well as the determination of the united peoples of Earth.

The forward door opened, and a disembarkation ramp was lowered. The diplomats waited expectantly, naturally curious but far from anxious. After all, the explorers had already communicated the fact that the aliens were unaggressive nitrox breathers. Shape and size and the style of visible organs of perception were no longer a novelty to the team of experienced professionals.

No one was prepared for what they saw, and the shock that ran through the small cluster of official greeters was almost palpable enough to set the seismographs located at the base of Mount Agung to stuttering. Despite intensive training, despite the presence of men and women who were experienced as well as highly qualified, despite the cushion of written procedure and the absence of a need to improvise for virtually any conceivable situation, for a long, long moment no one in the clutch of official greeters and welcomers had anything to say. It was extraordinary. It was unprecedented.

Most remarkably of all, the temporary paralysis extended even to the perpetually jaded representatives of the media who were on hand for the occasion.

Siringh Pranchavit, the leader of the survey team that had been exploring Argus V, led the way, accompanied by several of his top aides. Not all were present, a number having been chosen to remain behind to continue the work on that promising new world. Accompanying the scientists and researchers were officers of the *Chagos* itself. Behind them and in advance of representative members of the ship's crew were the aliens. As attested, there were twelve of them. Half were male, the other half female. It could have been otherwise, of course, but among the diplomats and media reps present none would have bet half a credit on the separation of alien genders being anything other than what it appeared.

The Pitar were gorgeous. Drop-dead, overpoweringly, stunningly gorgeous. As beautiful as they were human. More properly, they were humanoid, but none present, least of all among the media reps who were now frantically scrambling to make certain their equipment was functioning properly, was prepared to bring up that distinction.

The males were magnificent. Without exception they were tall, though not intimidatingly so, with finely finessed lean musculature and faces that were devoid of blemish or whisker. Their countenances demanded revision of all previous descriptions of "chiseled" features. They were, as far as both the human men and women present were concerned, visually perfect.

As for the Pitarian females, the females were . . . The representatives of the media competed among themselves in a desperate search for superlatives that were neither jejune nor overworked.

Neither Pitarian gender manifested visible discomfort, though a certain understandable nervousness was reflected in their initial comments. After all, despite the reaction of the greeting team, they were participating in initial representations with a newly contacted space-traveling species, physical similarities notwithstanding. The warmth of the greeting that followed as soon as the dumfounded diplomats and their associates recovered their senses soon put the visitors at ease.

Their skin was a homogenous, unvarying bronze hue, made all the more striking by the extreme variance in hair and eye color that the *Chagos*'s scientists assured the members of the receiving team was natural. Blue hair and violet eyes were not uncommon. There were combinations of white and yellow, green and red, lavender and pink that would have seemed shocking on a human but which on the entirely perfect Pitar appeared utterly natural. Their voices, hastily trained in basic Terranglo during the space-plus journey from Argus, were uniformly resonant and mellifluous. They moved with the easy, pantherish grace of natural athletes and politely tolerated the wide-eyed stares of media and diplomatic personnel alike. Only occasional indications of nervousness betrayed what otherwise would have been a confrontation between two species completely at ease with one another.

As the shock wore off, the visitors were escorted into the receiving area. While stunned personnel took over and began processing the Pitarian representatives, Pranchavit and the senior members of his team were quickly drawn aside and hurried into a small conference room whose atmosphere was filled with disbelief mixed wildly with speculation. Kept outside, the desire of certain media reps to gain admittance bordered on the hysterical. Through it all the chief of the

Chagos's scientific complement maintained a calm, though clearly amused, composure.

"What kind of a joke is this?" As an assistant general secretary specializing in human-alien protocol, Dosei Anchpura carried more weight than her slight frame suggested. Presently she had parked her diplomatic skills just inside the door. Immediately behind her, on the other side of the soundproof barrier, media representatives fought to aim their pickup lenses over the shoulders of immovable security personnel.

"Joke?" Smiling absently, Pranchavit considered her question rhetorically. "What joke?" Next to him Werther Baumgartner, a sober xenologist pushing an active seventy, smirked and nudged his companion. "There is no joke."

"This is impossible!" Anchpura looked to her colleagues for support. "These Pitar—those people out there being guided through the processing lines—aren't aliens. They're human. Where'd you pick them up? From a live show on one of the orbiting stations before you came down? Without clearance, I might add, and here instead of across the strait at Lombok, where you belong. Although now that I see the joke, I understand your reasons, if not your motivation."

"Aye," Colin Brookstone put in. "What's come over you? It's a fine joke, I admit, but you'll soon have to call a halt to it."

"Siringh is telling you the truth." Smirk gone, Baumgartner was all serious now, and all scientist. "Believe me, the first time we set eyes on them our reaction was, if anything, more disbelieving than yours."

Ambassador-at-large al-Namqiz, who until now had been silent, sputtered a response. "But how can this be? They are as human as you or I, as anyone in this room." His attention shifted to the tightly packed horde of frantic media representatives who were still fighting to gain entrance to the meeting room. "More human."

Lionel Harris-Ferrolk, Baumgartner's companion in subdued mirth, was the possessor of a reputation that exceeded even that of his two nominal superiors. "Remarkable how after all these years of contact with sapient extraterrestrials we are still hostage to the superficiality of appearance." His reconstructed eyes, small but penetrating, swept over the diplomats assembled in the room. "You are all right, and you are all wrong. They are human to a remarkable degree—and yet not. Not quite."

Al-Namqiz sighed as he took a seat. What had promised to be a traditionally impressive yet routine meet-and-greet had turned into something extraordinary. Eventually he was going to have to face the media. He was not a man, after thirty-four years in the diplomatic service, who desired to do so without answers.

As his two slightly senior colleagues appeared willing to let him do the explaining, Harris-Ferrolk continued. "What we have in the Pitar is either the most remarkable instance of convergent evolution ever encountered, much less demonstrated, or else possible proof of the old theory that the dispersal of the origins of at least certain kinds of life throughout the galaxy, if not the universe, was by some form of seeds or spores, whether aboard meteorites, comets, or some as yet unidentified vector. The Pitar have been very cooperative. I ask you to keep in mind that despite the astonishing physical similarities, which I might add include internal as well as external features, preliminary studies reveal significant differences in DNA. As well, there are other factors at work that would never permit a Pitar to pass for human, or for that matter a human as Pitar."

From the back of the tense, crowded room, a terse question. "What about interbreeding?"

When Harris-Ferrolk looked nonplussed, the more relaxed Pranchavit spoke up. "That is a question I would have expected to come from a representative of the general media, not a member of the diplomatic corps. However, since it has been asked, based on our studies to date we do not believe that would be possible. The mere act of intercourse, which requires nothing more biologically complex than crude physical coupling, is another matter." For confirmation he glanced at his two colleagues, who both nodded.

"Physiological similarities extending beyond physical symmetry and external features suggest the latter should be possible. As we have explained, the Pitar have been most co-operative." He added drily, "You understand this is speculation only. There has been no experimental confirmation of any of this."

"They seem very subdued," someone else ventured.

"They are not demonstrative by nature. Certainly less so than a comparable group of humans would be," Pranchavit replied. "We do not know if this is a representative social trait or if they are simply being restrained in our presence. I can tell you that this is not a function of their isolation here on a strange world. Their manner was identical on Argus V, when they were in the company of their own people. Do not make the mistake of confusing their appearance with that of comparable human counterparts." The researcher shrugged. "Perhaps they are simply quiet by nature. Personally, I find it refreshing."

"Life spans?" someone else wondered aloud.

Pranchavit did not miss a beat. "From what we have told and been able to glean, they are more long-lived than humans. Perhaps on the order of ten to fifteen percent."

"This may not be a properly framed scientific or diplomatic query," inquired one of the younger staff members restlessly, "but—do they *all* look like that?"

Baumgartner nodded somberly. "This group could be taken as typical, yes." In the back, someone whistled softly.

The others could indulge their curiosity. Al-Namqiz, charged with officially welcoming these unexpectedly attractive representatives of an alien species to Earth, was compelled to consider more practical concerns.

"What do they want? Have you talked with them about such things?"

Pranchavit nodded. "Good relations with us and everyone else they may meet. Beyond that we did not much go. Cultural exchanges, tourism, economic cooperation—my colleagues and I felt that these specific concerns did not fall within our purview to discuss."

Then he had not been cut out of the loop. Al-Namqiz felt

much better. "I take it these are not formally accredited ambassadors, and therefore they cannot speak for their government on such matters."

"Only informally," Harris-Ferrolk admitted. "Remember that they were as surprised to encounter us at Argus as we were to see them. They no more had diplomats on board their vessel than we did on board the *Chagos*. Both our ship and theirs were on journeys of exploration. But it was felt by them that contact would be expedited if some of their people returned with us to present themselves to the rest of humankind."

"Expedited isn't the word." Al-Namqiz gestured in the direction of the door, against which the representatives of the media continued to throw themselves like seals heaving themselves up onto a beach. "As soon as they are presented on the tridee, there's going to be a frenzy of volunteers to go and 'visit' Pitar. Or accommodate their representatives here."

"We know." Pranchavit smiled thinly. "Most of our waking hours may be devoted to our research and the rest of our work, but my colleagues and I are not strangers to the human condition. We have been just as affected by their appearance as you all were when they stepped down from the shuttle. They are forthright and accommodating, but somewhat shy. They are willing to cooperate in mutual studies and learning, but only via formal, academic, accredited channels. They have no desire to stroll casually among us, or to allow us to do so among them. At least, that is the situation as it was explained to us. Whether it will change in the future or whether that is a firm and unalterable expression of the Pitarian social ethos it is much too early to say."

"When can you introduce us to them?" The face of the youngest member of the diplomatic team was alert and anxious.

In lieu of Pranchavit's sigh, Harris-Ferrolk responded. "We understand your eagerness. Following the usual final medical checks they must be officially welcomed and then queried. All this they have readily agreed to." He eyed the junior staff member sternly. "We must insist that they be treated no differently than the representatives of any other sapient species, such as the Quillp or the thranx."

"The thranx!" Someone in the back hooted in a reflexively derisive manner.

"Sure," another staff member murmured. "I'll treat them just like I would a thranx. Especially the one with the turquoise hair and the—"

"Quiet, all of you!" Turning in his seat, al-Namqiz glared at his clustered staff. "Difficult as it may be, we will do exactly as Mr. Harris-Ferrolk says. You are all of you professionals. Or at least, I have been given to believe that is the case. A position in a different service can readily be found for anyone who prefers to demonstrate otherwise." For the first time since the visiting scientist-explorers had arrived, there was complete silence in the conference room.

"That's better." The ambassador turned back to the grateful researchers. "If there is anything we need to know before commencing official interaction, however disagreeable or difficult it might be, I will rely on you to inform us and we will deal with it accordingly. Your work must be the foundation upon which we build our relations with these people. Thranx or Pitar, Quillp or anything else, the government of Earth and its colonies treats equally with all other intelligences." For the second time he glared at his staff. "Anyone here have a problem with that?" A single strained, uneasy cough was the only response. "Thank you."

Rising from his seat, he smiled at the three scientists and gestured toward the door. "Gentlemen and lady, if you will lead the way, we will make an attempt to deal with what I expect is by now a rapidly swelling and frenziedly impatient clutch of representatives of the world and off-world media. Meanwhile the immigration and medical people will have a chance to complete their work, and then you may introduce me to our newest interstellar friends. I would appreciate any additional information you can give me that might aid in my dealing with the media, not to mention the government, and that might facilitate the subsequent exchanges between myself, my staff, and our visitors."

It was not easy. While the ambassador took the podium and parceled out answers, the junior members of the diplomatic team and the crew of the *Chagos* were assailed by media reps promising ever-ballooning rewards for any information on the Pitar. Names, statistics, histories, preferences, dislikes, interviews, recorded images—small and then large fortunes were promised to those staff members who could provide them. On an exclusive basis, of course. Bidding reached a fever pitch when it was disclosed by one harried member of the starship's crew that at least a few of the Pitar had mastered a minimum of Terranglo on the journey out from Argus. The prospect of a first interview with one of the magnificent humanoids who could actually respond to questions sent the media reps into a veritable feeding frenzy.

Despite their best efforts and their most enticing blandishments, nothing came of their desperate entreaties. The aliens remained isolated and in media quarantine until such time as ambassador-at-large al-Namqiz and his staff felt they would be ready to meet the general public. Having been placed under the strictest of injunctions, none of the other members of the *Chagos*'s crew would talk, and the diplomatic staff had little hard information to dispense. As they learned more about their visitors, and with their permission, tiny dribbles of information were passed on to the salivating media.

Not everyone was instantly welcoming. There existed among the population of Earth a sizable minority whose opinion of intelligent aliens could best be described as cautiously paranoid and a smaller segment that was openly and vociferously xenophobic. The revelation years earlier of the secret thranx colony-base in the Reserva Amazonia had not hurt their cause, and they railed continuously and loudly in the media and in the hallways of government against forming anything like a close relationship with any alien species.

But even they were hard-pressed to find much mud to sling at the Pitar. Superficial it might be, but physical appearance went a long way toward swaying public opinion. In that respect humankind had changed little since the dawn of civilization.

Rightly or not, it was much easier for people sitting before their tridee to envision welcoming a Pitar into their home than a thranx whose appearance might well put them in mind of a cockroach or a giant ant. Still, there was commendable caution and a desire to proceed slowly and carefully among members of all pertinent scientific and governmental agencies.

Then the two Pitar who had become the most fluent of their brethren in Terranglo appeared on the global tridee. As soon as the first one smiled in response to a question, and before he could even answer, systematic caution and scientific restraint was overwhelmed by an outpouring of popular interest that would brook no further interference from any mere official source.

The government tried to keep matters under control but was overwhelmed. Against such a tsunamic outpouring of emotion from its constituents, confronted by an unprecedented outpouring of goodwill and even love, the inherent caution of elected representatives could not stand. The public wanted access to these beauteous, wondrous Pitar, and they wanted it *now*.

Some of the more critical who had contact with the Pitarian representatives thought them standoffish, but the majority put this down to an inherent shyness made all the more charming by their irresistible attractiveness. While not forthcoming, neither were they especially insular. Restricted despite the clamor for their presence to the official contact sites on Bali/Lombok and Zurich, they were quite willing to meet and speak with any humans who desired to pursue personal contact.

Permission to do so was highly sought after, and not only by researchers and professional xenologists. Members of the lay public proffered all sorts of blandishments to those in charge, who were hard put to turn down bribes for access that were often as inventive as they were compelling. But the authorities in charge of interspecies relations were admirably adamant. The Pitar could not be permitted to journey freely among humankind for at least a year, until formal relations had been cemented and all appropriate medical and scientific tests had been carried out. In this the Pitar themselves concurred, for if anything they were even more demanding and insistent that their own procedures be rigorously followed.

Through the world and off-world media humankind was

treated to daily updates on the activities of the aliens. A craze for all things Pitarian swept the globe and spread rapidly to the colonies. Clothing, attitudes, gestures, words, phrases, hair colors—a host of Pitar imitations and imitators made their presence felt culturally. As for scientific advances the Pitar apparently had little to offer that was not already known to their hosts, though they were eager, in their formal and restrained fashion, to learn from humankind.

It would be fair to say that while humans became obsessed with their new acquaintances, the progress of interspecies relations with other intelligences suffered. The thranx in particular were neglected. Perhaps it was understandable that xenologists and specialists found it hard to find the time or enthusiasm to study chest-high bug-eyed antennae-waving insectoids when they could examine in detail physically perfect mammalian males and females instead. Similar sentiments were manifest among the general public.

While tens of thousands of requests for Pitarian attendance at innumerable social occasions poured into contact headquarters on Bali, not one asked for a date with a thranx—not even to talk. It was left to the professionals to maintain the minimum necessary contacts and to assuage hurt insectoid feelings.

Unfortunately, in order to know how to do that properly, considerable further human-thranx interaction was necessary. It was not immediately forthcoming.

3

Hathvupredek stood among the carefully tended jungle plants that thrived in the rich soil that overlay the subterranean, unseen colony and reflected on the alien world around her. She did not fear being seen. Ever since the premature but fortunately conciliatory revelation of the colony's existence some twenty human years previous, it had been possible for those dwelling in the hive below to walk freely on the surface of the world its dominant species egocentrically called Earth—within carefully prescribed parameters, of course. The councilor availed herself of the chance at every opportunity.

It was not Hivehom or Willow-Wane, but it was a beautiful world whose densest and least-disturbed tropical regions were reasonably close in general feel and appearance to that of home. Her ovipositors twitched as she settled herself down on a bench disguised to look like a fallen log, all six legs straddling the supportive cylinder.

In the undergrowth on her left a small, stealthy presence made itself known via a pungency that dominated everything in its vicinity. Her antennae dipped in its direction as she smelled the margay before she saw it. The secretive jungle cat dipped its head, eyes wide, as it took the measure of something too large and alien to eat. Like a puff of mottled yellow smoke, it evaporated into the surrounding verdure.

She did not turn as the organic crackle of crunching leaves and other forest detritus grew louder behind her. The voice was familiar, as was the gently brooding tone. A recent visitor to the colony, Adjami was a world representative from northern Africa. Fascinated by the thranx, he had chosen to linger beyond his designated time frame. In that time, he and the thranx senior councilor had struck up a more than professional acquaintance.

Eschewing ceremony, he sat down beside her, crossing his legs and heedless of the plant matter beneath that might stain his cool-suit. The heat did not trouble him, but he was thankful for the thermosensitive attire that relieved some of the onerous burden of the constant humidity.

They remained that way for some time: resting, soaking in the unspoken pleasure of one another's company, contemplating the surrounding undisturbed rain forest. Then Hathvupredek gestured and clicked a greeting with her mandibles and turned to look down at her companion of the moment. She did not have to hesitate or search for words or sounds, having reason to be proud of her fluency in Terranglo.

"What news for the hive from Bali?"

Reaching up, Adjami stroked his neatly trimmed black beard. His reply was peppered with clicks and whistles acquired from intense study of High Thranx. Many humans in the diplomatic service now utilized such thranx vocalizations, certain sounds providing efficacious shortcuts to specific phrases and intentions. Uncharted and largely unnoticed, a joint manner of speaking was evolving between the two species, or at least among those individuals whose work placed them in close contact with one another. A human diplomat whose hobby was linguistics had even proposed a name for it: Symbospeech. Begun as a game, a diversion, it was maturing into something much more significant. For the most part, the general population of both species remained unaware of its existence.

Especially since the advent of the Pitar.

"The proposed commerce treaty is still under discussion, with the usual adherents champing at the bit and the predictable opponents raining their suspicion on the slightest proposal." He flicked an inch-long ant off his left boot. Gnashing its jaws furiously, it landed in the leaves with an audible *plunk* before righting itself and scrambling away. "Two more cultural exchanges have been agreed upon, and there is finally some progress on the question of allowing the colony here to expand." That was the delicate matter that had brought him to the Reserva Amazonia in the first place.

"These individual humans who object to the details of the commerce treaty," she asked, "why are they so angry at us? Such exchanges can only benefit both our respective economies."

"As you know, the colonies are more enthusiastic." His sarcastic bent, never very far below the surface of his personality, singed the remembrance. "Swap all the painters and sculptors, poets and musicians you want and no one will say much against it. But when money is involved, tempers emerge and blood pressure rises."

"Our blood pressure does not fluctuate as wildly as yours," Hathvupredek murmured. "It can't, or we would blow up."

"Some of us do." Adjami sighed. "Politics can be such a disagreeable business. There are so many times when I wish I had followed my heart and studied archeology instead."

"I can sympathize. Myself, I wanted to be a *pin!!ster*."

He blinked uncertainly. "That is a term I am not familiar with."

"Someone who grows edible plants in an aesthetic manner. It combines your functions of farmer and sculptor. Easier to nurture a covenant with vegetables than with people. Plants do not argue."

Adjami grunted. "The ones in my homeland do. They grow reluctantly if at all. The ground there is obstinate." Reaching down, he dug through the leaf litter to raise up a fistful of dirt. "Not like here, where a little spit will bring forth all kinds of surprising growth."

"Perhaps we should expectorate more on behalf of mutual relations." Hathvupredek was not one to miss the opportunity to prod.

Adjami did not miss the gentle nudge. "I am impatient as well. Formalities should be moving along much faster. So they would be, if not for this recent distraction."

He did not need to elaborate. Ever since the discovery and

subsequent arrival on Earth of the representatives of the species that called itself the Pitar, the expansion of human-thranx relations had been placed on a slow track. The government was devoting the majority of its attention in off-world matters to the new visitors, as its constituents demanded. Relations with the thranx were cast by the wayside, contact delegated to lower-ranking functionaries such as Adjami. Who wanted to meet with bugs when they could sit across the negotiating table from the shimmering, incredibly glamorous Slyl-Wett and her handsome corepresentative Coub-Baku?

Too polite to raise a ruckus, too stratified in their conduct to insist that the humans pay more attention to the development of relations, the thranx ground their mandibles in silence and tried to content themselves with what progress continued to be made. And there was progress, albeit at a glacial pace. Alliances and affiliations that the thranx felt should have been formalized in months now looked set to take years, perhaps decades. There was nothing they could do about it. They were trapped by the admiration humankind felt for the Pitar. Cause trouble, make noise, demand the attention and respect they deserved, and they would only be giving ammunition to their xenophobic enemies within the human community. Naturally patient, their limits were being tested.

They had no choice—not if they wanted relations to continue to progress and improve. Meanwhile, influential thranx who felt humankind wasn't worth the time and trouble were agitating the Grand Council on Hivehom to break off all attempts at multiplying and enhancing relations in favor of maintaining only the loosest and most formal of associations. Who needed the humans, anyway? Yes, they were a numerous and powerful expanding species, but space was vast and there were others, like the Quillp, who were not so easily distracted.

Against this background of measured indifference from the human government and active opposition from the malcontents of both species, concerned individuals like Hathvupredek and Adjami struggled to sustain and strengthen the tenuous bonds between the two intelligences.

"Tell me." Adjami was rubbing a recently fallen leaf between his fingers, wondering what wondrous esoteric pharmaceuticals it might contain. "What do your people think about the Pitar? Officially they've been very reticent on the subject, but I've spent enough time in the company of your kind to recognize that more is being discussed in private than is being said openly." He smiled, showing a number of ceramic teeth. "Though short the requisite number of limbs, I have managed to acquire a small vocabulary of gestures."

She whistled softly, matching his amusement. "I have seen you watching. Many humans watch but do not see. Many see but do not learn. Many learn but easily forget." Truhands flashed. "There is no general consensus on the Pitar. The Grand Council continues to receive and absorb information. As you well know, this new intelligence is reluctant to disclose much about themselves. This invariably makes some of us suspicious."

Adjami looked away. Atop a dead tree, an oropendula was warbling. "It's said they are shy."

"Who says this?" Her tone was sharper than she intended; while more controlled than any human, neither were the thranx devoid of emotion. To calm herself, she recited one of the fifty-five mantras of Desvendapur. "Not the Pitar. To them their reticence to discuss and deal with many subjects is normal. It is the human media who have branded them bashful." Antennae coiled. "Humans evidently find such racial coyness becoming. My people are of a different mind."

"You said some of you find their ongoing restraint suspicious." Adjami gazed curiously into unfathomable, golden, compound eyes. "In what way?"

As would any thranx caught out by a direct question, Hathvupredek first considered what was known and then what was suspected before replying.

"We realize that despite appearances, the Pitar are not you. We are hardly experts in the analysis of mammalian behavior, much of which we regard as impulsive and indicative of an intelligence that occasionally veers into the retrograde. It is not even that we suspect the Pitar of hiding something."

"What could they hide?" Adjami added. "They immediately provided us with the coordinates for their twin homeworlds, which have subsequently been verified. I know of at least two KK-drive ships that have already made passing visits to both. They encountered nothing untoward at either stop, and were greeted in the same cordial, curious, restrained manner that the Pitar have demonstrated during their stay on Earth. There was no ambush, no indication of enormous fleets of armed vessels lying in wait or hiding to avoid discovery. It must be accepted that the Pitar are simply a reticent folk."

"So are the thranx." Despite the human's persuasive reasoning, the councilor knew that her superiors were far from ready to concede the Pitar's benevolence. "It is not that we are distrustful or even especially suspicious. We are simply more cautious in our dealings with other species." She shifted her position on the log bench. "This is not only a racial characteristic. Some of it certainly arises from our delicate dance of disharmony with the AAnn that has been ongoing now for more than three hundred and fifty of your years."

Adjami could not resist a dig. "We've been dealing with the AAnn for less than a hundred years and we've managed to get along. Sure, there have been occasional misunderstandings and minor confrontations, but we've always managed to smooth things over."

"The AAnn are spontaneous. In that they are far more like you than us. But when it suits their needs and aims they can also show patience. They are like a recurring virus that will not go away." All four hands gestured simultaneously. "We desire only to make certain that in the Pitar you have not encountered a species that is even more patient than the AAnn."

"A nicely diplomatic oblique damnation." Bending forward, Adjami picked up a long, thin leaf and chewed experimentally on the stem. It had a slight minty flavor characteristic of many of the alkaloid-laden plants that grew in the vicinity of the colony. "We're being careful."

"No you are not." Hathvupredek's atypical bluntness caught the visiting diplomat by surprise. "You are overcome by these

Pitar, who so nearly resemble physically idealized visions of yourselves. You are dazzled. We are more analytical, more systematic in our appraisal of other intelligences."

Adjami spoke around the stem of the leaf that protruded from between his teeth. "So you're saying we're being naïve."

The councilor's ovipositors flattened slightly, the lowermost curl pressing against the back of her abdomen. "We think you are too welcoming. An engaging trait, but a dangerous one."

Adjami laughed gently. "We're not as ingenuous as you seem to believe. Sure, we've received the Pitar readily, even enthusiastically. But that doesn't mean they've been given the run of the planet or the colonies, or that the appropriate agencies aren't keeping an eye on them."

"We hope so." Hathvupredek's antennae abruptly snapped forward. "What is that?"

Adjami allowed his gaze to be led by the councilor's. "I don't see anything."

"Neither do I," his companion of the morning admitted, "but I smell it. Humans, coming this way. Many of them."

Scanning the trees, Adjami found himself unable to suppress a smile. "You're sure they're not Pitar?"

Hathvupredek missed the sarcasm. Or perhaps the councilor simply chose to overlook it. "Your bodily odors differ significantly. That of humans is much . . . stronger."

"Yes," Adjami confessed a bit reluctantly. "The variance has been noted." He continued to gaze into the forest. "I wonder what a large group is doing here? I'd think that researchers interested in the Reserva's wildlife would avoid the colony site, now that they know it's here."

"They do." Compound eyes and weaving antennae continued to take the measure of whatever was approaching. "As you are aware, visitation to the colony is strictly monitored and is restricted to accredited representatives of your governmental and scientific agencies. Random tourism is neither permitted nor encouraged."

Detecting a rising rustle of leaf litter being crushed underfoot, Adjami rose from his cross-legged seat. "Then I wonder who these could be?"

Man and thranx found out together when the band of perhaps thirty men and women emerged from the trees. The grim, focused expression on each camouflage-painted face was not encouraging, nor was the especially wild-eyed look worn by more than one. Their jungle clothing was in keeping with their obvious desire to blend into the rain forest background. While unsettling, none of this alarmed Adjami. The weapons they carried did.

"Praise be unto Him, what the hell is this?" His startled attention flicked swiftly between implacable, uncompromising countenances. "Who are you people, and how dare you infringe on a species sanctuary! Do you have any idea where you're trespassing?"

A middle-aged man wearing a loose, floppy camouflage hat turned and strode belligerently over to the diplomat. His tone was grindingly cold.

"We know exactly where we are, bug lover."

These people were well equipped, Adjami saw. Were they sufficiently well equipped to steal through the automatic sentries and security apparatus that protected the colony? Any unsanctioned intrusion might logically be expected to come from the air. How well was the colony prepared to protect itself from unauthorized encroachment on the ground?

"If you want to insult me you'll have to do better than that." Behind him, Adjami noted that Hathvupredek had quietly slipped off her bench and had begun to edge backward, toward the portal that led down into the hive.

Grunting an expletive, the armed intruder roughly shoved Adjami aside. The diplomat stumbled but managed to maintain his balance. Several of the trespassing humans had already hurried on ahead to cut off the councilor's retreat. Adjami's eyes grew wide as the full implications of what he was seeing sunk in.

"What do you think you're doing? This is a restricted, controlled area. I am Adjami L'Hafira, an elected representative to the world council! Leave at once before you force me to summon Reserva Security."

Looking him up and down, the man grinned unpleasantly. "With what? I don't see a communicator." With the muzzle of his rifle he gestured in Hathvupredek's direction. "You're just out for a morning stroll with your favorite roach, ain't you? Dirty bug lover. Traitor."

Fanatics, Adjami realized. These were the most extreme representatives of the sizable xenophobic contingent that was opposed to any human-thranx rapprochement. Every political group spawned its fringe element. Here before him were the most radical of that radical band.

"What are you going to do?" he heard himself stammering. He cursed himself for the fear that shook in his voice.

A calm reply can never overcome the wildness of a madman's expression. "Drive them out. Get them off our planet. Send them back to where they belong." The gun muzzle twitched. "We had too many bugs before they came here and we'll have too many after they've packed up and left, but at least we won't be expected to share our lives and homes and resources with them."

Adjami was not sure why he found himself backing up. It was not instinct. That would have dictated that he try to run, in which case they might ignore him. He was not their target, after all. As an experienced politician he could have tried arguing with them, if only to stall for time until local security became aware of the breach in its perimeter. Instead, he backed up, stumbled over and through the forest litter until he was standing in front of the thranx councilor. He could feel hard chitin bumping against his back, and his nostrils were filled with the sweet fragrance of blooming amaryllis.

"I . . . I won't permit this. If you people leave now, if you renew any complaints you may have through the proper channels, I will personally see to it that your views receive a hearing."

"We're done with hearings," snapped a short, frail woman who looked to be drowning in her bulky camouflage gear. To Adjami it appeared that the gun she was cradling was much too big for her. "Half the planetary government is composed of shortsighted idiots who don't see what these filthy creatures are up to, and the other half has sold out in return for commerce we don't need and promises of shared technology that haven't materialized. What's needed is for real humans to stand up and make a statement." With one hand she stroked the inside of her rifle, and in response several telltales sprang to life within the barrel. "A loud statement."

"Get out of the way," someone else said. Inside himself, Adjami shuddered. The voice that had spoken was neither hot nor cold, but something far worse. It was dead inside, the sound of a soul that had already committed ritual suicide and was prepared for death.

Nevertheless, the politician in him would not quit. He had dealt with difficult people all his life. Even when coping with fanatics there was often room to compromise.

"You've already made a strong statement simply by showing up here like this and successfully penetrating hive security." He gestured with a shake of his head. "Go on then; go further. Set off some noisy explosions and make a lot of smoke. The media will lap it up and be all over you for your opinions. There might be some fines assessed for trespassing, but you'll get your views splashed all over the tridee, and nobody will get hurt." Silence greeted his proposal. "What do you say?"

If the group had a leader, and such fringe organizations usually did, that personage chose not to manifest at that time. The middle-aged man who had spoken first provided a response.

"I say that we'll still have just as many bugs to deal with, and we won't tolerate being fined for 'trespassing' on our own soil." Using his rifle, he directed Adjami to move out of the line of fire. "You're a putrid, contaminated bug lover, but you're still human. Get out of the way."

One of the most overlooked components of true heroism is an abiding stubbornness in the face of danger. Lifting his arms out from his sides, Adjami held his ground. As with many accidental heroes, who are the most honest kind, if he had taken the time to consider what he was doing he probably would not have done it.

"No. I won't let you do this." The shakiness had vanished from his voice.

"You can't stop us," a voice in the armed crowd declared.

"And you cannot do this," he replied firmly.

"Sure we can." Raising her weapon, the frail woman with the too-large eyes fired.

Adjami looked down at himself in disbelief. The old-fashioned but still effective projectile weapon had produced a small hole in his shirt. The stain that was spreading from it resembled the rapidly expanding penumbra of a sunspot. It did not hurt in the way the representative believed it might. There was no stabbing pain, no overwhelming throb. Instead, the wound burned as if he had been jabbed with a hot fireplace poker.

Weakness overcame him, and he fell to his knees. Behind him a mellow, calm voice was murmuring in Terranglo. "Thank you for trying, my friend. Intelligence knows no shape. Neither does compassion. *Tchik ua! re!iq.*"

The rest of what Hathvupredek the councilor said was lost in the ensuing staccato of gunfire. When it was over the two bodies, one mammalian, the other insectoid, lay on the ground. The intruders resumed their advance, stepping over and ignoring them both.

There were no weapons in the hive. As guests of an indecisive planetary government representing a mistrustful species, it would have been impolite to stockpile anything that could have been construed as offensive. No one foresaw a need for guns or their presence on what was presumed to be hospitable ground.

Breaking in through one of the lightly barred surface entrances that had been constructed subsequent to official recognition of the colony's existence, the wrathful intruders met little resistance. Distributing grenades and bullets at every opportunity, they rampaged through the stunned hive firing indiscriminately at everyone and everything in their path, making no distinction between thranx "invaders" and human "traitors."

Peaceful though they were, thranx history was a litany of battle, of hive striving for supremacy over hive. More recently, they had been forced to deal with a frustrating, seemingly endless confrontation with the more militaristic AAnn. So the species was not unfamiliar with conflict, either on an individual or racial scale.

As soon as the scope and ferocity of the incursion became known, internal barriers were closed to restrict the range and movement of the aggressors. Arming themselves with tools and kitchen implements, lines of silent, determined thranx converged on the invaders. There was no question of waiting for help from the human authorities, who in response to the distress call from the colony were already on their way to the Reserva. The hive was in danger, and the hive had to be defended.

Many more thranx perished in repeated attempts to staunch the mindless slaughter. So too did several humans who were working or studying in the confines of the hive. The fanatics had come armed and ready to fight. But despite their determination and their murderous weaponry, they were not trained soldiers. The close confines of the hive, whose details were known to its inhabitants but foreign to the attackers, was likewise a detriment to their barbarous cause.

By the time the Reserva rangers arrived, many of the invaders were already deceased or dying, surrounded by small mountains of thranx dead. When the first soldiers disembarked from a transport hastily ordered inland from the nearest military base at Recife, it was nearly all over.

Acclaimed as martyrs by their fellow fanatics and accorded grudging admiration in less demonstrative quarters by their "civilized" xenophobic supporters, the ravagers of the Amazon hive achieved the media exposure the brave, luckless Adjami had foreseen for them. Fortunately, the response of the majority of the population was embarrassment and apology. Reparations proposed by a guilty government were refused with the explanation that the thranx did not believe in materialistic expressions of sorrow. On the other hand, the many letters and expressions of regret from ordinary citizens were received thankfully and with elaborate gestures of gratitude.

Not even such a catastrophe could obscure the effect the Pitar, who considerately offered condolences of their own to their fellow visitors to Earth, were having on human society. A pair (they never traveled alone) even visited the devastated hive to investigate the tragedy and offer commiseration on behalf of their government. Their compassionate presence was duly noted and monitored by the planetary media, who managed to give greater play to the mission of the Pitar than to the suffering of the hive's inhabitants, many of whom had lost friends, coworkers, and even relatives in the debacle.

While the media focused on the origins of the small but lethal fraternity of fanatics and strove to trace their sponsors, and the government representatives assigned to study the disaster tried to piece together evidence that might lead to proof of conspiracy and complicity beyond what was readily apparent, a meeting took place immediately after the confrontation that was to have much more far-reaching consequences for human-thranx relations than the aftermath of the savage raid itself. None present could have foreseen the results. Certainly none could have predicted the direction they would eventually take. In retrospect this was not surprising.

Who could have suspected that greater things would arise from dealing with the future of the dead than the future of the living?

4

Father Pyreau picked up the gun without thinking. Here, in the depths of the alien hive, he was having difficulty breathing. He was mildly claustrophobic, and wide-open spaces and lofty cathedrals were his preferred venue. Deep beneath the surface of the Amazonian earth, lost in a warren of high-tech thranx tunnels, he had long ago loosened his collar.

Lately there were many times, too many times, when he wanted to forget it altogether, to resign his position in the clergy and seek elsewhere the fulfillment that the church no longer gave him. He had been preparing for the regular Sunday service at the base when the emergency call had sounded. Swept up in the uncharacteristic alarm that followed, he had found himself on the transport rocketing inland before he knew what was going on. A superior officer had spotted him and, despite his initial protests, requisitioned his presence.

"I have a feeling your services are liable to be in demand, Padre." The major had not been very informative, but Pyreau could hardly disobey.

Before he knew what was happening they had descended rapidly into seemingly unbroken rain forest, only to find themselves welcomed into a subterranean flight hangar by a milling mass of whistling, clicking, frantically chattering insects. No, not insects, he'd reminded himself. The exotic, visiting thranx were insect*like*.

He had never received a full explanation of the proceedings, not even when he'd found himself thrust forward and carried along with the rest of the hastily organized strike team. The soldiers surrounding him had seemed to know little more than he, but gradually the word trickled back that a small but fanatical band of xenophobes had infiltrated the colony and were killing every thranx in sight as well as any visiting humans who tried to interfere with their bloodthirsty spree. A visiting diplomat and several esteemed researchers had been among the earliest casualties.

Swept into the depths, he had found himself caught in conditions that more closely resembled the traditional biblical hell than anything he had ever experienced before. A professional life that had previously been confined to conferring communion and counseling soldiers stationed at a peaceful tropical military base exploded in a succession of corridor-constricted concussions, flying body parts, the screams and shouts and whistles and clicks of the wounded and dying. Covered in blood both alien and human he had made his stunned, dazed way through the tunnels of death, bestowing what comfort he could on the injured and last rites on the deceased. This he had done in a spirit of faith and desperation regardless of the actual convictions of the departed. Atheists, agnostics, and true believers had received equal attention, there being no time to run dead soldiers' personal identity chits through his chaplain's scanner to ascertain the specifics of individual beliefs. Swirling, acrid smoke and the pungent stink of death had been his companions, and no angels had stepped out of the fiery gloom to assist his ministrations or ease his personal pain.

He had not run out of bodies when he suddenly realized that he had run out of companions. He was alone except for the righteous dead. Alone, and lost.

No, not quite lost. Another figure was stumbling down the fume-filled corridor toward him. It was human, male, its clothes torn and its exposed skin scarred. Dark blood smeared its face and arms, mixing with greasy camouflage paint. Against this grisly, dark smutch the whites of the man's eyes stood out like sculpted marbles. He carried a large, battered rifle and wore camouflage gear but no uniform.

He was not a soldier.

Espying the figure of the padre kneeling beside an inert thranx and a dead corporal, the half-mad, half-dead xenophobe drew his own conclusion. "Dirty bug lover! You're all gonna die! We're gonna kill every one of you egg mother suckers!" The muzzle of the rifle started to come up.

"I was only . . . !" Pyreau began. He did not finish the thought. It would do no good. Whatever reason the raving lunatic before him might once have possessed had been abandoned on the surface prior to his homicidal entry into the hive. It flared in his eyes and resounded in his voice.

All chaplains receive basic military training as a matter of course. At Pyreau's right hand lay a neuronic pistol. The green telltale pulsing in its handle showed that it still held a half charge. Whatever guided his fingers might have been divine intervention or simply the most basic, primitive need to survive. Picking up the pistol, he raised it as something loud and concussive echoed in his ears. A hot blade bit into the flesh of his left shoulder. Aiming more from reflex than training, he fired.

The figure of the xenophobe shuddered even as the madman got off a second shot. It missed Pyreau entirely, slamming into the corridor wall behind him and to his left. Nerves paralyzed, his assailant went down in a heap, the rifle tumbling from his fingers. Silence roared. Once again, Father Pyreau was the only one alive in the tunnel.

Mouth open in shock, he put the pistol down and thought to examine his shoulder. Blood leaked from what was no worse than a graze. Trying to rise, he found that his muscles had turned to rubber, his bones to putty. He could not stand.

Then hands were levering him to his feet, and they were not human. The voice that accompanied the helping digits was firm but soft, almost whispery, the consonants oddly musical, the vowels separately enunciated only with difficulty. What he remembered most of all later was a piquancy redolent of damp honeysuckle.

"Please try to use your legs. I cannot lift you by myself."

Admonished brain activated muscles, and Pyreau found

himself erect amidst Armageddon. Stepping back, the thranx looked him up and down. "You wear the uniform of a soldier."

"I . . . I am a soldier, but a chaplain. Do you know what that is?"

Antennae searched in opposing directions to parse as much of the acrid atmosphere as possible. "I'm afraid not. You are with the rescue team that arrived promptly but too late."

"Yes." Pyreau nodded. "I'm sorry about that. We got here as fast as we could."

"I am certain that you did." A truhand gestured at the quiescent carnage surrounding them: waves of dead flesh frozen in midcollapse. "There will be trouble over this. Loud whistling and clicking and abundant recriminations to go around." Golden compound eyes rose to meet the padre's. "Enough for both species. What does a chaplain do?"

Pyreau gestured helplessly at the massed bodies, the majority of which were thranx. "I represent one of humankind's principal religions and, when necessary, all of them. I provide spiritual counsel to the men and women of the unit I happen to be assigned to, lead them in prayer on certain traditional days and also in private, minister to the sick at heart, and perform specific ceremonies that have religious overtones, such as the burying of the dead."

A truhand and foothand rose to gesture in the direction of the fanatic Pyreau had just shot. "You certainly ministered to him."

Pyreau did not look back—not because he was incapable of it, but because he did not want to. "I had no choice. It was him or me. Although I believe in a life after death, I'm in no hurry to trade this one for the other. It will come in its proper sequence, as it does to all of us."

"An interesting assertion of belief." Reaching up and across with a foothand, the thranx tapped his own right shoulder with all four fingers. In the manner of thranx body decoration, a small, glistening black circle was inlaid in the hard blue-green chitin. Even in the dim light of the damaged corridor it shimmered with iridescence. "Do you know what this insignia signifies?"

"I'm afraid I don't." The young priest badly wanted a drink of water. "I haven't paid much attention to the details of contact between your kind and mine. There hasn't been much new information available."

"I know." The thranx made a gesture that the good father did not recognize for the expression of resignation that it was. "Your people are preoccupied with the Pitar. About them you want to know everything." This observation was quietly stated and in no way accusing, but Pyreau felt oddly embarrassed just the same.

"It's not my job to decide what appears on the tridee. I have nothing to do with the media. If it means anything, I'd like to know more about both species." To prove that he'd been listening, he nodded slightly in the direction of the black inlay. "What does it signify?"

This time all four hands wove a quick but complex pattern in the air. "It means that we are colleagues."

"Excuse me?"

"I am . . . I do not have an exact translation that would fit a Terranglo term with which I am familiar. You might call me a consulting physicist of the soul. I am also a counselor. It is a traditional calling that was in place even in pretechnological times. When a member of the hive has a question that cannot be answered by anyone else, by a specialist or teacher or artist, they come to such as myself. We attempt to comprehend the incomprehensible, to understand that which has no explanation, and to provide some solace in the absence of cognition. We are the last resort when reason and logic fail, a repository of compassion in the face of a cold and indifferent universe." He ambled forward on four legs to examine the body of the xenophobe Pyreau had just killed. "Of course, we make a lot of it up as we go along, but in searching there is truth, and sometimes, even to our own astonishment, we manage to get something right."

"You—you're a priest?" Pyreau struggled to recall what was known about the thranx, or at least what he himself had studied. "I didn't think . . . didn't know you people had priests. I didn't even know you had religion."

"That by any other name, as one of your famous writers once avowed." With its largely fixed, inflexible countenance the thranx could not smile, but Pyreau had the impression of gentle amusement nonetheless. "Semantics are irrelevant in the face of the spirit."

"Do you believe in God?" Pyreau asked without thinking.

"In your sense, no. In ours . . . This is not a question easily or casually answered. Do you find it so?" The valentine-shaped head cocked sideways.

"Some of my superiors do. I don't. I was taught to believe, but I was also taught to question."

"Ah, *crri!kk,* those eternal antagonists. Always making existence more difficult and complicated than we would like it to be. But no one asked us, did they? My name is Shanvordesep." The soft alien voice grew suddenly alarmed. "Are you going to lose consciousness? You do not look so good."

"Just . . . thirsty. I am Cirey Pyreau." Pyreau muttered the response as he looked past the thranx and down the corridor, wondering when someone would find him. He had completely lost contact with the rest of his unit.

"As opposed to ultimate questions of divinity and existence, that much is easily remedied." Reaching back with a truhand, the thranx drew a cylinder of some shiny spun material from the pouch slung across his thorax and held it out to Pyreau, who eyed it uncertainly. The coiled drinking spout was unfamiliar to him.

"Like this." The thranx demonstrated briefly before passing the cylinder back to the padre.

Pyreau took it shakily. Probably he ought to have first smelled of the contents, but he was too tired and thirsty to care. Besides, there were times when a man had to take the word and judgment of another on faith, even if the individual in question came equipped with one too many pair of limbs.

The water was cold, fresh, and tasted better than the finest Chardonnay. Despite his desperate thirst he was mindful not to drink all of it, making sure to hand it back to its owner at least half full. With his right forearm he wiped the back of his mouth. The blood on the sleeve had already dried.

"What do we do now?" he wondered aloud.

Although the blue-green body remained facing him, the head swiveled an astonishing amount, enabling the thranx to look almost directly back over its shoulder. "I suppose we wait. I could go for help, but in the confusion I'm not sure your comrades would respond readily to my entreaties. If they are proper soldiers they will be following the orders of their superiors. In such a situation they are unlikely to listen to someone such as myself." Antennae twitched and mandibles clicked. "I am sure someone will find us before long."

Without pause or obvious attempt to change the subject, Shanvordesep crouched to examine the body of the nearest thranx. Curled tightly, all eight limbs had been drawn up against the body. Its head was missing, blown to bits by an explosive shell, nerves and longitudinal supportive muscle protruding from the open neck.

"I am given to understand that you recycle your dead differently from us."

Pyreau was appalled, though he was careful to control his expression in the event the thranx might comprehend it. "We don't recycle our dead. We give them, in most cases, a proper and dignified burial."

Still investigating the corpse, Shanvordesep looked back and up at the human. "You bury them in the ground. Then what happens to them?"

"They rest there." Pyreau wondered why he was being asked to explain the obvious.

"And then what happens to them? Later?"

Pyreau shrugged. "Unless special preservative techniques or coffins have been employed, they remain so until their containers break down. After that, their bodies are—"

"Recycled," the thranx finished for him. "There are only small differences in our approach, primarily in the matter of enclosure. We choose to recycle immediately, your kind over time. It has always been thus in the hive. Admittedly, there are details that do demarcate certain specific differences, but taken as a whole our traditions are not so very different." He straightened, his head coming just up to the priest's chest.

"I believe there are other similarities that might usefully be explored." A truhand gestured toward a section of corridor comparatively free of corpses. "Would you like to discuss them? It seems that for the foreseeable future we have nothing if not time."

Debate religion with an alien? One that reminded him more of the large mantids he had seen delicately poised beneath the eaves of the buildings back at the base than a fellow seminarian? Why not? As Shanvordesep sensibly pointed out, the only thing they had to kill now was time.

The last thing he expected was for a bug-eyed, eight-limbed alien insectoid to reinforce his faltering faith, but that was exactly what happened. For his part, he was able to enlighten the intensely curious thranx on matters of human spirituality. It developed in the course of their conversation that Shanvordesep was less than satisfied with the present organization of the ancient order to which he belonged and from which he drew his calling. It had not kept pace with the culture, he felt, or with such unanticipated revelations as the existence of other intelligent species elsewhere in the cosmos.

The longer they talked, the more Father Pyreau felt that here, beneath his gleaming exoskeleton, was a fellow spirit. Initial half-serious thoughts of trying to convert the thranx, if such a thing were even acceptable or possible, gave way to an open mutual exchange of beliefs and disbeliefs, of certitudes and unanswered queries, of a desire to understand the great mysteries while carrying out useful and practical work in the only reality they knew.

They were alone together in the corridor for a long time. When the first patrolling triad of hive gleaners found them, man and thranx were locked in animated conversation. Returned to troops who had thought him lost, Pyreau was accorded a hero's welcome. He did his best to demur in the face of all the accolades, pointing out that he had done little more than survive and wait for rescue. But his comrades would have none of it. He was recommended for several citations.

As a matter of course and though chaplains rarely wore such decorations, he was awarded the same battle ribbon as was the hastily engaged infantry who had fought to save the hive: crossed antennae on a field of blue-green. He found the ornate medal altogether too embarrassing and kept it hidden away in its sealed presentation box.

When he requested a leave of absence from duty it was readily granted. Given what he had been through, it was understandable to his superiors that he might require some rest and relaxation. Subjected to combat conditions, even a chaplain could suffer the contemporary high-tech equivalent of shell shock.

It was an assessment Father Pyreau made no effort to confirm or deny. All that mattered was that he be set free to resume his dialogue with the thranx advisor Shanvordesep. For his part, the thranx readily welcomed his new friend into the hive. Together they plunged into weeks of intense discussion of matters spiritual, studying one another's beliefs, learning their histories, discovering how representatives of both species perceived the same eternal conundrums.

Months later, they had done much more than exchange views and acquire wisdom. They had ascertained possibilities and identified solutions. They had determined how best to apply insubstantialties to reality and resolve contradictions. They were ready to act.

All they needed now was a sponsor.

"Found a new church? Are you both crazy?" Martine Herzalt Lorengau sat upright and stiff in a chair as she regarded the pair of unlikely visitors. "I'm assuming that blatant insanity manifests itself similarly among the thranx, of course."

"I can assure you that we are not mad." The insectoid gestured casually, in a manner the gangly, pinch-faced human might recognize. "Only hopeful."

Beside him, Father Pyreau hastened to support and reaffirm his friend. "We came to you because we have been turned down everywhere else."

A hint of a smile struggled with the corners of Lorengau's

mouth but could not break through. The barriers were too great. "As a businesswoman of some repute, let me tell you that is about as piss-poor an opening for a request for investment as I have ever heard. Nothing like starting out by telling me that everyone else you've talked to thinks that you're fools."

"This is to be an investment in people, and the future." Pyreau met the woman's unnervingly deep-set, large eyes without flinching and tried not to squirm in his chair. He ought to be used to this by now, he told himself. The milieu as well as the rejection. Nevertheless, he persevered. What else could he do?

"Even if I wanted to waste money on such a ludicrous enterprise, why would I choose to support one that purports, according to your proposal, to spiritually link humans with thranx? Why not humans with Pitar? In that, at least, I could see some possible return."

"The return from such an investment would not be monetary," Pyreau replied earnestly.

"With the Pitar involved, it might be." Her voice falling, she grumbled under her breath. "Missed the boat on that one. But we're catching up." Leaning forward slightly, the high, black leather back of the expensive chair rising behind her like a throne, she regarded each of them in turn. "I'm still not sure how you managed to secure an appointment with me. My time is valuable." Her tone darkened. "If nothing comes of this meeting, and I fail to see how it can, someone else is going to end up paying for it."

"There are those who do sympathize with our aspirations." Shanvordesep concluded his reply with a soft, descending whistle.

The industrialist's demeanor remained unencouraging. "If you did any research at all before coming here you should know that I am an atheist."

Pyreau nodded. "We know. Our proposed religious venue would be open to all."

This time the smile emerged. It was a smile that had on more than one occasion struck terror into the heart of a competitor. "Now you are simply being asinine and worse, wasting my time." A hand moved toward a row of tactile perceivers.

"We mean to do this thing. If we can establish a congregation capable of accommodating the beliefs and feelings of two entirely different species, making room for the different beliefs inherent in one species will be simple by comparison."

The dismissive fingers that terminated in perfect nails hesitated. "It won't include me. I don't believe in anything."

"But you do," Pyreau argued energetically. "Everyone believes in something. If you don't believe in a supreme deity, then you are convinced of its nonexistence. Conviction is founded on dogma, which is supported by belief."

Martine Lorengau blinked. "I am a businesswoman, not a philosopher. I have neither the time nor the inclination to waste on theology or metaphysics."

"You have a soul," Pyreau assured her softly.

This time she laughed, a sound that contrasted startlingly with her speaking voice. "I could cite you hundreds of people who would disagree."

"That which lies within every sapient being and cannot be quantified needs feeding." Truhands reflexively wove a complex pattern in the air before the intimidating desk. Knowing that the female human comprehended not a single wave of fingers or hands complicated Shanvordesep's response. Trying to communicate without gestures was akin to speaking with only half the words at one's command. Nevertheless, he tried.

"I assure you," she replied, smiling, "that I am fully fed. All of my psychological needs are well taken care of."

"Then you have completely recovered from and are entirely over the unfortunate deaths of your husband and daughter," Pyreau said.

Jaws slightly parted, Lorengau turned to stare sharply and unblinkingly at the unrepentant priest. When next she spoke, her tone was icy and dangerous.

"How dare you. How *dare* you mention that in my presence."

This time Pyreau was not intimidated. "One who stands

every day naked before God can dare anything." Simultaneously relentless and compassionate, he continued. "The accident was eleven years ago. One of your company planes was returning to Gauteng from Harare. To this day no one is sure why it went down into the Zambezi. Everyone on board was killed."

"I know what happened." Slumping slowly back in the great leather chair, Lorengau suddenly seemed in danger of being swallowed by it, of becoming even thinner, until she disappeared into one of the supple ebony tucks. "I wasn't much of a believer before that. Afterward . . ." Her gaze rose. "I'm curious. What sort of colossal personal arrogance makes you think your proposed denomination has anything to offer someone like me?"

"We can't say for certain that it would," Pyreau replied without hesitation. "We can be certain that nothing else does. Who knows what revelations may manifest themselves in the commingling of the beliefs of two entirely different species? Different ways of thinking, of looking at the universe, of both approaching and answering abstruse questions."

"There will be no restrictions, no constricting internal laws requiring adherence to unprovable dogmas," Shanvordesep added. "It will be open to all. Not only humans and thranx, but members of any other species who wish to join. It will remain resolutely apolitical, a noted concern of your kind, and as equally accommodating of traditional thranx hierarchical concerns, an interest of my people."

There was silence in the room. "What do you hope to achieve with this?" Lorengau finally asked. "Power, wealth? Inner peace? Acclamation within your own vocations?"

Pyreau looked over at his companion and saw Shanvordesep gesture encouragingly. "We don't know. That is, we're not sure. A place where individuals who are in need but who feel unsatisfied by other ideologies can come for succor and assistance. A refuge capable of offering more than words. We know that regardless of the beliefs it propounds, every church is ultimately accountable to a secular bottom line." He indicated his companion. "Shanvordesep has experience in such matters, far more so than I."

Lorengau pursed her lips. "So not only am I being asked to support this dubious, unfocused enterprise, I am also supposed to turn over control of a large sum of credit to an alien. Not even a Pitar, at that."

"It is a wonderful thing about mathematics that it responds with equanimity to skilled manipulation regardless of shape." The thranx calmly ignored the slight.

If the industrialist was testing him, he evidently passed. "This is a waste of time and money. In that my opinion obviously does not differ from that of everyone else you have contacted in search of support. However . . ."

If a divine blessing could be accounted in one word, Father Pyreau thought, the woman seated grandly before them had just intoned it.

"I have no time to waste—but I do have a lot of money. As you are aware, after the accident I never remarried. Mwithi was the finest man I ever met, and the only one who never expressed the slightest interest in my money. I've been looking for someone like him ever since. So far I have been grievously disappointed. As for my daughter . . ." She did not choke, Pyreau noted, but she did pause ever so briefly to gather herself. "You have your angels; I have mine. So, you want my money? To underwrite this numinous folly of yours?"

"We do, *crri!kk,*" Shanvordesep acknowledged.

"I suppose you'll want to lease or build a headquarters, or temple, or whatever kind of specialized structure you end up conceptualizing."

"We intend to keep our facilities as modest as our goals," Pyreau assured her. "I have always been doubtful of vast cathedrals and temples and mosques and the like. If God, or some great spirit, or whatever it is that we cannot yet give a name to is truly within us, then I don't see why it matters that what lies without be constructed on such a grand scale. All my life I have wondered about preachers who shout, as if God were deaf."

"All I know is that when that plane went down he didn't listen to me," she snapped. "But that's in the past."

"Then you will support us?" Unable to sit in a human chair, Shanvordesep had been forced to stand the entire time on all six legs. Now he rose, sitting back on four, the better to see eye to eye with the industrialist.

"I will underwrite your foolishness, yes. For as long as it continues to amuse me." Adopting a mocking tone, one slim hand fluttered diffidently in the air. "Who knows? I might even pay you a visit now and again, just to see how you are wasting my money."

Shanvordesep fumbled with his thorax pouch. "We intend to become self-supporting within the first year."

"Indeed?" She waved off his efforts to find whatever it was that he was searching for. "No, no. Don't show me any projections, any figures. I'll just spot the holes in them and discourage you. Madness needs to remain insular or it becomes hostage to reality and loses its charm. I'm not doing this because I think you're going to make money, or even repay me. I'm doing it for a diversion. As an amusement."

Having accomplished what they had come for, Pyreau knew they ought to depart. Shanvordesep was gesturing precisely that. But the good father had never been one to leave well enough alone. If that had been the case he would not have found himself in his present circumstances, sharing a hypothesized future with an alien bug while begging money from the contemptuous and cynical affluent.

"We don't consider the undertaking amusing. Despite what you may think, this is not farce. We see a need that is not being fulfilled."

For a horrible moment he feared he had gone too far, that he had abused this powerful woman's hospitality to the point where she would withdraw her offer. Then she laughed for a second time, and he relaxed.

"If you're not in the business of amusing, then why am I enjoying this so much? Why do I find the whole endeavor so comical?"

"Perhaps," ventured Shanvordesep quietly, "because it has satisfied a need."

She turned on him. "A need? I don't have any 'need.' What need?"

"One that you have yet to identify, obviously." The thranx bowed slightly and began to back away from the desk. "You are a fascinating species. I never cease to be amazed at your ability to pretend things that exist do not, and to ignore logic and reason in favor of what you would like to believe."

Lorengau shrugged slightly. "So our nature is more whimsical than that of the thranx. Whose wouldn't be?" Activating a screen set into her desk that was shielded from their view, she manipulated controls with the fingers of one hand. "I'll want my husband and daughter's names prominently displayed on the list of contributors, of course, as well as on the front of your first tabernacle, or whatever you end up calling your places of gathering."

Pyreau glanced at his eight-limbed colleague. "We don't plan to do that sort of thing. This is to be a refuge from the realities of the world, not a reminder of them. I have always found that the prominent placement of contributors' names on the outside of structures intended for religious purposes only reminds those who are unable to do likewise of their comparative insignificance, if only in a temporal, nonspiritual way. We are trying to get away from such things."

"But we will find a way to acknowledge your gift," Shanvordesep put in quickly. "One that I believe will more than satisfy your wishes."

Shaking her head slowly, Lorengau's speculative gaze passed from human to thranx. "I can't make up my mind if you two are truly dedicated or just arrogant." She sighed softly. "People are going to find out about this, you know."

"We intend that they should," Shanvordesep declared.

"There's going to be a lot more amusement, much of it directed my way. Not to my face, of course. But people will laugh at me."

"Someday they will bless you." Pyreau made the assurance with as much feeling as he could muster.

"Oh, I'm sure," she muttered sardonically. "What name have you picked for this creed of yours, anyway?"

That much, at least, he and Shanvordesep had worked out beforehand, Pyreau thought with relief. "Nothing complex. Nothing overbearing or intimidating. We were thinking of calling it the United Church."

"How original. And yourselves?" She eyed him with some interest. "Will you still be a priest, Father Pyreau?"

"I think so, though that is still to be worked out."

"And your many-legged, golden-eyed friend?"

Pyreau turned to the thranx, and this time it was the solemn-visaged pastor who smiled. "In a difficult moment early in our encounter Shanvordesep once referred to himself as the 'last resort' of his . . . flock is not quite the right word, but it will do. And that is what he will be once we begin: the last resort."

5

As it had for thousands of years, Mount Agung was steaming softly. The thranx who were strolling along the beach hardly glanced in its direction. They had never questioned why humankind had chosen to situate one of the two original sites for greeting and processing visitors to their world in the midst of a necklace of islands noted for their exceptional volcanic activity. Perhaps this question had occurred to their hosts, who had on more than one occasion alluded to the possibility of moving the facility to the large land mass that lay to the south.

There were three thranx: Nilwengerex, a specialist in human culture; Joshumabad, recently arrived from Hivehom; and Yeicurpilal, the second-highest-ranking representative of her species on Earth. In the company of the two younger males she made her way along the shore, careful to keep well away from the water. The protection from large, potentially deadly waves afforded by the offshore reef was not adequate to completely reassure any thranx.

Joshumabad would not, and perhaps could not, let go of the theme that prevented him as well as his companions from enjoying their morning stroll beneath the warm equatorial sun. It was understandable. The concern he continued to express was the reason for his being there.

"Those on the Grand Council feel like they are caught at the terminus of a dead-end tunnel with a starving *memn!!toct* at the open end. They do not know whether to run, estivate, or start digging."

Yeicurpilal's six unshod feet left multiple impressions in

the slightly damp sand. A warm tropical breeze whispered through her ovipositors. Though past the age suitable for procreation and unable to vent any more eggs, she was still straight and sturdy of limb. The delicate lavender tint maturity had imparted to her exoskeleton was highlighted by the angle taken by the rays of the still rising sun, and her compound eyes glistened with intelligence.

"Why are they so upset?" Yeicurpilal gestured with a truhand in the direction of the island of Bali that lay just across the deep, swift body of water known as the Selat Lombok. "Our relations with the humans are good. Negotiations are proceeding on a host of mutually important matters, from trade and commerce to exchanges in the arts. I realize that agreements are not being finalized as rapidly as some might like, but neither are they at a standstill."

Less comfortable in the alien surroundings than his companions, the recently arrived Joshumabad kept much of his attention focused on the ground beneath his feet. He was careful to avoid anything that hinted of the organic. While he had confidence in the greater experience of his associates, neither of them were experts on local life-forms. Though the likelihood of them encountering anything that could prove toxic to their offworld biologies was small, he was not the type to take chances.

"Everyone is nervous. Not only those on the council, but those who are assigned to many of the advisory committees. These mammals are aggressive, intelligent, and technologically advanced. The council very much wants them as a counterweight, if not as formal allies, in this part of the Arm to restrain the adventurism of the AAnn."

"We are on course to achieve that." Yeicurpilal bent to pick up a piece of driftwood. It had a lovely grain. Swinging it back and forth in the manner of strolling humans she had observed, she caused the nervous Joshumabad to put more distance between them. Disturbed at the pleasure she felt as a consequence of the result she had produced, she flung the stick aside. It landed in the water and began to drift away on the slight current. Was the same likely to happen to thranx hopes for this world and its peculiar, frustrating, sometimes maddening inhabitants?

"What is the council afraid of?" she asked when she had disposed of the stick.

"Being preempted by these Pitar. We have perused all the reports. It has been noted how the humans are far more comfortable in the presence of the Pitar than they are with us."

"They are not more comfortable," Nilwengerex declared firmly, speaking for the first time. "They are infatuated. I have some limited experience in intraspecies contact, with the Quillp as well as the AAnn, and I have never seen anything like this. It is not so much that they believe everything the Pitar say, or take all of it at face value, as the fact that they want so desperately to believe their own perceptions. These are, as you know, colored by the external appearance of the Pitar, who according to what my human colleagues have told me in response to my inquiries represent everything that is physically perfect in the human imagination."

Joshumabad considered. A bird, one of this fecund world's many acrobatic aerial life-forms, momentarily distracted him as it flew by overhead. He would have had even a harder time concentrating had he known that the sea eagle was evaluating him as a potential meal.

"How can they be so accepting? Physical appearance has nothing to do with the trustworthiness and dependability of another. It does not matter if one is speaking of an individual or, as in this instance, an entire species. Even a *hou!p* knows to look deeper."

"They are mesmerized by the superficiality of external beauty as embodied in these visitors." Nilwengerex was a staid, humorless male, Yeicurpilal mused, but ruthlessly good at his work. She ranked him near the bottom of potential companions and at the very top as an advisor. Whether he was aware of her opinion she did not know. Males did not challenge senior females in matters of personality. He knew his position within the hive and was content with it.

"I do not understand." Joshumabad executed a complex

gesture indicative of internal confusion. "They are manifestly intelligent, fast learners, enthusiastic explorers. Yet in the presence of these Pitar they slough off several hundred years of social maturity. If we were to encounter a sapient species that resembled the thranx ideal we would be welcoming, but not . . ."

"Sappy." Nilwengerex picked up a shell and began to examine the intricate, brightly tinted calcareous whorls. "As usual, the humans have a word for it, even if that is one they themselves would not apply to their present condition. However, nothing prevents me from using it." He handed the shell to Joshumabad, who extended a truhand to accept it reluctantly. To have refused would have constituted a small but inescapable insult.

"Interestingly," the culture specialist continued, "they are very much aware of their own insupportable reaction. At least, the more intelligent among them are. The great fevered mass of humankind seems largely oblivious. They wish only to expand and enhance contact with their new friends. Deeper consequences do not concern them."

"What about the reception accorded our delegation by these Pitar?" The representative of the Grand Council was not at all comfortable with the information he was receiving.

"Formal and polite," Yeicurpilal told him. "Insofar as we have been able to determine by cross-referencing with our human friends, these new aliens are treating us no differently than they are their human hosts. In that respect they are displaying more diplomatic maturity than the humans themselves."

"What is the opinion of our perceivers?" Joshumabad matched her stride for stride while Nilwengerex wandered off to inspect the gelatinous mass of some tentacled creature that the sea had regurgitated onto the shore.

"Inconclusive. Contact is too recent and infrequent to reach any formal conclusions." She glanced sideways at him. "The council has been kept fully informed by space-minus communications. They know all this. Why are you asking questions to which answers have already been given?"

Feeling a chill, Joshumabad found himself longing for the low-lying clouds of Hivehom. "I wanted to hear it directly from you. Oftentimes official reports inadvertently leave out the most significant particulars. Even visual transcripts can neglect information that is inherent in person-to-person gestures and glances." He turned his attention back to the cultural specialist, who had concluded his examination of the dying jellyfish and hurried to rejoin them.

"I am interested in your informal opinion, Nilwengerex. What do you, personally, think of these Pitar? Beyond what you have contributed to the official reports."

Nilwengerex pondered a reply. The sky was very blue, and beyond it, Hivehom very far away. Yet he did not feel as estranged on this world as he had on Trix, for example, or even at his first posting, on the benign globe known as Willow-Wane.

"I haven't made up my mind. Nor have any of my colleagues. We felt that we were just beginning to comprehend these humans, to come to some understanding of how their very different minds work, when one of their deep-space exploration teams returned with these Pitar in tow. Their unannounced appearance was as much of a shock to us as it was to the rest of humankind. So we have been forced to adjust our work and reallocate our resources to study not one but two new alien, mammalian species. It has been something of a strain. Under such circumstances, you and the council will have to learn to be patient. We are learning as much as we can as fast as we can.

"Unfortunately, access to the Pitar is restricted. More than restricted: It is virtually unattainable. Constantly attended and surrounded as they are by ardent humans, it is almost impossible to procure unescorted contact with them."

"They are willing enough to talk to us," Yeicurpilal put in, "but reluctant to insist lest they irritate the humans. After all, it is their world on which we all are visitors. A polite guest does not make demands that might displease their hosts."

"I know that the Pitar claim to occupy only two worlds, in conjoining orbits in the same system. Though they possess vessels capable of journeying in space-plus they are not eager colonizers. By way of contrast, we have to date settled five worlds and the humans seven. Population disparities aside, do you think they are dangerous, these Pitar?" It was a question Joshumabad had put off asking until he felt more comfortable in the cultural specialist's presence.

A sharp, high whistle sounded from Nilwengerex. Startled by the unnatural alien sound, several small, rainbow-colored lorikeets burst from the cover of nearby brush and took wing. When the whistling laughter finally died down, the smallest of the three strolling thranx readily replied.

"We do not know enough about them to say, but one thing I do know: They can't be any more dangerous than these humans."

It was not the kind of response Joshumabad had expected, and his responsive gestures showed clearly that he was taken aback. "How can you avow such a thing? We have not only many representatives on this world, but an expanding, functioning colony. If what you say now is true, then there are lives at risk."

"I do not deny it." The dour attaché appeared engrossed in the pale blue sea, as though he had a death wish of his own. Joshumabad did not like him very much, but he respected the other male's knowledge. "Yet each day I spend on this world I find myself liking these humans more and more."

Joshumabad halted abruptly, the sand warm beneath his feet. "Now I am thoroughly confused. Which is it? Which observation do I convey to my superiors when I return to Hivehom to make my report in person? Are these bipeds dangerous or not?"

He might have expected clarification from the senior diplomat among them. Instead, Yeicurpilal only succeeded in muddying the waters further. "That's it exactly."

Joshumabad held firm. "That cannot be it exactly. Either these humans are a threat to us or they are not."

Yeicurpilal was not swayed by the visiting representative's determination to secure a straight answer. "They are warlike and peaceful, brutal and sensitive, ignorant and understanding. This planet is a big ball of raging contradictions. And the worst of it is, while they recognize these inconsistencies within themselves, they seem powerless to do anything about them."

"You have to give me something more," Joshumabad pleaded. "I can't present myself to the Grand Council with conclusions like that!"

"First of all," Nilwengerex assured him, "they are only observations, not conclusions. I can *tell* you that my colleagues and I who have been studying these people do not believe they pose any direct threat to the thranx."

"*Crri!kk,* that's something, anyway." Joshumabad was visibly relieved.

"I said no 'direct' threat," the attaché reminded him. "Their racial volatility makes their future actions unpredictable. We have been making progress in many areas of cooperation, most notably in the matter of commercial and scientific exchanges. The greatest difficulty we are being forced to try to overcome is the fact that in shape we so nearly resemble the small arthropods that are, numerically at least, the dominant life-form on this world, and with whom humans have been engaged in a battle for survival since the dawn of their own evolution. As you must know by now, they attach an enormous and irrational importance to physical appearance." His tone had turned even drier than usual. "Witness their immediate and unwarranted attraction to these Pitar. Through no fault of their own, these newly contacted bipeds are inadvertently responsible for the marked setback in our developing relations with the humans."

The council representative was silent for a while as the three resumed their stroll. Much more at home on the alien beach, Yeicurpilal and Nilwengerex reviewed every plant and animal they encountered, striving to identify them according to the taxonomy that had been supplied by human scientists.

"Then I am to inform the council that relations continue to advance successfully, but at a slower pace than previously?"

Yeicurpilal gestured concurrence. "That is what I would report."

"And when might they be expected to accelerate again?"

Yeicurpilal looked to Nilwengerex for a considered response. The attaché was reluctant to commit himself. "It is difficult to say. My own personal opinion, based on observation and the small knowledge I have gained of these people, is that it will not happen until the novelty of the Pitars' appearance has run its course. Unfortunately, it shows no signs of relenting. The humans are as entranced by their newfound near-duplicates today as they were when first they were brought here."

"Is there nothing we can do to regain appropriate attention?" The unexpected situation was new and confusing, as unprecedented in Joshumabad's experience as it was in everyone else's. They had not had such trouble relating to the Quillp, or even to the AAnn.

"If we are too forceful in our demands," Yeicurpilal informed him, "I fear that the humans will take umbrage at our attempts, thus rendering the situation even more awkward than it is now. It is my recommendation—and Eint Gowendormet, who is chief of our mission here, concurs—that we proceed according to our standard plan of contact while waiting for the ferment surrounding the discovery of the Pitar to run its course."

Joshumabad brooded on this. "The council will not be pleased. The desire to fully engage a strong species such as this as a counterweight to the endless adventurism of the AAnn is resolute."

Yeicurpilal gestured powerlessness. "It cannot be helped. During my sojourn on this world I have learned a number of things about our hosts. One is that they cannot be pushed, shoved, forced, or cajoled into doing something that does not originate with them, even if it is manifestly to their benefit. It is better to hint and suggest and let them believe that the idea originates with them. When dealing with humans, patience is not merely to be advocated, it is imperative. There is no other way to work with them."

"I am sorry," Nilwengerex added, "but that is the way of things here. If these Pitar had not revealed themselves to a human exploration team, maturation of our mutual relations would be on schedule. You cannot imagine the exceptional forbearance we are required to show in our daily dealings with them. Whatever its wishes and needs, the Grand Council must learn to do the same."

A visibly unhappy Joshumabad indicated understanding. "And our tentative connection with the Pitar? We of course must seek to establish formal relations with them as well. Though it does not fall within your purview, I presume your staff has taken the necessary preliminary steps forced upon them by circumstance?"

Yeicurpilal replied thoughtfully. "We have made the appropriate overtures. It is not so much that they have been rebuffed as that the Pitar have no time for us. They seem to be as ensnared by the humans as the humans are by them, though for the Pitar this fascination is reflected in a more intense and subdued attitude. Unable to study them firsthand, our specialists are reduced to speculating on their motivations. It cannot be determined if they are reclusive, wary, secretive, guarded, paranoid, fearful, all of the aforementioned, or simply shy. Without more intimate contact their racial psychology cannot be resolved. It is hoped time will provide us with access."

Joshumabad considered. "What is your personal opinion of them? Aside from the knowledge that has been compiled by such as this one." He indicated Nilwengerex, who took no offense at being referred to obliquely.

Antennae twitched meaningfully. "I don't like them."

The representative of the council gestured tersely. "*Crri!!kk,* that is concise, anyway. Why not?"

Yeicurpilal looked away. "You asked for an opinion not based on known fact. That is my opinion."

"Foolish," Nilwengerex proclaimed. "Xenologically impertinent. Even an opinion must be founded on a base of knowledge." He inclined both antennae in Joshumabad's direction. "I have no fear of these Pitar, nor love of them. I feel the same about the humans. My reactions and published convictions are based on factual material."

"There is room here for maneuver." In his mind Joshumabad was already compiling the report he would make to the

Grand Council. "We will continue on course with the humans without forcing the issue of closer relations. These must develop as a consequence of natural processes. As for the Pitar, you will maintain contact with their representatives here on Earth until we can make arrangements to have a separate delegation received on Hivehom. Separated from humans, relations between us will advance at an acceptable pace." A seagull defecated nearby, and he observed the process with interest.

"Meanwhile, the current pace of diplomacy is not acceptable."

Yeicurpilal looked at him sharply. "But we have just told you that—"

"It does not matter." Joshumabad's interruption conveyed the importance of what he was saying far more than mere words and gestures could have. "The council is not satisfied." He used all four hands for emphasis. "If you cannot accelerate the signing of agreements with humankind, the council is perfectly willing to appoint others to your present positions in the hopes they may do better. This is not a threat, but merely a communication to be taken under advisement."

"I'm so glad it's not a threat." Even when he appeared to be ignoring his companions, Nilwengerex heard everything. "It does not matter. According to what you have been telling us, the council wants us to stay the course, not force matters but speed things up. I am sorry that does not strike you as a contradiction."

"It does not matter what I think." Being possessed of a highly amenable and easygoing personality, Joshumabad was noticeably unhappy at the direction the conversation had taken. Not that he had any choice. His mandate called for him to visit, learn, report, and deliver instructions. This he had done and would continue to do, no matter how unpleasantly he was received.

Yeicurpilal hastened to intervene between the two, conversationally as well as physically. "Nilwengerex is right. We are doing our best here. All the wishes of the council will not make the humans move any faster."

"Not even as fast as that larva." With a foothand, Nilwengerex pointed off to his left.

The girl who was running out of the palm trees and down onto the beach could not have been more than eight or nine. Even when inclined fully forward to make use of all six legs, the three thranx were taller. Leaning back on trulegs only, they would tower over her. She was as brown as the scattered pieces of shattered driftwood that studded the shore like so many gypsy hieroglyphs, with straight dark hair and dancing eyes the color of small black shells. Laughing and giggling, she bent to pick up a stick and throw it toward Sulawesi. It did not quite reach the water.

Turning slightly and bending in quest of another missile, she caught sight of the thranx. Having halted at her unscheduled intrusion, the aliens stood watching quietly. Joshumabad in particular was at once captivated and repelled. From his preflight studies he knew what very young humans looked like, but this was the first time he had seen one in the flesh. The unexpected encounter left him only momentarily speechless.

"Is . . . is it dangerous?"

"Not usually." Nilwengerex responded in his usual dry, clipped tones. "Not one this small. The adolescents are potentially lethal. Unlike us, their bodies assume adult form and bulk preposterously in advance of their minds. But one such as this should be quite harmless, though even infants are capable of surprising violence."

Straightening, the little girl came toward them. She was wide-eyed and unafraid.

"What should we do?" Joshumabad fought hard to suppress the panic that was rising within him.

"Nothing," Yeicurpilal informed him. "Remain as you are. Let the larva come to us."

Not without some concern, Joshumabad did as he was told. The girl halted a couple of arm's lengths away, one finger pressing against her lower lip. "Hello, bugs. What are you doing here?"

"What are *you* doing here?" Nilwengerex asked her in Terranglo so fluent that Joshumabad was startled. He knew the specialist was competent in the local language, but he'd had no idea he was so skilled. "This is a restricted area. Only authorized adult humans are supposed to have access." He looked beyond her. "How did you get in?"

"Hole in the fence," she replied without hesitation. "Maman says the big storm last week made it." She glanced back over a shoulder, though not to the degree a thranx could manage, and gestured importantly with one finger. "We're having a picnic."

Nilwengerex looked to his superior. "We must report this violation."

Yeicurpilal indicated resignation. "Of course. The humans will be most upset."

"At this point any kind of reaction we can get from them would be welcome. The council's official impatience notwithstanding—" He arched his antennae significantly in Joshumabad's direction. "—I look forward to the resumption of proper negotiations and exchanges." So saying, he stepped toward the child.

Joshumabad's instinctive reaction was to restrain the other male. Aware that Nilwengerex was the specialist in thranx-human interaction and he only a recently arrived newcomer, he held back. Lowering his head, Nilwengerex extended a truhand in an odd fashion.

"I am Nilwengerex. These are my friends, Yeicurpilal and Joshumabad. We are pleased to meet you."

"Hi. I'm Tomea." Reaching out, she took the extended truhand and shook it up and down. Joshumabad was impressed at how readily and easily Nilwengerex flowed with the gesture, which the representative quickly recognized as the most common human method of greeting. "It's nice to meet you. I've heard Maman and her friends talking about you." The doubly perforated organ located in the center of her face expanded and contracted several times. Following this, the corners of the flexible mouth curved upward and the jaws parted, exposing white teeth.

"You smell nice."

"Tomea!" The voice was deeper than the girl's, the tone agitated. "Tomea, where are y—?"

A subjective peroration split the air, startling Joshumabad who instinctively retreated several body lengths. Yeicurpilal did likewise, but Nilwengerex released the girl's fingers and stepped back only reluctantly. Chances to study human larvae were rare. He had yet to encounter one that readily accepted contact.

The female who came running down the beach was not very large. The thin, loose folds of her single garment fluttered like bird wings around her slim body. Reaching the girl, she clutched her by the shoulder with a severity that stunned Joshumabad. Turning her away, the mature female lectured her offspring as they walked back the way they had come. Occasionally the adult human glanced back at the three motionless thranx as if fearing pursuit. Joshumabad could not be sure, but it appeared to him that the larva was protesting the intervention.

"Do they always treat their progeny so roughly?" The visiting representative watched the adult human march her young off the sand and back into the trees.

"Frequently." Nilwengerex did not turn away until the two humans had been swallowed up by the palm grove. "It is a component of the naturally aggressive nature of the adults that is passed down to their brood. From my studies, it is clear to me that the humans themselves have little idea why they act in such a fashion, except that they always have."

"It may be a reflection of the fact that among mammals the young do not go through a pupal stage where all they can do is passively listen and learn." Yeicurpilal had evidently done ample reading and research on her own into the habits of these peculiar creatures.

"The break in the fence must be reported so it can be repaired." Nilwengerex glanced again at the representative of the Grand Council. "Not to keep us from wandering beyond the restricted area, but to keep curious and potentially dangerous humans out. No one wants a repetition of the Amazon hive incident."

"Certainly not I," Joshumabad agreed with feeling. He turned back. "It is growing late, and I would rather not be caught outside the compound after dark. You two may be comfortable in the night of this world, but I am not." Reflecting his agitation, his antennae bobbed and weaved aimlessly. "Yet despite such revelations, all reports indicate that those of you stationed here enjoy your contact with these humans."

"They are all right," Nilwengerex conceded. "They simply have a surplus of energy that they have never been able to channel properly. When our relations have become sufficiently close, it is hypothesized by those specialists concerned with such matters that we may be able to offer them some assistance in such matters."

"*If* our relations become sufficiently close," a brooding Joshumabad reminded him. "Too much energy, you say?"

"Not I," Nilwengerex corrected him. "Our students of alien psychology. Though I would not dispute their assessment."

"*Chrri!k,* at least it has done them well. They have advanced rapidly."

Yeicurpilal had been silent for a while. Now she spoke anew. "Only technologically."

Joshumabad eyed her curiously. "Your words are straightforward, but your gestures are circumspect. What else do you mean to say?"

The Grand Council's second-in-command on Earth regarded the visitor evenly. "You saw the reaction of the adult to our interaction with the larva. It does not matter if juveniles are involved or not, or only adults, or specialists, or even those who seek to help us bond with their kind. Beneath every interaction, whether successful or a failure, hopeful or uncertain, enthusiastic or rote, the undertones are the same. Sometimes they are subtle, sometimes blatant, but they are almost never absent."

Indicating confusion, Joshumabad turned to Nilwengerex for clarification. "What is she talking about?"

"These humans," the specialist informed him. "They are indeed technologically advanced. Even a cursory study of their history shows that they have overcome extraordinary odds and exceptional difficulties to reach the place where they are today, having successfully preserved their own world while settling many others. In spite of this, what the senior female says is indisputable. One does not have to be a qualified xenologist to see it."

"See what?" Joshumabad demanded impatiently.

Nilwengerex regarded the visitor quietly. "That they are not happy."

6

Minister Saluafata was not nervous about meeting his Pitarian counterpart. Having on occasion dealt with the eminently reasonable yet harrowingly grotesque-looking thranx, he anticipated no difficulty in sitting down at the table with one or more nonhumans who resembled tridee luminaries more than visiting aliens. He looked forward to the forthcoming interaction. Only the outcome concerned him.

This was to be no ordinary meeting. Much more was at stake today than superficial agreements on cultural exchange or travel rights. Such matters could be, and were being, handled by assistant ministers and second-echelon diplomats. Only for something as important as this was someone of Saluafata's stature personally involved.

That stature extended to his physical as well as mental proportions. Though not particularly rangy, the minister was huge. A legacy of his chiefly forefathers, he was almost as wide as he was tall, and very little of it was fat. A walking door plug, some of his colleagues and underlings had called him. More adept at plugging crises than doorways, Saluafata was used to disarming initially intimidated adversaries with a smile as wide as the lagoon that framed his island home. When that failed to soothe nervous opposites, a song or two sung in his startlingly accomplished falsetto inevitably produced grins and delighted laughter.

Like a whale that had been subjected to reverse evolution and had reclaimed its hind legs, he settled himself into the chair at one end of the table. His personal secretary Ymir sat down on his left while the prim and always correct second undersecretary for Extraterrestrial Affairs, Mandan HoOdam, assumed the empty seat on his right. Carafes of chilled water were positioned in front of the delegates, along with small cobalt crystal bowls of assorted nuts. The Pitarians, it had been learned, had developed a liking for such terrestrial food.

A guard stood at either end of the room. Neither of them carried visible weapons—the operative word, Saluafata knew, being *visible*. The meeting place was a cheerful hemisphere with a single wide window that overlooked the placid tropical sea beyond. Set high on a Balinese hillside, the carefree beaches of Sanur were visible in the distance. They were filled with visitors cavorting in the warm waters, none of whom were aware of the somber significance of the meeting that was about to take place. All but a few were employed by the planetary government in the service of extraterrestrial relations. Overdeveloped Bali had long since ceased to be a stopping point for gallivanting tourists.

The entire facility needed to be moved, Saluafata mused. With the increase in deep space exploration and expansion, it had outgrown the available site. Nor did he suspect that he was the only diplomat or worker who felt uneasy laboring in the shadow of the periodically active volcanoes that dominated the island and this part of the world. Already, bureaus and agencies in need of additional room were being shifted southward, to the east coast of the southern continent. There was a surplus of flat, empty land there, and an enormous shuttleport was being built to service the increasing volume of offworld travel.

HoOdam murmured while scanning the privatized contents of her reader. An invisible beam from the reader periodically bounced off her retinas and back to the device, indicating that the individual gazing down at it was lawfully entitled to do so. If that proved not to be the case, the print on the screen would have remained as invisible as the security beam.

"What do you think, Api? Will they be difficult?"

He shrugged, and the movement took measurable time to travel from his columnar neck all the way down his enormous shoulders to his upper arms. "There's no way to tell in advance,

Mandy. So far it's our government that has been doing most of the giving. The Pitar have been more than friendly; they've proven themselves amenable. But this is the first time we've proposed anything on this scale." Reaching forward, he poured himself a glass of water. Since there was no established protocol for dealing with the Pitar, he had no basis to fear that his simple gesture might be breaking it.

"What if they refuse?" Recorder at the ready, Ymir was running a hand repeatedly through his short, blonde hair. Saluafata recognized the nervous habit but did not point it out. Everyone was edgy, and it was a harmless enough release. The Pitar were not like the thranx, who saw every gesture, no matter how inconsequential, as the equivalent of a verbal comment. When dealing with the insectoids, a person had to be conscious of his every movement lest unexpected confusion or, worse, unintended offense be given. The Pitar did use their hands occasionally, but not as a component of interpersonal communication. That a hardworking handful of them had already become fluent in Terranglo only added to the ease of interchange. They were much better at it than the thranx.

Of course, he reminded himself, their speaking apparatus was far better suited to the task. Technically, the higher compliments were due the thranx who had mastered human speech. As always, when compared to the Pitar, the insectoids came off looking bad. But who wouldn't, the minister mused? Alongside the Pitar, everyone tended to appear ungainly and graceless.

He had resolved that the conference would not be affected by such superficialities of aspect. Personalities would not become involved. The forthcoming talks were too important, the matter at hand too consequential, to founder in a sea of perfunctory perception. He would not allow himself to be distracted. Besides, if not as attractive as the Pitar, he could be much more charming.

A soft musical tone chimed twice. Pushing back the specially ordered oversized chair, he and his colleagues rose as the Pitarian delegation entered. He recognized Urin-Delm and Jpar-Vhet from previous encounters. Both males were tall, muscular, perfectly formed, and wore the familiar blank Pitarian expression of noncommittal. They were clad in simple gray jumpsuits unadorned except for embroidered insignia that identified them as to both name and function. They flanked a mature female who . . . They flanked . . .

The minister swallowed hard as humans and Pitar alike took their seats more or less simultaneously. To his secretary he whispered, "Close your mouth."

Even by Pitarian standards of beauty the female was extraordinary. Hair the hue of turquoise framed her face like the ultimate expression of the Zuni silversmith's art. Her eyes were a deep royal purple. Lips that did not belong in any species' diplomatic service were lightly parted, and the molecules of air that rode in and out of that exquisite mouth were repeatedly blessed. As for the rest of her, perfection was too mild a word to serve as an adequate description. In a space of less than a minute, Apileaa Saluafata, minister for Extraterrestrial Affairs, virtually forgot who he was.

A nudge in his capacious side rudely induced his fall from heaven. Though much taken by the appearance of all three Pitar, Undersecretary HoOdam had retained a semblance of self-control.

"You're staring, Api. And we have business to do."

Indeed, having taken their seats, the three Pitar were observing their human counterparts in expectant silence. One had already begun sorting through the salted nuts on the table in front of him.

Unable to meet the ameythstine eyes of the alien seated across from him, a disconcerted Saluafata removed his own reader from its case and scrolled down the list of items that had been placed on the agenda. The cool, detached print helped him to regain his personal and professional equilibrium. But it was not easy. Every time he looked up, the purple eyes of his counterpart were there, gazing across the conference table in his direction. They made him want to think of anything except business. It did not help when she spoke first.

"The Dominion of the Twin Worlds extends its greetings to

the people of Earth on this congenial day. We look forward to listening to whatever you have to say."

Diplomats should not have voices like that, the minister felt. It conferred an unfair advantage on the speaker that had nothing whatsoever to do with the issues under discussion. It made him think of somnolent days on deserted beaches, of hammocks caressed by emollient breezes, and cold, tangy fruit drinks placed close at hand. It made him think of . . .

"We receive the representatives of the Dominion," he heard himself responding, "in friendship and with high hopes for a mutually agreeable and successful culmination of our discussions. I presume that you have all had an opportunity to examine the formal proposal that was conveyed to your equivalent agency or department?"

To Saluafata's disappointment, it was the male seated across from Ymir who next spoke. As for himself, he wanted only to sit and listen to the female speak, to have her words nuzzle his ears like the lingering warmth of a perfect sunset on the eyes. Not that there was anything wrong with the male's voice, as the first cracks in HoOdam's armor of diplomatic distance showed.

"The matter has been studied," the irresponsibly handsome male responded. "You wish our permission to begin settling your people on the world you have chosen to call Argus Five, also Treetrunk."

Saluafata nodded. Flanking him, Ymir and HoOdam struggled to present a businesslike demeanor. That did not keep them from stealing surreptitious glances at the radiant comeliness of the three Pitar. If the visitors noticed this unprofessional attention or took exception to it they gave no sign. Presumably, the minister thought, they were used to it by now.

"That is correct." The special chair provided enough room for him to shift importantly on the reinforced seat. "Naturally, we understand that you may have hesitations. Let me assure you that my government is prepared to compensate or negotiate further on any particular objectionable aspects of this proposal, no matter how numerous. We are willing to work with you on this for as long as may be necessary to ensure that both sides are completely comfortable with the ultimate resolution of the matter. We can offer you . . ."

"There are no hesitations." The female cut him off softly. "There are no objections. The Dominion of the Twin Worlds does not object to the settlement of the world known as Treetrunk by the people of Earth."

Having prepared himself and his staff for lengthy, difficult negotiations, for an extended period of give-and-take, for argument and dissention, the minister was more than a little taken aback by the unexpected and to all intents and purposes unqualified grant of rights. He stalled for a few moments to gather his swirling thoughts.

"I need to make certain we understand one another." He addressed the female. For him her companions had ceased to exist, though not for Ymir or HoOdam. "You are saying that you grant us permission to settle as many colonists as we wish on the one habitable world of the system in question, without restriction or covenant?"

The male on the left of the woman with the look of a shallow sea replied. "Without restriction or covenant, yes. You may begin whenever you wish. We will not interfere."

"I don't understand." HoOdam felt compelled to speak up. "The extremes for favorable existence of your species fall within the same tolerances as ours. You could settle Argus Five as readily as we. Furthermore, it lies much nearer your homeworlds than does Earth or any of its developed colonies. Why are you leaving it to us?"

As they so often did, the three Pitar put their heads close together and conferred in whispers that were even softer than their usual speech. When they moved apart again, the woman in the middle explained.

"We explore, as your first ship to visit Treetrunk discovered. But we do not settle. We do not colonize." She smiled, and her countenance far outshone the light from the overhead glowstrips. "Our population is stable and has been so for some time. Believing as we do that the Twin Worlds are the most perfect of all habitable places in this galaxy, or at least in this part of this arm, we see no reason to stray from them.

None of our people would willingly do so, even if our government was to offer incentives. They are quite happy where they are, and know that their offspring will be as content there as are they. We do not seek to spread ourselves more widely throughout the firmament."

The other male spoke up. "The stars are home to dangerous, uncouth, uncivilized creatures. We wish to know they are there so we can defend against any that might prove hostile. Among those we have met only yours suits our limited desire for offworld contact. We want as little as possible to do with the others." He shivered visibly. "Such as these overbearing AAnn and hideous thranx."

Frowning, Ymir piped up. "The thranx aren't so hid—*umph!*" Turning a hurt face to Saluafata, the secretary used the bottom of one foot to rub the other where the minister's heavy shoe had descended. Discarding laborious diplomatic niceties in favor of alacrity, Saluafata had cut the secretary off in mid objection.

Let them find every space-going sapient species except homo sapiens abhorrent, the minister mused. Unreasonable and xenophobic such an attitude might be, but it only increased humankind's leverage in relations and negotiations. Still, he could hardly believe his good fortune. Not only would the council be delighted, such an astoundingly successful arrangement could only enhance his personal prospects for advancement.

Still, he could not escape the feeling that he was overlooking something significant. He sought certitude.

"Though colonizable space on Treetrunk is limited due to the conditions that prevail over much of the northern and southern portions of the planet, there is room for settlement by more than one species. You are certain your people do not want to share? We already have such an arrangement with the thranx, both here on Earth and elsewhere."

"No thank you," replied the female evenly. "In addition to the reasons I have already given, we find Treetrunk both too cold and too barren to be enticing. Also, our present thrust of exploration lies in the direction of the galactic center, away from your Earth as well as the Argus system. Even if we sought it, there is no reason for potential conflict."

"Better for you to concern yourselves with the expansionist AAnn, thranx, and other aggressive colonizing species than with us," the male on the right proclaimed. "Bearing such considerations in mind, you would do well to begin your settlement of Treetrunk as quickly as possible."

"I'm sure that when I convey the results of this conference to my government it will want to do just that," the minister assured the Pitar. "Local climatic considerations on Treetrunk will keep the pace of development below that of such worlds as Amropolous and New Riviera, but I know that as a first step the scientific outpost that is there now will be expanded as rapidly as possible." Putting both massive hands together, he leaned forward and rested them on the table.

"Now that I have your most gracious concession on the principal matter at hand, we can proceed to a discussion of congruous minutiae. Specifically, how much and what sort of compensation does your government want in return for allowing us unrestricted settlement privileges on Treetrunk? I would imagine that trade credits would prove the most amenable, provided we have anything you want. If there is something else you wish that is within my government's power to grant, I have the authority to recommend that it be given to you."

For a second time the three Pitar conferred, giving Saluafata and his cohorts the opportunity to gaze long and lingeringly at their fetching alien counterparts.

"I am not sure we understand," the female finally declared. "We want nothing from you."

"Nothing?" HoOdam blurted. "No compensation at all?" So stupefied was she by the response that bordered on the ingenuous that she did not even notice Saluafata's disapproving glower.

"How can we claim compensation?" The female concluded with one of the few, restrained Pitarian body gestures. Saluafata recognized it and enjoyed it. "Treetrunk is not ours to give. It is an empty world. We wish only to see you, our friends and close relations, settle and enjoy and populate it. The coincidence of stellar proximity grants us no special claim to it."

Saluafata took the risk of pointing out something now in the hopes of avoiding disagreement or confusion later. Everything said at the conference was being recorded. Neither he nor the council wanted the Pitar or anyone else coming back years later insisting that a certain right had not been granted, that specific permissions had not been obtained.

"By galactic standards the Argus system lies much nearer the Twin Worlds than it does to Earth or any of its colonies. Members of the scientific team that you encountered there were told that your people had visited Treetrunk previously. To our way of thinking, that does give you the right of prior claim. Yet you wish to waive this privilege without recompense?"

"Quite," the male on the right stated. "We have no use for the place. We are certain your people will find much success there, will multiply and fill the narrow ecological niche that is suited to mammals. We encourage you in this."

"After all," the other male added with an inviting smile, "why waste it? You want the place; we do not. Take it and welcome, and in friendship."

"We will of course make periodic visits to monitor your progress." The female's smile, aimed exclusively at Saluafata, melted any lingering concerns. "It should be interesting to observe how your people spread themselves across a new world, since it is something we do not do and have never done ourselves."

The minister found himself beaming back. "Naturally your people will always be welcome on the world you have so generously yielded to us, as well as here on Earth."

"Then if there is nothing more to discuss . . ." The Pitarian representative left the implication dangling.

"Your people are fond of markings on documents," one of the two males pointed out.

Saluafata would rather have spent the next hour staring into the amethyst windows that were the female's eyes, but while he might be feeling like a love-struck schoolboy, he was not one. With regret, he broke the hypnotic connection and sat back in his seat. The buttressed chair groaned as he shifted his weight.

"Yes, I'm afraid it's a tradition even a contemporary government adheres to. If you do not object, that is," he added hastily, wondering what he would do if they did.

"We do not," the female replied, to the minister's relief. "We only find it a curious but harmless anachronism." Again the supple smile that could melt lead. "We will be happy to put the written equivalent of our names to any material of your choosing."

The official signing of the settlement agreement took place in the rooftop assembly chamber, a dome of iridescent, polarized glass that provided a much more dramatic backdrop to the ceremonies than the tiny conference room in which the unexpectedly meteoric negotiations had taken place two weeks previously. Given the presence of not one but several of the glamorous Pitar there was no shortage of media coverage and attention.

Though outranked by several more prominent signees, a restrained Saluafata dominated the proceedings with his sheer presence, his royal dimensions invariably singled out for comment by the tridee commentators. And when senior representatives of the world government returned to their homes and offices in distant Zurich, Washington, Beijing, and Delhi, it was the minister who remained behind to conclude the ceremonies and to see to the ultimate satisfaction of the visiting aliens. This appeared to be as much to their liking as to his.

Much as he luxuriated in the presence of the seductive Pitar, it was not all pleasure. There was business to be conducted. There had to be, or the aliens would have ignored him. Frivolity and fun did not seem to be part of their interspecies lexicon. Polite, pleasant, ingratiating even, they drew the line at convivial intimacy. It was a wall that the immensely gregarious minister was determined to break down. Within the government, subordinates and superiors alike were fond of remarking that Saluafata's girth was exceeded only by his charm. The contrast between sharp mind and boyish charisma struck everyone who came in contact with him, if one could call a man who weighed nearly two hundred kilos "boyish."

Yet his most sincere efforts to break down their inherent reserve resulted in nothing more than courteous smiles from the Pitar. Masking his disappointment, he persisted in his attempts, all the while conducting the people's business.

This was difficult to do on a beach, where accompanied by Ymir he met four of the Pitar for an informal discussion on issues of mutual interest. It was difficult because one of them was the female who had presided over the negotiations that gave rights of colonization of Argus V to the people of Earth.

Slightly more hot natured than the average human, the Pitar enjoyed relaxing if not stiffly basking in the tropical sun. This they normally did in the absence of clothes. Even though the beach lay within the diplomatic compound and was screened and guarded, they had reluctantly agreed to make concessions to the inexplicable vagaries of contemporary human culture. Swimsuits had been provided for all four. The most they would tolerate were small swimsuits. Very small. Guards and privacy screens notwithstanding, the utter absence of these strategic strips of fabric might well have provoked a riot among the ever-hungry media.

Focusing on the business of diplomacy, or anything else for that matter, in the presence of the gem-eyed, statuesque female was not easy. Despite the envy others might feel at his perceived good fortune, Saluafata actually worked harder at such times to earn his stipend than he did in more formal surroundings.

As they sat in folding beach chairs that were the property of the government and gazed at the unruffled silken surface of the lagoon, the minister confined his comments to matters of mutual interest. He did not try to make small talk. The Pitar did not engage in small talk, a characteristic that had been noted and remarked upon as early as their initial contact with the crew of the *Chagos*. But that did not mean that a speaker as voluble as Saluafata could not insinuate casual queries into an otherwise formal diplomatic conversation.

Noting that Ymir was cavorting in the water with a pair of support personnel from Administration, the minister leaned into the sun shadow of the female Pitar's shape. "The water here is safe and warm, but I don't see any of your people enjoying it."

Piercing eyes turned to meet his, and she smiled at him: the standard polite, noncommittal Pitarian smile. "We see oceans as a resource. There is no other reason to enter them except for harvesting and development."

To someone like Saluafata, raised on an island in the middle of the Pacific, such an opinion constituted a kind of heresy. Or would have, had it come from a human. Still, he found it hard to believe that the oh-so-similar Pitar did not even indulge in recreational bathing. It was an observation, however, that allowed him to segue to a minor but curious point of diplomatic contention.

"You know that my government has now made more than several appeals to allow some of our representatives to visit the Twin Worlds." Though his smile was far more open and genuine than hers, it won him no response. "Reciprocal cultural exchanges are a useful way of building and cementing long-term friendships."

"We have no objection to such exchanges," she reminded him. As she shifted in the seat, her barely covered golden alien backside only centimeters above the hot sand, he struggled to keep his thoughts focused on the current business. "We have already concluded numerous agreements permitting such contact."

"Yes, but all of them call for Pitarian cultural groups to visit Earth, or one of the colonies. No permission has yet been granted allowing the equivalent human organizations access to either of the Twin Worlds."

"It is just a matter of time." This time when she smiled, it struck him as just a smidgen more genuine and less academic. Or was he reading into her expression that which he wanted to be there? "Your people have to understand, Minister Saluafata, that the natural reticence and shyness of my kind far exceeds their own. Confined as we are to the two homeworlds of our origin, we are intimidated by races that have spread themselves to other worlds, other star systems. This feeling is not restricted to humankind. We have yet to allow the thranx or any other newly contacted species access to the Twin Worlds." Still speaking, she turned away from him to face the lagoon.

"I am sure it will come with time. But your government has to understand that access to the ancestral home of the Dominion is for us a most sensitive matter. Your people must be patient and not try to force the issue, especially when relations between us are maturing at such a satisfactory pace." Reaching over, she touched the side of his forearm with long, lissome fingers. Though manifestly casual and anything but overtly erotic, the contact sent a shock through his entire expansive frame.

"It's just that we don't see any reason for your hesitation." Despite his pleasurable unease, he refused to be distracted. "If true friendship is to be extended across the parsecs . . ."

She touched him again, and this time her fingers ran down his exposed skin from elbow to wrist. "Please, Minister Saluafata. It is very much such a pleasant day, and so good to—how is it said?—take a break from the relentlessness of duty. Do not spoil it by pressing me or my colleagues for a response we are not authorized to give. I can only reiterate that your people must have some patience with us." This time he chose to believe that the scintillating smile came from the heart. "After all, we have not even been aware of one another's existence for but a short time. Allow us our privacy."

He grinned back. "It's not for me to take away. I'm just doing my job by conveying the petitions of my superiors. Myself, I don't care if your people choose to keep your homeworlds cloistered forever, so long as you come and visit us once in a while and we maintain amicable relations."

"You are a gracious and understanding representative of your kind, Minister Saluafata. I can see why your people appointed you to such a significant position."

"I've seen how your kind favor formality in interspecies relations." He gestured amiably in the direction of the sand, the sea, and the tropical sky. "But just here, just now, couldn't you break with your tradition for a few hours? Long enough to call me 'Api'? It would please me." His grin widened irresistibly. "Think of it as a diplomatic concession to improved relations."

" 'Api.' " She considered him thoughtfully. "A small name for so large an individual."

"It's a common trait among my particular, very small tribe."

"You are a tribe all by yourself, Api."

It was the first time he, or perhaps anyone else, had heard a representative of the Pitar make a joke. He was encouraged beyond reason.

"I'm not involved with the extensive studies that have been undertaken and are still ongoing in attempts to resolve our respective biologies, but I have read the reports—at least, the informal ones. I have neither the time nor the training to delve into the scientific literature. One thing I believe we've had some trouble resolving is the matter of aging. You seem to do it so much better than us."

She executed a Pitarian gesture of understanding. "It is not something we work at. Biology is what it is. It does not play favorites. Believe me, there are aspects to it where your abilities far exceed ours."

"There are millions of humans who, after seeing you, would disagree. Take yourself, for example. Unlike with most human females, it's impossible to tell if you've had or have not had children."

The look she turned on him was so sharp and sudden it shocked him. "What makes you ask that?"

He hastened to recover. "Nothing particular. I was just making conversation." His smile seemed to settle her. "I did not mean to intrude, or to violate any social taboos. Remember, we are still learning about each other."

"That is true. You should excuse me. I should not have reacted the way that I did."

But she had, Saluafata reflected, and he could not help wondering why. He proceeded gently. "Then if I'm not probing an area that's restricted or off-limits, may I ask if you have had children?"

"No, I have not given birth to any offspring." She smiled as she said it, but to the perceptive Saluafata she still seemed sensitive about the matter.

He was about to investigate further when she suddenly turned to him and once more placed a hand on his arm. The difference was that this time, she did not remove it.

"As long as you have brought forth the subject of mutually investigative biology," she murmured in a voice that was as unchanged as it was inherently seductive, "you must know that it has been theorized that sexual relations between Pitar and human are regarded as physically possible. All preliminary studies of the relevant architecture would seem to favor it. There can of course be no issue as a consequence of such contact. All that is wanting for confirmed results to be promulgated is a sufficiency of experimental data."

"I actually wasn't aware that much of anything had been done to resolve the conjectures." He swallowed with some difficulty. "Such matters are reserved for study by the scientific community and do not fall within the ken of the diplomatic ministry." Glancing up the beach, he saw that the other three Pitar had wandered off by themselves. Frolicking in the shallow water, Ymir and the two administrative assistants had moved far away.

The alien was very close to him now, and the sun and sand were very warm. "We have more latitude in such matters." As she whispered to him, her hand moved from his arm. "As a dedicated servant of the Dominion, I am always ready to add to the growing body of scientific and cultural knowledge my people are accumulating about your kind. Experiments in the field need not always be officially authorized."

There were questions he wanted to ask her, elucidations he sought, but as her hand moved he forgot all about them.

7

Heather Wixom struggled triumphantly to the top of the ridge. She could have taken a lifter there and had herself dropped off, but that would have denied her the sense of accomplishment she felt from having made the time-consuming ascent on her own. Technically, it had been easy: dense but navigable native forest; pauses to examine the indigenous wildlife while it hesitated long enough to stare at the slim, alien, human intrusion; and at the top, tolerant slopes that were kind to her booted feet.

From one of the larger boles directly below her rose the dirge of a gnarter. The tree itself put her in mind of a spruce with a skin problem, many of the evergreens that gave Treetrunk its popular name tending to shed copious amounts of bark at the slightest shift in the weather. As for the gnarter, it was a lumpy, eight-legged mass of slow-moving brown and dark blue fur that lived in selected tree hollows while regarding the world out of large, mournful eyes dominated by hourglass-shaped blue pupils. It had been suggested that it looked like the product of a union between a cuttlefish, a koala, and a caterpillar. A prolific inhabitant of the boreal forests, it did not often stray this far south.

It was luxuriating in the "warm" weather, Wixom decided as she tugged the sealfast of her insulating coat tighter around her neck. Treetrunk had rapidly revealed to its new inhabitants how fecund the frigid northern and far southern climes were. The temperate zone that tracked the equator was home to a correspondingly greater variety of life, of which the gnarter was by no means the most outlandish example.

Another was the hoat, a puma-sized predator that impaled its prey on spikelike teeth that grew horizontally from its expansive mouth and flattened jaws. Alone on the hilltop, she kept a careful eye out for it and its less imposing relations. Treetrunk was far from being tamed, its indigenous life-forms anything but domesticated. That was one of the great joys of settling a new world, she knew. It was one of the reasons that, restless and unmarried, she had traded a comfortable and predictable life as an up-and-coming urban planner on New Riviera for the incertitude of laying out new communities from scratch on Argus V.

The weight of the shocker in her left pocket made her grin to herself. No need for quite so potent a weapon of self-defense on placid, easygoing, semitropical New Riviera. There, unwelcome advances could usually be discouraged by the judicious application of a few sharp words.

Unlimbering her backpack, she unfolded the extensible stabilizing pod and attached the siter to the clip on top. Activated, the unit provided a heads-up display that allowed her to place buildings and infrastructure wherever she wished, creating a virtual community anywhere the unit's viewfinder was aimed. Warehouses, shuttleport, access roads, communications, water and sewerage, power transmission pylons—everything could be constructed with the touch of a few controls, could be sized to fit and arranged as she preferred without a single spadeful of dirt having to be overturned.

As she began to lay out the access routes from the growing town of Rajput to the proposed suburban extension, she made adjustments for the terrain, utilizing the unit to banish rock and earth that was in the wrong place and move it to where it was needed. As many trees as possible would be spared, but it was not really a major concern. Between the tundra lines, Treetrunk was a solid belt of native forest, and provisions had already been made to preserve the bulk of it in reserves. A renewable resource if properly looked after, its woods would provide income to the colonists in the form of everything from exotic furniture to tourism.

As she contrived the new town the unit recorded those decisions that she wished to convey to the planning board. In so doing she allowed herself room to maneuver, occasionally indulging in personal fancies that she knew the board would disavow. It was a game: She did as she pleased, the board remonstrated with her, and they compromised. In the end she got what she wanted while permitting the board members to believe that they had prevailed in every matter. The ego involved in the repetitive confrontations meant nothing to her: It was the results that mattered. Her psychological skills had contributed as much to her success on New Riviera as had her talent for organizing and planning.

The board would want the power distribution center to go there, she suspected. She moved it six blocks east. After due debate, she would concede the point, thereby allowing herself room to place the observation and restaurant complex exactly where she wanted it. That mattered. She didn't give two gnarter moans about the location of the power center.

"You are very intense."

The comment did not cause her to jump out of her skin, but her heart certainly thumped momentarily harder. Whirling, she prepared to unload a choice selection of suitably modified expletives on the head of whoever had snuck up behind her. Thinking she was alone and concentrating on the work at hand, she had been doubly oblivious to her immediate surroundings. The surprise had been total, and someone was going to pay.

The instant she caught sight of her soft-footed visitor, the flood of insults she was ready to deliver caught in her throat. From past experience ruefully familiar with their propensity for elaborate gags, she was expecting one or more of her colleagues from Rajput. What she got instead was an alien.

To be precise, a Pitar.

She was better prepared to deal with a marauding hoat.

He gazed down at her with interest, his expression noncommittal, his mouth set in a thin, inscrutable line. The heavy cold-weather attire he wore obscured most of the famed Olympian alien torso, but she could see enough to tell that from the neck downward his build did not differ significantly from the bronzed Greek-god proportions that were the Pitarian norm. She knew they often visited Treetrunk to offer their quiet assistance and to monitor, out of curiosity, the progress of the colony's development. Since they laid claim to nothing, and in fact were effusive in offering their help to the small but steady stream of arriving settlers, the government saw no reason why they should not be granted unrestricted access to the burgeoning, energetic new communities.

Wixom knew of several occasions where the aliens' assistance had been vital in helping small new municipalities overcome difficult local conditions. How the Pitar knew when an outlying hamlet was in trouble no one knew, but when it was they invariably appeared in their sleek shuttles, providing aid and support without having to be asked. No thranx vessel ever did anything like that, she reflected, shuddering a little at the thought of the giant, grotesque bugs running freely through the colony. Admittedly, the nearest thranx system lay a respectable distance from Treetrunk while the Twin Worlds of the Dominion were near neighbors in terms of space-plus travel. Nor was it that the thranx were indifferent or standoffish. They simply preferred to follow procedure in all things, including matters of aid and assistance. In this as in everything else they were methodical where humans were impulsive. Pitarian methodology appeared to fall somewhere in-between.

In any event, she relaxed as soon as she identified her visitor. He had steel-gray eyes and pale orange hair that put her in mind of ripening tangerines. Framed by a soft, protective hood, his features were predictably perfect. As he stood there on the windswept rock slope she grew aware that he was waiting for her to say something. The fact that she had never met a Pitar and knew nothing of their language was a poor excuse for her continued nonresponsiveness, but it was all that she had. Quick-witted, sharp-tongued, and completely at ease as she was among members of the opposite gender of her own kind, in the presence of this minor male mammalian divinity, she stood as if struck dumb, completely at a loss for movement as well as for words.

Apparently detecting that something was amiss, the visitor

spoke again. "I seem to have startled you. Such was not my intent. Do you require medical attention?"

I am not going to swoon, she told herself firmly. Women of my experience and education do not swoon. Besides which, swooning is an atavistic reaction more properly applicable to the proper ladies of the nineteenth century. This facile forensic explication, however, did nothing to reconcile the physical and emotional insurrection that was raging within her.

The Pitarian male helped. He helped by moving: by bending and picking up a rock. He examined it before tossing it casually aside. It clattered against the scree, and the sound and motion served to jolt her out of her trance. Forging an effort of will, she turned away from him and back to her work. Her mind, however, was not intent on laying out accessways, waterlines, or communication lines-of-sight.

The alien was very close to her. She wanted to tell him—no, to order him—to move away, but for some reason her brain seemed to have lost contact with her vocal apparatus. All she could say was "Yes, I'm an intense person, both in my work and in the rest of my life."

"Intensity is good." Leaning close, the Pitar tried to resolve her heads-up display. This put his head very near to her own. She could smell the flat but not unpleasant alien scent, could feel the gossamer caress of inhuman breath. Her fingers on the controls of the siter started to tremble, and she angrily thrust them down at her side.

"What are you doing here?" I sound inane, she thought angrily. An inane twelve-year-old; that's what I've become. Conscious of the fact that she was bringing no credit either to herself or to her species, she fought to reestablish the kind of control that the alien's unexpected appearance had shattered.

"Only having a quiet look around, as you humans say."

Just as she was starting to recover some equilibrium, he smiled at her, and she found that she had to begin all over again.

"As you know, we are fascinated by the entire concept of leaving the comforting confines of a homeworld to settle upon another. It is a concept entirely foreign to us. But we want to see you succeed here, on Treetrunk. So in order to learn how to be of better assistance, we travel and we observe." His expression flattened once again. "You do not mind if I observe you?"

"Suit yourself," she replied indifferently. Within, she was yearning for him to observe her for a good, long time. Oh, how she wanted him to observe her! She had heard stories, they had all heard stories, about the . . . relationships that under just the right circumstances could develop between individual humans and Pitar. There were those who insisted these were nothing more than that—just stories. Rumors fed and fueled by the perversely imaginative. Though looking at this Pitar, tall and straight and so obviously muscular beneath his cold-weather gear, she could well believe that . . .

Stop it, she told herself! Male he may be, but he's also an alien. Don't ignore him, but don't trade your dignity and self-respect for some unsupportable foolish flight of fancy. Respond to his questions, and to nothing else.

"You are doing what?" he inquired politely, and the slight grammatical deviation helped to remind her of who and what he was. She returned her attention to her instrumentation.

"I work for the planetary planning agency. It's my job to search out and recommend the best locations for the individual components of a new development, as well as to design and suggest overall schematics. It's a task that does require some intensity of purpose, as you observed."

"I am very impressed," the Pitar told her, and for utterly inexplicable reasons this perfunctory comment caused her breathing to accelerate. "I am only a simple observer and could never manage the complex interdisciplinary tools necessary to perform such a task."

"It's not that difficult," she responded. "Having a new, state-of-the-art siter helps a lot. Here, I'll show you." Stepping aside, she allowed him to peer directly into the eyepiece that queued the heads-up display.

The Pitar asked several questions, struggling with his command of Terranglo, before stepping back. "It appears to be a very efficient device. Your technology is good."

She could not decide if she was blushing or if her cheeks were simply reddened from having been exposed to the cold air during the climb. "I don't make it; I'm just trained to use it. From what I read and see on the tridee, your technology's good, too."

"We have done well enough. Concentrating solely on developing the Twin Worlds has both helped and forced us to concentrate our energies. Our two local asteroid belts supply ample resources, and we are careful not to overexploit those that are not renewable. Of late our society has grown somewhat stagnant, but contact with your people has suggested ways and means of revitalizing our development, as well as solving problems that previously seemed insurmountable. For that we thank you, and are most grateful for the contact between our two species. We are especially glad to see you doing so well here on Treetrunk."

"Your people have been so helpful ever since the first settlement went in." She hesitated briefly, fearful of committing some unseen faux pas. She was a planner, not a diplomat. "Some of us have become . . . fond of you."

"Your demonstrations of affection have been remarked upon." His tone was dry and formal, and she wasn't sure whether she was grateful for that or not. "We find it peculiar that a great deal of it has to do with our appearance, which we ourselves find in no way remarkable and over which we have no control. Nevertheless, anything that facilitates better relations between us is to be welcomed." From within his protective hood a smile emerged that warmed her to the tips of her boots. "Your mate must be proud to be conjoined to so competent a worker."

"Thanks for the compliment, but I'm not marri . . . mated."

"No children, then?" His tone was unchanged, academic.

"Not yet, but I'm hoping to have a couple someday." She fiddled absently with the controls of the siter.

He looked past her, into the shallow valley that would soon be home to another two or three thousand humans. "As am I. Our reproductive and birth systems are extraordinarily similar."

"So I've heard." She looked away from the siter and back up at him. "Why haven't you had any children?"

His smile faded, and he made a gesture she did not recognize. "For one thing, the time is not right for me. That is one area where our physiologies differ. Not only are our females fertile only for a limited time each year, but the same is true for the males. We do not enjoy the flexibility of year-round breeding that you do."

"Oh, I don't know." She responded with a mixture of consideration and playfulness. "I know plenty of people who would prefer that kind of biological arrangement. It would make a lot of things easier." Reaching out, she tentatively placed a hand on his arm. She could feel the power even through layers of winter clothing that exceeded her own. "So that means you can't get anyone pregnant right now?"

He made the Pitarian gesture for agreement, a smooth dipping of the right shoulder. "That is correct."

"Not that you could anyhow," she murmured as she embarked on a fairly explicit explanation of the intricacies of how certain specific on-site structures ought to be erected.

From the preliminary settlement of Chagos Downs to the carefully laid-out capital city of Weald, the colony grew rapidly. The pure, unpolluted air energized new colonists the instant they stepped off their transport shuttles. Sometimes bitterly cold winters, when it seemed as if the entire planet were about to succumb to the glaciers that were advancing slowly from both north and south to squeeze the habitable belt around the planet's midsection in an icy vise, gave way to an explosively vibrant spring and therapeutic summer. As predicted by its discoverers, Treetrunk was no New Riviera, but it was a highly amenable place to live. Those who arrived from other worlds to make their homes there generally had few regrets.

There were always malcontents who would never be happy anywhere, who really believed they *could* get all their squirrels up one tree. Grumbling and complaining, they packed up and left, always in search of the paradise world that existed only in their imaginations. Their number was a trickle compared to the steady stream of satisfied newcomers. Families began to put down roots, new enterprises were begun, education centers expanded rapidly.

Operating out of her own tiny prefabricated habitation, a crazy lady preached the gospel of a church that as yet had no recognized name but which aimed to include and encompass all forms of intelligent life. Bound by tradition and unable as yet to envision themselves praying alongside, for example, a brace of thranx, colonists new and old laughed at and teased the earnest evangelist. A few, a very few, occasionally stopped to listen, finding the ravings of what appeared to be a rational fanatic entertaining if not convincing.

Following in the gridded footsteps of the planners, the colony expanded. Outposts became waypoints; waypoints became stations; stations became the cores of small communities. Imports gave way to locally produced goods and services. New industries congealed, from small crafts and manufacturing that made use of the planet's extensive hardwood forests to a pair of mines that extracted useful metals from beneath the surface.

The colony was well on its way to advancing from dependent to transitional autonomous status, with its own independent world government, when the *Glistener* entered into orbit above Weald. A small, compact deep-space vessel engaged in scientific exploration, it stopped to pay its respects to the inhabitants of the new human colony world before continuing on its planned course through the upper Orion Arm in the general direction of the galactic center.

Visitors from the ship were greeted with full courtesy and formalities, if not warmly. Though naturally suspicious of outsiders, the settlers could not very well refuse to welcome representatives of a race with which humankind enjoyed officially cordial relations. The thranx were granted permission to visit several communities. Each group was accompanied by experienced members of the planetary government who saw to it that the visitors' plans and itineraries were well publicized in advance. The majority of colonists had never seen a thranx, and it would not do to have children or susceptible individuals panic at the sight of them. That would have been discourteous.

There was little need to worry. The thranx intended a short visit at best. A species that favored 100 percent humidity and air temperature to match, they were not at all comfortable in the brisk, wintry atmosphere of Treetrunk. Despite their personal discomfort, their inborn concern and curiosity caused them to persevere, if only for the brief duration of their stay.

Dutifully, they admired the energy exhibited by the human settlers and gestured approvingly at the skill with which the colony had been laid out and was being developed. Their hosts thanked them when appropriate while privately wishing to be rid of the inquisitive, talkative, pleasantly odiferous bugs so they could get back to the business of building the colony.

Unlike her fellows, there was one senior thranx who seemed, in spite of the unkind climate, reluctant to leave. Every question her hosts answered sparked another two or three. Interested in everything, she was satisfied by nothing. While her hosts despaired of satisfying her, she continued blithely on her way, inquiring endlessly about the most inconsequential matters.

"The local population is approaching six hundred thousand," her weary guide informed her. "Of these, some two hundred thousand plus are concentrated in and around Weald, with another ninety-five thousand at Chagos Downs. Allowing for geological constraints, the rest are scattered in small communities and outlying camps that follow the equator."

"You are not expanding to north and south as well?" Cocooned within cold-weather gear that exceeded in insulating properties anything a human would wear except at the poles, the thranx's face was barely visible. Twin antennae peeped hesitantly from beneath the brim of the headgear.

The guide sighed tiredly. "Of course we will, but for right now there's no reason to do so. The most amenable zone is being promoted first. When our settlements meet on the other side of the planet, that will be the time to expand into the colder forests."

The senior thranx nodded, a gesture they had developed the habit of using among themselves as well as in the presence of humans. "Then you are doing well here?"

"Extremely well." The guide could not help but add, "In addition to the regular runs from Earth and the occasional visit from New Riviera or Proycon, the Pitar have been really supportive. Not just with verbal encouragement, but with material assistance as well. Especially during the first two years of settlement, the help they provided was invaluable."

If the thranx understood this observation to be a dig at her kind for not offering more, she did not acknowledge its tone. "We are glad that you received the aid that you needed. You are fortunate. The expanding colonization efforts in our own sphere of exploration require our full attention, as no species has offered to assist *our* efforts. In addition, we have a long-running, ongoing disputation with the race you know as the AAnn, which complicates and inhibits our efforts."

"The AAnn don't bother us here." Unwittingly, the guide had assumed a marginally superior air.

"*Chur!kk,* the AAnn are very shrewd." A truhand encased in insulating fabric waved at the much taller guide, who comprehended nothing of the meaning behind the gesture. "Thinking oneself safe from them, bound by alliances and agreements, secure behind a thin barrier of treaties and covenants, is the most dangerous attitude a people can have."

"Well, I'm not a diplomat, but all I can say is that they haven't given us any trouble."

"Have they paid you a visit?"

The guide blinked. "Several times, I believe. I only settled here last year myself. But yes, ships of the Empire have called at Treetrunk. If I remember correctly they had a look around, extended their hopes for a successful enterprise on the part of the colonial government, took some straightforward and innocuous scientific readings, and left. I understand that their visits were very brief." He couldn't keep from smiling. "No doubt they found it a bit nippy for their liking."

Once more the thranx gestured. "The AAnn require an ambient temperature similar to ours, but infinitely drier than even your kind prefers." A pair of hands wagged in his direction. "Ensure that those who monitor your scanning instrumentation are well trained and remain alert. Nothing is more dangerous than a well-wishing AAnn."

"We'll have a care," the guide replied with polite nonchalance.

Whether the thranx detected something in her host's voice or if she simply decided to have a further say in the matter the man never knew, but the heavily bundled insectoid turned to him with an effort and met his eyes with hers. Leastwise, he thought she did. When gazing at compound eyes, it is difficult to tell for certain exactly where they are focused.

"We are always astonished at the confidence you humans display in the face of a lethal and indifferent universe. Have a care that your confidence does not exceed your ability to sustain it."

"Thank you for that solicitous homily," he replied tartly. "We know what we're doing here."

"Does anyone know what they're doing anywhere? Individual or species, it does not seem to matter. We are all of us sapients adrift together in a cosmos in which the largest single constituent of matter seems to be composed of unanswered questions." Turning away, she started up along the path that would lead them back to the terminus where the ground skimmer would pick them up. "I have seen enough. I'm cold, and ready to return to my cubicle on board the *Glistener*.

I'm ready for you to do so too, he murmured silently. Most of us here on Treetrunk have better things to do than escort garrulous bugs around, answering their inane questions while trying to ponder their cryptic aphorisms. Even if, he reflected, one or two did smell like attar of frangipani.

8

Trohanov was relaxing in his cabin with one of the few tridee recordings he hadn't already watched on the run out from Earth. It was some trifle about a genetically engineered lone avenger on an endless voyage of self-discovery whose ultimate denouement the creators of the entertainment had left purposely obscure. The protagonist struck him as shallow and his paramour devoid of depth, but they were both pleasant to look upon.

Presently, their beguiling three-dimensional forms were occupied in an activity that, while not in any wise significant to the advancement of the plot, was nonetheless engaging. So it was with some ire that he acknowledged the insistent hail from the bridge.

"Hollis, I'm off duty!" he barked, knowing that the omnidirectional pickup would convey his tone as well as his words to the ship's second-in-command. "Maybe that doesn't mean much to you, but when you reach my age you learn to treasure every little—"

The second officer interrupted him, which while not unprecedented, was unusual. She also sounded worried, but that was normal for Hollis. "Captain, you'd better come up here."

"Why?" Even as he objected, he was swinging his legs out of the bed. "We made the transition from space-plus without incident, and this system holds no surprises. What's wrong with the ship?"

"It's not the ship, sir. At least, Kharall says it's not."

"All right, all right!" Grumbling to himself as he slipped into his one-piece duty suit, he damned the regulations that required a vessel's captain and senior officers to always be available for consultation.

No one confronted him as he made his way via lift and corridor to the bridge. Whatever had upset Hollis, it had not caused any panic on the ship. He encountered no frightened faces, no individuals racing to and fro in panic. This had better be a real problem, he thought irritably, or he was going to have serious words with his second.

Nor did there appear to be any reason for distress on the bridge itself. There was Kharall, bent toward his console as if by bringing his face a few millimeters closer to the readouts he could discern details that would not otherwise be evident. Everyone else assigned to the second shift was in position and to all intents and purposes engrossed in their work. A few chatted softly, their attitudes anything but indicative of imminent disaster. No voices were raised, though the expressions on several faces as he entered were expectant.

Expectant of what? He had no idea yet what was going on, or why Hollis had thought it necessary to summon him from the middle of his rest period. Only one thing was he certain of: He would have some answers very quickly.

Turning slightly to his right, he strode purposefully over to where Hollis was conferring with Meeker, the ship's communications specialist. Both looked up at his approach. Hollis didn't wait for the captain to speak.

"We're a fraction of an au out from Treetrunk, just cutting the orbit of Argus Six, and there's still no response."

He replied instantly. "So their beacon's down."

"All of them?" She met his gaze unflinchingly. "All three?"

"It's possible," he shot back, though internally he was already beginning to argue with himself.

Meeker joined in. She was a small woman with big ears, ragged black hair cropped short in what Trohanov had always thought a very unflattering cut, and she had a surprisingly large voice that was the aural equivalent of her occasional opinions.

"One okay. Two maybe. Three never."

"Never say never." Trohanov was not ready to concede,

though if professionally challenged he would have been compelled to agree with his communications officer. "Treetrunk's still a new world, only been settled for a few years."

"Four," Meeker corrected him.

"Okay, four, dammit." Ahead, through the narrow, curved port, could be seen only stars and the still distant dot of Argus V, their destination. "A multiple beacon failure is still possible, especially on a world as recently colonized as this one."

"There's no response from the shuttleport at Weald, either." Meeker was conciliatory but insistent.

"So their communications are down also. It means they're having some problems, that's all." As he spoke he leaned closer to the communications console, studying the readouts closely.

Meeker turned her child-troll's face up to his. "There's no background noise. No tridee, no chat, nothing. Not even a hiss. From a communications standpoint, the planet's dead."

Her choice of words upset Trohanov, but he didn't let it show. "Okay, that's bad. Maybe real bad. Let's not anybody jump to any conclusions. I've known several people who jumped to conclusions and they invariably came to a bad end."

"What happened to them?" Hollis asked softly.

He flicked deep-set cinnamon eyes at her. "They landed in holes. Maintain preset course for orbital insertion. There's nothing to suggest we should do otherwise. Keep everyone on alert."

"What about the rest of the crew?"

"Leave 'em alone. There's no reason to tell them anything until we have something definite to tell. Those who are sleeping might need all they can get." Reaching down, he put a strong hand on Meeker's shoulder. "Keep monitoring everything that sputters and let me know the instant you hear anything, even if it's just bad language." She nodded once. In charge of words, Meeker was not one to waste them.

Hollis regarded the captain speculatively. "I suppose there's no reason for you to stay here, sir. You might as well go back to bed. We'll call you when we know something."

He glanced sideways at the starship's silent, flickering instrumentation, his expression set. "Like hell," he growled softly.

They settled into orbit without incident. As expected, they were the only vessel present. Treetrunk was an outpost, a comparatively new settlement far from Earth and the other colonies. KK-drive ships called infrequently, and only on official business. In the ellipsoidal cargo compartment that comprised the bulk of the vessel's superstructure was a consignment of goods from New Riviera. Subsequent to delivery, the space-plus transport would move on to Proycon. Everything about the run, from its payload to its course, was conventional.

On the chill world below, however, something was not.

Meeker had been at it for another six hours straight when Trohanov finally lost patience. By now all three shifts were awake, with rumor and controversy rampant among the crew. It was time to resolve ignorance.

"Run the check on shuttle number two. I'm going down. Hollis, as per procedure you're in charge until I get back." He turned to leave.

"What about the cargo, sir? We have three full loads. The company will scream if we have to make an extra drop."

"Let 'em howl. There's some kind of trouble down below, and until we know the nature, extent, and degree of the local emergency it's more prudent to hold onto the shipment than to start delivering it. As soon as we know what's going on we'll start shifting containers. Until then, ship is to remain on alert and everyone is to stand by. I'll field complaints from those who are supposed to be on downtime later. Right now the first thing we need to do is find out why this place is electronically comatose."

Nothing untoward materialized to interfere with the shuttle's descent. The view out the small, thick ports was uneventful, the surface a watercolor wash of white, brown, and green. Trohanov and the half dozen crew he'd chosen to accompany him spoke little as the shuttle struck atmosphere and began to vibrate. At such times each man and woman had thoughts enough to occupy their minds. At the captain's direction, all wore sidearms. Procedure, he thought. In the absence of knowledge it was always reassuring to be able to fall back on procedure.

Nothing in the literature, or the regulations, or his experience prepared him for what they found, however.

As the shuttle dropped beneath the thick clouds and into calm air the pilot reported the absence of any signal from the capital's port. There was heavy overcast but no rain or snow, the atmosphere being as eerily silent as the surface. In the absence of the usual datastream to take control of the shuttle's instruments and guide it in, the pilots were forced to locate the landing strip themselves. "On final approach," one of the pilots said, and Trohanov and his people scrunched a little deeper back into their seats. Down, down . . .

The shuttle accelerated violently and without warning. He found himself wrenched sideways, then pressed back into the seat. Several of the crew gasped, but no one screamed and there was no panic. They were still airborne, and the shuttle's engines throbbed with restored power. Moments later the voice of the pilot echoed through the passenger compartment.

"Sorry about that, everyone. Obviously, we made a last-second pull-up. We're going to have to try and find a field or something to set down in. We can't use either of the two landing strips at Weald shuttleport." There was a short pause while the atmospheric craft began to bend around in a tight curve, though the arc it executed was no more constricted than the pilot's voice. "They've been destroyed."

It took some time for the pilots to locate a suitable site. Relying on the shuttle's landing skids, they made a bumpy, jolting, but successful touchdown. Before the craft had slid to a stop Trohanov was out of his seat and harness and racing forward.

The view out the cockpit's wide double port was maddeningly uninformative: tall evergreens, distant tree-swathed hills, a nearby pond whose inhabitants were only now starting to return following the shuttle's noisy landing. Everything appeared peaceful and serene.

"Where are we?"

Solnhofen, the copilot, pointed to a readout. "About two kilometers southwest of the southern runway. This appears to be a natural meadow."

Bending over to peer out the port, Trohanov nodded once. "I don't see any signs of catastrophe. You said the landing strips were destroyed?"

"Yes, sir." The pilot's face was ashen. "We didn't get a good look at the city itself—too busy with the descent. Neither Lillie nor I have had to do a manual landing since flight school."

"Forget it. You both did great. Could you tell what caused the damage?"

The two pilots exchanged a glance. "No, Captain," a regretful Solnhofen told him. "It was as Dik said. We were too busy just trying to get down in one piece."

"Right." Turning, a couple of steps brought Trohanov back into the passenger compartment. Everyone was out of harness, fidgety and anticipative. "We're going for a walk. Check your sidearms and make sure they're not just decorative. I want everyone's weapon and communications gear fully powered up." They stared at him expectantly, and he realized they were waiting for an explanation. In the absence of one, he improvised as best he could.

"Something bad has happened here. We don't know what yet, but we're going to find out."

"That's not our job, Captain," someone pointed out. "We're a class three KK-drive deep-space cargo carrier, and that's all we are."

"You can file a formal complaint about being forced to function outside your job classification with the company later. Right now everybody here comes with me. I've been in Weald twice before, once as recently as last year, so I'm at least sort of familiar with the municipal layout. Stick close and don't wander off. No matter what we find, we'll be back here before dark." He looked over his shoulder, toward the cockpit.

"You two stay on board. I don't want you going outside, not

even to smell the tree sap. If anything real disturbing should start to show itself, you lift off and return to ship."

"Disturbing?" The pilot looked uncertain. "Like what, Captain?"

"Like I don't know—yet. Use your own judgment." He tapped the communicator on his duty belt. "We'll keep in touch."

Stepping out of the shuttle, it was difficult to believe that anything was amiss. Indigenous wildlife filled the nearby forest and the open meadow with intermittent alien song. Arboreal life-forms flitted among the trees and skittered through the waist-high blue-bladed ground cover. Plotting a simple straight line, Trohanov led his people away from the shuttle and into the woods.

The gently rolling ground did not slow them, and the absence of dense underbrush except in isolated copses allowed rapid progress. With the shuttleport lying to their northeast, Trohanov calculated, if they maintained their current pace they ought to reach the southernmost outskirts of the city by midafternoon. That would not allow much time for exploring, but they ought to be able to secure transport into the city center. Someone at Administration would be able to clear things up and to explain the nature of whatever emergency had befallen the colony.

But there was no transport readily available in the southern suburbs of Weald. There was very little left of the suburb they entered, or for that matter of the rest of the city.

Its inhabitants, it was revealed, were as dead as their communications.

Whatever smoke and flame had risen from the ruins had long since burned itself out. Except for the occasional darting shape of a native scavenger working the dead, the city was devoid of movement. Finding and righting a small skimmer that still retained half its power charge, they succeeded in covering considerably more ground than they would have been able to do on foot.

The destruction was selective as opposed to total. Many of the city's buildings were still intact, from individual or group habitations to municipal facilities such as the central water-treatment plant. But the center of the city, where Administration had been located, was a spacious, silent crater. Ramparts of fused glass sloped down to a pile of vitreous slag in the center. On the northern outskirts of the city, a similar pit marked the spot where the colony's intersystem space-minus communications shaft and facility had been located.

All that afternoon they scoured the capital in search of survivors, and found none. Those bodies that had not been incinerated by shot or subsequent fire displayed indisputable evidence of having been shattered by violence. Come early evening Trohanov found himself kneeling alongside an entire family. Trapped inside a small shop, they had evidently attempted to make a stand against whatever had ravaged their community. Signs that a blockaded doorway had been smashed inward lay scattered everywhere.

Whatever weapon had been used to kill them was thorough and messy. Though no forensic pathologist, Trohanov could see as clearly as anyone that something had struck each of the bodies and blown them apart. The remains of the father lay in the middle of the floor, where he had apparently attempted to intercept the intruders. Back in a corner they found the corpse of the mother splattered over those of two preadolescent boys. In a warmer climate the stench in the room, as elsewhere in the city, would have been overpowering. The cold, clear air of Treetrunk had helped to slow decomposition and decay. Otherwise, it would have been impossible for the crew to have continued their investigation.

As it was, several of the small group became sick at different times that afternoon. The slaughter gave every indication of having been carried out in a relentless and methodical fashion. Returning to the shuttle, Trohanov informed Hollis and the rest of his crew of what he and the others had found and took care to relay the visual information they had managed to collect. Returning to the ship, they compressed and sent it on its way to Earth, entangling it with the first quantum receiver that acknowledged their transmission.

In the silence of the bulbous ship no one slept. As soon

as Trohanov felt able, he took a larger team back down to the surface. This time they set down near the colony's first community and second city, the municipality that had been named Chagos Downs after the ship that had originally explored the Argus system. There was no shuttleport at the Downs, but there were landing facilities for suborbital aircraft. Unfortunately, those facilities had suffered the same fate as their much larger counterpart at Weald, and the crew once again had to set down in the nearest available field.

Chagos Downs was a mirror image of disaster, albeit on a smaller scale. The same conditions applied as they had encountered in the capital: Many structures had been left standing and intact, some with no sign of damage at all, while others had been completely reduced. As before, there were no survivors. Like the inhabitants of Weald, the citizens of the Downs had been slaughtered where they had been found; attempting to surrender to unknown assailants, lying in bed, slumped over instruments and other devices while busy at work, caught preparing meals, on the streets, and in hallways. From the eldest patient in the hospital to the youngest infant, no one had been spared.

Whoever, whatever had committed the atrocity had been relentlessly thorough in seeing to it that not one survivor was left breathing to comment on the cataclysm. Trohanov knew it was not his responsibility to try and find out who was responsible. The crew member who had spoken out earlier doubtless had being doing no more than voicing the concerns and opinion of many of his colleagues. They were crew on a deep-space transport: not soldiers, not mass-homicide investigators, not government operatives. Whatever had happened on Treetrunk was terrible, but it was not their business to try and fix responsibility. Nor could Trohanov leave his ship under Hollis's command to resume its voyage while he remained behind to await the first official response from Earth. Pragmatically, he and his companions could do nothing with the anger and helpless fury that boiled within them except bottle it.

Reluctantly, they returned to the ship and resumed their itinerary. Until the day and hour of their deaths, the memory of what they had seen never left them, remaining as clear and sharp as the air of the devastated world itself.

Little had changed when the three warships emerged from space-plus dangerously close to the planetary mass. Settling into equidistant orbit, their instrumentation between them covering and monitoring every meter of the cloud-swathed globe beneath, they dropped nine shuttle craft into the clouds and clear air below. Each was far larger than that of the cargo ship that had preceded them. On board were soldiers as coldly efficient and highly trained as Earth and its colonies could produce, armed with the most advanced weaponry their military research institutes could manufacture.

Setting down simultaneously at predetermined locations in the planet's habitable equatorial zone, the independently functional squads immediately established defensible perimeters around their respective shuttles. Once these landing sites were secured, ground transports were unloaded from the craft and boarded by half of each squadron's personnel. Leaving the entrenched perimeters that now surrounded the heavily defended shuttle craft, these armed skimmers and their smaller escorts moved out in carefully designated search-and-rescue patterns.

They found little changed and nothing significantly different from the halting, barely adequate pair of reports that had been filed by the crew of the cargo transport that had first made the grisly discovery. Fanning out from their landing sites, they checked the towns first, then moved on to isolated hamlets, individual farms, mines, and tiny frontier outposts. The degree of physical destruction varied, but nowhere did they find anyone alive, nor any record in any of the surviving instrumentalities of what had happened.

As soon as the military commander of the expedition was satisfied that no threat remained on the surface, at least insofar as his troops could determine, the members of the scientific team were allowed to descend. Forced to remain on their assigned ship while the soldiers secured the ground, they were in a quiet frenzy of fervor to begin their work. Over their protests each was assigned an armed guard. Until some answers were forthcoming the military was taking no chances. Pathologists and recorders, biologists and scanners were forced to operate under the watchful eyes of edgy soldiers.

The scientists' escorts were not uneasy because they feared attack. Indeed, they would have welcomed it. To the last man and woman they had seen too much death on what had previously been considered a mellow, pastoral, even boring world. Women clutching infants, old men slain in the doorways of their homes, children shot down in the street: It was too much for some of them. Those who gutted their way through the last of the patrols wanted something to shoot at, something to kill. No plague had wiped out the inhabitants of Argus V, no secretive native uprising had surprised the colonists in their beds. The evidence was indisputable that advanced killing technology had been at work in the peaceful forests and meadows.

The question that was on everyone's mind—soldier, scientist, and starship crew alike—was, Whose?

Derwent was tired of trideeing bodies. After the first sickening couple of days his stomach settled down and he was able to go about his job more or less normally and at a faster pace. The labor was necessary, he knew. Not only so that relatives on other worlds could identify slain relations but so that the research team being put together back on Earth would have as much information to work with as possible. Hudson, his partner, was reciting into her recorder in her familiar monotone. It was her job to render a preliminary judgment on cause of death.

Dozens of additional personnel were active in other districts. Since landing, no one had enjoyed a day off. Given the condition of many of the bodies there was no time to spare. Not with hundreds of thousands of corpses to evaluate. For teams such as Derwent and Hudson, long hours in unpleasant conditions had become the norm. Every body, or remnant thereof, had to be dutifully recorded and evaluated.

Outside the ruins of the small country inn a corporal and two privates stood guard, *stood* being perhaps too strong a word. Derwent didn't mind when the three sat down and set their weapons aside, conversing quietly among themselves. The small skimmer that had transported the team and its supplies rested nearby, powered down and open to intrusion. The recording specialist was not worried. From the time the first squad of marines had touched down they had encountered no opposition. Nor had any trouble manifested itself since. Nothing interfered with the work of the pathologists or coroners.

Whatever had exterminated the population of Argus V was nowhere in evidence. If the relentless and thorough attackers had suffered casualties they had been careful to take their dead and wounded away with them, as well as erase any evidence of their existence. Only human bloodstains and fragments of human bodies were found. The use of generic and not especially sophisticated weapons of destruction precluded the rapid identification of the killers. Nothing remained of their handiwork except the corpses of their victims.

To the psychologists, that suggested that the assailants feared retribution. As well they should. There wasn't a soldier among the relieving force who did not go to bed night after night dreaming of imaginary alien necks to wring.

Derwent was more of a realist. Knowing nothing of those who had destroyed the colony, it was premature to assign blame even to imaginary enemies. For all they knew the invading force might have been renegade humans from one of the other colony worlds.

"What motivation could another colony possibly have for carrying out a massacre like this?" Hudson had challenged him. Light glinted off her implanted lenses. She was a pert, spirited lady whom the adjective *vivacious* fit in more ways than one, and she was not slow to defend an opinion.

Phlegmatic and blunt, Derwent argued for the sake of dissention. They were not a particularly well-matched team, but their personal disagreements did not hamper their work.

"How should I know? Not having the mind-set of a mass murderer myself, I can't begin to imagine a reason." He stepped over the body of an eight-year-old boy whose head and legs had gone missing.

"Then shut up," she told him curtly. "If you can't give reasons, you don't have a hypothesis."

"Oh so?" Swinging his recorder around the front room of the inn, he made sure to keep the extensive damage to the back wall in frame. "All right, I'll guess. Maybe somebody was jealous about the amount of aid these people were receiving. Maybe they thought they could steal whatever was really valuable and save themselves some hard work. Maybe a grudge developed between this colony and another."

"None of those makes any sense." She was bent over the remains of a middle-aged couple who had died in each other's arms. "Even if one of them did, or if several of them did, all of them taken together with another half dozen added don't serve to rationalize the annihilation of six hundred thousand people. Humans don't do this sort of thing."

Derwent laughed curtly. "Read your prehistory."

"All right," she conceded, "they don't do it *anymore*. We haven't turned on ourselves to this extent since the conclusion of the Second Dark Ages."

"Then aliens are responsible."

"Nothing is certain yet," she reminded him. "No conclusions have been drawn. It's too soon, and the evidence is still being assembled. We won't be the ones to render the final judgment anyway. You know that. It will be decided back on Earth." She fell to murmuring into her recorder.

Derwent had already finished upstairs. Four guests had been staying at the inn at the time of the attack. Besides the proprietor's family there was also a second couple who had worked for the owners. The number of deceased jibed with the records a search team had accessed in the nearest town, except for a Sithwa Pirivi, age twenty, whose body had not yet been located. That meant nothing, he knew. The young woman might have been elsewhere at the time of the attack, visiting friends, shopping in town, or simply out hiking, and would have been killed there instead of in the vicinity of the inn where she worked. It was going to take time to fill in the blanks in the record of Treetrunk's exterminated population.

People traveled, both for reasons of work and recreation, and did not always perish where they lived.

The chore of recording and evaluating the tens of thousands of decomposing dead was a distressing and difficult task. Not everyone adjusted as efficiently or pragmatically as the team of Derwent and Hudson. As time wore on many had to be relieved, some only long enough to recover their equilibrium, others permanently. Throughout the appalling work the teams and their support groups persevered. The number of identified dead rose from the tens of thousands into the hundreds of thousands.

And still there were no answers. Working alongside their conscripted civilian counterparts, practitioners of military forensics struggled with the available evidence in an increasingly frustrating and futile attempt to try and identify the perpetrators of the atrocity. The executioners had left nothing behind, not even footprints. If they had utilized weapons firing explosive projectiles they had gathered up every shell casing, intact or fragmentary, so its origin could not be identified.

One aspect of the attack the researchers felt confident in propounding: It had taken the colonists completely by surprise. How else to explain the utter absence in surviving records of any reference to the invasion? If someone had jotted a report or warning down on a piece of paper, or whispered frantically into a personal recorder, there was no record of it. It was as if the population had stood blithely by while whoever was responsible for their brutal demise had proceeded methodically with their gruesome work. The pathology teams were specifically instructed to look for any such surviving testimony.

"You'd think there'd be a note somewhere." Having finished his work at the inn, Derwent was wandering through the reception area while Hudson tidied up the last of her responsibilities. "A sketch drawn by some poor terrified kid, or a description buried in a coded file."

"There isn't an intact file left on the planet subsequent to the day of the final encounter." Hudson rose from where she had been crouching. "Not only were these people surprised by their attackers, they were surprised repeatedly. It's crazy. But I agree with you. No matter how much of a shock this attack was to the populace, someone ought to have left a recoverable message somewhere." She looked up at him out of her colorless implants. "It wouldn't take much. A couple of words. 'Humans did this' would be enough to get started on. Or 'Thranx here, killing everybody.' Or 'Unknown aliens have landed.' Anything, anything at all."

Derwent nodded as he lowered his instrument and started outside. "Anything's better than nothing. And right now, nothing is what we got. I don't suppose you've heard any different from any of the other teams?" As he strode toward the skimmer, their military escort reluctantly bestirred themselves.

She shook her head. "It doesn't seem to matter if you're working out in the country, like us, or downtown in one of the bigger communities. It's the same everywhere. All dead, and nothing to implicate the possible killers." She hazarded a thin smile. "Somebody'll find something somewhere. You don't slaughter six hundred thousand people without leaving a few clues behind. It's only a matter of time."

"Better be soon." Climbing into the skimmer, Derwent settled himself into his seat. Their next stop was a small vegetable farm located six kilometers northwest of the inn. He had no doubt what they would find there. "I hear that back on Earth and the colonies people are raging at their local government ministers. That's not surprising. They want a face to attach to this enemy."

"Revenge may be a primitive emotion, but it's one that's likely to always be with us." Given her smaller frame, it required more of an effort on Hudson's part to board the vehicle. As the soldiers began to pile in and take up their positions she strapped herself in next to Derwent, making sure first that her precious recorder was secured. "I'd like to personally eviscerate a few of whoever's responsible for this myself."

As the skimmer whined to life and began to lift he looked at her in surprise. "Seriously? You never struck me as the violent type."

She glanced over at him, her petite features not far from his own. The optiplants glittered like herkimer diamonds. “I never saw two hundred dead children all huddled together in one place before, either.”

Derwent remembered the school, and his teeth clenched. Everyone had their limits. Despite his outwardly stoic demeanor he wanted to find something to hold responsible as badly as did everyone else. He wanted something to kill. Sure, he was first and foremost a professional, and he prided himself on his professional detachment.

But when it came down to it, no matter how hard he tried to affect an air of indifference and aloofness, he was only human.

9

The outrage and anger felt by the rest of humankind at the awful butchery that had taken place on Treetrunk were shared by every known sentient species. Ships of the thranx, the Pitar, the Quillp, and others were instructed as well as warned to be on the lookout for any unfamiliar or infrequently encountered species that might have the technological capability to perpetrate planetary genocide on the scale it had been committed on Argus V. This request from Earth was readily, even eagerly, complied with. In addition, the thranx and the Pitar of their own accord sent out ships whose mission was specifically to search for the home of an as yet unidentified and unknown race of maniacal aliens.

Nor did humans neglect to investigate possible motivations that might have arisen from within their own tortured racial history. Like any colony, Treetrunk had been settled by a heterogeneous broth of folk of every ethnic, religious, and social background. Nevertheless, the possibility that some powerful group, either from Earth itself or one of its distant colonies, held a grudge against a significant component of Treetrunk's population could not be and was not ex officio ruled out. In the absence of explanation, no prospect, no matter how outrageous, was automatically discounted. Every theory was investigated, every suggestion taken, every lead acted upon.

But despite the remorseless and dedicated perseverance of both humans and their alien allies alike, nearly a year passed without so much as a single hint or clue emerging as to the identity of the perpetrators of the carnage. Human exploration and development of Earth's recognized sphere of influence were slowed as xenophobia and fear on Earth and its existing colonies gained sway over those who favored continued expansion. Few people were anxious to settle on new worlds knowing that the butchers of Treetrunk's six hundred thousand were still out there—unpunished, unidentified, and unknown—ready to annihilate the next rush of humans rash enough to try and settle themselves on yet another empty, inviting world.

On Earth and elsewhere recriminations raged among a distraught and frustrated populace. How could such a catastrophe have been allowed to happen? Who had been negligent? In the absence of answers blame was readily placed elsewhere. Many who were innocent of oversight or neglect became inevitable scapegoats. There was finger-pointing in the media and in private, there were riots and accusations, while lawsuits and calumny raged aplenty. The only thing there was a dearth of was answers.

Inevitably, gradually, the rotating military and forensic teams that were assigned to investigate Treetrunk completed their work. As one contingent after another was withdrawn, that hospitable world with its ringing waterfalls, racing streams, and globe-girdling forests was abandoned to its indigenous life-forms. No possibility had been overlooked, not even the remote chance that some advanced native civilization had managed to keep in hiding while their planet was settled, only to emerge one day to murder every unwary, unprepared settler. The highest form of life on Argus V was an arboreal saurian with sloe eyes and an accusative yip. Although it displayed some rudimentary tool-using behavior, it could not cope with the larger, dull-witted carnivores that preyed upon it, much less wipe out so much as a handful of well-armed humans.

Reldmuurtinjak was a member of one of several thranx teams that had offered their services to help try to resolve the appalling riddle. Together with specialists from the Pitar and Quillp worlds, they, along with their human counterparts, poured over and through the scant available evidence, finding very little light in the unwholesome darkness that now shrouded the planet.

If anything, the exceedingly organized thranx were more frustrated than their human colleagues. Such things simply did not happen in a part of the galaxy where sentience and civilization held sway. Yes, death and dissention and violent disagreement were still present, but they could always be explained if not justified. In the absence of reason, there were still reasons.

Reldmuurtinjak was working in the ruins of one of Weald's few surviving administrative buildings when he looked up long enough to observe the tall human advancing toward him. He had never met a human being prior to being assigned to this grim duty. Scrutinizing the barren devastation for clues was difficult enough for him: He could only imagine what it must have been like for the first human crews forced to deal with thousands of corpses lying amidst the destruction.

Like the rest of his kind he had heard a lot about the humans. Visuals had helped to put to rest some of the more outrageous tales that had been told about them. They did not tower over thranx; they were simply tall. Most could not bend their bodies into rubbery knots; they were merely flexible. And despite their ridiculous tailless longitudinal axis, they did not fall over. At least, not very often. While excitable and edgy, they could also relax and be pleasant. Personally, he found this last open to dispute. During his sojourn on Treetrunk, the researcher had not seen very many of them relax.

The one who now approached looked uneasy but not nervous. His name was Lee, and Reldmuurtinjak had struck up a causal, casual relationship with him as their respective groups labored side by side in search of answers in the ruins of Argus V's capital city. Unusually intense even for a human, he spent more time in the company of the thranx than did any other of his colleagues. Reldmuurtinjak wondered at this. He was soon to find out the reason why.

Lee peered down at where the thranx was working in a

slight depression in the floor. The space had somehow survived the collapse of the upper two floors. Lying within the shallow bowl was an intact desk together with contents. Typically, none of the desk's linking electronics had survived the devastation, but there were always hopes of finding notes, scribblings, jottings that might shed some light on what had happened. Using a translating scanner, Reldmuurtinjak was examining these now, neatly filing each sheet of treated synthesized cellulose into one of three piles.

"Any luck?" the pale-haired human inquired rhetorically.

Reldmuurtinjak replied as expected. "There is much surviving information. Unfortunately, none of it is relevant to our inquiry."

Nodding to indicate that he understood, the human turned sideways and slip-slid cautiously down into the dimple in the stelacrete floor. "Your people are very good at this kind of work. You never seem to get tired, or bored."

Reldmuurtinjak struggled to reply in his recently acquired Terranglo, even as the lanky human sought to address him in Low Thranx. Their conversation was a melange of both, an uncertain brew of slippery human vowels and fricative thranx clicks and whistles. The ungainly but evolving interspecies patois had unofficially been dubbed Symbospeech, and the name had stuck. As yet, the results were far from justifying even so semigrandiose an appellation. But with each encounter between the species, the shared vernacular grew.

"We are accustomed to slow, methodical work." Reldmuurtinjak did not look up from his labor. It was not necessary, since there were few human gestures critical to interpret. Aural conversation conveyed the majority of their communication. "We are glad to help."

"You know, some of my coworkers—not myself, understand—have wondered about that. Of all the other intelligent species, you and the Pitar were the first to volunteer your assistance." He looked distinctly uncomfortable, but Reldmuurtinjak had not dealt with enough humans for long enough to be able to interpret the extravagant range of human facial expressions. "There's been talk—I haven't participated in it myself—that maybe, and I hope you won't be offended by this, that maybe a rogue element of your people might have had something to do with this."

It took a moment for the import of the human's words to sink in and for the thranx to review it in his mind to make certain that he had not heard incorrectly.

" 'With this'?" Putting down the four tools he was handling simultaneously, he now turned face and antennae up to the human. "I believe I understand the implications of what you are saying. I just do not want to."

Lee raised both hands in a gesture unfamiliar to Reldmuurtinjak. "Hey, it's not me! I don't give any credence to it for a moment." To emphasize his stance on the matter he concluded with a fairly fluent double click from the back of his throat. "I just think you ought to know what's being said about you. Not about you personally, understand. About some hypothetical thranx who might have had a hypothetical part in the real tragedy."

Utilizing the by-now common human gesture, the researcher nodded deliberately. "There is tragedy in what you say, but it has nothing to do with what happened to this world." He turned slowly back to his work.

The human started to edge a little closer and then, uncertain, held his ground. "I don't believe a word of it, of course. I mean, it doesn't make any sense. What would the thranx, any thranx, have to gain by participating in such a bloodbath? Not new lands to settle. Your kind get chilled in Earth's tropical regions. You'd be uncomfortable here on a midsummer's afternoon, like today. Most of the year you'd just freeze."

"Quite true," Reldmuurtinjak agreed, trying to bundle his own cold-climate attire more tightly around his thorax. "We have no use for this world."

"And we've had contact with each other for more than half a century now, with no major conflicts or disputes. Just the usual ranting and raving from xenophobes on both sides." He went silent.

As the human appeared to be awaiting a response, Reldmuurtinjak supplied the one he thought the biped might be waiting to hear. "Those thranx who are suspicious of and wish no contact with your kind inveigh against it because they are frightened of your unpredictability."

Lee frowned uncertainly. "Not our proclivity to violence?"

"No. Recognizing that aggressiveness is not an uncommon characteristic among sentient species, we are not unsettled to find it among your kind. Our ancestors fought one another as ruthlessly as did yours. And we have been dealing with the feints and depredations of the far more belligerent AAnn for more than two hundred and fifty of your years. But the actions of the AAnn are more or less predictable. Those of your kind are not." Now he looked up from his work. "At least, the formula for mutual understanding is still in the developmental stage."

Kneeling down alongside the insectoid, Lee was caught up in a pervasive scent of gardenia. "Look, I want to apologize for my friends. You have to understand that every human, here and on all our worlds, is intensely frustrated at our inability to identify the people or peoples who were responsible for the horror that happened here."

Glistening compound eyes considered the flexible, enigmatic alien face. Reldmuurtinjak could not decipher what might be hidden there, but he did detect the concern in the mammal's voice. "We are frustrated too, but it does not lead us to make groundless accusations."

An embarrassed Lee looked away. "It's a human thing. In the absence of someone to blame, blame anyone. I'm afraid that's not going to change until we find out what happened here."

"Then relations between us are likely to be poisoned for some time." The thranx's voice was soft as always, the tone cool and uninflected. "Because my people have found nothing any more conclusive here than have yours."

This time they were silent in tandem for a while before Lee spoke again. "It does strike some of us as peculiar that among the known sentient species capable of rendering assistance only the AAnn have declined to send research teams here to help with the search for leads."

"*Kil!!ck,* that does not surprise us. The AAnn are a treacherous and dangerous people. They will kill when it is to their advantage and retreat in a confusion of apologies when strongly confronted. That is what makes dealing with them so infuriating. One moment they will be happy to trade keenly but fairly, the next they will ambush and destroy. If caught out, they are masters of repentance. In the absence of surety one must always be on guard against them."

Lee considered thoughtfully. "You're not the first to hint that the AAnn might be responsible for this. Until the puzzle is solved, everyone is suspect. Even apostate humans."

That startled the thranx researcher. "You would suspect your own kind of such an atrocity?"

"Such things have happened in the past. In the First and Second Dark Ages."

"But why? What possible motivation could there be?"

As his legs began to cramp, Lee settled himself into a more comfortable seated position. "You spoke of the xenophobes among your own kind who don't want to have more than the most minimal contact with us. Ours are more zealous than yours. There are fanatics who'll do anything to keep our respective species from growing closer together." With a sweep of one arm he gestured at the devastation that surrounded them. "It's not out of the realm of possibility that they might resort to measures as extreme as this so they could blame the result on the thranx, or on nonhumans in general."

"Then you have motivation." Although he spoke the words, the possibility that the scenario the human had just described might actually have taken place remained barely conceivable to Reldmuurtinjak.

"Motivation, yes, but seemingly insupportable means of acting on it." Lee shifted his backside against the hard floor. "Though powerful, with many undeclared supporters, it's hard to envision how the xenophobes could have mustered sufficient military-style strength to carry out such a devastating assault on another world—much less erase any and all evidence of their participation. What happened to the Amazon hive was one thing. Obliterating the population of an entire colony is something else again. If such was actually the case it would answer one question, though."

"Which one?" Reldmuurtinjak executed a gesture of ongoing confusion. "There are so many."

Lee was not sophisticated enough to catch the delicate hint of humor. "How the invaders were able to achieve such complete surprise. Battalions of arriving fellow humans, even heavily armed fellow humans, would not be questioned. Not until it was too late. They could have spread themselves throughout the colony before attacking simultaneously at multiple points in response to some prearranged signal. Evidence of their perfidy could have been gathered up and destroyed after the fact." His tone was flat. "As I said, in the absence of the guilty, everyone is suspect. Even ourselves."

"I am glad to know that we are not alone." The thranx had a well-developed sense of sarcasm. "Better your people should look to the AAnn, press them on their absence from the collective effort to unearth explanations, and watch the skies of your other colonies."

"Everyone from New Riviera to Cachalot is on alert," Lee assured the bug. "Every arriving ship has to undergo checks and quarantine that would have been unthinkable just a couple of years ago. It's a monumental inconvenience, but most people understand the need."

"Inconvenience is better than genocide." Examining a torn length of the familiar white human writing material, Reldmuurtinjak patiently set it in one of the three piles that were rising slowly beside him. "What have you heard from the central coordinating authority? Is there any news?"

Leaning back against a melted mass of plastic that had once been a storage locker, Lee sighed resignedly. They were all tired from their fruitless researches. Arriving in orbit around Treetrunk, everyone had been flush with energy and enthusiasm, each man and woman in his complement certain they would be the one to find the key that would unlock the mystery of the colony's destruction. As the days wore on and became weeks, then months, nascent eagerness gave way to uncertainty, then to resignation, and lastly to a kind of professional ennui. No one expected the next building, the next box, the next electronic file, to provide anything more informative than the routine details of everyday life leading up to the disaster. He wondered if the thranx ran a similar gauntlet of discouraging emotion. If so, they did not show it—at least, not in any fashion a watching, wondering human could decipher.

"No," he replied. "Not a thing. I heard that a Quillp team working east of Chagos Downs thought they'd stumbled onto the wreckage of a downed nonhuman shuttle, but it turned out to be a privately registered aircraft. Strictly suborbital. Hundred percent human design and manufacture." In response to the unasked corollary he added, "No evidence of arms or armament was found in its vicinity, so it must have been local."

Reldmuurtinjak was intrigued. "Among my kind individuals do not have access to their own shuttlecraft. There are private suborbital vehicles capable of very high-speed flight, but nothing that is competent for extraatmospheric travel. No individual entity smaller than a hive operates its own flights into orbit."

"In that we are different," Lee explained. "Among my kind large nongovernmental organizations engaged in trade and commerce often operate their own vessels, which are naturally equipped with proprietary shuttles. There are also certain very wealthy individuals who have access to privately owned and operated ships, even starships, together with their associated shuttlecraft. It's not common, but it's not unheard of, either. That's the most likely explanation for what the Quillp found. Remember what I told you earlier about the possibility of fanatic human xenophobes mounting their own attack on the settlements. The first step in plotting something like that would be to obtain adequate untraceable interstellar transportation. That means acquiring not only starships, but also unused or unregistered landing capability."

Reldmuurtinjak indicated that he understood. "Nothing else, then?"

Lee shook his head regretfully. "Only rumors that the money and resolve to keep our work here going is drying up.

There are people on Earth and the colonies who want to concentrate the relevant research resources elsewhere."

"As in finding a species to blame for what took place."

Lee did not dispute the thranx's observation. How could he, when he had alluded to as much himself? "I'm afraid so."

"Would that not play into the hands of renegade humans, if it is indeed such who are responsible?" Truhands and foothands worked through the mass of debris in a digital ballet.

"Possibly. I hope those in charge keep that in mind when they make their final decision." Raising up, he looked around the ravaged interior of the building. "Personally, I'd hate to see the last humans abandon this beautiful world without taking some answers away with them."

"You said 'abandon.' If I grasp the meaning correctly, your authorities are not planning a recolonization?"

Lee eyed the insectoid in dismay before realizing that the thranx doubtless felt different about such matters, as they did about so many things. "It wouldn't matter if they were or not. No human would settle here now, no matter how potentially profitable or life affirming. Despite its physical beauty, Treetrunk is seen as a world of death. Humans are . . . not always scientific in their response to such occurrences. For any of my kind to even think of resettling the Argus system, an incontrovertible explanation of what happened here must first be presented. Even then, I'm not sure very many people would want to live in the psychic vicinity of six hundred thousand dead."

" 'Psychic vicinity'? What is that? Is it near Weald?"

Despite the serious turn of conversation, Lee had to smile. "It's a state of mind, not an administrative boundary. Just take my word for it. No one will move here until they know for certain what annihilated their predecessors, and maybe not even then."

"Six hundred thousand dead." Reldmuurtinjak repeated the figure in Low Thranx. To Lee the melancholy mantra was a succession of ephemeral whisperings framed by an eloquence of musical whistles and clicks. It sounded even more foreboding in Low Thranx than it did in Terranglo. "All the dead have been accounted for, then?"

"Less some twenty-two thousand presumed incinerated or otherwise utterly obliterated." Along with the rest of his associates the young researcher had been compelled to deal with such deranged statistics daily, but that did not make them any easier to take, or the images they conjured up unbidden any simpler to banish. Six . . . hundred . . . thousand. An inconceivable number, an unreal chronicle of annihilation.

As for the identities of the missing twenty-two thousand, they had been culled from the litany of the known deceased. There would be no burial for them, and their memorials would be anonymous. Lee had seen pictures, tridee recordings, drawings from life that had survived in schools and residences. The faces of the exterminated swam before him: wide-eyed, innocent, oblivious to the fate that was soon to befall them. The weight of the dead was crushing.

All of a sudden he wanted out. He'd had enough. Let someone else be the hero. To an unknown more perspicacious than himself he bequeathed the honor of unraveling the great enigma. Climbing to his feet, he regarded the industrious, methodical thranx without envy.

"That's it. I've done my share here. I'm going to put in for transfer. I can't take this anymore." Focusing on the alien helped him to avoid looking at the surrounding desolation, kept him from hearing the screams of the dying or envisioning their helpless, terrified faces.

Reldmuurtinjak looked up from his work, his valentine-shaped head facing that of the taller human squarely. In the subdued light that filtered into the depression between floors, his blue-green exoskeleton shone dully. "Psychic vicinity beginning to affect you?"

"Something like that." Glancing around to see if any of his colleagues were watching, he lowered his voice. "I hope it's one of your kind that finds the answer. I hope it's a thranx."

Reldmuurtinjak gestured to express curiosity, even though he knew the human would in all probability not be familiar enough with thranx body language to appreciate the sensitivity of the response.

"Why? What difference does it make to the ultimate resolution?"

"Because I don't want to think that your people are responsible. Not even a group of fanatics. Because I enjoy talking with you and others of your kind. Because unlike some of my uncertain, suspicious colleagues and friends and relatives back home I want to see that relationship deepen." Reaching out, he extended a hand, palm downward and fingers slightly apart, toward the insectoid's smooth, shiny skull. "Because I like you."

Twisting his inflexible upper body around as much as he was able, Reldmuurtinjak dipped his head forward until both antennae made contact with the human's hand. It was a gesture of greeting and farewell that was becoming more common among mammalian and insectoid acquaintances, one that took into account humankind's regrettable lack of a flexible cerebral sensing mechanism. Smiling, Lee turned and moved to rejoin his friends.

Reldmuurtinjak regarded him for a moment longer, then returned to his work. It was as monotonous, boring, and unrewarding as ever—but without pausing to consider the reasons, he found that he was feeling a little better about it.

10

As starships went, the battered, downsized craft that stumbled inelegantly out of space-plus in the vicinity of Argus VII was singularly unimpressive. The parabolic fan that promulgated its KK-type drive field was inefficiently aligned and indicative of low-grade manufacture. Further proof that the vessel was the product of a struggling as opposed to a surging technology could be found in the design and execution of the main body. Any ship of human, thranx, or AAnn fabrication was superior.

But it was no derelict. It moved, and it was guided by its builders, who took what pride they could in a vessel that represented the pinnacle of their own meager science. All ships might not be equal, nor their engineering, but the crew of the odd little craft took pride in their species and its limited yet very real accomplishments.

The Unop-Patha were not well known. They occupied a single system whose sun they called Unatha, after the Great Being they traditionally believed had given birth to the first of their kind. Ill equipped for long-range exploring, they kept close to home and sent out no more than a couple of ships at a time to maintain contact and relations with the far more vigorous sentients who occupied the same general area of the Arm. Humankind knew of them largely through the thranx, who had enjoyed contact with the species for well over a hundred years.

The Unop-Patha were neither bold nor threatening, finding the maintenance of even formal relations with other intelligent races a strain on their limited resources. An easy conquest for an aggressive, expansionist people like the AAnn, their world and its scanty assets were not even worthy of the force required to take it over. Their very worthlessness assured their continued independence.

Occasionally they sent one of their few space-plus-capable ships voyaging. Not in search of resources they were unable to exploit, or worlds they were incapable of settling, but because they were as curious as any developed people, albeit with a timorous curiosity. Treetrunk drew their attention not so much because of the tragedy that had befallen that human colony but because it lay within the limited range of the best of their vessels. They were aware of the catastrophe, of course. Every intelligence within that part of the Arm that had access to travel in space-plus or that had space-minus communications capabilities knew.

Their arrival was immediately noted and their presence challenged by one of the two warships from Earth that remained in orbit around the planet. It took a few moments for the analysts on board the cruiser *Shaka* to convince themselves of the identity of the visitors. Setting aside initial impressions, they did not take the abused, apparently innocuous appearance of the much smaller vessel at face value. Everything and anything in Treetrunk's vicinity had to be thoroughly checked out.

As soon as ship-to-ship communications were established and the taxonomy of the Unop-Patha crew confirmed, the visitors were allowed to proceed as they wished. Travel to or visitation of the surface of Treetrunk was circumscribed but not forbidden, provided that any landing parties first obtained appropriate clearance from the military authorities on board the *Shaka*.

The Unop-Patha accepted these restrictions obeisantly, having neither the desire nor the inclination to challenge the far more powerful human craft. Their own carried virtually no armament, its crew instead relying for defense on their transparent helplessness. Nevertheless, their presence and actions were closely monitored by sensitive instruments on both warships. Though nearly a year had passed since the destruction of Argus V, no one had forgotten that whatever had extirpated its population had accomplished the evil with the aid of complete surprise. Certainly the Unop-Patha and their pitiable vessel looked harmless, but they would nevertheless be watched carefully and scanned periodically until they left the system or reentered space-plus.

The Unop-Patha did not avail themselves of the opportunity to descend to the surface of Treetrunk. They could not afford nor could their single shuttle craft tolerate more than a few such trips, and they chose not to expend one visiting a world whose horrors were well known. Instead, they contented themselves with dropping into as low an orbit as they could manage and making observations from altitude, even though they would have found the climate congenial and the gravity light.

A week of such scrutiny proved sufficient to satisfy their modest scientific needs. Signaling their intention to move on, their polite appreciation was acknowledged by the officer on board the *Shaka* who had been given charge of such matters. A request to take measurements and readings throughout the remainder of the Argus system was promptly granted. The unassuming scientists on board the Unop-Patha craft were particularly interested in Argus VI, a gas giant of unusual composition. Though located in an orbit comparatively close to Treetrunk, its banded bulk did not appear to exert any gravitational effect on that far more salubrious world, hinting at the absence of a solid core. While much material on the gaseous sphere and the rest of the Argus system was obtainable from human sources, the Unop-Patha humbly preferred to carry out their own investigations.

Accelerating slowly away from Treetrunk, the Unop-Patha navigators plotted a course that would insert them into orbit around the sixth planet of Argus within a couple of days. As they moved off, tugged along by the greatly subdued glow of their minimally powered drive, they were traveling slowly enough to take readings on the two moons of Treetrunk. Rocky, airless, small, and astronomically undistinguished, these had been of no especial interest to the colonizing humans. Their dimensions, composition, and other relevant information had been automatically recorded, filed, and forgotten in the rush to settle the glamorous, accommodating world nearby.

The Unop-Patha were not sophisticated, but they were thorough. Patience was a virtue of science that did not demand advanced technology to practice. So they slowed still further, to ensure that their specialists would be able to complete their readings.

It was while passing the inner and smaller of the two chunks of rock that one of the three communications technicians, engaged in monitoring background noise, thought she might have detected an anomaly. Accorded only minimal attention by her colleagues at first, she persisted, finding the duration and bandwidth of the noise perplexing. Her perseverance finally engaged the interest of a superior, who while initially skeptical, soon found himself studying the relevant readouts through the twin lenses of puzzlement and surprise.

The electromagnetic nonconformity was brought to the attention of the family group that was in command. After due debate and discussion it was decided to pause in the vicinity of the moon just long enough to investigate the abnormality before moving on to the sixth planet as planned. A cursory inquiry would cost little and would not involve the use of much time or equipment. The very low gravity of the moon meant that the coddled and sometimes troublesome shuttle craft would not have to be used. A pair of much smaller repair vehicles could be employed to explore the cratered surface.

Each utilitarian vessel could accommodate a maximum of four, but two were adequate to fly and operate the compact craft. Taking silent leave of their respective air locks, they fired programmed bursts from their tiny engines as they descended toward the scabrous surface of the noticeably ellipsoidal moon. The feeble electronic anomaly that had sparked the unplanned visit grew no stronger as they tracked it, suggesting emission from a natural source.

The reality turned out to be anything but.

The pilot of the first ship altered his trajectory as soon as visual contact was made, directing his backup to do the same.

Anxious communications flew back and forth between the two repair craft and the starship.

"A vessel of some kind it is, MotherTwo." The pilot and his companion did not have to use instruments to reach their conclusion. The silhouette that was floating above the crater was unmistakably synthetic.

"Can you it identify, TwelveSon?" came the apprehensive response.

Both Unop-Patha stared at the quiescent, shadowed object that lay in front of and below them. "Ours it is not, but that without saying goes." Alongside the pilot, his companion hazarded a guess.

"FortyDaughter here being. Human maybe it is, because it on a moon sits that a human world orbits it does."

"Real you speak, FortyDaughter," came the reply. "However any space-going species belonging to it could. Including maybe sentience unknown that the population of this world made dead."

However reasonable and indeed, unavoidable, the verbalization of such a possibility was, it was seriously disconcerting to the crew of both observing repair craft. Yet there was no sign of movement or life from the unidentifiable ship, nor any indication that anything aboard, organic or artificial, was aware of their presence.

"Very small it is," the pilot of the second repair vessel reported. "No larger than our own. Not capable of space-plus travel it is, would I estimate."

His colleague in the other ship continued the reportage. "No generating projector visible is, nor anything that an analogous structure might be called. Old it looks. If elsewhere encountered, not capable of flight of any kind would I think it. Almost at the end of a decelerating synchronous orbit it appears to be. If not for the slightness of this moon's weak gravity I imagine it long ago into the surface would have crashed." When no response was forthcoming, he inquired hesitantly, "Closer looking should we take?"

This time the ensuing silence from the starship was understandable: The commanding family was taking the request under advisement and discussing it with the heads of the other dominant families. The pilot was not sure whether to be happy or despondent when the response that was finally forthcoming was affirmative.

"Distance where and when possible keep," the pilots of the two investigating craft were admonished. "Remove yourselves if any hint of trouble or hostility there is. Scrutiny we perform will, recordings you take will, and when done all a report to the human authorities we make will."

TwelveSon waited for FortyDaughter to bring her little ship up alongside his. Together they advanced on the silent, inactive alien craft. No, silent not, he reminded himself. It continued to emit its feeble, intermittent electronic sputter.

What if a scout ship of the unknown ravening species that had annihilated Argus V it was? He could feel his copilot shivering and shuddering alongside him. Together they sloughed off an inordinate amount of nervous energy. He knew that FortyDaughter and her companion must be experiencing similar terrors. He wanted to turn around, to flee this dark, dead place and return to the familiar family warmth and comfort of the starship. Wanted to, but did not. The Unop-Patha were not particularly courageous, but they were persistent. Oftentimes all that kept them stumbling down the road of progress was the fear of being laughed at.

The two investigating repair craft were soon close enough to the alien vessel for their integral manipulative armature to reach out and touch it, should the pilots wish to do so.

"How the emission is?" FortyDaughter inquired.

"Unchanged still," came the reply from the starship. "No reaction from the subject craft?"

"Nothing," TwelveSon reported. "No movement, no lights internal or external visible are." Carefully he edged his ship along the length of the silent vessel. Within the repair craft all was hushed. "A lock I have maybe found. Sealed it is." Plaintively he inquired, "Can return to ship now maybe?"

"No. Families further information wish. Conclusiveness is sought."

"Conclusiveness points to nothing living here," Twelve-

Son's copilot murmured. "Automatic emission only there is. Not even signal we are sure it is. Energy release from broken equipment or failed instrumentation could well be. Let the humans further probe." Tilting his round, heavily furred head back, he surveyed their grim surroundings. "Unpleasant this place is. Dead ship in a dying orbit above a dead moon."

"Conclusiveness sought is." The directive from the starship was tranquil but unrelenting. "Search lock external release for. Try."

"Not even certain builder-owners of ship oxygen breathe." Grumbling, FortyDaughter maneuvered the manipulative arms of her craft into position above the possible lock door that TwelveSon had located. Unfortunately, there were indications of exactly the sort of controls they were looking for. Unfortunately, these responded to the pilot's gentle, precise handling. The lock or seal slid into its retaining wall, revealing a small alcove beyond. Both pilots maneuvered their ships close enough to shine lights within. They were unable to ascertain the identity of the instrumentation and internal engineering. Both dreaded the directives that reached them subsequently.

"Enter and explore. The source of the emission try to establish."

"I here will remain to keep watch," TwelveSon immediately offered.

"No," argued FortyDaughter. "You better at such exploration than we are. You enter, watch we will keep."

The dispute was settled from the ship. "TwelveSon and ThirtyOneSon enter will. FortyDaughter watch will keep. Care to be taken."

"Care to be taken." Muttering, TwelveSon released himself from his restraints, disconnected himself from the repair craft, and prepared to follow his copilot into the repair craft's tiny lock.

It was a cramped space whose confines made donning a suit for outside work more difficult than it ought to have been. Normally, such suits would be put on in one of the much larger main locks on board the starship. When they had dropped away, no one had anticipated any reason why they might have to make use of pressure suits. It took some scrambling, but after dancing awkwardly around each other for a while, both pilots were suitably outfitted.

They exchanged a brief but intense clinch before turning and opening the door to the outside. Gravity barely strong enough to keep the alien vessel from drifting off into space allowed them to float gently down to its curved metal skin. Ahead, the open alien lock loomed. Above and behind them, they could see the concerned faces of FortyDaughter and her companion anxiously following their progress through the viewport of their hovering repair craft.

The sooner they completed their examination, the faster they could return to the warm embrace of the starship. TwelveSon led the way forward. Memories of the empty, shattered world below rose unbidden into his consciousness. Something had utterly annihilated the population of a seemingly benign world. Admittedly, the six hundred thousand who had perished had been aliens, but they had been intelligent and warm-blooded like the Unop-Patha. Whatever had ruthlessly slaughtered them might not be discriminatory in its taste for extermination. True, the ship they were about to board was unpretentious, far too small to harbor weapons of mass destruction or very many warlike individuals even if they were smaller in stature than the Unop-Patha. But it was more than a matter of numbers. TwelveSon did not want to encounter even one rampaging, murderous alien.

As they entered the lock both he and ThirtyOneSon agreed that the placement of controls and instruments suggested that the lock, and by inference the rest of the derelict vessel, had been designed with beings bigger than the Unop-Patha in mind. TwelveSon was not sure whether to be relieved or further intimidated by this conclusion. Trying to determine its composition, he studied a blank screen of alien manufacture while his companion scanned the inner door and its seals. The screen and its design were far more sophisticated than anything comparable aboard the starship.

ThirtyOneSon turned to him, staring out of his suit's head

bubble. "There's no atmosphere on this craft. If there ever was one it has all away leaked."

"It could be there was aboard never anyone." Moving to the inner door, TwelveSon began running his four stubby fingers around the edge. It was darker here, away from the outer portal. "It might have been accidentally from the surface of the fifth planet launched, or from a human starship, or from a vessel of the attacking species. Or it might a true derelict be that has here for generations lain."

"Not many generations," ThirtyOneSon reminded him. "The colonizing humans had not this world for very long occupied before they wiped out were."

"I realize that, but there is still—"

He let out an involuntary yelp and leaped backward as the inner door began to open. The paltry gravity would have sent him crashing headfirst into the ceiling had not an alert ThirtyOneSon reacted in time to grab his companion's lower leg as he began to soar past. Even as ThirtyOneSon pulled his friend back down toward the floor, he was already stumbling toward the outer portal.

"What is it, what happening is?" FortyDaughter's alarmed voice crackled over their simple bubbleset speakers.

"The inner lock door cycling is," TwelveSon reported as he regained both his emotional and physical equilibrium. Together, he and ThirtyOneSon halted themselves in the frame of the outer doorway, watching and waiting.

The inner barrier continued to withdraw until the way was clear. Beyond, they could make out a corridor and more alien instrumentation. A few lights shone dimly. In the stillness of the airless moon, nothing moved.

"In the course of your inspection one of your hands must a still active control have brushed," ThirtyOneSon remarked to his companion. When the pilot, still breathing hard, did not reply, the slightly larger of the pair added, "We should a survey of the interior make."

TwelveSon looked over at him. "I would rather not."

ThirtyOneSon did not possess an especially imaginative personality, a quality that was a definite asset in their present circumstance. His tone was maternal-stern. "We should a survey make," he insisted firmly. "Having been the opportunity granted, we will chastised be if we without doing so return."

"No one will know if . . . oh, wait," an unhappy TwelveSon muttered. They had already reported to the other repair ship that the inner lock was open. Even if ThirtyOneSon had concurred, it was too late to back out now. With great reluctance, the pilot started back into the lock and toward the ominously gaping inner gateway.

The absence of breathable atmosphere was encouraging. Surely there was nothing left alive aboard the solitary little vessel. As they penetrated deeper within, keeping close to one another, growing confidence began to override his unease. As an exemplar of alien engineering the ship struck him as more primitive than what he had seen of the best of contemporary human and thranx and AAnn technology, but it was still more advanced than anything aboard his own vessel. A sudden thought struck him: If by chance the humans did not know this was here, perhaps he and his people could claim right of salvage. There might be much to learn from the empty, abandoned craft. It depended how advanced it actually was. Arrogated technology was of little use to those who appropriated it if its design and details were beyond comprehension.

ThirtyOneSon bumped into him, knocking him slightly forward and in the light gravity, nearly off his feet. TwelveSon whirled irritably on his companion. "Watch where you stepping are! And don't so close follow. There plenty of room in here for the two of us is."

That was when he noticed that the hair on his friend's head, face, and neck was standing straight out. ThirtyOneSon was looking to their left, and pointing. "You mean, there plenty of room for the three of us is."

A shape was rising from the shadows. It continued to rise until it towered over the two terrified Unop-Patha. TwelveSon was too frightened to move forward, back, or scramble for a hiding place. More than four times their mass, the ghostly apparition had a similar bipolar body but with much longer limbs. What they could see of its face and head inside a helmet were almost as shaggy as those of an Unop-Patha, but the eyes were far too small and the mouth too large. As details continued to resolve themselves in the feeble light, he and his companion began to relax.

It was a human. Then this was a human vessel, or so they now supposed. But where had the human come from, and why was there only one of them? If this was a scientific vessel engaged in an exploratory jaunt from one of the two huge warships orbiting the planet, TwelveSon would have expected it to house several scientists. And if that was the case, why was this individual wearing an environment suit and not working in a pressurized compartment?

An accident! They had stumbled across a human survey or scientific craft engaged in exploration of this moon. It had run into difficulty and become stranded here. It might be from one of the warships or—he hardly dared countenance the possibility—it might have been caught and trapped here when Treetrunk had been set upon by its unknown homicidal invaders. Overlooked by the otherwise maniacally thorough attackers, its crew had survived.

Except there did not seem to be any crew. Looking past the single tottering figure TwelveSon was unable to discern any others, either erect or lying down. The little vessel was large enough to accommodate a number of individuals the size of the average human. Possibly they were active in another compartment. If this craft was not a component of the present orbiting human detachment and if it had been here since the attack on the fifth planet, then supplies of every kind would be running very low. Retiring to the confines of sealed suits would have allowed the marooned crew to conserve their remaining air by in effect pressurizing only their bodies in lieu of their surroundings. He marveled at the environmental technology that would let so small a craft keep its occupants alive for such an extended period.

Of course, how far and how long any onboard supplies lasted was in direct proportion to the number of crew. The fewer the occupants, the longer the reserves would last. Once again he peered past the awkward bulk of the human. There was still no sign of the rest of the crew.

"Why is it not to communicate trying?" ThirtyOneSon was eying the human intently. This was the first one either of them had ever encountered in person instead of via a communications transmission or study manual.

"Perhaps it see us does not." TwelveSon weighed how best to proceed. "Or perhaps it is not to open communications authorized and is for one of its superiors waiting."

"That may be," ThirtyOneSon conceded, "but I sure it sees us am. How could it not? We right here in front of it are."

"Protocol it from acknowledging us may prevent. The AAnn like that are, and the thranx somewhat less so. We far less about this species know than we do many others."

"So what do we do? Just here for the rest of them to show up wait?" ThirtyOneSon looked around uneasily. "I this place do not like. I want to back on the ship be."

"No less than I." Protocol be damned, TwelveSon decided. He was not going to stand here waiting on the aliens forever. If his actions resulted in a reprimand, he would accept it with good grace. Anything to accelerate matters so he and his friend could return to their vessel. ThirtyOneSon would support his actions.

Moving forward, he reached out and touched the leg of the human. When it failed to react, he grabbed the flexible material of its suit and tugged on it. This finally produced a response. Turning toward the two Unop-Patha the human glanced down. His eyes widened, the framing flesh pulling back to expose more of the whitish orb, and his mouth opened and began to move.

Wrenching himself away from the Unop-Patha's grasp, the human stumbled backward until it was pressed up against the wall. It stood there staring at them, its mouth still working, arms splayed wide and flattened tightly against the composite material of the bulwark.

TwelveSon took a step forward, then hesitated. Hardly a

specialist in interspecies contact, he was once again unsure how to proceed. "Is it to communicate trying or not? It looking right at us is."

"No." In his stolid, unimaginative way ThirtyOneSon was firm. "It not looking at us is. It looking behind us is." Turning as one, the two Unop-Patha examined the space behind them. They saw nothing exceptional, nothing to differentiate it from the rest of the vessel's interior.

"Whatever it is seeing not here is, but in its mind is." ThirtyOneSon's tone was somber. "I don't think I to see it want."

"But at it look! Surely it trying to communicate is." Baffled by the human's reactions, TwelveSon was at a loss as to what to do next. "See how open and active its mouth is? Humans communicate that way, as we do know; by means of modulated sound waves."

"Different frequencies," ThirtyOneSon commented thoughtfully. "We would not its words anyway understand, but specialists on the ship have to the principal human tongue access. Our people may not fluent be, but the necessary data in the library should be." He contemplated the task at hand. "We must back to the ship get this one."

TwelveSon reluctantly agreed. Since he and his companion could not talk to the human, they would have to somehow induce it to follow them into the presence of those who could. Stepping forward, he executed several simple gestures, hoping the human would get the idea. Then he and ThirtyOneSon turned to start back the way they had come.

"It not following is," ThirtyOneSon observed. "It still just standing there staring at the opposite wall is." He peered past the human and down the empty corridor. "Maybe for the rest of the crew it waiting is."

"I'm beginning to think there no rest of the crew is." TwelveSon's thoughts were tumbling. "If there were they ought to have by now arrived. This a very small ship is."

A contemplative ThirtyOneSon was quiet for a moment. "Then this being a sole survivor of the accident that trapped this vessel here is."

"I beginning to think so am." TwelveSon hesitated. "Unless the others, if there are others, are all dead, or otherwise immobilized."

"I don't know about you, but I not looking am." The larger Unop-Patha was adamant. "We our family mandate here and more have fulfilled, by this craft entering and one human finding. Let FortyDaughter or others from the ship explore further. We leavetaking are owed."

"I agree. But one last time let us try." He turned back toward the human, who had not shifted from its splayed stance against the wall. "If it will with us come and our communications people can with it make contact, others may not hunt for answers to difficult questions have to."

"Yes," his companion readily agreed, "and if it a lost craft from one of the orbiting warships is, we valuable merit for performing a rescue should acquire."

"Wonder make one it does, though." TwelveSon had approached to within arm's reach of the much more massive human. "If that the case is you would expect the humans both of these moons to be scouring, as well as the planetary surface in search of their lost comrade. And to have informed our ship upon arriving here that one of theirs had missing gone."

"Communication the key is," ThirtyOneSon observed. "Once that established is, then the human all such questions for us can answer."

Reaching out for the second time TwelveSon grabbed the human, this time reaching up over his head to tug on the creature's arm. Its helmeted head jerked around sharply, and the Unop-Patha could see the large facial orifice gaping and moving once again. But the human would not leave its place flattened against the wall.

Bemused, TwelveSon stepped back—only to see that his companion had retreated several steps and was staring mutely up at the alien. "Now what is it?"

It took ThirtyOneSon a moment to respond. "Your suit's transmission pickup. Off internal communication switch and change to—" He glanced down at the wrist console he had been fingering. "—eighty-six point three dash eleven."

"Why, what the point is?" TwelveSon looked from his friend back up at the immovable alien. "Don't tell me you understand it can?"

"Yes." ThirtyOneSon's words were barely audible. "Yes, I can understand it. Just listen, and you will, too."

Bewildered and a bit angry, TwelveSon proceeded to do as his companion suggested. As soon as he entered the recommended frequency into his suit instrumentation his ears were assailed by the voice of the alien, and he understood the truth of what ThirtyOneSon had told him. He found that he could indeed understand the human.

It screaming was.

11

"They're saying *what*?"

Having not been told to stand at ease, the orderly remained at attention in the anteroom, surrounded by the Victorian-era bric-a-brac that was the commander's favored décor. "They claim to have rescued a human from the inner moon, sir. They say—" The orderly glanced down at his reader to the printout of the report to make certain he was recounting everything accurately. "—that they found one live human in a single small vessel on the far side of the moon. Beyond being alive, they cannot testify as to his condition, though they believe it to be marginal."

"This is preposterous." As she spoke, Commander Lahtehoja was sealing up the sides of her lightweight duty boots. "Neither we nor the *Shaka* are missing any personnel, and I would be more than a little upset to learn that all shuttle craft and lifeboats were not accounted for. I know that the level of boredom is high among the crews, but if some people have gone for an unauthorized joyride I am not going to be pleased."

With each sentence the commander's voice had diminished. Eyes set front, body stiff and ramrod straight, the orderly knew what that meant. In contrast to others, when Lahtehoja grew quiet it meant she was really angry. When a soldier had to strain to hear the commander's words, it was time to look for a hole to hide in.

He pivoted sharply to follow her as she exited the commander's quarters and headed for the bridge, moving with the same long, purposeful, relentless strides that had made her a champion quintathlete in her days at the Academy. Crew they encountered stopped whatever they were doing to snap to attention and salute, gestures that she acknowledged perfunctorily. Anyone who had thought that inspection and survey duty at ill-fated Treetrunk would be a walk through an aerogel had neglected to note the name of the commander currently in charge.

A lift carried them to the auxiliary bridge blister situated on the upper-middle portion of the big ship. Far forward, the immense projection fan of the KK drive dominated the field of vision. With the warship rotated to face the planet, the white-girdled globe of Treetrunk loomed in the view dome.

More salutes and salutations greeted her arrival. Lahtehoja did not move to take her seat but instead strode directly over to confront the officer on duty. Captain Miles vaan Leuderwolk was a paunchy, easygoing career officer who favored a shaved head and imposing beard. For all his rough appearance he was known to laugh frequently and easily. He looked like he should have been spending his days serving lager in a beer garden instead of directing a warship. Those who served under him were inordinately fond of their easygoing master. No such rumor had ever been attached to Lahtehoja.

"What do we have, Miles?" The commander's eyes were black, small, and intense as a laser. You had to look for them, but nobody wanted to find them.

The captain of the *Ronin* wore his bemusement as artlessly as his beard. "You read the report from central communications?"

"I've heard it." A flick of the head in the orderly's direction was sufficient to explain. "Who are these Unop-Patha? I'm not familiar with their kind."

"I'll tell you on the way to B hold." Vaan Leuderwolk smiled through his beard. "I don't know much about them, either. Just the basics. They have very little contact with us, and we with them. When they popped out of space-plus here a few weeks ago they requested and were subsequently granted permission to do some cultural and scientific survey work."

Lahtehoja led the way, forcing the captain and the orderly

to have to hurry to keep up. "I don't remember being notified of this arrival."

Leuderwolk shrugged. "It happened when you were on sleep shift. "Buthefasi over on the *Alexander Nevsky* didn't deem it important enough to bother you."

Lahtehoja muttered something under her breath but did not comment further. She knew it was a failing of hers that she felt the need to know everything about everything that was going on under her command. A good commander had to know how to delegate, a skill that was not among her strengths. Nevertheless, although Buthefasi had acted properly, this was one particular she was sorry she had missed.

Her ignorance was soon to be rectified, however.

Having just listened to as concise a briefing as the relevant department had been able to prepare with virtually no notice at all, vaan Leuderwolk filled her in on what was known about the Unop-Patha as it had been related to him. Occasionally she would nod her understanding or interrupt to ask a precise, terse question. By the time they reached B hold she felt she knew as much about these Unop-Patha as did the captain of the *Ronin*.

They were waiting for her: half a dozen child-sized aliens with round, almost tubby bodies, big eyes, and no visible ears. What she could see of their bodies was covered with a thick, coarse, green-brown hair. They wore miniature space suits and had removed their headgear. Small black noses with four openings peeped out from near the top of the skull, just barely visible within the dense fur.

Lahtehoja and her small entourage halted before them. A specialist eighth-class wearing the insignia of communications walked over, saluted, and accepted the commander's admonition to stand easy with obvious relief.

Lahtehoja glanced automatically at the man's ident. "What do we have here, Mr. Waitangi?"

The specialist was prepared. "Their vessel hailed ours, Commander, and requested permission to come alongside. They claimed to have found and picked up a lone human from a marooned ship drifting in low synchronous orbit on the far side of the nearer moon." As he spoke the specialist frequently glanced down at the oversized reader he held, the rapid but controlled movement of his eyes automatically scrolling the information it displayed. "We had to run the transmission three times to make sure we had it straight." He smiled tolerantly at the waiting, curious aliens. "Their communications technology is pretty primitive."

"Apparently it was good enough to find this person when neither we nor any of our predecessors in this system could."

The specialist's smile vanished instantly. "Naturally, they want to transfer him, but they say that they can't."

Lahtehoja's neatly highlighted brows drew together, and her voice fell slightly. "Why not?"

The young man hurried his response. "They say that when they try, he—we've determined from their description that the individual in question is male—he resists. Sometimes violently."

The commander nodded knowingly. "And they're afraid he'll hurt one of them or do some damage to their ship. I can understand that, noting the disparity in our respective sizes."

"Excuse me, Commander, but that's not the reason." The specialist assumed an apologetic air. "They say that they have him safely isolated on their ship, but they're afraid he'll hurt himself."

"Hmm." Lahtehoja eyed the inquisitive, clearly awed visitors with new respect. "So we don't know much about these Unop-Patha, but we see that they understand compassion. I'll accept that as a basis for working with any alien species. Ask them if they will permit some of our medical personnel to go aboard their ship and remove this person they have so obligingly rescued."

With a nod, the specialist turned to face the visitors. As he spoke through the translator that hung from around his neck he crouched to bring his face more in line with those of the aliens he was addressing—and also to assume a less intimidating aspect.

It took a few moments, what with the specialist's need to adjust the translator each time human or alien spoke. Unlike

High Thranx, for example, or Pitar, no one on board the warship spoke Unathian. There was no need for it.

Eventually the specialist rose. The look of satisfaction on his face preceded his announcement. "They say that they have no objection, but suggest that anyone we wish to send to visit their vessel be chosen as much for physical dimensions as for pertinent skills."

"Thoughtful of them." The commander turned her head in vaan Leuderwolk's direction. "Find me some short doctors and nurses and have them assembled here. Let's see what these people have found." In a less authoritative tone she added, "What the devil is one lone individual doing stuck out here, of all places, and where the hell did he come from?"

"I'm as curious to know as you are, Ludmilla." The captain watched as the petite aliens began redonning their rudimentary suit helmets. "Who wouldn't be?"

It took several hours for the hastily assembled medical team to be transported to the Unathian vessel and to return. They made the transfer in a couple of the *Ronin*'s accessory craft—not because Lahtehoja and vaan Leuderwolk did not trust the patently inoffensive Unop-Patha, but because the transportation the aliens courteously offered to provide would have been too cramped even for the purposely diminutive group of physicians and assistants.

Lahtehoja was back on the bridge attending to the normal workday duties of a task-group commander when she was notified that the medical team had returned. Leaving the *Ronin* under designated cluster command, she and vaan Leuderwolk took an express lift to the infirmary. Lieutenant Colonel Holomusa, chief of medical staff, was waiting for them in the reception area. Cursed with the face and frame of a caricatured undertaker, he resorted to scanning makeup to enliven his otherwise doleful appearance. For all that, he was an upbeat and merry fellow, exactly the sort a patient confined in an infirmary would want to see coming toward them.

He was not smiling now, however. Lahtehoja did not like to see confusion and uncertainty spread like a mask across the faces of those under her command. She especially did not like to see it dominating the usually cheerful countenance of a ranking physician.

"I can see the prognosis in your face." She sighed. "Educate me."

Holomusa glanced down at his reader. "Anglo-Oceanic male, height one hundred and seventy-two centimeters, weight fifty-one kilos." Noting her questioning look he added, "The reduced body weight doesn't appear to fit naturally on his frame. He has the underlying musculature of a much stockier man. One doesn't have to be a physician to be able to tell just by looking at him that his health has suffered—psychologically as well as physiologically. In other words, he's had to deal with shock to his nervous system as well as an insufficiency of food. Naturally, each magnifies the deleterious effects of the other." The chief medical officer swallowed. "After examining him, I'd say it's a wonder he's not in worse shape. Given his condition, it's something of a surprise that he's even alive."

Vaan Leuderwolk spoke up. "To what do you attribute his survival, Ben?"

The physician made a noncommittal gesture with his reader. "Better to ask him that. It certainly wasn't a sound and satisfying diet. He's suffering from an impressive catalogue of nutritional deficiencies." He nodded in the direction of the recovery chamber. "Not vitamins, though. Pills can help, but they're no substitute for solid food."

Lahtehoja turned toward the silent, shuttered chamber where their mysterious visitant lay. "You're feeding him now?"

"In a manner of speaking." Holomusa chuckled softly. "He's receiving a steady flow of osmotic fluids."

Vaan Leuderwolk nodded knowingly. "When will he be able to sit up and take solid food?"

"Yes, and how soon can we talk to him?" Lahtehoja had to restrain herself from carrying the conversation into the recovery room. Commander of the visiting force she might be, but within the confines of the infirmary it was Holomusa who was in charge.

"I don't know," the chief medical officer replied candidly.

The commander ground her teeth—a bad habit she had never quite been able to break. "That's not the kind of answer I expect from my staff. I don't deal in incertitude."

"You think I like to?" Among the complement of the *Ronin*, the chief physician was one of the few the commander could not intimidate. "Nonspecific as it is, that's my prognosis. The man's comatose. I'm not going to try and force him out of it. Push his condition and we could lose him permanently."

As always, Lahtehoja was ready with a sharp retort. Instead of delivering it to the unblinking physician, she sighed again and raised her gaze ceilingward. "All right, Ben. It's your call. What happened when you went aboard the Unathian ship?"

"They took us to the room where they were holding him." Holomusa's tone was even, professional, but vaan Leuderwolk could tell that the physician had been shaken by the incident. "He was curled up in a corner, not quite fully fetal, but on the way. As soon as I saw the state he was in I ordered everyone else to remain in the corridor and out of his line of sight. I'm not a big man, but the Unop-Patha are a lot smaller, and I had to bend low to fit through the doorway."

"What did he do when you entered his 'space'?" Lahtehoja's voice was flat, unemotional, analyzing.

"Started whimpering," the physician told her without missing a beat. "I've seen disturbed men and women, people who have suffered a severe mental shock, try to dig their way into the floor or climb through the walls. This is the first time I've seen one try to crawl into himself." Behind the three officers, the commander's orderly stood mesmerized by the doctor's tale.

"As soon as I saw that there was a very real chance of him hurting himself, I stopped where I was. Trying to make eye contact, I just started talking to him. Anything I could think of, whatever came to mind, so he would hear a familiar, nonthreatening, hopefully soothing human voice. My object was to get him to relax, to slow his heart rate, which I supposed might be dangerously high, and to get him to trust me."

"And did you?" With one ear Lahtehoja was straining to hear sounds from the recovery chamber, but the only audible noise besides that of their own voices were the soft beeps and hums of efficient, indifferent instruments.

"Long enough to stick him with an osmotic hypo that pumped him full of tranquilizer. I was ready to jump him, to call for help, or to flee back out the doorway depending on his reaction. Funny—all he did was slip quietly into unconsciousness. Never uttered a sound. We squeezed him back through the door, off that claustrophobic Unathian ship and onto one of ours. He's been sleeping soundly until about an hour ago, when he woke up."

"Woke up?" Vaan Leuderwolk blinked. "I thought you said he was comatose."

"All right, maybe 'woke up' is an overstatement. He opened his eyes and he's breathing on his own. Other than that, there's nothing there. Severe trauma." He spread his hands helplessly. "Not much I can do here. Sure, we're trained and equipped to deal with a whole range of combat psychoses, but wherever this guy has retreated to, he's gone deep. I could try to pull him out—"

"Why don't you?" Lahtehoja prompted him.

"Like I said. Because if I make a mistake, I could drive him down deeper into the pit. Deep enough so that he might never come out. I'm not prepared to take that responsibility."

"Suppose I change my mind and order you to try?"

The chief medical officer stiffened slightly. "Then I would respectfully relinquish my post and report to the brig. I assure you that in that event every one of my subordinates will follow me, one by one."

"Take it easy, Ben," she soothed him. "I had to ask. I have no intention of trying to countermand or supersede a medical decision. Damn! That means we'll have to take him back to Earth for treatment without knowing his history. We'll end up seeing his story on the tridee like everyone else."

"If he ever recovers enough to tell his story," the cautious physician reminded her.

"What about physical details?" vaan Leuderwolk prompted

the other man. "Identification, clothing, indication of possible origin?"

"His garments were filthy." Fastidious physician that he was, Holomusa's expression wrinkled at the distasteful memory. "My inclination was to have them burned." At the look of alarm that spread over the faces of the commander and the captain the physician hastened to reassure them. "Ai, don't have a stroke in my presence! Rest assured that everything has been properly preserved for future examination. I can tell you that his garments disclosed nothing spectacular or specific, which was in itself telling. They were clothes such as anyone might wear around the house—or on a ship. Casual and domestic. No uniform. Nothing in his pockets or sealed secretively in the fabric of his clothing.

"He carried no identification. Nothing. I have been informed that the suit he was wearing when the Unop-Patha found him is a very old model. It was in bad shape, barely pressure-safe. Certainly would never have passed inspection on this ship, or on any private vessel that valued its certificate. It showed evidence of having been repaired, restored, and refitted more times than is legal. I spoke of burning our mystery man's clothing. His space suit should have been burned before he stepped into it."

"Yet it kept him alive," vaan Leuderwolk pointed out. "On the inner moon."

"In what circumstances?" Lahtehoja's brain was running hot. "Did the colony have a scientific station there? Some kind of observation post, perhaps for weather watchers?"

"Sorry to disappoint you, Commander." Vaan Leuderwolk knew what his superior was thinking. His thoughts had rushed down the same path of possibilities—until some basic research had shot them down. "According to every available record on Treetrunk there was not recently and never was any kind of colonial outpost or base of any kind on either of the planet's two moons. They're too small and their orbits are too irregular to make them of much use in that regard, and like most relatively new, rapidly expanding colonies, this one had no resources to spare on scientific frivolities. Their standard-issue communications satellites did the same kind of work more easily and cheaper." He paused briefly.

"Of course, whatever annihilated the population took the time and care to destroy anything that might have been capable of recording what was taking place at the time. Including all communications and monitoring satellites."

Lahtehoja grunted. "So we don't even know where this poor bastard is from."

Holomusa shook his head sadly. "Not based on his appearance, his suit, or his clothes, no. We can't even say if he's from Treetrunk or some passing ship that subsequently vanished. And that's all we have to go on."

"Not quite," the always calculating commander countered. "There's the vessel the Unop-Patha found him in." Badly as she wanted to speak to the survivor, it could wait. Turning to the *Ronin*'s captain, she issued the order for a change of orbit.

Starting at opposite ends, two teams of investigators would examine the exterior of the unknown survivor's ship while a third plumbed its interior. Should they encounter anything of significance, it would be removed to the cruiser's labs for more detailed analysis. Following this preliminary survey and investigation the tiny ship itself would be brought aboard the warship, where further studies could continue in a controlled environment during the flight back to Earth.

Even if the Unop-Patha had not provided details of the vessel's location, it would have been easy to find. The inner moon was not large. But anyone not making a deliberate search of its far side, she reflected, would never have picked up the incredibly feeble remnant of a signal that the diminutive craft was emitting. Identifying it proved surprisingly easy.

It was a lifeboat. A lifeboat from a KK-drive ship. What it was doing crewed by a single psychotic on the inner moon of Argus V no one could say. It was only when the *Ronin* was several days out from Treetrunk and deep in space-plus that a team of inspecting engineers brought the news.

Certain details had led them to one unlikely but inescapable conclusion. The lifeboat had not been launched from a ship. Leastwise, not in recent memory. Instead, it had been used to travel from a planetary surface to the satellite where it had been found. A one-way trip with no possibility of return or of traveling anywhere else. A suicide run—or one of ultimate desperation. Tests of microscopic particles clinging to its interior confirmed the obvious: that Treetrunk had been the origin of the battered vessel's most recent and final flight.

What was an ancient, oft-repaired, and amateurishly refitted lifeboat doing on a colony world like Treetrunk in the first place? That was a question for which the most detailed examination of the boat failed to supply an answer. The craft's on-board instruments had recorded only flight data, and there was no magic bottle full of answers hidden away in a cabinet or storage locker waiting to be opened. Only its presumed pilot, navigator, crew, and sole survivor could provide an explanation.

And he wasn't talking.

The government intended to keep the matter as quiet as possible for as long as possible. Revelation that someone might have survived the Treetrunk massacre, much less have been a living witness to its destruction, would have sparked an outcry and concurrent media frenzy unprecedented in the history of interstellar colonization. Under the resultant pressure for information it might have proven well-nigh impossible for the physicians assigned to the case to perform their work properly. It was decided at the highest levels that the comatose survivor's privacy would be protected at all costs, along with that of the specialists who were charged with doing their utmost to try to revive him.

The hospital was located in a quiet suburb of Kavieng, on the Pacific island of New Ireland. It was as isolated from the mainstream of world culture and tridee attention as it was possible for such a facility to be while remaining close to relevant government centers of operation on Bali and in Brisbane. Originally a center for research into and treatment of tropical diseases, over the years it had been expanded and modified to serve the needs of a wide area, including and beyond the Bismarck Sea. Workers on the regional tuna and lobster farms were among its regular clients.

Not everyone knew what the unconscious man in room fifty-four had been admitted for, nor the cause of his condition. An unusually large number of visiting doctors came and went from his bedside, prescribing, consulting, and conversing among themselves. Some were rumored to be specialists from as far away as Europe and North America, and several members of the staff recognized one especially famous neurosurgeon who was noted for never leaving his distinguished practice in Gangzhou.

It did not matter how many physicians visited room fifty-four, however. The condition and status of the patient it housed did not change.

The hospital's regular staff attended to his conventional, daily needs. He was fed and hydrated intravenously. Fifth-floor nurses bathed and changed him, making sure the monopole braces that suspended him in a clinical magnetic field above his resting place did not fail and drop him to the bed or surge and fling him against the ceiling. Such lifters, which held a patient aloft in a strong magnetic field, were usually reserved for seriously injured patients such as critical burn victims, and its employment simply to ensure the comfort of one who could not express feelings of pain puzzled some of the staff. But orders were orders, and since the facility was notably free of critical cases at that time it did not become anything more serious than a topic of conversation.

That the patient was someone special was evident not only from the parade of specialists who visited his room but from the presence of the two plainclothes guards who were always present outside his door. These men and women were polite but uninformative, insisting to inquisitive staff that they had no more idea who the man in room fifty-four's bed was than they did. They had been assigned to watch and protect. There was no need for them to know anything more, and frankly, they preferred it that way.

So the equatorial days slid into equatorial nights, with the tropical sun dropping systematically behind the distant high island of New Hanover, without more than a few people at the very top level of hospital administration knowing that the silent, unimpressive figure who lay motionless in corner room fifty-four was the most important patient on the entire planet.

Certainly Irene Tse was unaware of his prominence. Unlike some of her colleagues, she worked the graveyard shift because it allowed her to spend many of her daylight hours diving. Wearing their compact rebreathers, she and her friends would spend endless hours in the waters framing the dozens of small islands that speckled the ocean surrounding New Ireland and New Hanover, observing what was still the world's most diverse and impressive aggregation of underwater life. Widowed at twenty-three when her husband had been crushed in a stampede of panicked three hundred kilo bluefin tuna, at thirty she had yet to remarry. A lively and spirited personality, she had been attracted to a number of men and several women, but attraction was not love, affection not passion.

As far as the motionless man in fifty-four was concerned, identified on his charts as a Mr. Jones, to her he was just another patient who needed to be cared for, an insensible lump of humanity who might or might not one day emerge to a greater or lesser degree from his present state of catalepsy. At two o'clock in the morning she greeted the guards, both of whom were engrossed in watching a live windsand race from central Asia. Even though they all knew each other by sight now, she was required to produce her ident as well as being physically recognized by both retinal and heartwave scanners.

Once passed into the room, she began by checking the monitors. It was not necessary for her to record their readings, as these were transmitted directly to the hospital's central monitoring facility. Activating the levitator, she changed the bed and sponge-bathed the patient while he hung suspended in the field, the atoms of his body temporarily magnetized. When she shut down the field he was lowered gently in fresh hospital gown onto the newly changed bed.

She was preparing to move the osmotic fluid injector to a new area of his torso when she felt something touch her arm.

She might have stopped breathing for a second or two. She wasn't sure. What she was certain of was that fingers had moved against her skin. Looking down, she saw that the patient's left hand had brushed her wrist. Fallen against it, no doubt. As she was preparing to make a note of the phenomenon, two of the fingers, the middle and the index, rose. Trembling, they lightly grazed her for a second time before falling back, as if exhausted by their own nominal weight.

Looking up, she saw that the two fingers were not all that had moved. The patient's head was inclined toward her—though that may simply have been where it fell, she reminded herself. The open eyes did not startle her—they opened every morning, to stare at nothing, and closed every night. It was the moisture at one corner that was unexpected. It could easily have been the result of a miss with the soft towel following the evening bath. There was a quick and easy way to tell.

Leaning forward and reaching over, she wiped at the bare trickle with a finger and brought it to her lips. Her tongue communicated the unmistakable taste of salt. The moisture was a tear.

Why she voiced her thoughts she never knew. It was not a conscious decision, simply part of an automatic response. "I'll call the duty doctor," she whispered tightly. As she started to turn to do so, all five of the fingers on the patient's left hand suddenly uncurled and reached up to grab her wrist in a grip of iron.

Lips fluttered, lips that had been kept moist through the judicious application of treated cloths and expensive salve. For the first time in the month and a day since the patient had been brought into the hospital and placed in his bed, a sound emerged from the hitherto unused throat. She had to lean close to sculpt a word from the whisper.

"Don't . . ."

Transfixed by the single word, by the man's blank stare, and by the utterly unexpected firmness of his grasp on her wrist, Tse stood there, not moving, waiting to see what would happen next. She could break the hold if she tried, she felt, but what effect might that have on the patient, who obviously wanted her to remain? He had spoken—she was certain of that. Could he also now hear?

"I'll stay," she told him, "but let go of my arm. You're hurting me."

The fingers relaxed, released her, slumped away from her wrist. In minutes, she knew, someone at Hospital Central would have noted the surge in physiological activity within the room. The duty doctor and staff might already be on their way.

Sure enough, they piled into the room a couple of minutes later, crowding around the bed as close as they dared without impeding the patient's access to air. Among the panting arrivals was an imposing woman in expensive designer garb and a tall, lanky older man wearing the uniform of a high-ranking military officer. They competed for space and attention with Dr. Chimbu, who bent low over the patient.

"Mr. Jones, can you hear me?" When no response was forthcoming from the motionless figure in the bed, the doctor looked expectantly up at the woman in the expensive suit. After exchanging a glance with the officer, he nodded solemnly and tried again—but differently.

"Mr. Mallory. Alwyn Mallory, can you hear me?" The doctor licked his lips. "If you can hear me, can you give us a sign of some kind?"

The single, barely perceptible nod the patient managed by way of response generated more activity in the room than a speech from the president of the world federation. Bodies flew through the outer door, startling the guards. More decorously dressed but heavily armed individuals appeared moments later. In the interim, a steadfast Dr. Chimbu tried to keep at a proper distance those who sought to crowd the bed. Only the woman in the suit would not be denied.

"Mr. Mallory," she whispered in a compassionate and gracious tone, "you are on Earth. You are safe. You were brought here from the inner moon of Argus Five. Treetrunk. You were found there on a badly jury-rigged lifeboat of outmoded design, in a spacesuit that was supplying you with a seriously reduced flow of air, presumably to conserve dwindling supplies." She swallowed delicately. "It is presumed by some that you came from Treetrunk itself. Others feel you reached the moon from a passing ship. We—everyone—would like very much to know which is the truth of the matter." When no response was forthcoming she glanced back at the stone-faced officer and tried again.

"Please, Mr. Mallory. If you can say anything, anything at all, do try to do so."

The prone shape on the bed lay still and silent. Its lips did not move; its arms remained listless at its sides. Then very suddenly, without any warning whatsoever, it began screaming.

"Out, everyone out!" Chimbu was already working on the patient, giving orders, directing nurses. The startled woman and her entourage were ejected from the room, despite the halfhearted protests of the man in uniform. Only Chimbu, two assistants who had arrived with him, and Tse, standing by the door, stayed.

When the patient had been sedated and was once more resting quietly, eyes closed, heart rate and other vitals stabilized, Chimbu drew the nurse aside.

"I saw what happened on the monitor replay. He grabbed your wrist. Is that correct?"

She nodded slowly. "First I felt something—him—touch me. Then he grabbed me."

"You touched his face in the vicinity of his left eye and then put your finger to your mouth." Chimbu's words were composed, professional. "What was that about?"

"I saw moisture there. I thought it might be left from the bath I had just administered. It was salty. He was tearing."

The doctor nodded. "He also moved his lips. The pickups that are in place are sensitive, but they're not perfect. *Did he say anything to you?*" The quiet intensity in the physician's voice unsettled her. Chimbu was no automaton, but around the hospital he was not noted for exhibiting a wide range of emotion.

She licked her lips before replying. "Yes. He said, 'Don't.' "

"That's all?" The doctor's expression wrinkled. " 'Don't'?"

She nodded, and he seemed disappointed. "Don't 'what'?"

"I had the impression he didn't want me to leave."

"Ah." Chimbu looked back at the stabilized, immobile patient for a long moment. "Then stay. If he even hinted that he might want you to stay, you should stay."

"Doctor? I have to complete my rounds." What was happening here? she found herself wondering.

"Not anymore," he informed her firmly. "As of right now you are relieved of all other duties. Replacements are already being scheduled. From this moment you are assigned to this patient exclusively. Furthermore, you are being placed on extended half-day shifts." Raising a hand, he forestalled her imminent objections. "You're also on double pay. No, triple." Murmuring more to himself than to her, he added, "Administration will approve it on my recommendation. They don't have any choice in the matter anyway." Raising his eyes back to hers, he remembered that he was speaking to another human being and not to a mechanical or a recorder.

"I would like to make arrangements to move another bed in here, so you can sleep in the room when you're not officially on duty."

She gaped at him. "Doctor? I take pride in my work, but I have a life outside it, you know."

"I know; I know." He made mollifying gestures. "You'll be fully compensated for your sacrifice. And if the patient begins speaking rationally to others, you will be permitted to leave. On extended vacation, at hospital expense."

Her eyes widened. " 'Permitted' to leave? What is this?" Looking past him, she focused on the man in the bed. The ordinary, now officially semicomatose man whose brief stirring had aroused an unexpected tidal wave of activity. "Who is this 'Mr. Jones' that you called Alwyn Mallory?"

"You're a good nurse, Tse. You don't miss much." Chimbu pushed his physician's probe back from his forehead to the crest of his skull so that it pressed tightly against the receding hairline. "You know about Treetrunk?"

She searched his face. He looked suddenly tired, weighed down by unexpected and unsought responsibility. "I'm not dead, so of course I know. What's that to do with this Mallory person?"

"If you're going to attend him you have to know, so you might as well know now." The hospital's chief of staff was as serious as Tse had ever seen him. "He *may* be a survivor of the massacre."

Overwhelmed by the implication, for a long moment she had nothing to say. Finally she stammered, "There are no survivors of what happened on Treetrunk."

"You heard what the woman from the bureau said. He was found in a lifeboat on the planet's inner moon, traumatized and speechless. He might be a refugee from a passing ship, or someone a disgruntled crew kicked out. Or . . . he might be a survivor of the catastrophe. The only survivor." He peered deep into her startled eyes. "You understand now? *Do you?*"

"Yes, Doctor." As much as anyone could understand the impossible, she thought.

"He wants you to stay. Or he might have meant something else when he whispered 'Don't' to you. We don't know yet. We don't know anything. No one knows except him." Turning, he gazed speculatively at the figure in the bed. "His reactiveness tonight might have been a one-time fluke. Or it might be the harbinger of future stirrings. We can't take any chances with this man. He might be nothing important. Or he might be able to manage only another sentence or two. They might be sentences twenty billion humans are waiting to hear." He took a step back from her.

"Until we know what he meant when he said 'Don't' to you, you are to stay with him. Continue with your usual duties. Bathe him, check his hydration and nutrients and medicine drip. Stay close." His tone softened. "I know you're not a statue, not a machine. You can use the room's tridee. Whatever you want to make you as personally comfortable as possible will be sent in. The room monitors will remain on, recording twenty-four hours a day just as they have been for more than a month, so you don't have to worry about missing something of significance. If one of his eyelids twitches, it will be noted and recorded."

"What—" She tried to gather herself, to make sense of everything that had happened in the past few frenetic minutes. "—what else should I do?"

Reaching out to her, Chimbu gently squeezed her shoulder. "Be here. For him. If he wants to whisper, you listen. If he wants to converse, you talk."

She nodded. "Do you want me . . . Do you want me to ask him about Treetrunk?"

The doctor considered. "No. The important thing right now is to encourage any progress in his condition. I'm still the Chief of Staff here, and I'll shield you. From the government, from the military. So will my colleagues. If he speaks, let him talk about whatever he wants. If he improves enough, we'll consider putting questions to him later. In the meantime his health is the most important thing. Don't worry—if he lets something important or relevant slip, it will be recorded." He released her shoulder.

Around them, curative instrumentation and devices hummed and clicked softly. On the bed, a single figure lay unmoving. Tse and Chimbu contemplated it together.

"Is there anything else, Doctor?"

"Yes," Chimbu murmured. "If the opportunity arises, be kind to him. He needs it."

12

Having heard only one word in the course of one month, Tse did not expect tirades to spill from the mouth of the afflicted. But she was surprised when, upon awakening on the morning of the fourth day after being moved into the room, she sat up rubbing sleep from her eyes to find Alwyn Mallory staring at her.

Nothing else had changed; nothing in the room had been disturbed, though she knew that down in Central doctors and other important people must by now be glued to viewscreens in response to the patient's action. It must be demanding a tremendous effort on their part, she reflected as she turned and slid her legs off the inflatable bed, for them to stay out of the room.

Not only was he staring at her, he had raised his head slightly to get a better look. Now it fell back, the inches it had inclined forward proving too much for the man's weakened muscles to sustain.

"Don't stress yourself," she heard herself saying to him. "I'll come over there." Aware that monitors were everywhere, including the bathroom, she simply slipped out of the sleeping gauze and into her uniform.

By the time she sat down in the chair that had been placed by the right side of the bed, he had ignored her advice to remain still and had turned his head to face her. Then he smiled. So brightly unexpected was it, so warm and full of thanks, of the simple joy of being alive, that this time it was her own eye she found herself daubing at.

"Well, that's better." It was all she could think of to say.

"Who are you? Where am I?" His lips moved slowly, with careful deliberation, as if each syllable had to be constructed and approved by a separate portion of his brain before he attempted its actual verbalization.

"You're in Golman Memorial Hospital, South Pacific Region. I am your duty nurse, Irene Tse."

"I'd shake your hand, Irene, but you told me not to stress myself." A different sort of smile this time, more calculating, reflective of looming uncertainties. "I don't like taking orders, but you I think I'll listen to. Not because I have to, but because it pleases me." Defying her admonition, he raised his head again, holding it up longer this time. With each movement, each word, he seemed to grow stronger, not weaker. "You said 'South Pacific Region.' I'm on Earth?"

As she glanced over at his readouts in what she hoped was an inconspicuous manner, she did not comment on the obvious. He looked around, inspecting the room.

"How long have I been asleep?" His eyebrows tried to knot. "They must have knocked me out for the jump here."

"No one knocked you out. You traveled to Earth and arrived here in a cataleptic state." Reflexively, she put a hand on his lower arm. "As of this morning, you've been here in hospital thirty-four days."

"Thirty-four . . . ?" Leaning back against the pillow, he gazed pensively at the ceiling. "Not asleep. In coma." She nodded gravely. "I didn't wake up at all? I mean, if I did I don't remember it, but it's hard to think of being unconscious all that time. I don't feel like I've been out for more than a day or two."

"The mind plays wonderful tricks on the body." She smiled reassuringly. "Sometimes the body plays back."

She was acutely aware of the omnidirectional pickups that were judiciously placed around the room, of the fact that everything that was being said or done was being observed and recorded by a multitude of devices. It shamed her. Whatever he had gone through, this man deserved his privacy. It might never be given back to him, she knew. Issues of an order of magnitude greater than the personal desires of one man were at stake.

"Who found me?" Though he had asked a question, it seemed to her that his thoughts were concentrated elsewhere. He had posed it almost absently.

"I don't know." Before she could finish, her recorder vibrated gently against her. Removing it, she found information on the remotely activated page. "Some people called the Unop-Patha. A minor race about which not much is known except that they're shy and inoffensive. They just happened to be in the right place to pick up the signal from your ship." A line of questions appeared on the screen immediately after this information. Consenting only to the first, she firmly tucked the recorder back in its holder. "I understand that the vessel they found you in was of an old, discontinued type and wasn't in very good condition."

He laughed then, a good sign. It was followed by a spate of coughing that was not. Unable to raise his hand all the way to manage it, he let her slip the drinking tube between his lips. When she felt he'd had enough, she gently withdrew it from his mouth.

"That's enough for now. You've been on osmotics for a long time, and you don't want to shock your system with too much real drink and food too soon."

"Yes I do," he shot back. "I want to shock the hell out of it. I want tea, and coffee, and twenty-year-old bourbon. I want fish, and canned goods, and crispy vegetables, and cremated dead cow."

Her mouth was firm. "How about some applesauce?"

"How about you—?" He broke off his rejoinder and inhaled deeply, slowly. "I can't argue with you. I can't argue with anybody right now. 'Applesauce'!" Astonishingly, his expression grew mischievous. It was about the last thing she would have expected. "Will you feed it to me?"

Mindful of their significant unseen audience, she kept her response coolly professional. "That is part of my job."

"Good! Then I will have some applesauce."

When he said nothing more, she hazarded a cautious prompt. "Don't you want to talk some more?"

Now he was grinning broadly. "Applesauce. Your idea."

Afterward he slept, ignorant of the frenzy of activity his awakening had galvanized within government and military circles. Indifferent to a flood of entreaties, she refused to wake him early or otherwise intrude on the peacefulness that seemed to have come over the rechristened Alwyn Mallory. True to his word, Dr. Chimbu and the rest of the medical team supervising the precious patient's care backed her decision.

Two more days passed in recovery for Mallory. Two days during which the inner workings of government lurched forward in a state of semiparalysis. Two days in which extraordinary efforts somehow succeeded in keeping an always ravenous media ignorant of the lone man in room fifty-four of the Golman Memorial Hospital on the island of New Ireland. The intentional isolation helped. Even in the latter half of the twenty-fourth century, New Ireland was not an easy place to visit.

In those forty-eight hours Mallory went from barely being able to raise his head to being able to feed himself, from hesitating in the clouded search for words to talking voluminously. His apparent progress was underlain by the very real medical fear that he could lapse back into coma at any moment. Chimbu and others put their careers on the line by supporting nurse Tse's determination not to pressure the man in their care for details or ask if he knew anything about what had happened on Treetrunk.

Following lunch on the third day, her forbearance and the medical staff's conviction were rewarded.

"A couple of days ago, when I mentioned the kind of ship you'd been found in, you laughed at me." She came toward the bed, having just dumped his lunch dishes and utensils in the room's recycler.

This time he only chuckled. "I remember. You said that it was old and not in very good condition. That's hardly surprising." When he was alert, like now, she found that his eyes had a wonderful twinkle. "It was an old lifeboat, freighter class. I got it cheap, since the masters of the cargo ship that left it behind on Treetrunk knew it would cost too much to renovate it to the point where it could pass a safety-board inspection again. Fixing it up, puttering around with its innards, was my hobby. Kept me busy whenever I started to think too much. I never expected it to actually fly anywhere again, much less offworld." His gaze met hers. "Did you know that I was a member of the original survey team of the *Chagos*?"

The name meant nothing to her, and she told him so. Down in Central, where hospital communications had been linked in half a dozen ways with centers of power all across the planet, technicians scrambled while several of their superiors digested the patient's disclosure in stunned silence.

To Mallory, however, the innocently ignorant Tse clearly required elaboration. "The *Chagos* was the starship that discovered and carried out the first surveys of Treetrunk. Since there was no reason for the people who brought me from there to here to presume that kind of personal connection, I guess no one made it. Also, I used to space under the name Alwyn Lleywynth." He grinned. "Finally got tired of people not being able to spell or say it, and had it changed officially when I settled on Treetrunk."

"That's interesting," she told him, nodding. "I have a feeling that you're right and that no one made the connection." They would be making it now, she knew without a glance at any of the pickups. Making connections and trying to draw conclusions.

"I was good at what I did. I'm also an accomplished bitcher, which didn't endear me to many of my colleagues, I'm afraid. But in spite of my customary complaining, I liked Treetrunk. Liked it a lot. Enough to ask for my release and stay behind when the *Chagos* finally left. I helped build the place, worked on some of the first infrastructure for Weald and a lot of smaller towns. Always kept to myself as much as I could, though. I didn't much care to be around people. It was one of the reasons I originally went into deep space. It was one of the reasons I chose a new world to be my home and final resting place." His voice fell slightly. "That's all changed now. When I get out of here I think I might like to settle down in New York, or Lala, or Joburg. I want people around me now. Lots of people. Swarms of 'em."

Without warning, he began to tremble, the covering sheet shivering above his torso like rapidly advancing bleached fog. The contrast between his strengthening voice and frail body could not have been more dramatic. When she started to rise, he lifted an arm to detain her.

"I'm all right," he whispered shakily. "I'm all right." His expression pleaded. "Would you—I swear I'm not trying anything here—would you just, hold me? For a moment. Just . . . hold me."

Rising from her chair, she tentatively took a seat on the bed alongside him. Bending low, she put her arms around his shoulders. Immediately his head slid into the crook of her arm, like a bird finding its nest. Hesitant at first, she brought her legs up onto the bed and slid them carefully next to his. Then she lay down beside him.

More than an hour had passed when she awoke, quietly surprised to discover that she had fallen asleep next to him. Around her the machines ticked and whispered. The room was unchanged. No one had disturbed them.

Moving her head, she found that he was awake, staring at her, his eyes swallowing every inch of her as if she were a cool, invigorating potion, a silent libation for the soul. Uncertain and a little confused at what she was feeling, she sat up quickly on the side of the bed.

"Relax. Take it easy," he told her. Then he smiled afresh. "Hey, did you hear what I just said? Me, telling you to relax and take it easy. Want me to check your vitals?"

She had to smile back. This man, who had obviously been through an experience too horrible to imagine, was irrepressible. She found herself liking him instead of pitying him. He sensed the shift in her attitude and was pleased.

"So you became a citizen of Treetrunk." She rested a hand on his upper arm, not entirely for therapeutic purposes this time.

"Yes," he told her. The smile faded away, and he began to

shake again. In response to her look of alarm he willed his body to relax, forced the muscles to still. "It's okay. I'm not going to scream again."

She blinked. "You remember screaming?"

"I remember." He nodded. "I just couldn't stop it. I didn't want to stop it. It was so easy, to scream. It blotted everything out. A little." He began to fidget beneath the sheet. "I'm sick of lying down. Help me sit up."

Immediately she reached for the bed's remote. "I can raise you to any angle you—"

"No, goddammit!" He was emphatic. "I want to sit up! Me, not the damn bed."

She assisted him, wondering as she did so what Dr. Chimbu would have to say about stressing the patient. But no one interrupted them, either in person or via communicator, and with her aid in a couple of minutes he was sitting up straight, his back propped against the pillows.

"How do you feel?" Her concern was a mixture of professionalism and—something else. "Any nausea? That would be normal."

"Not for me it wouldn't. A little dizzy, maybe. That's all." Looking past her, his gaze focused for the first time on the view through the room's large window. From his location in a top-floor corner of the hospital he could see palm trees and ships in the harbor and the blue, blue water of a tropical sea. A flock of flying foxes was flapping from east to west over the harbor, a dark motile cloud scattered among towering white cumulus.

Turning to her, he asked in a calm, quiet voice and without warning, "Would you like to know what happened to my adopted home? To Argus Five, also known as Treetrunk?"

Down in Central, and in linked monitoring stations all across the globe, instant pandemonium ensued.

13

It was a good life. Mallory was happy with his decision to resign his position on the *Chagos* in order to become one of the first settlers of the new world. That choice would not make him rich, but perhaps his progeny, if he ever had any, would one day find it useful to be able to boast that their great-grandfather, or whatever, had been among the original surveyors and colonizers of Argus V.

Despite his irascible, often contentious personality, he had no difficulty finding work. As a jack-of-all-trades on KK-drive craft like the *Chagos* and a retired ship's engineer—and at a precocious age, at that—he was a master of many skills that were highly valued in the new colony. Disdaining seductive offers from the rapidly burgeoning municipality of Weald and the innumerable companies and concerns that specialized in abetting the development of new colonies, he set himself up as an independent consultant. Wealth did not flow in his direction, but he made a more than adequate living. In his ample free time he visited many of the beautiful and as yet unexplored regions of the temperate equatorial belt or enjoyed the home and shop whose construction he had supervised. Its isolation on an uninhabited mountainside deep within a choice patch of virgin alien woods gave him the freedom to tinker with the surplus freighter-class lifeboat he had purchased on a whim for an astonishingly modest sum.

When he needed credit he would choose from among the many standing assignments on offer. Given the headlong forward expansion of the colony, these were always in plentiful supply. There were few newly arriving settlers with his knowledge and experience. His expertise was eagerly sought.

In this manner five years passed during which Mallory, while not entirely happy—such a state of existence not being in his nature—was forced to concede that he was less discontented than usual. When compelled to visit the city for those necessary items he could not manufacture or grow himself, he tolerated the occasional company of others. As a known recluse who was irritable by nature, he was not sought out except when his professional abilities were in demand. This suited both him and everyone else on the planet just fine.

He did not hear the general announcement that interrupted all tridee programming. That particular morning was unusually bright and clear, even for pristine, unpolluted Treetrunk. As the sun rose and warmed his mountainside he ate a leisurely breakfast on the hand-hewn porch and then prepared to spend a stimulating and enjoyable day working in the simple shed that housed his shop and hobbies.

The walk from his home to the outbuilding was a short one. Though he had built a covered walkway to shield him from the rain and snow of Argus V's wet season, he had no need of it that day. The sun was out, and there was hardly a cloud in the sky. The shed itself was a single large enclosed structure stained brown and green to match the surrounding trees. Such a large, unmasked building would have attracted the attention of the passing curious. Having no wish to be disturbed and being fanatical in his desire for privacy, Mallory had caused both his home and workplace to be camouflaged from the rapidly expanding population. Newcomers in particular he sought to avoid. They were invariably effusive and friendly, two qualities he did not seek in neighbors.

Four months before, he had taken the old lifeboat out for a short flight from the capital district over to Demure and back. While successful and as smooth as could be expected, the journey had predictably loosened some internal components. Entering the open boat, he found his tools where he had last left them and settled down happily to effect the necessary repairs.

Several times during the morning he thought he heard the echo of distant, dull booming. Despite the absence of clouds when he had made the walk from home to shop, he put the noise down to an approaching thunderstorm. Rough weather could blow up on Treetrunk at any time, and with summer approaching abrupt atmospheric disturbances could be expected. Or it might have been a construction team excavating new foundations for large buildings on the outskirts of Weald itself. Or perhaps it was simply boisterous adolescents working mischief closer to his home. He gave the random, sporadic echoes barely a second thought.

It was nearly two when, sweaty but satisfied, he set the industrial-strength tools aside and resolved to get something to eat. As he often did, he'd labored through the lunch hour. One of the pleasures of working for oneself, he reflected as he wiped at his face and rose to leave the lifeboat, was the freedom to eat when one was hungry instead of when it was expected.

Exiting the shed, he started back toward the house—and stopped. Shading his eyes with one hand, he stared in the direction of the capital. Rising into the crystalline air, smoke from numerous sources drifted together to form an enormous dirty brown cloud that had begun to block out the sun. *What the hell . . . ?* he thought.

Moving a little faster, he hurried back to the house. Some kind of widespread industrial disaster had struck Weald. At the moment he could not imagine its nature. Modern fire prevention techniques prevented destructive blazes from spreading freely from house to house, building to building. Yet the distant glow of flames and widely separated pillars of smoke suggested not only spreading, but that the conflagration had broken out simultaneously in different parts of the city.

Hurrying straight to his den, he activated the tridee and waited for the first three-dimensional image to congeal above the floor. Colors and shapes appeared, but did not coalesce. No matter how much he fiddled with the controls he could not induce the flickering polygons and sparking clouds to come together into anything recognizable. Similar static dominated every infochute. Then he lost the static, too. The air in the room was silent.

Something was very wrong.

Not panicked yet, but anxious and concerned, he rushed back outside. If anything, the smoke cloud had grown larger in his absence. He couldn't be certain, but it seemed as if new smoke pillars were appearing even as he watched. The recurrent booms he had heard before were sounding more frequently now.

He had never seen a city under attack, but he had seen tridee recordings, both fictional and historical. Who would assault a defenseless colony and why, he struggled to imagine. His first thought was of the AAnn. The thranx insisted the aggressive reptilian species would jump on any advantage it could find. But Treetrunk was much too cold to suit them, far from the nearest of their own worlds, and did not even lie along a potentially Empire-threatening vector. Nor was it a storehouse of valuable resources that could not be found elsewhere.

The same reasons only more so applied to the thranx. Like the great majority of humankind his feelings toward the insectoids was ambivalent. They wanted to be friends, but most people were not anxious to jump at the opportunity. Distance remained largely because of the species' appearance. Having spent thousands of years battling the thranx's much smaller very distant terrestrial relatives, it would take time before people were ready to invite them into their homes.

Who else, then? he wondered as he stood stunned and watching the distant destruction blossom. Surely not the Quillp, as inoffensive a species as humans had yet encountered. Still, the Quillp were colonizers and settlers, too, and their sphere of influence lay much closer to that of the rapidly expanding humans than did the empire of the AAnn, though not the thranx.

Might it be a new, previously unencountered race? Standing there on the mountainside watching the city he had helped to found burn, that seemed to him at that moment the most likely explanation. Whoever it was, they were technologically sophisticated.

Retreating back into the house, he returned to the porch carrying a handheld scoper. Methodically, he played it over the perimeter of the great cloud, then scanned the interior. There was no sign of aircraft. The descending explosives were extra-atmospheric. They were being launched from orbit and then guided to their targets with precision. A more distant pillar of rising smoke marked the location of the city's shuttleport. Two others indicated the sites of outlying towns.

While thorough, the intent of the attack was apparently not to annihilate completely. Had that been the case, he would not have heard multiple booms while he had been working on his salvaged lifeboat: only one overwhelming one as a single nuke obliterated the entire city. Instead, it was still there, albeit burning furiously. He did not doubt that the attackers, whoever they were, possessed such weapons of mass destruction or the ability to manufacture them. Any sentience sufficiently advanced to negotiate space-plus had to first achieve nuclear technology. You couldn't learn to manipulate the components of other space until you had mastered the minutiae of this one.

What were they after? What did they want? If total obliteration was not their aim, it suggested they wanted something intact. He couldn't imagine anything that an invading force could not have acquired simply through threat. The only explanation, he decided, was that the attackers wanted to protect their identity. Based on the collapse of planetary communications and on what he could see from the front of his home, it was a hypothesis that gained credence with every passing moment. He had no doubt that the space-minus communications facility near the shuttleport was one of the first sites to be targeted. Almost certainly the other one at Chagos Downs had suffered a similar fate.

If so, it suggested that the aliens knew what targets to hit first and where to find them. That put the lie to the notion that the attackers were a new, previously unknown and unencountered species. There were always KK-drive ships in orbit around Treetrunk, and they would have noted and communicated the presence of any alien vessels embarked on a survey of strategically important locations. Therefore the attackers must have arrived with a carefully laid-out, premeditated plan of assault based on prior research already in hand.

Even so, the unannounced arrival of one or more large alien craft would have been noted by the government and as a matter of course passed along to the citizenry through the usual media channels. He had seen no such bulletin on the tridee, not the previous night or this morning during breakfast, when everything had been operating fine.

He was missing something, he realized. Something important. Whatever it was, the authorities had missed it as well. Not that there was much they could do to stave off a determined attack by a properly equipped military force. As a new, developing colony Treetrunk had only domestic policing weaponry of its own. Humankind was not at war with any of the known intelligent species. Disagreements that revolved around matters of commerce and settlement were settled by discussion, sometimes loud but never physical. Interstellar war on a large scale was too complex and expensive a proposition to be viable. Even the AAnn realized that and limited their occasional depredations, usually in thranx territory, to isolated, confinable piratical acts. No one thought of assaulting an entire world.

Until now, he told himself grimly.

Having returned to the notably aggressive AAnn, his thoughts once again considered what reason the bipedal reptilians might have for launching so violent an assault on an innocuous colony world. Try as he might, he could not conceive of one. Of course, he was speculating from the standpoint of human motivation. The AAnn might have reasons for attacking Treetrunk that were quite incomprehensible to him or to any other human.

He needed information. In the absence of the usual tridee chutes, he would have to try something else.

Rushing back into the shop, he activated the antique communications console on board the lifeboat. Designed to scan and decipher every possible corner of the spectrum that might contain downloadable information, under his direction it began by checking the bands that carried information from ship to ship and ship to ground. There was plenty of chatter, but it was all in colors and hisses unknown to the unit. It was the attackers, he decided. Talking among themselves. It was maddening to know that he was seeing and hearing the answers to his most pressing questions but could not decrypt them.

Changing focus, he sampled more familiar bandwidth. As expected, all the usual tridee chutes were either dead or suffocating in visual static. Weald was silent. So were Chagos Downs and Waldburg and every other town that boasted its own chute or uplink. Nothing came from above, the dozen or so communications satellites proving as quiet as their land-based transmitters and translators. Destroyed during the initial attack, most probably. It was what he would have done. Blind and isolate your prey first, then butcher at leisure.

He had almost given up hope and had decided to fly his truck as close to the city's outskirts as he dared in hopes of learning what was happening when something flickered in the lifeboat's viewing alcove. It was smaller than similar images would have been in his house because the display space was smaller.

What he was picking up, distorted and intermittent, came from a mobile remote, an automated unit that was the property of one of Treetrunk's two independent media concerns. He identified it by the small rotating logo that hovered above the floor of the lifeboat. There was sound but no commentary. Whoever had been traveling with the unit was quite likely dead, murdered by the invaders. Since communications both local and extraplanetary had been among the invaders' first targets it was not unreasonable to assume that everyone back at the media concern's main offices were dead by now as well.

Unconcerned and oblivious to the fate of its human operators, the independently powered robot soldiered on, obediently transmitting tridee images to a base unit that probably no longer existed. No home or commercial receiver could pick up its pictures. For one thing, such interception of a commercial signal would have been illegal. It would take a skilled technician working with specialized equipment to make the grab. Someone like Mallory, for example, working with something like a lifeboat's all-encompassing emergency instrumentation.

Sitting alone in the boat's cockpit, he watched in stunned silence as the mobile unit's pickup roved the city. There was fire everywhere, and smoke that obscured many of the images. Trained to seek out the visible, the unit kept moving. In the absence of directives from an accompanying commentator or its home base, it relied on the fallback instructions programmed into its memory.

Not every building was on fire. Some had been spared or missed. Others had been melted, and gaping, smoking craters marked the prior location of those that had been completely obliterated. A man appeared from off-image left, running at an angle across the pickup's field of view. Dirty and bleeding, his clothes torn, he carried a baby in his arms while a teenage boy ran along parallel to him. The man kept looking around as if in search of help or a refuge. He might have been an office worker or a technician or a civil servant.

The boy looked back, and as he did so, his head vanished in a rainbow puff of blood, brains, bone, and flame. Ducking to his left, the man tried to bend as low as possible while shielding the child in his arms. One of his legs exploded, and he went down. Unlike the teen, who had perished in silence, a horrified Mallory heard him scream. The mobile remote picked up the shrill sound with detached efficiency.

Dumped from cradling arms, the infant went rolling across the street. It too was screaming. One leg gone, the man began to pull himself across the street toward the child. As Mallory bit down on the back of one index finger hard enough to draw blood, shapes appeared out of the smoke, advancing from the left. There were two of them, tall and straight, clad in protective helmets and bulky body armor. One of them walked up to the crawling man, put the tip of a long, unrecognizable instrument against the side of his head, and activated the device. The man's head blew apart, blood and fragments of bone splattering against the armored legs. The killer's companion walked over to the squalling infant and without hesitation repeated the action. Mallory ordered his body to breathe.

The mobile unit moved sideways, traveling along the street, emotionlessly following its programming. When it found a scene that would trip something within its set of internal commands, it would stop and focus, then move on again. Twice Mallory lost the image; both times frantic manipulation of the lifeboat's outdated but still functional instrumentation brought it back. As he worked at the controls something large and powerful screamed past overhead, loud enough to be heard within the lifeboat that was inside the shed. Transfixed by the images he was seeing on the tridee, he ignored the sonorous echo of the object's passing.

Drifting aimlessly in a fallback news search pattern, the mobile reached Weald's central plaza. Carefully and lovingly laid out to resemble a series of concentric gardens, the square had been planted with blossoming plants and exotic growths gathered from all over Treetrunk. Many of these careful transplants were dead or dying now, incinerated or blasted from their planters. The square's central fountain, a gift from the populace of the enormously successful colony of New Riviera, was a shapeless lump of ceramic and composite slag. Water from broken source pipes ran in a steady, aimless stream into surrounding drains.

Several air repulsion-type vehicles were clustered together near the center of the square, hard by the demolished fountain. All boasted protrusions that, while not immediately identifiable, were easily recognized as weapons. More of the armored body shapes were moving about nearby. In addition, there were a large number of figures engaged in other activities.

The mobile moved in closer. For some reason it was not immediately noticed by the invaders. Or perhaps, having already destroyed all known communications facilities, they felt no urgency to eliminate a single mobile device of obviously mechanical origins. The tridee image in the lifeboat flickered and danced. Cursing, hammering on the console, Mallory fought to stabilize it.

A small vehicle arrived and halted. Several of the more

lightly clad figures moved to its side and helped those aboard to unload. Mallory leaned forward slightly, expecting to see valuable electronic components or containers full of informational recordings. The objects the aliens disbursed were somewhat larger, though equally recognizable.

Bodies.

Whether they were dead or simply paralyzed Mallory could not tell. In any event, none of the dozen or so exhibited any visible signs of damage. They were all, insofar as he could tell from the unsteady, intermittent image, female. Ranging in approximate age from fourteen to forty, they were carefully laid out on a prepared portable platform.

Other figures came forward. They carried small devices that Mallory at first thought were sidearms. They were not. Three of the figures immediately set to work on the nearest of the neatly laid out torsos. Silently, stolidly, having no one to lament with, Mallory watched as the aliens carefully and efficiently sliced into the abdomen and removed, insofar as he was able to tell, the complete set of female reproductive organs: uterus, fallopian tubes, ovaries, everything. Wet and glistening, these were smoothly transferred to a waiting container from which smoke/mist drifted, indicating that its interior was either very hot or very cold.

Their excision completed, they moved on to the next body in line, that of a girl who looked to be close to but not quite twenty. Whether the woman they left behind was still alive or not Mallory could not tell. It did not matter to the aliens, who made no attempt to close the gaping wound they left behind, and he found that he did not want to know.

He wanted to look away, to stare at something else, to put what he was seeing out of his mind, but he could not. The mobile unit, following its programming, continued to focus on the grisly biopsies, following the horribly inevitable course of one after another. So stunned was Mallory's system by what he was witnessing that the shock was sufficient to suppress even his nausea reflex. At least, it was until he saw one of the eviscerated women twitch and try to sit up. Not through any dint of empathy but operating strictly from efficiency, one of the patrolling armored figures noticed the movement and shot her before she could rise far enough to comprehend the gaping crater in her belly. She had been granted the mercy of indifference.

Devoid of involvement beyond its unemotional programming, the mobile was relentless. It watched, it transmitted, it commented not. Pausing before the seventh helpless, prone figure, one of the alien exenteraters paused to adjust his protective gear. In the course of so doing it momentarily removed its helmet. Reacting to this action, a companion did likewise. Mallory stared. Humans. Other humans. Then he took note of the subtle differences, of the prismatically colored hair, the too-perfect posture, the sculpted countenances. Not human.

Pitar.

Why? he felt himself screaming silently. Why, why, why? What reason could there be for the Pitar to attack an inoffensive and harmless colony like Treetrunk without warning, without reason? It made no sense. Exultant madness ruled the day, and dementia had taken control of the plenum. And what were the invaders doing, what could they possibly want, with the preserved reproductive organs of human females?

To these hopeless questions he could configure no rational answers. It made no sense, none whatsoever. Surely the Pitar knew the consequences of their actions! Not only humankind but sentience throughout the Arm would react with outrage, with anger, and then with retribution. Whatever they hoped to gain through the successful fulfillment of this atrocity would be infinitely transcended by the devastation a united and fully mobilized humankind would wreak on the perpetrators of the outrage.

Which would only happen, he realized with abrupt, exquisite clarity, if the identity of the perpetrators became known.

He was already moving when one of the body-armored Pitar finally took notice of the hovering mobile, turned directly toward it, raised a weapon, and fired. By the time the tridee image vanished, Mallory was out of the shed and racing back toward the house.

There was no need for structures and facilities on Treetrunk to be camouflaged. Who would want to attack a colony with a restricted habitation zone, limited industry, and still underexploited resources? Only someone who wished to be avoided by his fellow settlers would seek to distance himself from them and to make an effort to conceal his abode. There were no true hermits on Argus V, but there were a number who cherished their privacy. Among these, only one had the skill and the wherewithal to render himself and his habitation semivisible.

That wouldn't save him, Mallory knew. It might keep him from discovery by the invading forces for a while, but eventually they would seek him out. They had to. The horrors they were committing demanded no one be left alive to speak of what had been done. The Pitar would scour the habitation zone for colonists and the cold wastes of the north and south for exploration parties. If they carried life detectors they would be able to track down and analyze even minor ambulatory patterns. On such instruments a human being left a signature as clear and sharp as a tridee paragon. Only a deep cave or oceanic environment could mask the individual autograph, and he didn't doubt that the Pitar would search beneath the ground and sea as well.

He couldn't remember from the last time he had viewed the news if any KK-drive ships were currently in orbit. If they were, none were likely to be warships. Undoubtedly their unlucky crews had been among the first to fall victim to the Pitarian treachery. Vessels stopping at Argus could not continue to disappear without notice, but given recent shipping patterns he estimated it might be several months before another called at Treetrunk. Several months would give the Pitar more than enough time to search the length and breadth of the planet for possible survivors and then depart without notice.

They would know where to look: what zones were being surveyed for minerals or development; what areas were under consideration for future expansion; where important communications, power-generating, and transportation facilities were situated. And why not? After the first several calls, their regular visits to Treetrunk had ceased to be restricted. Why circumscribe the movements of amiable, considerate, congenial friends? All the time they had been helping the colony to expand, they had been recording and consolidating data for the day of the attack.

They might not immediately notice his home and shop, isolated and concealed as they were on the side of the mountain. But after securing the few cities they would methodically move on to the larger towns, then the smaller villages, and finally to outlying farms, infrastructure postings, and individual structures. Even the forest would be no refuge. It would be expected that some people would flee into the Argusian wilderness in search of safety. Ruthless and relentless, the well-prepared Pitar would have anticipated that and would have come prepared for it. Mallory's expression tightened. After the cities and towns, there would be hunts. Human hunts.

Any ships, satellites, or free-orbiting maintenance craft would already have been captured or destroyed. A competent attacking force would first secure the space around a world before turning its attention to the helpless surface. Shuttleports and airfields would be next in line for destruction or occupation, together with any craft capable of flight that happened to be on the ground. Once confident of having eliminated a target's ability to fight or flee in atmosphere or free space, invaders could settle down to methodically exterminating the local population.

A few companies and citizens operated aircraft of their own, he knew. But such craft, while they might preserve their owners for a while longer, could not escape the attentions of much faster, higher-flying, orbit-capable shuttle craft. Anything with the ability to reach orbit required the long runways and support facilities of a port, or in an emergency a spacious open field or dry lake. Nothing robust enough to escape the pull of the planet's gravity could take off straight up. That would require a craft with a short, explosive propulsion system: one designed to generate a single sustained but brief burst of speed before its motive source gave out.

In short, a lifeboat. Alwyn Mallory had a lifeboat. It was intact, more or less. It was internally equipped and provisioned, more or less.

The question was, could it exceed orbital velocity, more or less?

Having no options, he did not hesitate. If he remained where he was he would undoubtedly survive longer than the great majority of his unfortunate fellow colonists. It might be a matter of days, it might be a matter of weeks, but eventually the Pitar would come for him, as they would for everyone else. He did not intend to wait helplessly for that moment, like a rat chittering impotently at the back of its burrow.

Without hesitation, he tore through his once orderly home, ripping into cabinets and storage lockers. Anything that might prove remotely useful he threw into the transport cart from his shop. Food, medical supplies, reading material, raw electronic components, clothing, small tools—all found their way into the bowels of the old lifeboat. There was plenty of room. Designed to carry and care for a dozen people, it would soon be serving as refuge for only one. He would be short of everything but space.

It took him less than a day to scavenge his home of several years, the home where he had expected to live out a long and reasonably contented life. With luck he might see it again someday, but he did not stand around dwelling on distant possibilities. The lifeboat would be his home now. Or it would if he could escape the attention of the Pitar. When the last bar of sustenance had been thrown aboard, the last potentially useful tool stowed away, he rigged a line to fill the boat's tanks with water. There was none aboard, just as the craft was devoid of food. It had been so when he had purchased it, everything useful and portable having long since been salvaged by the previous owners.

One tank leaked copiously before he noticed it. Despite the urgency and desperation of the moment he had to laugh at the idea of fleeing into the cold, heartless vacuum of space with water sloshing around his feet. It was a short, terse laugh. He had neither the time nor the inclination to indulge in any extended bouts of hilarity. Outside, down the mountain and beyond the woods, the beautiful, the glamorous, the estimable Pitar were slaughtering and eviscerating. The noble Pitar. The neighborly Pitar.

He had to get away. Somehow he had to avoid the blanket of detection they must even now be expanding across the planet. It was possible that the spider's web was not yet complete. All that was necessary was for one fly to get through. Throughout the night he slaved intently on readying his wings.

Two hours before sunrise he was ready. As to whether the lifeboat was, the answer would come from the trying. The proof would be in the doing. If his preparations proved inadequate, if trouble arose that was beyond his power to amend, well then, he would die no slower than if he fell into the hands of the invaders.

Settling himself into the cockpit he ran a final check. Those instruments that still functioned, many of which he had personally repaired or replaced, insisted that their respective components were functional. He found himself wishing he had spent more time with each and every one, that he had taken a little extra effort with each installation and connection. But it had all been a lark, a time killer, something to amuse himself with in his idle hours. Now his life would depend on the skill with which he had indulged in a hobby.

Was there anything he had forgotten, anything that had been omitted? Once committed to the launch sequence he would not be able to change his mind, to remember something overlooked. He did not trust the old lifeboat, or for that matter his own skill at restoration, to recover from an abort sequence. Deciding to go, he would go, and devil take the consequences.

Then he did remember something. Spending as much time as he did in the shop, and away from home attending to various work assignments, he tended to miss a good deal of live entertainment and news. When not watching the tridee, it was set to record. It would have recorded informational bulletins. It would have recorded presentations and sports from the capital and elsewhere throughout the colony. Unfortunately, the last transmissions it would have recorded were unwatchable garbage.

But the images he had recently viewed on the lifeboat, the singular movements and images that had been transmitted by the orphaned media mobile, would have been recorded by its own built-in unit, and should be available for playback.

He did not have time to check. Opening the console, he dug inside until he found what he was looking for. Removing the tiny mollysphere, he slipped incontrovertible proof of Pitarian perfidy into a pocket, shut himself into the lifeboat, force-sealed the reluctant lock, and settled into the pilot's seat and harness. He was no qualified pilot, not of a craft the size of the lifeboat or of anything else. But the whole concept behind such a vessel, the notion that underlay its very design, was that it had to be able to be operated in a moment of emergency by utterly unqualified passengers. As an ex–ship's engineer he was far better prepared than the average citizen to operate a lifeboat's instrumentation, even a design as antiquated as the one that now enfolded him.

The star Argus would soon be making its presence known above the eastern horizon. While the Pitar were certainly equipped with all manner of sophisticated tracking devices, he saw no reason to make their search any easier by providing the additional possibility of visual identification. He could do nothing about the lifeboat's initial liftoff signature. It would be noisy and bright, but only until he reached escape velocity. At that point he would have to risk shutting it down.

A preflight check of the weather indicated the presence of a small storm to the northwest. What he wanted was a hurricane, or some severe thunderstorms. Anything to help mask evidence of his liftoff. The modest rain event would have to do. Programming the shed's roof and the boat's navigation to the best of his ability, he tightened the harness as much as his body would tolerate, then waited.

Even if he was detected lifting off, nothing but a shuttle that happened to be in the immediate vicinity stood a chance of intercepting the vertically ascending lifeboat. Not that it mattered. Once out in space, drifting free, he could be tracked down and eliminated by an orbiting shuttle. Or, if he was extremely lucky, a warship might actually have to bestir itself for a moment or two to chase him down. If nothing else, he might at least inconvenience a few of the invaders.

Or having analyzed his craft and realizing it had no spaceplus capability, they might simply decide to ignore him, letting him float aimlessly in the vastness of space until his supplies and atmosphere ran out. He suspected that was a forlorn hope. Having already witnessed evidence of their thoroughness, he did not expect that the Pitar would leave anyone alive, not even a lone soul adrift between worlds without any hope of returning to one. He might be found, and that they could not permit.

He had to try, though. Anything was better than sitting and waiting for death to come knocking. Better to kick back and keep on kicking for as long as was possible.

A pleasant feminine voice announced that departure was imminent. He had taken special care with reprogramming the boat's methodical, businesslike tone. Now he was glad that he had. It might be the last voice besides his own he ever heard. A loud whine permeated the air, and the cockpit began to vibrate around him. There was no port, but the forward viewscreen showed the roof of the shed parting like a pair of flat, featureless hands. Beyond, black sky and scattered stars became visible in the lucent night of Treetrunk. The whine became an irritation, the vibration in his seat and harness almost soothing. A final massage, he mused. The solicitous attentions of a mechanical undertaker.

Something shoved him hard in the chest, and he gasped sharply. The receded roof panels disappeared, and the stars rotated wildly. In minutes he had punctured roiling cloud—the storm that was drenching the forest to the northwest. Minutes later he burst free, like a fist punching through stuffing, to find that the stars had multiplied beyond counting. The pressure on his chest lessened; the hand that had shoved him gradually withdrew. Small unstowed objects began floating about the cockpit. His stomach churned, and his inner ear insisted he was falling. And so he was—falling up.

Free of Treetrunk's gravity, he was still alive, the embracing lifeboat still intact around him. Loosening his restraints, he hastened to check the readouts. Designed to locate and skew a vector for any nearby ship, the lifeboat was already searching for presumptive help. Prior to liftoff he had thoroughly disabled the automatic beacon designed to signal the lifeboat's presence to other vessels. There was no help to be found here, and he did not want any nearby craft to pick him up. He would blow the lock first and die cleanly in the emptiness of the void.

The relevant readouts made no sense. Testing for malfunctions, he found none. There were no ships within detection range, which meant that it was possible there was nothing to detect him as he raced, silent and small, away from the surface of Argus V. That was impossible. Where were the Pitarian starships, their transports and shuttles? They could only be one place, he realized.

On the other side of the planet. For the moment, Treetrunk was screening him from detection.

It was not how he would have conducted an invasion. But the more he thought about it, and he had time for nothing else, the more he realized that his extraordinary luck was the product not of alien stupidity but of a quite understandable succession of factors. Having destroyed or captured everything in orbit around Treetrunk before commencing the actual physical invasion, the Pitar had no doubt already secured or rendered useless all three of the colony's shuttleports and any orbit-capable craft located on the ground. That and the two space-minus interstellar communications facilities would have been their first ground-based targets.

With the ports and their complement of vessels accounted for in the first stages of the attack, there was no reason to suppose anything like a rogue lifeboat might be present elsewhere on the planet, much less anything in operable condition. In the first flush of what surely must look to be a complete and unqualified triumph, they might relax their surveillance just a little—just enough for a single minuscule, almost undetectable craft to make its escape ridiculously perpendicular from the planet's surface on the opposite side of the world from the attacking armada. No shuttle craft would lift off at the angle he had taken.

He wanted badly to record the size and strength of that invading force, but even if he had possessed the maneuvering capability necessary to sufficiently alter the lifeboat's course he would not have done it. If he tried to move into a position to observe them, then surely the far more sophisticated instrumentation on board a modern warship would detect his presence first.

So he continued to speed outward from the devastated surface, leaving warmth and atmosphere and ongoing horror behind, heading for the only destination the lifeboat had a chance of reaching before its limited supplies began to run out. He had programmed the boat to aim for the inner moon. Not because it was closer, but because it was far smaller than its more distant relative. It was a less likely place to hide, a much more modest potential refuge. As such, if the Pitar thought to consider such possibilities, there was the chance they might conduct a cursory survey of the more accommodating satellite while passing over its relatively insignificant cousin.

The inner moon of Argus V generated barely enough gravity to hold itself together, let alone affix anything to its surface. Maneuvering the lifeboat as delicately as his limited skills and the remaining propulsive capability allowed, he dropped the craft into lower and lower orbit until eventually it was hovering only a short distance above the floor of a suitable impact crater. With the boat's motive power all but exhausted, he ran multiple checks of the restored vessel's status.

He had power. He had air. There were no detectable leaks. Hull integrity was intact. Having positioned himself to the best of his ability, he settled down to wait and to deal with dangers as serious as those posed by the Pitar: loneliness and silence.

The first days and weeks were a cycle of rising, eating, and watching the readouts for signs of passing or patrolling ships. With each succeeding day that the instruments remained quiet and the screens blank his confidence grew. By the end of the first month he felt certain he had escaped the notice of the invading Pitar entirely. As the end of the second month approached he began to fear that he had.

It was terrible in the lifeboat. The psychic weight of airless void on one side and lifeless rock on the other began to press inexorably on his spirit. He felt his very self squeezed between resignation and isolation. Yes, he had foiled the Pitar. Yes, he was still alive when every other human being on Treetrunk was probably dead. But to what end? To thumb his nose at invaders who were not now and never had been aware of his existence? So he could die out here, alone, not even surrounded by the corpses of his fellow settlers? As the days continued to pass, the minutes slowing to a visible crawl, he began to wonder if he had made the right decision. Resistance, survival at any cost—what was it worth? Did it have meaning, or had it been nothing more than the instinctive reflex of a clever ape?

Growing desperate, he even risked some of his precious air by going outside in a suit. The barren, lifeless surface of the dwarf moon drove him back inside where at least there was warmth and recorded sound and visuals. After a while he stopped watching them, too, unable to bear the sight of happy, living humans. The boat was stable in its absurdly low orbit, but his mind began to drift. Gravity is only a local constant and does not hold thoughts.

By the third month his hastily assembled supplies began to run out. He found that he did not care. To conserve air he began to live in a suit, choosing to shrink the available atmosphere around him. He did it because it was expected of him, to preserve life, and not because he had any especial desire any longer to do so. A sufficiency of water to sustain existence for a little while longer remained, but he was out of food. That was a good thing, he decided. He would weaken and eventually pass out and not know when the last air available to his suit was exhausted. His body would remain untouched by Pitar or decomposition, preserved in the perfect coldness of space that had already established its imperturbable grasp on the rest of the ship.

He had been drifting, drifting, for a long time, sucking less and less often at the plastic teat of the water tube in his helmet, when something hazarded to ruffle his sleep. Irritated at the interruption, he rose from his seat and moved to locate the source of the disturbance. Before he could find it, it found him, and he started to scream. After that, he remembered little except the screaming.

As it turned out, except for a few inexplicable outbursts, no one could hear the screaming but him. It went on and on, forever . . .

14

". . . Forever."

Tse said nothing. Sliding her hand down his arm, she took his right hand in both of hers. Lifting it, she brought it up to her lips and kissed it gently, then pressed it against her cheek, not giving a damn what any vexed bureaucrats or disapproving hospital personnel watching on distant monitors might think. As he continued to stare out the window at the blue water and gently swaying palms, tears were running down Mallory's cheeks, copious and unstoppable. His respiration was normal, his heart rate steady, but he could not stop crying. Eventually, he simply ran out of water.

"A part of me is here, alive. Another part is back on Treetrunk, with my friends and associates, dead. A third and last part is floating, floating on an inner moon, raving mad."

"I'm here," she told him softly. "I'm alive."

"Yes." Smiling again, he wiped at his eyes with the sleeve of his hospital gown. "Thank God for small favors. Not you, Irene. There's nothing 'small' about you. May I call you Irene?"

"Mr. Mallory, you may call me anything you want." Lowering his hand, she squeezed it very tightly before lowering it back to the bed. "You've earned that right."

"I don't want it as a 'right.' I want it from a friend."

"However you wish," she told him softly.

The moment was broken, though not shattered, as Dr. Chimbu, several military and civilian personnel Tse did not recognize, and two medical technicians entered the room. Though they filled it, there was no frenzy, no pushing or shoving. Everyone, including the solemn-visaged officers, was quiet and respectful.

"Mr. Mallory," Chimbu began gently, "we don't want to crowd you. If there are too many people in here now, just say so and we'll have some leave."

The man in the bed grinned. He had not let go of the nurse's hand, and she did not draw it away. "Too many people? There aren't enough. There can never be enough for me, not ever again."

Standing behind the chief medical officer, a handsome woman in a colonel's uniform was no longer able to restrain herself. It was an attitude plainly shared by everyone around her.

"Mr. Mallory, as I'm sure you can understand there are some of us who very badly would like to ask you some questions. If you don't feel up to it . . ."

"Ask away." He smiled up at Tse. "And how about some real food? Applesauce is fine—preferably on a large eland sirloin, with fried potatoes. And gravy. And shellfish—any kind of shellfish."

Tse glanced expectantly at Chimbu, who looked reluctant but eventually nodded. "A *small* sirloin," he could not forbear from adding.

The elegant soldier was hesitating, spurring Mallory to prompt her. "Go ahead and ask what you will. You won't upset me. I've done my time in upset land."

"Very well. Mr. Mallory, I'm sure you know that everything that has happened in your vicinity since you were brought here has been carefully monitored. I'm sure you must understand that given the reception the Pitar have been accorded here on Earth and elsewhere, coupled with the fact that over a period of some five years they have displayed nothing even remotely like the behavior you have described—the story you just told is difficult for the rest of us to accept." The hospital room was dead silent as everyone waited to see how the patient would react.

Mallory's reply was low, but perfectly intelligible. "So you think I'm a liar?"

"Nobody said that," another officer hastened to add. "Nobody's calling you a liar." He looked to the woman, then back down at the ravaged figure in the bed. "You've been through a terrible ordeal, sir. It's a miracle that you survived, much less with your body and your . . ." Aware he had stumbled into awkward territory, he broke off.

Mallory finished the thought for him. "My mind intact?" His eyes searched the attentive gathering. "You think I may have hallucinated what happened on Treetrunk? How about the six hundred thousand dead or missing?" His voice rose perceptibly. "That's one hell of a hallucination."

"No one disputes the destruction of Treetrunk." The female officer's tone was tender, but hardly condescending. "That is something no human being would dare try to deny. What Major Rothenburg and the rest of us are wondering is if you actually saw what you say you saw, or if your mind, overwhelmed by the horror, invented something, however implausible, to mask or blot out an even worse reality."

"Worse reality? Worse than genocide? Worse than female reproductive organ evisceration and theft?" He shook his head slowly. "Ma'am, all I can say is, you must have a greater capacity for inventing horror than I do."

From his position near the end of the bed, Chimbu spoke up. "Mr. Mallory, Colonel Nadurovina is an eminent military psychiatrist specializing in combat and combat-related disorders. She doesn't mean to impugn your veracity. Like the rest of us, she only wants what's best for you—and to get at the truth."

"The truth!?!" His voice bordering on hysteria, the patient leaned sharply forward in the bed. Nearby, a medtech activated the osmotic hypo he held behind his back and started forward. Startled by the unexpected violence of his response, Tse let go of Mallory's hand. But she did not stand up or retreat from her position alongside him. Seeing the sudden fear in her face, he made an effort to regain his composure.

"I've told you the truth. Whether you believe it or not is up to you." Staring hard at the circle of the curious, he added warningly, "You'd better, because there's no guarantee the

Pitar won't try something like it again. Unless, of course, they got everything they needed from Treetrunk."

"Human female reproductive organs?" Rothenburg's tone laid bare his skepticism. "You'll excuse me, Mr. Mallory, if that doesn't strike some of us as unsound grounds for rationalizing an assault on a colony. To gain a strategic advantage or base, yes; to acquire a world rich in rare metals and minerals, perhaps; or even to try and intimidate the occupying species into conceding possession, possibly. But what you say makes no sense."

"Deliver us from the blindered workings of the military mind," he muttered. "What's the military doing here anyway?"

"When six hundred thousand people are slaughtered without mercy or warning, it becomes a military matter," a man behind Rothenburg replied stiffly.

Mallory grunted and leaned back against his pillows. "For what it's worth, it doesn't make any sense to me, either. Pitar and human can't generate offspring, but at the same time I can't put the kind of organized organ-gathering I witnessed down to morbid scientific curiosity or aimless disemboweling. The Pitar I saw looked like they knew exactly what they wanted and how to go about getting it. They had storage containers ready to store their . . . handiwork. What they did was for a reason. If they had other motives for annihilating Treetrunk, then they're the only ones who can tell you about them." He made an obscene gesture, heedless of who might be watching via relay on distant monitors.

"Me, I think we should put every weapon we can find on every ship that can be mustered and blow them out of existence all the way back to their beloved bastard Dominion, and then seed both their precious Twin Worlds with radioactive dust that has a nice, long half-life. How about it? Why don't you put the question to a couple of their local representatives? Gauge their reaction. They'll lie, of course. Fluently. They're doubtless convinced they obliterated any evidence of their treachery. Which they did—except for me." The bluster and bravado abruptly leaked out of him like the air from a balloon subject to deep-sea pressures. His voice became small and frightened, as if two distinct personalities were fighting for space in the same body.

"They don't know about me, do they? They don't know I'm here . . . ?"

"Easy," Tse told him, leaning closer and stroking his arm with her fingers. "Be calm, Alwyn. Nobody knows you're here." She looked anxiously over at Chimbu. "Do they?"

The chief physician shook his head. His words spelled confidence. "Only the upper echelon of the hospital staff knows about Mr. Mallory's origins. Beyond the people presently assembled in this room, there are a handful of government officials who had to be informed."

Colonel Nadurovina added soothingly, "You would be surprised who knows and who does not, who was deliberately informed and who was kept in the dark. You are safe here, Mr. Mallory. If you look in the hallway you will not see much, if you look out your window you will see less, but it would take vaster weaponry than we believe the Pitar or any other species possesses to reach you." She smiled, and it did not seem forced or artificial. "At this moment you may very well be, Mr. Mallory, the best-protected individual in this portion of the Orion Arm. The members of the world council are not as well looked after."

"Then you do believe me." She might not be in charge, but Nadurovina acted as if she was, so he directed half his attention to her. Whether she was aware of it or not, the rest had been settled on Irene Tse.

"We believe you saw something. We believe that a powerful and inimical sentience is responsible for the eradication of human life on Treetrunk. Whether those two things are one and the same we cannot accept on the word of one man found drifting in space starving, near death, and out of his mind." This time her smile was wry. "Surely you can appreciate the sensitivity of my position and that of my colleagues who are charged with rendering a decision in this matter."

"Question the Pitar," Mallory shot back. "Corner them and press them. Ask them what they might want with human organs and judge their reaction."

A plump man in civilian clothes who had hitherto been silent now pushed his way forward. "I am Jenju Burriyip. I represent the world council." His lips curved upward. "Those members who have been informed, anyway. Please tell me, Mr. Mallory, how I am supposed to confront the representatives of what to this point has been a likeable, good-natured species and inquire politely if they might perchance have in an off moment slaughtered six hundred thousand of my fellow beings?"

"How should I know?" the patient snapped curtly. "I'm no diplomat."

Burriyip nodded solemnly. "That is exactly my point, Mr. Mallory. If, and please bear with me when I say 'if,' what you have told us has somehow become confused by your condition, or distorted because you have suffered physically, or has otherwise been altered in your mind, and we wrongly accuse the Pitar, however obliquely, then we stand to forfeit some nice, useful, popular new friends. If word got out, the government could fall."

"Listen to me." Mallory chose his words slowly and carefully. "The Pitar are not nice. They are not ever going to be 'useful.' They murdered six hundred thousand men, women, and children, for what depraved reasons of their own I can't say. And if they only had to do it once to get what they wanted or needed, and never do anything like it again, then they will have done worse than what they did. They will have gotten away with it."

Burriyip was immovable. "I said 'if,' Mr. Mallory. No one is ready to discount your theory out of hand."

"Goddammit, it's not a theory!" He looked as if he was going to start crying again but pulled himself together with an effort. The hypo wielder held his ground. "Then you won't confront the Pitar?"

The representative sighed heavily. "I am sorry, Mr. Mallory, but to accuse an entire race of interspecies genocide on the word of one man . . . We cannot. You have to understand that. You do not have to like it, but you do have to understand."

"I understand that if you don't do something you're going to have humankind dancing and laughing down through the years hand in hand with the worst enemies in its history, and that they're the ones who are going to be laughing the hardest. If they do laugh, that is."

"We will do something, Mr. Mallory." Nadurovina tried her best to mollify him. "We will find out who is lying and who is telling the truth."

"And most of all," Rothenburg added, "we're going to find out who or what was responsible for what happened on Argus V."

"Not if you don't ask the right people the right questions." Closing his eyes, Mallory slumped deeper into the pillows.

Tse held his wrist, not trusting the machines. "That's enough. He's only recently emerged from his coma, and this is more activity than he should have to endure."

Chimbu rose. "Nurse Tse is right. We should leave so he can get some rest."

"When can we talk to him again?" Despite his professional skepticism, Rothenburg felt concern for the man in the bed.

"Not before tomorrow." Chimbu began to urge everyone out of the room, an insistent father herding his flock. "If you don't want to communicate with a mind that might be playing tricks on itself, allow it to rest. If his vitals continue to strengthen and he is willing, we'll try this again tomorrow."

"Maybe once he's rested some more he'll remember something else," Rothenburg murmured as he stepped out into the corridor.

"Like who actually committed the atrocity?" Nadurovina followed her colleague down the hall.

"Then you don't believe his story?" Absently, Rothenburg saluted the two guards who were posted at the far end of the walkway.

"I don't know. The Pitar as exterminators? And for such an obscure reason? One that might well devolve from some unhappy or repressed childhood sexual experience of the patient's? I could not find anything in his records, but that does not mean there is nothing of the kind buried deep within his memories." They entered the hospital lift and stood back from the closing doors. "That does not mean he is not telling the truth. The question remains, is it the truth as it actually is or merely the truth as his traumatized self sees it?"

Rothenburg considered. "Burriyip meant it when he said the government couldn't confront the Pitar."

"I know. We cannot, either. Not without a specific directive from above, one that I do not think will be forthcoming. Ever since the first encounter, people have been mesmerized by the Pitar."

Rothenburg nodded knowingly. "My wife has two outfits inspired by Pitarian design. She'd find the very idea of them killing one human grotesquely laughable, let alone hundreds of thousands. If we challenge or accuse them in any way, there'll be diplomatic bedlam. Careers will be ruined, or at the very least any hopes for advancement aborted. In that respect Burriyip wasn't understating the gravity of the situation. Such a confrontation really could bring down the government."

"I agree. Neither the government nor the military can directly confront the Pitar. But someone else can."

"Someone else?" Rothenburg's uncertainty showed in his expression. "Who else could possibly . . . ?" He halted in mid-query. "You can't be thinking what I think you're thinking."

Nadurovina did not smile. Her posture was as regimented as her thinking. "Tell me true, Erhard: Haven't you ever, watching such happenings on the tridee, had the desire one time in your life to gamble a million credits or so on a single throw of the dice, or spin of the futures' globe?"

They stepped out of the lift and into a main hallway, busy with nurses and medtechs, doctors and support personnel. The two by now familiar uniformed officers hardly rated a glance.

"We could lose him," Rothenburg warned her. "The shock might be too much, even if the Pitar are involved only in his imagination. Fantasy can kill as readily as reality."

"I'll speak to Chimbu about it. Medication and specialists

will be standing by at all times in the next room, ready to intervene."

"What about the Pitar? What makes you think one of them will agree to see him?"

The colonel's mouth twitched. "How could they refuse? Compassionate and neighborly as they are, it would look funny if they declined to offer their deepest sympathies to the sole survivor of the Treetrunk holocaust. Anyone who agrees to pay their respects will be intimately screened for the carrying of anything even potentially inimical, of course, before being allowed to come within a hundred kilometers of this island, much less this hospital. Much less Mr. Alwyn Mallory's presence."

"Even so," Rothenburg felt compelled to point out as they turned a corner, "determined assassins invariably find a way."

Nadurovina nodded thoughtfully. "In that event we would have something of an answer by roundabout means, wouldn't we?" Rothenburg did not know what to say in response to this cool, detached calculation. "But I do not think that will be a problem. The Pitar may very well believe that we are testing them with words. If they are the responsible party, as Mallory continues to insist, then they will gladly go along with any test they believe will help to remove them from the list of suspected peoples. If they are not responsible and their participation in the atrocity is nothing more than a figment of Mr. Mallory's addled imagination, no harm will have been done."

"Not to human-Pitar relations, maybe," Rothenburg objected, "but what about to the patient?"

"Time to roll the dice, Erhard."

He smiled thinly at his colleague. "Easy to say when it's not your sanity that's at stake."

His retort clearly troubled her. "In spite of what you may think, I don't recommend this course of action easily or without qualms, Major. However inchoate, I am quite aware that Mr. Mallory is our only connection with whatever happened on Treetrunk. I have no more desire to see him lose his strengthening grasp on reality than you or anyone else. But I am the senior officer here, and I am the one being pressured for answers. Not informed speculation, not reasoned hypotheses, but answers. Whatever happens if we confront Mr. Mallory with his terrors, whatever the consequences, I am the one who will have to answer for them. I am prepared to take that risk."

"Again, with somebody else's dice." Rothenburg refused to let his colleague and superior off the hook. "In spite of initial impressions I find myself liking this Mallory."

"It is not his likability that is at stake here. For what it is worth, I like him, too. But in the resolution of this frightful mystery, neither his life, nor mine, nor yours, means anything."

"All right. I'll cosign on the requisite directives so long as you accept ultimate responsibility."

She found herself walking toward the exit. Outside were languid breezes and the scent of orchids, the warm, moist aroma of mother Earth. Upstairs lay a lonely, frightened man who might hold the key to cataclysm, if only they could drag the proof or denial of it out of him.

"As senior officer on site, I have no choice. So I might as well do it willingly. You will commence the necessary arrangements?"

He nodded. "I'll handle my end of things. How long before you think you can have one or more of them here?"

"One should do, I think. If we make too much of a show of it they may become suspicious. We want them to react, not anticipate. I will discuss with Dr. Chimbu a means of monitoring Mr. Mallory's reactions even more effectively than we do now. We will need to record everything that happens in the finest detail for study later."

"In case he locks up, or blanks out again, or dies?" Resigned to the turn of events Rothenburg might be, but he was not happy about them.

Nadurovina ignored the sarcasm. "Yes. In case any of those eventualities unfortunately come to pass. I hope they will not."

"What about having the nurse present—Tsue or Tsoy or whatever her name is?"

"Irene Tse. She should be there. She is good for him. She does a lot of little things."

Rothenburg was moved to reluctant admiration. "You don't miss much, do you, Colonel?"

"No, Major. It is my job not to."

15

He was tall and bronzed, regal of posture and sleek of muscle, faultless of demeanor and enchanting of smile. Wherever they went, heads turned; men out of admiration, women from a plethora of confused but animated emotion. In other words, he was a typical Pitarian male, no more or less spectacular than any other of his kind. Walking alongside him Nadurovina felt slighted, but not overawed.

His name was Dmis-Atel. A tertiary assistant from the southwest branch of his embassy, he had flown to New Ireland at the request of the authorities there to pay his respects, it was said, to a survivor of the Treetrunk bloodbath. Protesting that no such survivors were known to exist, the Pitar had been informed through the most secret channels that this was most probably the case, but in the event it was not, it would be gracious of them to bestow their guileless commiserations in person. And in the far more likely event that it was a clever falsehood being perpetrated by certain unscrupulous individuals for amoral reasons of their own, perhaps a perceptive Pitar could shed some light on the matter by examining it from a nonhuman perspective.

Once the situation had been explained to them thus, the Pitar did not hesitate. Representative Dmis was placed by his embassy on the first available aerial transport and charged with rendering whatever sympathy or service he could in the matter, as the occasion might demand. Rothenburg had met him at the airport and escorted him to the hospital, where he had been taken in hand by a calm, unruffled Nadurovina.

"I am anxious to see this person."

The Pitar moved with effortless, graceful strides that gave him the appearance of flowing over the floor. One was tempted to bend low for a look at the bottoms of his feet to see if they were actually touching the ground. The Pitar did everything effortlessly and well. Nadurovina was no more immune than her friends to the spell they cast. Only her innate professionalism allowed her to maintain a greater degree of detachment. Did they also slaughter the innocent effortlessly and without strain?

"He does not know that you are coming." They turned into a corridor through double doors that shouted *Restricted Entry—Authorized Personnel Only* and headed for the lift. Every step of the way, hidden scanners were examining every aspect of their bodies, from the material of their clothing to the contents of their digestive systems. Specific instruments searched for explosive components in their bloodstreams and toxins in their saliva. By the time they reached the corner room on the northwest end of the fifth floor they had been subjected to as thorough a noninvasive analysis as contemporary technology could contrive. This despite the fact that Nadurovina and her associates were fairly certain that the Pitar would not make an attempt on the patient's person. To do so would amount to an admission of guilt or, at the very least, a stain on their saintly mien that would be difficult to wash away. Armed and highly trained personnel would be close at hand in any case, ready to intervene at the slightest provocation.

The Pitar did not give indication of being under any unusual stress, but then, the Pitar never did. It was difficult for the most perceptive at the best of times to tell what they were thinking. They never lost their temper or burst out in uncontrolled laughter. Like their physical appearance, their demeanor was always perfect.

They were alone in the lift. Nadurovina knew that a battery of observers was waiting in the room next to the patient's, with dozens more cemented to remote monitors and pickups. Every movement of the visiting Pitar would be scrutinized, every word deconstructed, every shift in expression analyzed.

The door loomed ahead. The Pitar looked over and down to smile gently at her. "Are the guards for us or for this individual?"

"For him. As you can imagine we've been very interested in what he's had to say about the destruction of his adopted homeworld."

"And what has he said?" The Hellenically perfect countenance betrayed no concern, the body movements no agitation.

The military psychiatrist smiled back. "You can ask him yourself." After identifying herself and her guest to the guards, they were allowed to pass. "I think you'll find him an interesting subject."

Still no visible reaction. Why should she have expected anything different? Opening the door, she entered first.

Mallory was sitting up in the bed with Tse in a chair at his side. It was a tableau that had become intimately familiar to Nadurovina over the past week. In that time the patient had put on weight and regained lost muscle tone. Much could be attributed to the attention he had received from the nurse, whose devotion to the single patient whose care she had been charged with looking after exceeded anything that could reasonably have been expected.

Here it was. The moment of confrontation. She could feel the eyes behind the multiple pickups glued to their screens, watching, waiting.

"Good morning, Mr. Mallory, Ms. Tse. I hope you do not mind, but I have brought a guest." Stepping aside, she bequeathed to the man in the bed an unobstructed view of the visitor.

Mallory's eyes shifted. He saw the Pitar. As importantly, the Pitar saw him. Nadurovina was not above holding her breath, ready to intervene, spring aside, or call for help as the occasion should demand. She did not know exactly what to expect. No one did. In their intense discussions prior to this moment she believed that she and her colleagues had imagined and discussed every possible scenario.

They were wrong.

"A Pitar." Mallory's voice was calm, controlled, absolutely

devoid of fear or panic. "Here." His gaze shifted to the psychiatrist, and he did something even more remarkable. He smiled. "Another of your tests? A little experiment, maybe?"

"Dmis is a member of the delegation that is headquartered on Lombok," she explained. "He is a real Pitar, not an actor made up to look like one."

"I can see that." Did his tone darken ever so slightly, or was Nadurovina reading into it one of the things for which she and her associates were searching? "I know what a Pitar looks like."

She tensed but made no move to interfere when the alien moved toward the bed. Outside, beyond the wall, she knew that the strike team of armed commandos would have reacted to the alien's approach by automatically advancing to another level of readiness. To her relief he halted at the foot of the bed.

"So. You survived the disturbing incident that overwhelmed Argus Five."

"That's right. I did." Mallory met the alien's inscrutable gaze without flinching. "I saw what happened there."

The Pitar made a small, almost imperceptible gesture whose meaning no one in the room comprehended. "My people are very concerned about what took place."

Mallory's mouth set in a tight line. There was no trembling, no quivering that Nadurovina could see. A glance at the readouts of the instruments that monitored the patient's vitals showed little change, certainly not enough to be considered significant.

"I'll bet they are."

"What did you see happen there, man?"

Seated next to Mallory, Tse listened quietly to the conversation, one hand resting on the patient's forearm. Reaching up, Mallory affected an air of mock forgetfulness.

"I'm not sure . . . Oh yeah, it's coming back to me now. Let's see. Your people were there." Once more the mocking smile. Did the Pitar stiffen? Again, the psychiatrist couldn't be certain. Being in the room, standing to one side and observing, was like watching a chess match with living pieces.

"Yes, that's right. Your people. I recall it quite clearly. They were killing everybody. Destroying anything and everything that might record or otherwise indicate what they were doing. Your people are real thorough. Real thorough motherfuckers."

Nadurovina felt compelled to play the role she had assigned herself. "Please, Mr. Mallory. Dmis is a diplomatic representative."

"That's kind of a contradiction, Doc. There's nothing diplomatic about the Pitar."

The alien's expression did not change. He seemed more fascinated than upset by the patient. "You are a very imaginative person, Mr. Mallory. Very inventive. The Pitar do not kill except in self-defense. I am no physician, but I think the dreadful experience you have obviously suffered must have at least temporarily unhinged your mind. Why my people should figure prominently in your delusions I cannot think, but it is not very flattering."

"I'm not delusional. It wasn't delusion. I know what I saw. Your people attacked without warning, trading on friendship acquired through five years of joyful, kindly contact to achieve complete surprise. You slaughtered anything on two legs. It didn't make any sense to me then, and it doesn't make any sense to me now."

"Ah," Dmis murmured, "an admission that confirms the diagnosis."

"No, you don't understand. What doesn't make any sense to me is what you needed with the reproductive organs of human females. I saw them being removed with surgical precision from one woman after another and carefully packed away in what I believe now to be cryogenic containers. What do you do with them? Eat 'em? Venerate them? Use them in some kind of unimaginably barbaric conceptual art? Tell me, diplomat Dmis. I'm really curious to know."

"As am I," the Pitar replied. "Curious to know what sort of human mind can invent such absurdities."

Nadurovina interrupted. "If this is upsetting you too much, Dmis, we can leave."

"No, no." The alien did not appear in the least perturbed by the accusations that were coming from the bed. "It is interesting. As do all of my kind, I want to know as much as possible about humans. Even their mental aberrations. This is a useful occasion."

Mallory nodded agreeably. "Useful for me, too. See, I want to know all about the Pitar, because it will help me to understand how better to kill you."

"I have to tell you, Mr. Mallory, that I understand what is happening here and that I truly sympathize. With ongoing care of the quality you are obviously receiving I am certain that your condition will improve. Meanwhile, I am intrigued by your misconceptions." He smiled over at Nadurovina. "Is there anything I can do to help?"

"Yeah," Mallory declared without hesitation. He proceeded to describe an act that was an anatomical impossibility, even for the limber Pitar. Nadurovina choked slightly, but the alien took no apparent offense.

"Another elaborate fantasy. Naturally, Mr. Mallory, you have proof to underline and support your fantasies. Images of this imaginary assault, perhaps, or voice records, or a corroborating witness."

"No," the man in the bed muttered. "You know damn well that I don't. If I did, you wouldn't be standing there grinning like an underfed Buddha. You wouldn't even have been brought here. Somebody would've shot you on sight." His smile widened. "I'd gladly do that myself except that where my mental state is concerned plenty of these 'specialists' happen to agree with you, or at least are willing to consider the possibility. I could get up from this bed, right now, and put my hands around your blemish-free throat and squeeze until all the life leaked out of you." For the second time, Nadurovina tensed.

"I do not think even if you were healthy you would be physically capable of such a feat," the much taller Dmis replied calmly. "As it is, you are weakened from your misfortune, and I am considerably larger and stronger than you."

"I can see that, but you've never experienced the kind of strength that uncontrolled fury can give a human being." He glanced at the anxious psychiatrist. "Don't worry, Doc. Much as I'd like to I'm not planning on leaving this bed for a while. Not even for the sheer pleasure of feeling a Pitarian neck under my fingers." He turned his attention back to the alien. "I'm saving myself, you see. I want to kill many more than just one of you."

Dmis looked to his escort. "I hope Mr. Mallory is receiving appropriate medication for his condition. It would distress me to think that he might one day attack someone else, perhaps believing that they were Pitar."

"I can assure you that his treatment regimen takes all possibilities into account," Nadurovina told the alien, succeeding in answering him truthfully without committing herself to any specifics.

"This has been most interesting." The Pitar leaned slightly over the foot of the bed in Mallory's direction and beamed benignly. "When you have invented some proof to give support to your expressive delusions, you must see to it that I am notified. It would be educational to continue this discussion. In the absence of anything additional, however, I must return to my mission and make a report." Stepping back, he turned his full attention to the psychiatrist.

"I would like to be kept informed of Mr. Mallory's progress, as a matter of personal interest. It is distressing to see any sentient being slide so far into fantasy. But it is quite understandable. Among my kind it is also common to build a mental wall around a terrible experience as a way of dealing with the consequences. In the absence of truth, the patient has invented elaborate imaginings to avoid having to deal with a large, threatening blank spot in his memory. I am sure that with time and your good offices these delusions will gradually begin to fade away."

"I'm sure he will continue to improve," she replied noncommittally as she gestured toward the doorway. The Pitar preceded her into the hall.

Nine and a half hours later Irene Tse burst from room fifty-four in panic. From behind her and within the room came a cacophony of instruments shattering and furniture breaking. Above it all rose an inhuman howling, the piteous shrieks of an unhinged mind teetering on the razor edge of sanity.

Nadurovina was interrupted in quarters where she had just sat down to dine with her husband. Tearing back to the hospital at velocities that threatened to send her vehicle spinning out of control, she blew through the entrance and past startled hospital personnel in her race to reach the building's top story.

Shoving her way through the crowd that had gathered at one end of the floor, she espied Tse and ungently forced a path to where the nurse was sitting. Though the psychiatrist was not in uniform, the medtech who was attending to the nurse recognized the officer and gave way.

Trembling, Tse was holding her face in her hands. Blood from a deep scratch had welled up to stain the upper right sleeve of her duty blouse. Settling in behind her, the medtech began to treat the wound.

Nadurovina had no time for niceties. "What happened?" Reaching forward, she grabbed the younger woman's wrists and roughly pulled them away from her face. "Look at me, nurse!" Tse's tear-stained face lifted to meet the psychiatrist's.

"I . . . I don't know. It just happened. One minute everything was fine. I was just clearing away the dinner tray when it happened."

Nadurovina glanced in the direction of the room but was unable to see anything but surging, swirling bodies. If it was this confused and chaotic now, she reflected, what must it have been like ten minutes ago?

"When what happened? Talk to me, nurse. Was it . . . Did the Pitar . . . ?"

"Pitar?" Blinking, Tse reached up and rubbed at her eyes with the unstained sleeve of her uniform. "What Pitar? There are no Pitar here." Realization penetrated the younger woman's understanding as Nadurovina heaved a vast sigh of relief. Despite every precaution, despite all the round-the-clock, state-of-the-art security, there was always the possibility, the fear, that if the aliens were guilty of Mallory's charges or if they had simply taken a severe disliking to him they might somehow manage to get to him. Evidently they had not.

On the other hand, their apparent absence and lack of involvement in whatever had taken place in the hospital room meant they were still, in the eyes of uncommitted justice, as innocent as Dmis had claimed.

Tse was babbling quietly. "He just went crazy. One minute he was finishing the last of his ice cream and passing me the tray, smiling and happy, and then . . ." The slow shaking of her head was visible evidence of her disbelief. "It was like a bomb went off inside him."

"Is he . . . all right?" With her initial concerns allayed, Nadurovina could afford to be more compassionate.

"I guess so. I don't know." The younger woman's expression pleaded for understanding. "I tried to help, tried to calm him down, but it was like he couldn't hear me. He started throwing things, breaking things." As if still not believing it was there, she reached up to feel the cut the medtech had just finished bandaging. "I ran, both to protect myself and to get help." She looked toward the room. "It's been quiet for a little while, so I guess they got him calmed down. I hope . . . I hope they didn't have to hurt him."

"He's had the best people the staff of this hospital can boast attending to him on permanent rotating duty." The psychiatrist tried to sound reassuring. "I am certain he will be all right."

"What do you think happened, Doctor?"

"I don't know, either, Irene. But I can hazard a guess. He has experienced a delayed psychological reaction to the Pitar's visit. You saw how calm he was in the alien's presence. It was the last thing I would have expected, whether his story is true or not. Somehow he held it all in, kept perfect control of his reactions and emotions. Then I expect he tried to forget all about it. And he managed to do it—until his system could not take any more. When you told me it was like a bomb went off inside him you were probably closer to the truth than you realize." She shook her head.

"People have this belief that fusionable material contains the most explosive type of energy." Reaching up, she tapped her forehead. "Myself, I have always believed it was trapped in here." Her expression somber, she knelt to face the shaken woman and put a comforting hand on the other's knee. "If you would like to be relieved of this assignment, I will see to it that the order is cut."

Tse swallowed and wiped at her eyes again. "No. I'll stay on."

Silently pleased, an admiring Nadurovina straightened. "Your devotion to your job is commendable. I will make sure that you are properly compensated for your dedication."

Tse looked up at her. "I'm not staying on because I'm devoted to my job."

Nadurovina hesitated only briefly. "Oh. So that is how it is."

The younger woman nodded. "That's how it is."

The psychiatrist's mouth tightened. "I don't approve. It is not professional."

Tse responded with an awkward, choking laugh. "You're telling me. I didn't plan it, you know. I had no idea anything like this would happen."

"I am not sure that any of us ever do, dear." The older woman sighed. "I won't say anything. As long as it does not appear to be interfering with your professional duties, I will not raise any objections to your staying on."

Reaching up, Tse took the other woman's hand in hers and mustered the best smile she could. "Thank you."

With a last nod, Nadurovina turned and pushed back into the crowd. This time she was held up by a guard, but from within the room Chimbu must have seen her because she heard his voice call out for her to be admitted.

The hospital room did indeed look as if a bomb had gone off within. Of the patient there was no sign.

"We moved him across the hall into fifty-two." A weary Chimbu looked harried and strained. "Along with anything else that was worth moving. He's sleeping now, under sedation." Without further comment he indicated their surroundings.

The destruction was impressive, Nadurovina saw. Hard to believe one short, malnourished, sick patient still in the middle stages of recovery had been able to wreak so much havoc in so brief a span. Chimbu saw the question in her face.

"Nurse Tse called the medtech staff on duty immediately,

but they hesitated to interfere out of concern he might seriously injure himself. It took the duty physician a few minutes to get here and issue orders. At that time the patient was still going strong. Five orderlies needed to coordinate their efforts to get him down long enough for one of them to administer a sedative. They finally made the decision to jump him when it looked like he was going to make a run for the window."

Nadurovina glanced in the direction of the specially retrofitted safety glass. It was strong enough to stop an explosive shell. She found herself wondering if it would have been enough to thwart the crazed Mallory. The window was still closed. "What about self-inflicted damage?"

"Nothing too serious. Minor cuts and bruises. I've talked to Tse, and I think it's pretty clear what set him off."

The psychiatrist nodded. "I have also spoken with her." As she conversed with the chief medical officer she scanned the room. Expensive instrumentation had been smashed, cables ripped from the walls and monitors, furniture crushed. Bent and twisted, a chair lay in one corner like a beached anemone. Even the bed coverings had been shredded. Bending to pick up a plastic cup, she saw that pieces had been chewed out of the rim. The tornado that had gone back to sleep in Alwyn Mallory's brain had reawakened. Remembering the shaken, frightened nurse, Nadurovina was thankful no one had been hurt.

What would Mallory do when he began to come out of his sedative-induced sleep? By that time if the hospital staff had done its job properly a new set of monitoring equipment should be in place and operational. There was no guarantee the patient would not resume where he had left off, raging and destructive, endangering all those around him as well as himself. Tse's intervention could be crucial, she knew. Steeling herself, she headed for the hallway to talk to the nurse.

Her considerable powers of persuasion were not required. Tse was anxious to return to Mallory's side. She listened quietly to the older woman's instructions, taking on that advice she thought useful and wordlessly ignoring the rest. By this time she felt she knew Alwyn Mallory better than anyone else. Ultimately, when he next awoke she was the one who would have to make the first, critical decisions.

In furniture, facilities, and layout room fifty-two was a mirror image of the one a berserking Mallory had wrecked. Under the influence of the powerful sedative he slept all through the rest of the day and on into the night. Tse dozed off beside him, unwilling to make use of the inflatable bed that had been provided for her. When she awoke, it was to find the first tendrils of daylight creeping through the window and the patient lying with eyes open, staring silently at her.

Surprised, she started slightly, relaxing only when he smiled.

"I was a bad boy, wasn't I, nurse?"

"How are you feeling?"

Even before he could answer she was automatically checking the monitors alongside his bed. She knew they would read more or less normal. If anything serious had manifested itself during the night, doctors and other nurses would have attended to the problem, invariably waking her in the process. But she had to ask.

"Tired. A little sore." Reaching up, he felt of the pellucid epidermal seal that had closed a cut on his forehead. "I don't remember many details. Just a lot of noise."

Her tone was quietly reproving. "That would have been you smashing up everything within reach in the other room."

"Other room?" Raising up slightly, he scrutinized his new surroundings, noting the reversed layout and the altered view through the large window. "I don't remember being moved."

"They had to knock you out. It took five orderlies."

"Five, eh?" He seemed perversely pleased. "I imagine this is going to go on my bill."

Putting a hand over her mouth she covered the laugh she was unable to suppress. This was supposed to be a serious moment, one in which she admonished the invalid for his unacceptable actions and discussed with him how to prevent a recurrence. Instead, she found herself giggling and grinning at the irrepressible patient's every other comment. Furthermore, she discovered that she didn't give a damn about the reactions of those individuals whose attention might be fixed to distant peeping monitors.

"I have a feeling the government is picking up the cost of your stay."

"Really?" Pushing down against the mattress, he sat up. "Maybe I'll trash this one later. Yeah, one room a week. That would fit the way I'm feeling."

Making an effort to be serious, she wagged a warning finger at him. "I'd think twice about that. Keep it up and you'll be spending most of your time under sedation. You won't be any good to anyone in that condition."

His smile evaporated and he looked away from her. "Who gives a good goddamn?"

"I do," she replied simply.

That brought his head back around. Outside, the equatorial sun was climbing rapidly, flooding the room with diffused but still sharply defining light. The window glass darkened slightly in response, moderating the illumination and temperature level in the room.

His tone was subdued, thankful. "I'd like to be able to say it was worth everything I went through just to hear those two words."

She put a hand on his. "I don't expect that kind of oblique praise, Alwyn. I don't need it."

"Then you believe me?" Despite his outward bravado, she could sense that veiled desperation underlined his words.

"I believe you," she replied sympathetically, "but to convince others will require more than your word. Surely you can see their side. You can't accuse an entire species of genocide and inconceivable acts without something more to back it up than the word of one man. Or even the words of a shipful. You mustn't feel singled out."

"But I do feel singled out," he told her. "I *was* singled out. I survived. I'm the only one who survived. Why me? Why not someone with a better nature, or great artistic talent? Why not a composer or a writer, or a mother with three kids? I'm a cynical, misanthropic, short-tempered, semiretired son of a bitch. If there was any justice in this universe I'd have been one of the first to die."

"That would have been a pity."

His gaze narrowed slightly. "Yeah? Why?"

Her fingers tightened around his. "Because then we couldn't be having this conversation."

He stared at her for a moment longer. Then he began to cry. Not silently this time, nor in great racking sobs, but normally, the way any man would cry when overwhelmed by irresistible emotion. The very ordinariness of it was a profound relief to her.

He stopped so suddenly that she was alarmed.

"Alwyn, what is it, what's wrong?"

"Nothing's wrong." He wiped at his eyes almost angrily, as if trying to punish them for their betrayal of his fancied indifference. "I just remembered something."

"Is it important?"

"I think so." He was nodding slowly. "It's proof."

Nadurovina was not the first into the room. Rothenburg was faster. Chimbu followed behind, accompanied by an orderly. There were others who wanted to join them, but the chief medical officer had ruled against any more being present at any one time. Given the patient's recent deranged outburst, the doctor did not want to do anything to make him feel pressured. That included crowding his space.

On the bed, Mallory was nodding wisely to himself. "This is about as much privacy as I thought I had."

Rothenburg would not be denied. "You said you remembered proof. I heard you. I heard you distinctly. What kind of proof?"

Mallory eyed the intelligence officer unflinchingly. "You think I invented that story about the Pitar. You all think I'm nuts, that my mind is conjuring illusions to cover what I actually saw. That's what that smiling Pitarian bastard you flew in to confront me with would like you to think, too."

"Change our minds." Ignoring the cautioning looks he was receiving from Nadurovina, Rothenburg challenged the other man openly. "Make us look stupid. Go on, do it! Shove the truth right in my face."

Mallory held the Major's eyes for a moment longer, then dropped his gaze and looked down at the bed. "I can't. Not yet."

An exasperated Nadurovina kept her voice level. "Why not? You said you had proof."

"That's the right tense, Colonel. *Had* is the operative word here."

Rothenburg wanted to lurch forward, to shove the seated nurse away from the bed, reach down, and violently shake the infuriating man hiding beneath the covers until he made sense. "All right. You 'had' proof. What kind? It would have to be convincing beyond doubt."

Mallory coolly met the officer's angry glare. "How about a few hours of verifiable media-grade recording of the Pitar ravaging Treetrunk? Shooting down adults and children, razing buildings, stalking through the streets in body armor? Surgical teams carefully eviscerating women and preserving their internal organs?" His body had begun to tremble again, but his voice held steady. "How about it, Major? Would that constitute sufficient 'proof'?"

"Yes." Rothenburg straightened. "Yes, once cleared beyond doubt of possible falsification and professionally verified, that would probably suffice. Where is it?"

The man in the bed was shaking his head slowly. "I don't know."

"You don't . . . ?" Rothenburg began, but held himself back when Nadurovina grabbed his shoulder.

"I mean," Mallory muttered as he struggled with himself, "I know, but I don't know. I *think* I can find it." He wore a look of honest helplessness. "I hid it."

Glancing up at a small dot in the ceiling, Rothenburg barked directives. "Security recheck! I want to know that this entire building is scan-shielded, not just this room. Do it now." When a reply in the affirmative sounded from a concealed speaker, he nodded sharply and turned back to Mallory. "Very well.

You have a recording, but you hid it somewhere. You think you can find it. Where do we look?"

"You'd never locate it. I'll have to do it. Retrace my steps." He smiled wanly and gripped Tse's hand tightly. "It's the only way."

"Why?" Rothenburg prompted him. "Just tell us where on Treetrunk you concealed this recording and there'll be a recovery team on site within days."

"It's not on Treetrunk," he told the officer. "It's on the inner moon." His expression turned apologetic. "Under a rock. I didn't want to leave it on the lifeboat in case the Pitar detected my emissions and picked me up."

Rothenburg looked like a fighter who had just taken a combination to the head and body. "After the Unop-Patha delivered you to the *Ronin*, your lifeboat was brought aboard and thoroughly checked over. Nothing was found, of course. But if that was your reference point for what you buried, how are you going to find it now? As moons go, I understand that Treetrunk One is pretty small. But it's still a moon."

"All I can do is try."

"You'll have help." Rothenburg's mind was racing ahead—planning, directing, plotting logistics. "What kind of container did you bury the recording in? Metal?" he concluded hopefully.

"Sorry. I used a small composite sealtight. Impervious to extremes of heat and cold, maintains a good vacuum."

"What was the recording medium?" Nadurovina asked.

"Standard home-recording mollysphere. A big one, centimeter in diameter. High grade—I could afford quality stuff. Also composite material, of course."

"Which means we'll have a hard time running a materials scan through rock." The major took a step back from the bed. "It doesn't matter. We'll find it if we have to take the whole planetoid apart grain by grain."

"I think I can save you a lot of time." Mallory leaned back against the pillows. "At least, I hope so."

"Just a minute." Chimbu broke his silence. "I'm not sure that's such a good idea. If you go back to where you were found, there's no telling how you'll react. The experience could cause you to flash back and relive the trauma you originally suffered. You could lapse back into coma."

"I'm sorry, Doctor," Rothenburg began, "but the overriding importance of this dictates that your authority is . . ."

Mallory cut him off. "Take it easy, Major. I'm coming." He shifted his attention to the troubled Chimbu. "I don't have any choice. I owe it to six hundred thousand dead neighbors."

"If you experience a serious relapse," the chief medical officer warned him stiffly, "this time you might not come out of it in as little as a month's time. You might not come out of it at all." He looked sharply at Rothenburg. "Then you'll have neither proof nor witness."

"A witness without proof is worthless," the officer shot back. Remembering the man in the bed, he added less stridently, "Nothing personal, Mallory."

"Up yours," the patient responded without hesitation. "I'm going."

"Good. I'll initiate the necessary arrangements." Rothenburg eyed the doctor. "You'll certify that he's well enough to travel."

"Since that wasn't phrased as a question," a diffident Chimbu replied, "I don't suppose it matters what I say."

"You'll come along," the officer continued inexorably, "to supervise his medical care." His gaze shifted to the side of the bed. "As will you, Nurse Tse."

"I have no problem with that." She continued to hold Mallory's hand in hers.

"A one-centimeter diameter composite mollysphere." Exhaling slowly, Nadurovina rubbed tiredly at her forehead. "I hope his mind will be clear enough to remember its location."

"Screw his mind," Rothenburg snapped. "His sense of direction is all I'm concerned about." Remembering the figure in the bed he added, "No offense."

"For a repeatedly offensive person, at least you're appropriately apologetic," a serene Mallory informed him.

16

The long journey to the Argus system was accomplished via military transport. Mallory was given a commanding officer's suite with two adjoining orderly's quarters. Tse was ensconced in one and Chimbu in the other. Though he objected strenuously to the profusion of monitoring instrumentation that had been placed in the suite, his protests were courteously ignored. Until the greater matter at hand was resolved, Alwyn Mallory would not be allowed to go to the bathroom unsupervised. He was too important—so important that the KK-drive dreadnought conveying him back to Treetrunk traveled englobed in a cruiser-and-destroyer convoy.

It was an incredibly costly escort for one man. But Rothenburg could have asked for half a fleet and had the request granted. Out of concern for secrecy, he did not. The movement of a small task force would not be overly remarked upon. Military vessels made the run to Argus periodically. Mallory's escort was certainly of unusual size, but not aberrantly so.

As one by one the ships executed the drop from space-plus back into space-normal, there was outwardly nothing wrong with the convoy's first passenger. How much he was holding inside only he knew. Nadurovina worried herself sick about him. To a lesser extent so did Chimbu and Rothenburg and the few others who knew what a full-strength task force was doing visiting the devastated Argus system. Of those close to medical science's most important patient, only Tse was relaxed and confident.

"He's stronger than you think," she told Nadurovina one morning over real coffee and calorie-free beignets.

"Taxonomically speaking, I realize that Alwyn Mallory is one tough son of a bitch." The psychiatrist sponged coffee with a beignet. "I also know that he puts up a strong defensive front that conceals what he is really feeling. He would not be human if it were otherwise. We are both aware that despite his jaunty demeanor and tough exterior he is never very far from the edge. He proved that when he became violent and wrecked his original hospital room." Her voice fell slightly. "What happened before can happen again. As the physician nominally in charge of overseeing his state of mind, I am far from prepared to piss off that possibility."

"I didn't mean to make light of it." Tse had lost weight during the past weeks, Nadurovina noticed, while Mallory had put it back on. Diet, concern, or fear? "I know Alwyn's sanity has survived a terrible shock." She smiled hesitantly over the rim of her cup. "He likes to say that the hinges of his mind are intact, but rusty."

"Has he said anything more about the location of this recording he claims to have made?"

Around them, crew shuffled back and forth from the food wall to tables, chattering in small groups or eating in solitude. The crew of the dreadnought knew only that they were making a visit to Treetrunk. Rumor had it that the stop was intended as a grisly object lesson, to emphasize that those who staffed the giant military KK-drive starships must never stray from alertness. This erroneous scuttlebutt was encouraged.

Not 'claims to,' " Tse countered primly. "Made. It's real. All we have to do is find it."

Nadurovina sipped at her coffee. She had taken quite a liking to the younger woman, motherly concern she kept well hidden. Nothing could be allowed to affect their professional relationship.

"I wish I had your confidence. This is a very expensive little excursion. We have no choice, of course, but to follow up on the only clue that has bequeathed itself to us. The world council realizes that. Even so, they were reluctant to authorize the escort force that Rothenburg insisted on. For his part, he refused to take your Mr. Mallory off-world without it."

"Major Rothenburg is afraid that the Pitar might try something, isn't he?"

"He just wants to be prepared. That's his nature. A consummate alpha personality."

"I want Alwyn to find the mollysphere, of course," Tse murmured, "but more to prove that he's been telling the truth all along than for any other reason."

Nadurovina was slightly taken aback. "What about bringing the butchers of the six hundred thousand to justice?"

Tse hesitated momentarily. "If Alwyn's right and the Pitar were responsible, if they did all the terrible things he says they did and he can bring forth proof of it, it will mean war, won't it?"

The psychiatrist nodded slowly. "One does not need an advanced degree in human psychology to envision the explosion of rage that would result. Personally, I cannot see anything less than all-out hostilities satisfying the atavistic revenge response that would ensue. The limits of such a conflict would remain to be defined, of course."

Tse looked unhappy. "There are interstellar wars with limits?"

"We have no experience in such matters, but if the thranx are to be believed, they have been engaged in just such a contest with the AAnn for more than two hundred and fifty years. I do not see anything that time-consuming happening in this case." She looked thoughtful. "We do not have the patience or the forbearance of the thranx. Or so the relevant literature insists. Myself, I have never met one of the bugs. Someday I think I would like to do so."

"Not me." Tse spoke with conviction. "I don't care how intelligent they are. Every time I see one I'm reminded of the time I snuck into my mother's pantry looking for candy and a bunch of cockroaches fell out on me. I was washing my hair for days afterwards."

"They do not look like cockroaches. Haven't you seen the tridees? More like mantids."

"I don't like them either." Tse pushed back from the table. "I don't like anything that eats with multiple mouthparts, or has honeycombed eyes, or walks on more than four legs."

"You are phobic. I am surprised. A woman with scientific training like yourself."

"I'm not perfect," Tse contended. "Everybody's afraid of something. Major Rothenburg is afraid of not having everything sufficiently organized. Dr. Chimbu is afraid of losing a patient. You are afraid of Alwyn losing his mind again."

"And Alwyn Mallory is afraid of the Pitar," the psychiatrist concluded.

"No. You're wrong there." There wasn't a hint of doubt in the nurse's voice. "Alwyn isn't afraid of the Pitar. He hates them. What he's afraid of is himself."

Consistent, disciplined activity was the norm on the bridge behind him as Rothenburg gazed out the port. Mallory was right, he reflected. Treetrunk One was not much of a moon. Easily overlooked, it was hardly worthy of the astronomical designation. Looking at it put him more in mind of a captured asteroid than a moon. But it was more than large enough to hide a small ship behind. Something as small as a lifeboat would be swallowed entirely.

He had seen the tridees of the tiny vessel Mallory had used to escape the holocaust that had swept over Treetrunk. The interior had immediately struck him as uninhabitable. The outside was worse. Somehow the irascible engineer had not only coerced it into lifting off without exploding on ignition, but had managed to coax it to the point of achieving escape velocity. Without its outmoded navigation equipment to automatically hone in on a destination, Rothenburg knew it would have gone sailing silently off into the starfield, never to be seen or heard from again.

Instead a quirk of luck had led to its being found by ingenuous aliens and its pilot being returned to his people. Subsequent events had precipitated a sequence of scarcely credible concurrences culminating in the arrival proximate to the minor satellite of Treetrunk of the most powerful expeditionary force this sector of starfield had ever seen. It was hardly to be believed.

Rothenburg believed it, just as he believed that in a very short while that same pilot was going to embark on a return visit to the scene of his recent madness. All the medical technology human science and experience could muster was going to be brought to bear on that singular individual to ensure that a recurrence of his dementia did not take place. Even so, Rothenburg knew that nothing was certain. The best minds and the most skilled techniques could not warrant that upon setting foot on Treetrunk One Alwyn Mallory would not go stark raving mad or lapse into coma or otherwise react in a fashion guaranteed to drive Rothenburg, Nadurovina, and everyone else connected with the current enterprise a little crazed themselves.

They could only hope and do their best and put more trust than they wanted to in the ministrations of an ordinary duty nurse with a less-than-extensive professional history.

As so often happens at such times, events progressed in ways unforeseen by even the most adept prognosticators. Mallory allowed himself to be suited up without complaint or hesitation, joking at the ongoing process and lending a hand when and where he was able. Meantime, while everyone was focusing on the indispensable patient, they neglected to consider the condition of his personal attendant. Having never worn an environment suit before, much less been outside a ship in space, Irene Tse was rapidly working herself into a state of near hysteria.

The consequences of this were as salutary as they were unforeseen. Instead of being left to worry about himself, Mallory spent the last moments before disembarking working to soothe and reassure the nurse. Only when he was convinced of her well-being did he condescend to board the military repair vehicle that would carry them from the vast cocoon of the dreadnought to the surface of the tiny moon below. This time it was he who gripped her hand reassuringly.

They were not alone. A small flotilla of armed lifeboats, repair craft, and other vessels awaited, hovering like so many incandescent bees around a darkened, mottled hive. Their operators had been primed to respond instantly to any requests from Mallory—once these had been quietly cleared by Major Rothenburg or one of the two extensively briefed lieutenants who were assisting him.

The major's declaration that if circumstances demanded it they would tear the moon apart to find the mollysphere was held in abeyance. Stir up the satellite's surface and they might bury the inestimably precious recording permanently. Or worse, the abysmally low gravity might allow it to drift off into space. In respect of everything that could go wrong, each ship kept its preassigned distance. Only one descended, with infinite deliberation and care, to the surface of the moon itself.

It did not quite achieve touchdown. Hovering just above the battered, eroded surface, it adjusted its position until the best records available insisted it was occupying the exact same coordinates as the patient's lifeboat had previously. Even the north-south axis of the repair craft was oriented identically. Stepping outside, Mallory theoretically should be able to recognize his surroundings, theoretically ought to be capable of retracing his steps to the spot where he had buried the recording.

Theoretically.

He entered the lock effortlessly and without apparent trepidation. Two techs preceded him while a third accompanied a visibly agitated Tse. She was controlling herself with an effort, insistent upon being included in the excursion, knowing that if Mallory suffered a relapse she wanted to be with him. She needed to be with him, and not just for his sake. Their relationship had progressed beyond that. Nadurovina followed her into the lock while a fourth tech signaled to those on the other side of the barrier that all was well and the landing party was ready to proceed.

All was not well, but Tse knew how to utilize various mind- and breath-control techniques to stabilize her system. Such skills were part of her training. It was the first time she had used them on herself, however, and not on a patient. Controlling her emotions was another matter entirely. Somehow she managed that as well.

The outer door opened, and the dusky light of Treetrunk's star poured in. The first pair of techs exited efficiently, one after the other floating gently down to the rocky surface. In defiance of proper procedure, Mallory insisted on taking Tse's hand and egressing with her. To everyone's unspoken relief, the tandem descent was accomplished without incident.

Once the entire landing party had left the repair craft, Mallory moved clear of the group and sought to establish his bearings. If the larger vessel was positioned exactly the same as his lifeboat had been when he had been marooned here, then there ought to be a hill resembling a broken tooth approximately forty degrees to his right. Turning in that direction, he was gratified to see that the landmark was exactly where and how he remembered it. Approximately fifty meters from where he was standing there would be a small, shallow crater. As he paced off the span, the others followed at a respectful distance. No one watched his movements with more intensity than Irene Tse.

The crater was a little farther than he remembered it, but it was unarguably the same depression. To make certain, he walked off the diameter. Seven meters, more or less. Remembrances were lining up like winning numbers on a gambling machine, with a jackpot payoff at the end no bigger than a fingernail. Looking back at the hovering repair craft to properly orient himself, he drew a mental line in the rock between the ship and the snaggle-topped hill. Walking to the half-meter-high rim of the crater, he looked down at its edge, searching for the large, flat rock he had placed there. It had a distinctive triangular shape, which was why he had chosen it.

The rock was not there.

Frowning behind the faceplate of his suit, he followed the crater's rim to the right. Still no sign of the marker he had carefully left behind. When he had walked perhaps a fifth of the way around the crater he retraced his steps and began searching in the other direction. Tse advanced to join him. The consequent intimacy was only physical. Anything they said to one another could be overheard clearly by everyone else in the group, as well as by the crew of the repair craft and, via relay, everyone listening back on board the dreadnought.

"It's here." Mallory paused long enough to look over at Tse, their faceplates nearly touching. "I know it's here."

"Of course it is," she told him reassuringly. "It's only natural for you to be a little disoriented. It's been a long time, and you had other things on your mind when you hid it."

"I'm not disoriented!" Seeing her flinch behind the faceplate he hastened to apologize. "Really, I know exactly where I am. Sometimes my words still get all mixed up, but not my actions. Everything is just as I remembered it." Turning, he indicated the location and position of the repair craft, the jagged hilltop looming in the distance, the shallow circular crater. "This is all correct. Everything is where it should be. Except for that damn rock."

"Which damn rock?" she inquired quietly. "I'll help you look for it." Turning her head, she glanced back in the direction of the assembled group. "We'll all help."

Mallory hesitated. It was his rock, his potential vindication, and he wanted to find the damn thing. But it wasn't where it was supposed to be. Maybe he was forgetting something. Or maybe he was imagining it after the fact. Maybe . . . maybe the Pitar who had visited him in the hospital room had been right all along and his brain was inventing elaborate cover-ups for his debased memory. Panic threatened to rise in his throat like vomit.

"Okay, sure. Why not? Everyone can have a look. The important thing is not who finds the rock but finding it, right?" Smiling tenderly behind her faceplate, Tse nodded encouragement. The others gathered around.

"We're looking for a flat stone about this big." Mallory used his hands to trace size and shape in the vacuum. "About eight centimeters thick. No other distinguishing features."

"What color is it?" asked one of the techs from the ship.

Mallory had to laugh. "Look around. You've got a choice of two: dark gray and darker gray. It's the shape that's significant."

The party split, half searching to the left, the other half

marching methodically in the opposite direction. When they met unsuccessfully on the other side of the crater they passed each other and kept going. By the time they met again, back at the original starting point, discouragement and the first flickerings of serious mistrust were beginning to make their psychological presence felt among several of the searchers.

"Are there any other identifying landmarks?" Nadurovina probed as gently as she could. It would not do to challenge the patient too forcefully or say anything accusatory. Upsetting him could only have deleterious mental consequences.

She need not have worried. Mallory was already actively upsetting himself. The strain showed clearly on his face.

If he had imagined burying the mollysphere, then maybe he had imagined having it. If he had imagined having it, who knows what else his mind had invented? The presence of the Pitar? Not the devastation of Treetrunk—that was real enough. All too much proof of the atrocity was hanging in the sky on the other side of the small moon. Under incredible psychological pressure and mental stress, had he written on the blank sheet of his memory an elaborate scenario that had never taken place, that was the product of an overheated imagination instead of cold, composed reportage?

He could see the faces of his companions through the transparencies of their faceplates, could see the skepticism stirring in their expressions. Outwardly they remained committed and supportive, but within themselves they were beginning to question, to wonder, and he lay square at the nexus of their mounting uncertainties.

Where was that damn rock? A man could contrive any number of chimeras, but a rock was a real thing: solid and unforgiving, a piece of stellar matter made hard and cold. Ignoring the accusing stares, he focused on the surface on both sides of the crater: scanning, searching, scrutinizing. There were plenty of rocks, hundreds of rocks. Some were the right size, but none were quite the proper shape, and not one was where it had been when he'd first decided on the hiding spot.

"We have to go back." The voice of the tech reverberated like a bell in Mallory's helmet: tolling failure, ringing fiasco.

He was studying a gauge. "Overall, group air is down to fifteen percent. Return to ship is standard security procedure."

Tse remained at Mallory's side. "It's okay, Alwyn. While the suits are recharged we'll have something to eat and drink. We'll talk about it, and you can collect your thoughts. Then we'll try again." She smiled hopefully. "Maybe all you need is a fresh start."

"That's right." Though it was not required of her, Nadurovina did her best to encourage him. "If you stepped out of the ship facing the wrong way, you could have started off on the wrong tangent right at the beginning."

"We'll recheck the location and orientation of the repair boat, too." Rothenburg's tone belied the helpfulness of his words. "If it's off even a few degrees it would mess everything up."

Everything was already messed up, Mallory thought apprehensively. The repair craft was properly positioned. He knew that was the case because the cracked hill stood exactly where it ought to be. So did the crater. He knew it was the right crater not only because it was situated precisely where it belonged, but because it was the proper size, shape, and depth. He *remembered*. There was nothing wrong with his memory—unless he was so seriously impaired that his imaginings had become that real to him. If that was the case, then maybe what he thought was reality was in fact the foundation of his madness. Maybe he wasn't even here, on this runt rock of a satellite. Maybe he was lying in a hospital somewhere back on Earth, with a solicitous but otherwise disinterested Tse bending over him. He'd been given a lot of medication, he knew. Maybe his return to Treetrunk was drug-induced instead of Kurita-Kinoshita powered.

"Alwyn, don't look like that!" Tse was at his side, gripping his suit and shaking him. "You're scaring me."

Blinking, he nodded slowly as he met her gaze. "It's nice to have company. I'm scaring me, too." Gently disengaging his arm, he turned to look at and past the crater rim. "This is *right*. Everything is right. It's just as I remember it. The rock should be here. The recording should be under it."

He became aware that the two techs were now flanking him. "Mr. Mallory, sir," one of them was saying inside his helmet, "we're running low on air. Regulations require that we return to the ship for recharging."

Angry and confused, he allowed himself to be led back toward the waiting repair boat. Aware that their words were common currency via the suit channel, none of his companions voiced their thoughts or feelings. Vacuum helped to dissipate the growing tension, but could not banish it entirely.

Halfway back to the ship, Mallory halted as if shot. When he whirled to confront Rothenburg, the officer recoiled slightly but held his ground. He did not care for the look on the patient's face.

"When the technicians from the *Ronin* retrieved my lifeboat, what method did they use?"

"Excuse me?" Taken aback by the abruptness of the question as well as the confrontation, Rothenburg stalled for time.

"How did they reclaim it?" Mallory was in a fit of impatience, not madness. "Did they use a tractor beam from the big ship, did service personnel adjust its position before signaling for it to be taken aboard, did they try to fire the boat's engine? What recovery techniques were employed?"

"I don't know," the major admitted. "But I can find out." Switching to suit to boat to mothership relay, Rothenburg conveyed the query while Mallory and the rest of the party waited. Not in silence, though, or in contentment.

"Really, Mr. Mallory," the tech standing on his right declared. "Suit air is approaching ten percent. We absolutely must return to the boat."

"You go on if you want to." All of Mallory's attention was focused on Rothenburg, waiting for a reply, waiting for an explanation. "I'm not finished here yet. Ten percent is more than I need." At his side, a hesitant but supportive Tse stood with him. With an effort of will, she avoided looking down at her own suit gauge.

Rothenburg finally switched back to suit-to-suit. "Two manned repair craft were used to move your old boat from here to the *Ronin*. They were smaller than the one we came down on, but larger than your lifeboat."

"Propulsion systems." With that Mallory turned and began to retrace their original line from the repair ship, not walking deliberately this time but moving in long, bounding strides through the low gravity. Each time he touched down his feet kicked up a cloud of slow-settling dust—dust and small rocks.

Nadurovina was visibly concerned, and Tse's expression bordered on the frantic; but Rothenburg saw and understood. By running Mallory was not just returning as rapidly as possible to the crater: He was delivering a lesson in physics. Ignoring the rising plaints of the technicians, the major raced after the retreating patient.

Arriving at the crater's edge he found Mallory once more searching thc terrain. Not along the crater's rim this time, but beyond. Well beyond. Without a word he moved off to one side and commenced hunting on his own. He heard Nadurovina long before she reached him.

"What's going on? You heard the tech. We have to return to the ship!"

"Five minutes," the excited officer told her. "Another five minutes. Then we'll all go back together. Right, Mallory?"

"Right," the spirited reply came. Some private epiphany had restored the patient's spirits even as they had revived Rothenburg's enthusiasm for the mission. "Five minutes. And if we don't find it then, we'll come back and spend some real time looking for it. Everybody, five minutes! Look for the rock."

Tse fell to searching alongside him. "I thought you told us that you placed it on the rim of the little crater, Alwyn. In a line between your lifeboat and the broken hill."

"I did." Not looking up, he continued moving methodically over the airless landscape, head down, searching, searching. "But when repair craft came from the *Ronin* to recover my lifeboat, one of them might have positioned itself with its grapplers facing that way." He rose just long enough to point directly behind them, back toward the waiting boat. "When it fired its thrusters to commence the return to the cruiser, the exhaust blast would have come *this* way." One arm swept around in a wide, swooping arc that terminated with his hand pointed toward the ragged promontory. "It would have blown dust and debris in the direction of the hill."

Her eyes widened slightly. "And rocks."

He nodded vigorously. "Maybe even a few big rocks. Maybe even one shaped like a triangle."

They found it with six percent air remaining in their suits. There was nothing under it. Another man might have been crushed by the sphere's absence, but not Mallory. He recognized every rill in the stone, every pore, every crack. It was his rock, the one he had positioned as a marker over the container holding the recording. Half mad at the time he might have been, but the sane half had known what it was doing. Of that infinitely priceless little sealtight there was no sign.

"It's here." Carefully he put the rock down. "For God's sake, everyone watch where you step." His head was in constant motion, minutely scrutinizing the surface around the feet of his companions as well as his own.

Nadurovina studied the gently rolling, dust- and grit-covered terrain. "We'll need dozens of searchers. Even with numbers it could take months to find anything in this."

"If the exhaust blast from the repair vehicle blew a rock this size so far from the crater's rim, the container holding the recording would have been blown ten times as far." Rothenburg was looking not at his feet, but off in the distance.

"Not necessarily," Mallory argued. "It could have been blasted down into the dust, or become caught up against another rock, or the rim of one of these smaller craters. It could be an arm's length from here, or a hundred."

The major was nodding. He was doing what he did best, what he most enjoyed: organizing. "Everyone will be properly instructed. We'll bring shape sensors in, and have some simple mesh boxes made up for sifting dust. We'll find it." His tone was decisive.

"Unless it was blown off into space," one of the techs contended. "The gravity here is so weak."

"That is a possibility." The ever-rational Rothenburg was

compelled to entertain the unthinkable. "But to push away from the surface the thrusters on the repair craft that retrieved his lifeboat would have been directed downward. I would lay odds that the container is still here somewhere, buried in the dust or jammed up against a redeeming rock." The muscles of his face were tight. "We have to believe that."

Had the Unop-Patha chanced to return to the inner moon of Argus V they would have been astonished to find more than a hundred space-suited humans busying themselves like ants on a portion of the insignificant satellite's surface. Finding humans more than a little baffling anyway, the frenetic activity being carried out in the complete silence of the void would only have added to their bewilderment.

Responding to Rothenburg's directive, thc task force was prepared to remain on station for a month. Settling in for a long, monotonous stay proved unnecessary.

The young ensign who entered the cafeteria two days later had not even taken the time to remove her sweat-stained undersuit. Accompanied by two companions and a senior officer she made her way to the table in the far corner and presented herself to a questioning Nadurovina with a crisp salute. Without further ado she swung a small metallic bag from her side to her front, unsealed it, reached inside, and removed an object that she placed gently on the table.

"Is this it?" she asked without preamble.

Resting on the table, between a chicken sandwich on cracked wheat and a rangeweed salad, was the most important single object in the Arm. It did not look like much. The tumble it had taken from the back blast of the rescuing repair craft's thrusters had left its surface pitted and one corner crumpled. The seal, however, was intact.

Mallory was surprised at how steady his fingers were as he reached across table and food to pick it up. Almost casually, he disregarded the seal. The lid flipped open. Inside lay a small, gleaming, one-centimeter-in-diameter silvery sphere that glistened metallically beneath the overhead lights of the cafeteria, even though there was no metal in it.

Unable to contain herself, Irene Tse threw her arms around Mallory's neck and shoulders and hugged him so hard that the psychiatrist feared he would drop the container. There was little chance of that. For the foreseeable future it was wedded to the patient's hand: a small, square, silvered sixth digit. The former patient, she corrected herself. Standing by the side of the table, the ensign who had found the box beamed proudly. No one had acknowledged her question. No one had to.

A somber Tse stared at the unprepossessing contents of the box. "So much tragedy in such a tiny space."

Mallory nodded. "It's full of death. Death, and justification. I wish the two weren't joined." Putting it back in the sealtight, he closed the lid but did not try to reactivate the container. Frankly, he was unsure if the battered seal could be repowered. "Intelligent beings are going to die because of what's on that mollysphere. A lot of intelligent beings."

"I hope so, sir," one of the other soldiers who had accompanied the ensign declared. Standing at attention, he was not smiling. "One of my cousins and his family were colonists on Treetrunk."

"Better no one jumps to any conclusions." Pushing back from the table, Nadurovina rose. "We must go inform Rothenburg and the rest of the staff. Meanwhile, let's pray that the sphere is still functional and that it contains more than tridee of Argusian fauna and scenes of settlement life." She started for the doorway.

Mallory and Tse followed. She was leaning against him. "I don't care what happens now, or if the sphere operates, or what's on it. Finding it vindicates you, Alwyn."

"I know. But I don't care if I'm absolved. I want what I saw and experienced to be vindicated. Not me." In what should have been a moment of triumph, his expression was forlorn, his tone bleak. "The psyche is exonerated. Let's hope the same holds true for the technology."

17

Herringale had been chosen by lot from the pool of qualified candidates. Inoffensive, gentle voiced, with a physical profile from which all the rough edges had long since been buffed by time, he was one of those faceless but professional bureaucrats who do most of the work for little of the recognition. An engraved plaque now and again or an extra day's paid vacation were all the extra reward someone of his position and demeanor could reasonably expect.

Now he was waiting to receive Suin-Bimt, the ranking Pitar on Earth. He was not nervous, and in fact was looking forward to it. He would control himself, he knew. His life had been spent in controlling himself. It was one of the reasons he had been chosen to conduct the interview.

The conference chamber was very large for two. An enormous curved window, seemingly poured in one piece and unsupported by braces throughout its length, overlooked the Bodensee. Ancient castles were visible along the lakeshore, and snow crowned the majestic rampart of the northern Alps. Gleaming golden, a meeting table capable of seating thirty in comfort shone behind him. He and Suin would not need it. They would use two comfortable chairs and a small round table instead.

The Pitar entered from the far corridor, the doors sliding silently apart to admit him. Locating Herringale as his host rose, Suin altered course toward him. When he extended a hand in the customary human fashion, the much smaller human took it politely, then gestured that they both should sit.

Outside, pleasure boats cruised the calm waters of the immense alpine lake. The sun shone brightly, filtered by the glass. On the small table between them stood two tall glasses and a citrine pitcher filled with ice water. Suin took in the view and smiled.

"This is very pleasant. I was told my presence was required here, so I came. Not for long, I hope. I have a full schedule today."

"It shouldn't take much of your time." Fingering the arm of his chair, Herringale activated the player. A large rectangular heads-up display darkened in the center of the window, blocking out a portion of the villatic view of the lake and mountains. "I've been asked to watch a recording with you and seek your comments. It's been cleaned up a little, but I'm told it's more or less identical to the original. There's water, and glasses. If you need anything else, ask me."

"What kind of recording?" The Dominion's ambassador settled back in the easy chair. "One of your frenetic entertainment features? Or is it music? I quite like your music."

"There's no music," Herringale told him quietly, "and it's not entertainment."

The display flickered briefly. An added title appeared, giving time, date, and length as well as other relevant vitals. Herringale was watching the Pitar, not the display. He had already seen the recording. More than once.

Everything that appeared was from the point of view of a moving recorder. The images drifted dreamily in the air in front of the window, rendered in soft tridee or what the ancients would have called bas-relief. Adjusting the display controls would have brought them forward in full three dimensions, but Herringale and his superiors saw no need for that. There was enough to comprehend in the reduced format.

Suin watched for a while without commenting. Insofar as Herringale could tell, the Pitar's expression did not change. Twice, he turned slightly to pour himself a glass of water. Only when the recording reached its end did the alien turn to regard his host. During the replay the ambassador had shown no emotion, had offered no comment.

"Very imaginative. And very insulting. I am forced to inquire as to the rationale behind such an expensive travesty. Your entertainment people are very clever, but this is not in any wise amusing."

"We are in agreement on that," Herringale informed him stiffly. "It is not amusing. Nor was what you have just seen the product of our 'entertainment' people. It is a tridee media recording, broadcast on Treetrunk at the time of its invasion and recorded by an alert citizen who had access to more professional equipment than the average resident."

"Absurd." The Pitar's voice was unchanged. "No record of the devastation of that unfortunate world exists. If it did, it would have come to light long before now."

"It was hidden," Herringale explained. "And only recently recovered."

The Pitar shifted his position in the cradling chair. "I had been given to understand that your people had scoured the surface of Argus Five and continue to do so without finding anything remotely like what you have just forced me to watch."

"That is so. However, this recording was not found on Treetrunk. It lay buried and unnoticed on Treetrunk One, the smaller of that martyred world's two moons. A refugee who fled during the invasion concealed it there. He is the same person who made the recording."

Ambassador Suin was repeatedly making the Pitarian gesture that signified negativity. "No one escaped the destruction. Your own people say so." He shifted his legs preparatory to rising. "I do not like this game, and I have important work to supervise."

"Oh, please." Herringale leaned forward sharply. "Humor me a moment longer. This really is very important."

Impatient and reluctant, the ambassador retained his seat. "I disagree, but very well. A few moments more, and then I really must go."

"Yes. Just a few moments. Does the name Alwyn Mallory mean anything to you?"

The Pitar's expression rippled. "No. Is this person attached to the diplomatic mission here?"

"Hardly. He's not even attached to the government. One of your people on the other side of the planet, a diplomatic attaché named Dmis, has met him."

"I do not know that name, either. I am not expected to know the names of everyone assigned to duty on your world, any more than you would be required to identify everyone working in the diplomatic arm of your government."

Herringale nodded. "Maybe you should contact and converse with Dmis. He met Mr. Mallory, so he knows that he is a real person. We also know that Mr. Mallory is a real person—an unusually independent and resourceful one. Among other things, Alwyn Mallory is an ex–starship engineer. As a hobby, he obtained and restored a ship's lifeboat of antiquated design. It was adequate to convey him to the far side of the moon in question, together with a copy he had made of this remote media broadcast. To ensure its safety, he buried the recording on the moon. It has only recently been recovered."

"A very disturbing story." Suin pressed outer edges of his hands together in the formal Pitarian manner. Like all his kind he was an extraordinarily handsome individual, tall and regal. Granted unlimited access to the skills of Earth's finest cosmetic surgeons, Herringale knew he could never look half so imposing.

"The recording has been authenticated. Among the methods employed to do this was the extensive excavation of the specific locales imaged in the tridee. Everything matches up, from the ruined buildings to the traces of blood found in the city of Weald's central square." He found that he was compelled to take a swallow of cold water. "I am told that such traces are extensive. Having viewed the recording several times previously, even as a nonexpert I can understand this."

"I am leaving now." The ambassador moved to rise. Herringale rose with him. The Pitar towered over the soft-bodied, middle-aged diplomat.

"We have many questions." Herringale's voice was as calm as when he had first greeted the alien. "Foremost among these is the desire to know the reason behind the careful evisceration of so many females and the concurrent careful preservation of their reproductive organs. I admit that I am personally interested. I have two daughters of approximately the same age as the young women who are shown in the recording being disemboweled while still alive." Without realizing what he was doing, he reached out to pluck at the ambassador's sleeve. "Please, won't you explain? I'm really, really curious."

Suin stared down at him. "I intend to register a formal protest with my government. To waste my time with such nonsense is bad enough, but to subject me to additional slander borders on wanton malice."

"Go ahead and register," Herringale told him. Something was rising within the career diplomat, and he fought hard to suppress it. Professional self-control was a major reason, after all, why he had been chosen for this morning's work. "It is possible your complaint will arrive before my government's formal declaration of war."

The ambassador finally showed some emotion, though it was as subdued as all such Pitarian reactions. "What kind of joke are you making? You can't mean that your people would begin a war based on a single recording purportedly made by a lone human?"

"The recording has been validated. Mr. Mallory's reminiscences have been validated. The decision of the world council was unanimous. The colonies have been informed, and their respective individual councils wholeheartedly concur. In effect, the war has already begun. It will be interesting to observe the consequences. There are those pundits who insist that interstellar war is an oxymoron. We are about to find out." Despite efforts to control himself, his tone darkened somewhat. "Your people are about to find out."

"Is there no stopping this travesty?"

Herringale gazed up at the much taller alien. He found that he was not intimidated. "Beginning at six o'clock tonight, Greenwich mean time, the recording made by Mr. Mallory will be broadcast across the planet and on all the colonies. It will be flanked by detailed information explaining the nature of the recording and how it came to be. The program will be followed by the official announcement of mobilization. Reservists are already reporting to their positions and their ships. I have been asked to conclude this meeting, Ambassador Suin, by informing you that you and your entire staff are under arrest, and heretofore should regard yourselves as prisoners of war." This time it was the sallow-faced human who smiled.

"You cannot reciprocate, of course, since you have never allowed us to establish a formal mission on either of the Twin Worlds. In the light of what we now know, such puzzling decisions on your part strike us as ever more suspicious."

"Are there to be no ends to these insults?" Suin drew himself up to his full, impressive height. "By your own laws, my staff and I have diplomatic immunity."

"I'm sorry, but after viewing that recording there is little inclination among any of my people, be they members of the diplomatic corps or the local janitorial staff or the general populace, to grant any kind of immunity to any Pitar. In fact, I can honestly say that if the privilege were bestowed upon me, I would take great pleasure in cutting you into smaller and smaller pieces of raw meat right here in this room, even at the risk of permanently staining a very expensive and historically important floor covering."

Suin was striding toward the doorway. "I refuse to stand here and be subjected to continued insult and innuendo."

"You don't have to," Herringale called after him. "You can keep going and be subject to continued insult and innuendo later."

Herringale was not quite finished with the ambassador. Confronted beyond the doorway by a quartet of heavily armed and armored security personnel, the Pitar surprised them by drawing a weapon of unknown type from a hidden compartment within his left pants leg. It must have been a well-shielded compartment in order for the diplomat to have successfully blinded the security scanners that monitored all comings and goings to the inner chancellery. There was no need for a diplomat to carry a weapon, Herringale mused as he ducked down behind one of the chairs, unless the possessor had something to fear—or was particularly paranoid.

They never found out in Suin's case because, after wounding two of the guards, the Pitarian ambassador died in a blaze of gunfire as he attempted to flee the building. An offer to remand the remainder of his colleagues into protective custody was declined with disdain. Following the general broadcast of the Mallory record, as it came to be known, a mob stormed the building housing the Pitarian embassy in Zurich. Defending themselves, the Pitar killed several dozen people before the military could intervene. The aliens perished to the last.

Similar confrontations took place wherever Pitar could be found, from the supposedly inviolate compound on Bali to more isolated urban facilities in Brisbane, Delhi, and Lala. Within twenty-four hours of the worldwide broadcast of the unexpurgated recording, not a Pitar was left alive on Earth.

At the time, there were two Pitarian vessels in orbit. In attempting to flee, one was blown apart while the other managed to escape. It being impossible to track a ship in space-plus, the pursuing humans terminated the chase halfway between the moon and distant Mars.

All the while, warships and supply vessels were in the process of assembling—not only in the vicinity of Earth, but around its far-flung colonies as well. From Proycon to Centaurus, from New Riviera to Mantis, ships and personnel gathered. There was no singing of patriotic songs, no mass rallies of fervid supporters. It was all business, serious business, and was organized and conducted accordingly.

Some hoped that the Pitar would admit their crime and capitulate, following which suitable punishment and penalization could be decided upon. Others prayed that the aliens would resist. As the Twin Worlds of the Dominion did not lie that far from either the galactic plane or the expanding human sphere of influence, an answer to these questions was expected soon.

Once they had been informed of Pitarian responsibility for the Treetrunk atrocity, outrage was general among every other civilized species. It did not translate into action, however. The quarrel was between humankind and Pitar, and it would be left to those two civilizations to settle the matter. The Quillp, the Unop-Patha, and everyone else expressed their regret and sorrow and then stood back to see which species would prevail. In this regard the AAnn proffered their condolences as fervently as anyone else, while quietly hoping that both powerful space-going races would permanently and severely incapacitate one another in the coming conflict.

Among the thranx the reaction was one of subdued fury. Arising as they did from an ancient line that had succeeded partly by venerating a single egg-laying queen, they were especially sensitive to any violation of the reproductive system. What the Pitar had done to and with human females sent a ripple of rage through every hive. Even as the humans methodically assembled a vast force to attack the Twin Worlds, vexatious debate seethed among the thranx on how best to respond to the unimaginable barbarity.

"It does not involve us."

Sprawled atop a convenient log, Wirmbatusek regarded the lake. It was a small body of water surrounded by dense tropical forest, a refuge high in the mountains of Lombok. Nearby, Asperveden was waltzing with a birdwing butterfly, letting it flutter from one truhand to another. Perhaps the huge, iridescent green ornithop recognized a distant alien cousin. More likely it just found the thranx's chitinous digits a convenient place to rest.

"Of course it involves us."

Raising a truhand, Asperveden examined the exquisite creature. Compound eye met compound eye. Beautiful, the attaché mused. What the butterfly felt was not recorded. Eventually it tired of the game and flew off, soaring up into the tall vine-draped hardwoods, a pair of thin emerald slabs throwing back the sun.

Wirmbatusek turned his head and antennae in the direction of his friend and coworker. "Keeping a constant watch on the AAnn is enough to worry about. Why would the Grand Council choose to weaken our own defenses to support a massive effort to punish a race that has done nothing to us?"

Exhibiting uncharacteristic daring, Asperveden walked forward until all four trulegs were in the water. Astonished at his own boldness, he stood and watched as the tepid, algae-stained green liquid swirled gently around his limbs. Where he was standing the lake was perhaps ten centimeters deep.

Wirmbatusek's antennae twitched nervously. "Are you insane? Get out of there! Suppose the soil is soft and you begin to sink? Don't expect me to pull you out."

The slightly smaller thranx gestured for his companion to be calm. "Have no fear. The surface underfoot is firm and unyielding. These Pitar have violated every accepted norm of civilized behavior."

"No one disputes that." Wirmbatusek watched a line of ants marching along the base of the log. To a single ant, the insectoid thranx might well have been a vision of God. "No one disagrees with the humans' urge to seek revenge. We would doubtless react similarly, albeit less noisily, if the barbarity had been visited upon us. But it was not. What happened on Argus Five does not concern us."

"Why not? Because only mammals died? Because only human females were dishonored?"

"It is too facile to say that we should help the humans." Sliding off the log, Wirmbatusek settled himself on his trulegs. Using all four hands he daintily picked bits of bark and other debris from his gleaming blue-green exoskeleton and the thorax pouch that hung from his second major body segment. "First, they have not asked us, or any other species, for assistance. Next, it is not incumbent on the thranx to aid them because there is no treaty or agreement between our two races particularizing any such action. There are no reasons for us to become involved and many why we should keep our distance. For one thing, like so much else about them the martial capability of these Pitar is unknown. We could end up having allied ourselves with the losing side." He flicked a fallen leaf from his abdomen.

"I would not bet against the humans in a war." Finally starting to grow uneasy at the feel of water lapping around his legs, Asperveden carefully backed out of the shallows.

"Nor would I, but neither would I choose to gamble with the neutrality that preserves our civilization unscathed. War is not a lark, and gambling on it not entertainment."

One foot at a time, Asperveden shook water from his impermeable chitin. "The estimable Desvendapur would have much to say about this situation."

"No doubt, if he was living. I wish I could have seen him perform. To my knowledge none of his poetry dealt with war, despite the gravity of his clan and family history." The larger thranx followed a pair of hornbills as they glided across the lake. "What makes you think the humans would accept our help even if it were to be offered? A great many of them despise us and cannot even stand to be in our presence. Those of us here and at the Amazon hive are isolated from such individual conflicts."

"I realize that our relations are still developing." Feeling the first pangs of morning hunger, Asperveden began to remove food from his own pouch. "I am not naïve. Much work remains to be done to bring our two peoples together to the point where trust is accepted instead of debated, and genuine friendship is not an isolated occurrence." Biting into a starch loaf with all four opposing jaws, he chewed reflectively. "This conflict would be a perfect opportunity to do just that."

Approaching his friend, Wirmbatusek waited to be offered food, withholding his own offering until the smaller thranx made the appropriate gesture. "More than strategic concerns are involved in this. As many thranx are suspicious of the humans as they are of us. It is hard enough to arrange for meetings, for cultural exchanges, for agreements on minor matters. An alliance that includes provisions for mutual defense lies far in the future."

"It need not require a formal association." Asperveden executed the appropriate hand gestures, following which his friend responded in kind. They exchanged food. "The arrangement could be temporary, and understood as such by both sides. Assistance in time of and solely for the duration of conflict, superseding all current agreements, after which the previous status is resumed."

Wirmbatusek considered. "I am envisioning several fully armed hive warships emerging from space-plus at safe distance beyond the orbit of this world's moon. I am envisioning the human reaction. I am not sanguine about what I am seeing."

"Hive ships need not enter this system. A mutual rendezvous point elsewhere could be agreed upon." Asperveden refused to acknowledge the impossibility of his hypothetical proposal. "The humans would be grateful. It would advance our relationship and improve our mutual prospects immeasurably."

Swallowing, Wirmbatusek began to hunt in his pouch for the spiral-spouted drink bottle. "If we are victorious. If the Pitar should win, we would have acquired their enmity for nothing."

"Not true," Asperveden argued. "We would still have gained the gratitude of the humans."

"Would we?" Slipping the decorated drinking tube between his jaws, the larger worker began to sip sugary, nutritious liquid. "You ascribe to humans a quality of gratefulness I have yet to see demonstrated." He passed the bottle over. "First I would like to see one invite me into its home without an expression of disgust on its face. Then I might consider rendering it some assistance. If we remain neutral we are detached in the eyes of Pitar and human alike. We risk nothing. That is what the Quillp, and the Unop-Patha, and even the AAnn are doing. Why should we do any differently?"

Asperveden contemplated the tranquil lake, the intriguingly different indigenous wildlife, the warm, clear, morning air, and felt himself troubled. "I do not know. Perhaps because we are better than they?"

Wirmbatusek chose to comment via a sequence of circumspect clicks. "Anything else?"

"Nothing that could be construed as conclusive. Only that,

unlike many who count themselves true progeny of the First Queen, I happen to *like* humans."

"So do I," Wirmbatusek confessed freely. "But that does not mean I am ready to march out of the hive to sacrifice limb and life alongside them."

18

The armada was unlike anything that humankind, or for that matter any of the other species that happened to dwell in that same portion of the Arm, had seen before. Less what was necessary to protect and defend Earth and its other colonies, every armed vessel propelled by a KK-drive was assigned a position and time to rendezvous on the outskirts of the Dominion. It was believed that the Pitar would meet them there, somewhere in the vicinity of their system's twelfth and outermost world. It was also conceded that Pitarian vessels ranging far and wide would at least make an attempt to assault one or more of the human populated worlds, if only to divert attention from their own.

Neither threat materialized. Human strategists were perplexed. The xenologists who had studied the Pitar were not.

Levi was one of those who was not. Others like him had been assigned to the armada, one to a ship so that in the event of catastrophe all the members of his group and the valuable knowledge they represented could not be lost in a single blow. If not the fleetest of mind or the most experienced member of the team that had studied the Pitar since first contact, he was acknowledged the senior member of the group. His opinion was solicited and respected. He found himself on the *Wellington*, seconded to the general staff.

It was subsequent to a meeting where the plan of first attack was being finalized that he found himself, thoroughly preoccupied with the critical matters at hand, strolling aimlessly through the great ship. As big as anything mobile that mankind had yet put in space, the *Wellington* was an impressive achievement. Four rings of armaments located in evenly spaced weapons blisters girdled the main body of the dreadnought. The KK-drive generating fan that spread out before it and pulled it through space-plus was the size of a small town. Between fan, hydrogen spark plug, and the main body of the ship were five defensive-screen generators. No more powerful or fearsome ship cruised the cosmos. It was a supreme example of contemporary human technology, an other-than-light vessel representing a confluence of all that human civilization had thus far accomplished.

That it was designed expressly to blow things up placed it squarely in the mainstream of human technological achievement.

Meyer Levi was a civilian attached to a military expedition. He was an old man who ought to have been reclining in a soft chair in a library, fronted by a tridee screen and surrounded by real books, a hot drink steaming on a nearby table, and a rumpled dog lying at his feet. Instead he found himself inconceivably far from home and anything akin to such imaginary comforts.

Despite the absence on the system's outer fringes of any armed confrontation, no one believed that the Pitar were simply going to allow the invading humans to put punishing landing parties down on the surface of the Twin Worlds unopposed. The timing and manner of their resistance was yet to be determined. But one by one, the warships of Earth and its colonies had emerged from space-plus into Pitarian space, uncontested and unchallenged. Now fully assembled in normal space, the armada was ready to take the next step of moving toward the system's sun and positioning itself around the Twin Worlds.

Nor had the Pitar sent ships to attack Earth itself or any of its more lightly defended colonies. There had been no reaction at all from the tall, elegant humanoids. Their representatives on Earth and elsewhere had died fighting, refusing to suffer imprisonment. All remaining Pitar, the entire population, was on their two homeworlds, presumably cognizant of and awaiting the arrival of a vast assemblage of ships crewed by tens of thousands of angry, revenge-minded humans.

What were they overlooking? Levi found himself wondering. Surely the Pitar were going to resist, were not going to commit racial suicide. But that was essentially what their isolated representatives on Earth had done. Did the entire species have a death wish that humankind had been put in the position of inadvertently satisfying?

The armada was in motion, a great swath of ships and science, when the answer came to him. Rushing as fast as his aged legs would carry him, he hurried toward the bridge. In the vastness of the great ship he lost his way several times, despite the instructions available to him in each lift.

When he finally succeeded in finding his way to the central, shielded core of the *Wellington*, he had to identify himself several times before he could gain access to Fouad. She was seated in the captain's command chair, in charge of the ship but not the strategy it would execute. That was the province of the group of general officers seated off to one side, facing one another across a wide, oval table from which projected upward a perfect three-dimensional portrait of the Pitarian system. A cloud of glowing pinpoints was moving toward the sun at its center, each pinpoint a ship. Levi was put in mind of midges attacking a dog.

"Hello, Mr. Levi." Her musician's hands rested on controls; her trained soprano voice commanded more destructive power than humankind had ignorantly unleashed upon itself since the beginning of its struggling civilization. "Feeling well?"

"Tired," he told her. "Tired, and worried."

"We're all worried," she replied. Before her hovered a tridimensional image similar to the one being closely scrutinized by the general staff, only somewhat reduced in scale. "Everyone is waiting for something to happen."

"What will you do if the Pitar do not respond?" Fascinated as always by technology he did not understand, Levi stared at the perfect, hovering representation of the space in which the ship was moving.

"Place ourselves in orbit around the first of the Twin Worlds.

Deliver the ultimatum drawn up by the world council." She shrugged without smiling. "React to their reaction. If they continue to do nothing, the first landing parties will go down. These will be backed by heavy armor and orbital firepower. Once our forces have acquired a beachhead on the surface the choices remaining to the Pitar will be considerably reduced. Basically, they'll have to decide whether to opt for capitulation or seppuku. After securing the outer of the Twin Worlds, the armada will move on to the second and hopefully repeat the process."

Levi nodded. "What happens if they do submit without a fight?"

Fouad looked at him closely. "Is that what you think is going to happen?"

"No, but at this point the possibility cannot be entirely discounted."

She turned away from him, back to the glowing, in-depth representation. "That's not my department. I'll do what the general staff tells me to do. They in turn have their orders from the world council. All I know is that there's a predetermined sequence of actions whose degree of reaction is calibrated according to how the Pitar respond." Her jawline firmed. "To one extent or another, they are to be punished for what they did on Treetrunk."

"You asked me what I thought was going to happen." Levi watched her expectantly.

The captain's interest was piqued. "You have an idea?"

"I think so. You know, among the original Twelve Tribes the Levites were the scholars. I do not feel like I belong here, on a warship, preparing to engage in mass destruction."

"Your unhappiness is noted," she replied curtly. "Tell me what you think."

"I've studied the Pitar ever since they first arrived on Earth aboard the *Chagos*."

"I know that." Her tone was impatient. "Get to the point, old man. In case you haven't noticed, there's an invasion in progress."

"Sorry. There are a number of ways I could put it scientifically, but I see no need to couch an opinion in complex systematic jargon. Suffice to say that the Pitar are homebodies."

"They don't colonize. They told us that from the first." Fouad tried to divide her attention between the clustered general staff, the view tridee before her and its accompanying heads-up displays, and the lugubrious sage standing next to her seat. "It was one of the reasons their complicity in the massacre was so hard for so many to accept."

"They're not just homebodies. They're fanatical about the Twin Worlds. Except for occasional excursions to places like Earth and Hivehom, and deviate adventures such as Treetrunk, they do not leave their home system. Not only are they not colonizers, they are not big on straightforward exploration. They simply do not like to leave home."

"Which means what? You do have a point, don't you?"

"I think so. What I am trying to say is that all the energy, and effort, and advanced technological development we have put into spreading ourselves outward, they have focused inward."

She frowned and idly adjusted the neural jack above her left ear that allowed her direct communication with the rest of the armada, her own staff, and the *Wellington*'s intelligence center. "So you're saying that . . . ?"

A little anxious himself now, Levi interrupted her in order to state the thought. "Everything we have put into offense, they may have concentrated on defense."

It was not long thereafter that the *Wellington* was rocked by explosion and near catastrophe, and the armada found itself fully and desperately engaged.

Extending in their respective orbits outward from Pitar's star were three worlds of various mien, none suitable for permanent habitation. Then the closely aligned planets numbered four and five, the Twin Worlds of the Pitarian Dominion. Between the fifth planet and the sixth, which happened also to be the first of four gas giants, was not one but two asteroid belts. While one lay in the normal plane of the ecliptic, the second occupied an orbit almost perpendicular to the first. Among this mass of planetary debris were a good many planetoidal objects of considerable size.

Every one of which had been transformed by the Pitar into an armed and shielded attack-and-support station.

In those first lunatic moments frantic commands ricocheted between ships at the speed of light. Humans and their machines slipped instantly into battle mode, each functioning efficiently and effectively. In this it was difficult to say who had the greater advantage. Machines offered speed and reliability, humans the ability to improvise in response to the unexpected. Organic and inorganic had spent several hundred years evolving in tandem to perfect the art of combat.

On the other hand, in spite of the unprecedented ferocity of the human assault and despite all their racial introspection and paranoia, the Pitar did not fold up and slink quietly back to their homeworlds.

Interstellar space is unimaginably vast. Even between planets there is room enough to lose a thousand ships. But the physics that can follow the tracks of tiny comets and minuscule asteroids are also adept at locating the operational drives designed to push vessels through space-plus. And a vessel that is propelled by anything less takes months to journey from one planetary body to another.

So while humans and Pitar swam in inky nothingness, their respective machines utilized far more sensitive instruments than eyes and ears to plot each other's courses. Every time a ship of the armada attempted to pass within the orbits of the intersecting asteroid belts it found itself confronted by two or more Pitarian warcraft. Each human vessel was parsecs from home while support for the defending ships was, astronomically speaking, an eye blink away.

And the Pitar were capable. Avoiding confrontation wherever possible, they concentrated exclusively on countering any approach to the Twin Worlds. Initially, fear of active counterattack dominated much of the general staff's strategic thinking. As the days became weeks and the weeks months it became clear that Pitarian tactics included such thrusts only insofar as they related to their defense. No attempt was made, even by a single suicidal ship, to threaten Earth or any of the colony worlds. Everything the Pitar had, every armed vessel they could throw into the conflict, remained close to home. Not one ventured beyond the Pitarian heliosphere.

The attacking humans tried everything. When a deliberate concentration of forces in one place was met by an energetic and equivalent Pitarian response, the battle planners went to the opposite extreme by suggesting an attempted englobement of one of the Twin Worlds. Reacting aggressively and quickly, the Pitar promptly dispersed their forces in precisely the most opportune fashion to counter the widespread assault. Probes of sectors presumed weak were beaten back by Pitarian forces of unexpected strength.

Missiles launched at the fifth world were detected, tracked, intercepted and destroyed. The residents of the Dominion suffered no casualties as a result of the invasion of their system. Requests to parley were met with strident animosity. It became clear that while humans had originally taken an immediate liking to the Pitar, the humanoid aliens felt very differently about their smaller mammalian counterparts. This did not take the form of outright loathing: The Pitar were too courtly for that. It was more on the order of a general contempt for the human species as a whole. The Pitar would not talk, would not discuss any sort of armistice with the lowly humans, until every last ship of the armada had left the sacred system of the Twin Worlds.

It didn't matter, since they refused to apologize for what they had done on Treetrunk or discuss handing over those responsible. One Pitar spoke for all, and all Pitar spoke for one. Admitting no guilt, they therefore dispersed it among themselves and repeatedly commanded the disgusting, detestable invading beings to depart, as their very presence constituted a corruption in the sight of the hallowed Dominion.

Their attitude helped Levi and his colleagues to unravel the rationale behind many prior enigmas: why no embassy had been allowed to open on either of the Twin Worlds, for example, and why visits to the Dominion had been prohibited. It had nothing to do with racial shyness or reticence. The Pitar were not coy—they were overbearing. Nasty, uncouth humans could not be allowed to defile the purity of the homeworlds.

To what end their plundering force had removed the reproductive organs of thousands of human females from Treetrunk continued to remain a mystery. Here it was left to an admixture of Levi's people and researching biologists to speculate on possible reasons. Many were put forth, some fantastic, not a few revolting. Among the facts that were assembled in the ongoing attempt to build an explanation was the realization that from the moment the Pitar had been contacted until the day when the armada had emerged from space-plus on the outskirts of the Dominion, no one had ever seen a Pitarian child.

Had some factor still unknown, psychological or biological, caused them to stop reproducing? In carrying out the atrocity on Treetrunk, were they seeking a means for ensuring the continuation of their species? Had that means been found and implemented, and if so, did humankind really want to be informed of the methodology? Many people on Earth and elsewhere had relatives who had perished in the extermination of intelligent life on Argus V. Levi and his colleagues were not so sure that they would be happier or otherwise better off to learn precisely what had happened to some of their deceased relations.

Certainly the Pitar did nothing to enlighten their attackers. Even tentative requests for explanations were dismissed out of hand. They would not talk, coldly refusing all attempts at communication with what they could now openly admit to regarding as an inferior life-form. Levi and the rest of the scientists and researchers who accompanied the armada grew increasingly frustrated. The uniformed masses who crewed the ships labored under no such mental strain. Some of them, too, had lost friends or kin on Treetrunk. Their interests were much more focused: They did not need to understand; all they wanted to do was kill Pitar.

Five months into the attack the ships of the armada and their frustrated personnel began to be rotated. New ships arrived from Earth and the colonies crewed by eager, fresh enlistees.

They opposed an enemy whose soldiers faced no long journeys through space-plus, who could find ease and relaxation within a day's flight of their duty station. In battle they found themselves confronting concentrations of ships that could be quickly and easily repaired and restocked. It was the classic battlefield situation of an overextended attacker trying to break down the defenses of a determined and well-entrenched enemy, translocated to an interstellar environment.

Eight months passed without any change in the line of battle. The Pitar would not permit a single human vessel of any size to cross beyond the orbits of the intersecting asteroid belts. The attacking humans would not give up. Determination and not skill or strategy became the defining factor on both sides.

While ships might stand still, weapons research did not. For every new means of attack the humans refined and threw into combat, the Pitar developed a counter. High-energy beams were met with high-energy deflectors. Subatomic particle guns designed to disrupt communications on board opposing vessels were intercepted and shunted harmlessly into space-plus by low-power versions of deep-space drives. Larger, faster missiles were met with small interceptors that were faster and more agile still. Space was filled with the scattering of shattered matter from fusion weapons that never reached their intended targets.

Now and then a ship engaged in skirmishing would take a hit, suffering damage or on rare occasions, implosion. At such moments hundreds, even thousands of lives would be snuffed out of existence, vanishing into the icy limbo of the void. Each such loss made the Pitar more intractable and the humans more unforgiving.

Finally admitting after ten months of failed attack that they were unable to break through the defenses of the Dominion, the general staff debated how best to proceed. Breaking off the offensive was unthinkable: Now spread across a number of worlds, humankind would not hear of it. Ending the confrontation would imply that the Pitar had won, that they had consummated their barbarism without suffering any penalty. Such an abomination could not be tolerated.

It was remarked that while no human warship had been able to reach either of the Pitar homeworlds, neither had any of the aliens' craft been able to travel a sufficiently safe distance from those twin planets to safely engage its full drive and make the jump to space-plus. Trapped in the glare of human vigilance, the Pitar were effectively confined to their homeworlds. Other species, however, were not.

On the face of it, the notion of a blockade in space seemed unworkable. Even the comparatively tiny distances between planets allowed ample room for a ship to enter into or emerge from space-plus. Once back in normal space, however, any and every such vessel was vulnerable.

The word was passed, though not without trepidation. How would neutral intelligences such as the Quillp react to being banned from an entire system with which they had no quarrel? More importantly, how would the combative and powerful AAnn react to a unilateral attempt to restrict their access to a people with whom they enjoyed amicable if not affectionate relations?

Before such a tactic could be tried, it was the turn of the diplomats to go on the offensive. The Quillp were puzzled. But while the ornithorps were expansionists, colonizing empty worlds in the manner of humankind, they were by nature inherently unaggressive. As might have been expected, the Unop-Patha wanted nothing whatsoever to do with the ongoing conflict, preferring to stay as far away from both the arrogant Pitar and the demonstrably demented humans as possible. Several minor species, each confined to a single inhabitable world, were not important enough to enter into the equation.

Among known intelligences with enough strength to affect the balance, that left the AAnn and the thranx. The insectoids were not only amenable to the pronouncement, but had from the start been quietly supportive of the human attack on the Dominion.

The AAnn were more difficult to factor. Following intense

lobbying by human diplomats, they agreed not to send any of their vessels into the Pitarian system until the military impasse there had been resolved in favor of one side or the other. Their understanding was marked by repeated thranx warnings to the effect that if the Pitar should succeed in seriously degrading humankind's military capability, it would not be past the AAnn to take advantage of the situation. In such an event, probing AAnn attacks on one or more human colonies could reasonably be anticipated.

The world council and the general staff separately advised the distressed thranx that even in the event of an unanticipated catastrophic human defeat in battle, sufficient forces had been held in reserve to ensure the safety of Earth and every one of its colonies. The thranx accepted this reassurance with a certain aplomb, but remained privately watchful and troubled. It was wonderful to observe the passionate confidence displayed by the humans, but confidence had never been of much use against the AAnn.

With every species that could possibly be impacted having been contacted and dealt with, the general staff formally announced the imposition of the blockade. Safe and assured on their twin homeworlds, the Pitar were neither impressed nor intimidated. Tens of thousands of individuals on hundreds of ships actively supported by the populations of multiple worlds maintained and strengthened the stalemate.

It was not a static standoff. From time to time specially designated components of the blockading human fleet would attempt to penetrate the seemingly immutable Pitarian defenses. Each time, utilizing newly conceived tactics and weaponry, their crews would set off full of faith and in high spirits. Each time they would return, thwarted and dispirited. And there were those terrible times when some did not return at all.

Wars of attrition are not always won by the besiegers, no matter how resourceful and resolved. Having nowhere to go, no hidden retreat, no refuge held in reserve, the Pitar fought with incredible tenacity and determination. Though their ships would hurl themselves entire, crew and all, into an enemy attacking pattern in order to disrupt it and preserve possession of a seemingly minor, insignificant asteroid, they would not commit a single vessel to an attack. Their philosophy of war was wholly defensive, to protect the twin homeworlds at all cost but not to otherwise directly challenge an invader.

The members of the armada's commanding general staff were rotated along with enlisted personnel and low-ranking civilian affiliates, but they were united in their frustration. As one admiral put it, the blockade was war conducted entirely under cover of night, where night covered nothing. There could be no surprise attacks launched on an alerted, technologically sophisticated species. Instrumentation that never slept saw to that. Mind could only do so much before it was necessary for machine to take over. For a soldier it was hard to sustain the energy and alertness demanded of a fight with an enemy one could not see. Even the enemy's worlds were no more than another bright couple of points of light in the galactic sky.

Yet no one thought of giving up. Treetrunk could not be forgotten. Even so, despite the comparative recentness of the outrage, it was already starting to fade a little in the minds of a small but growing segment of the population. The media strove to maintain interest, but a blockade is not like a series of dramatic encounters in space. The battle for control of stasis did not play as well on the evening tridee as an invasion.

Something had to be done. Something had to happen to change the unacceptable status quo, and both military and civilian strategists realized that in that regard sooner would be better than later. By now more than a year had passed since the *Wellington* and the rest of the armada had entered the system of the Pitarian Dominion to the cheers and vengeful shouts of the majority of humankind. Almost that much time had passed since there had been any perceptible change in that status. In the interim, the cheers had given way to grudging acceptance of the blockade, and the vengeful shouts to orchestrated growlings of support. The military was aware of the threat of germinating discontent, but there was nothing more they could do than what they were already doing.

Others, however, had different ideas.

19

"Why should we help them any more than we already have? Why should the hives, *cruk!ck*, get involved?"

"Yes," another member of the circle agreed. "There is no compelling reason for putting thranx lives at risk." Leaning back, the speaker raised all four hands in order to gesture simultaneously. "These humans do not even like us!"

"I can just see," still a third sarcastically declared, "these humans risking their own lives to aid us if the situation were reversed. Put them in a tunnel with only us facing danger, and they will turn and run the other way."

When the dissenters had had their say, the Tri-Eint Debreljinav activated the pickup before her and was respectfully conceded queen's dominance. Since the advent of hormonal extracts that had enabled any thranx female to lay fertile eggs, the lineage of hereditary queendom had vanished from thranx civilization. Subsequent to the enforced abdication of procreative royalty, many heraldic vestiges of those primitive times had assumed highly formalized places in thranx culture. One such was the rotating speaking position of queen's dominance.

No member of the Grand Council was more respected than Debreljinav. Not many were older; few were as perceptive. Chosen leader of both the hive Jin and the clan Av, she had advanced to the exalted position of eint at an unusually early age, retaining the post while acquiring honor and prestige over the years. Now she could rise no higher, being one of those the great mass hive of thranx had chosen to govern not only Hivehom but the colony worlds as well.

"It is clear what benefits accrue to us if we remain neutral, like the Quillp. But what might we lose by doing so, and what more might we gain by becoming actively involved?"

An eint seated among the opposition responded without hesitation. "We lose nothing because we have nothing to gain." Sympathetic stridulation by those of like mind momentarily filled the room with the din of a hundred improperly tuned violas.

"Nothing?" a supporter of intervention argued. "We have cordial relations with the humans. Aiding them in their war would, if not make formal allies of them, leave them in our debt. When the next serious confrontation with the AAnn arises—and make no mistake, it will arise—we will be able to call upon these tumultuous mammals for assistance. Just the ability to do that will give even the most belligerent among the emperor's court pause."

"Who says the AAnn fear the humans?" a voice shouted from the other side. "What makes you think the scaled people factor the mammals into their equations?"

"Because while the AAnn may be malicious and rapacious, they are not stupid." This time it was supportive stridulations that rose in volume from the other side of the table.

The racing noise receded as Debreljinav prefigured her speech with an appropriate gesture. "Do the humans truly hate us so much that they would even refuse our help?"

A representative of one of the technical classifications rose. He was not an eint and was present, along with a number of others, because he possessed the ability to contribute special insight into specific aspects of the debate.

"Only a small number of xenophobes and fanatics among the bipeds actually hate us. Among the rest there are many who openly enjoy our company and are not afraid to say so." Compound eyes swept the attentive chamber. "The vast majority of humans belong to neither grouping. This mass remains unsure of us and our motives."

"Ingrates!" a leader of the opposition bellowed. There was discord until the Tri-Eint Sevrepesut could restore order and return dominance to the patient female standing off to his left.

Intimidated, the specialist waited for Debreljinav's gesture of encouragement to respond to the interruptive expletive. "Humans have short memories but—"

"Fine candidates for allies in time of trouble!" another representative of the skeptical shouted.

"But they are capable of grand kindnesses and gratitude. I believe that those who advocate intercession are correct. In so doing we would gain valuable allies against the AAnn, and against any others who might one day threaten the great hive." Whistles of derision and rising stridulation threatened to drown him out, but this time the specialist would not be denied.

"The AAnn Empire is strong and growing more powerful by the day! If we will not aid the humans in their just fight against the Pitar to make them our allies, then we must aid them so that the AAnn cannot. Or is that a possibility that the distinguished eints prefer not to ponder?"

The reaction from supporters of intervention as well as those of the opposition showed that it was a notion that had not been much discussed. Everyone hoped that in an ideal cosmos the humans would ally themselves with the thranx against the AAnn. Few cared to contemplate the consequences should the aggressive, militaristically accomplished mammals choose to take the side of the predacious reptilians instead.

"The humans would never support the AAnn in a disagreement with us." The eint who ventured this observation did not sound very convincing even to herself.

"Why not?" a supporter of intervention countered. "One of your own has just pointed out how much they dislike us."

"We must make them like us." Debreljinav's declaration carried the full force and weight of her considerable personality. "We cannot afford it to be otherwise."

"It will not be any easy task." The Eint Jouteszimfeq was anything but encouraging as he looked around the circle. "I have tried to study everything there is to be known about the humans. Individually they are sound, but their mass psychology is unstable. Small, insignificant things can induce vast swings in their collective consciousness. Worse, these critical effectives can in themselves be meaningless and unsupported. But by the time realization sets in, the damage has already been done." His antennae parted to sense the greatest possible number of his fellow debaters.

"We must move actively to prevent this from happening. Although it does not sound in and of itself especially scientific, making the humans 'like' us should be among our very first priorities. Simultaneously, we must endeavor to deal with those thranx who have difficulty tolerating the sight, sound, and presence of humans."

"Don't you mean the smell?" someone who wished not to be identified interjected. General whistling followed, eventually to be suppressed by Debreljinav's four-armed gesturing.

"I myself am rather more concerned with the eventual disposition of human muscle than their scent." Respectful quiet again filled the chamber. "If we cannot induce the humans to become our allies, then we must strive to make them our friends. Since we can do nothing about our shape and ancestry, which is what appears to constitute the principal basis of human dislike for us, we must find other ways of convincing them that we are worthy of their trust." Antennae spread and at the ready, she gazed around the chamber. "As a tri-eint among you, I am open to suggestions."

There were almost as many positive suggestions as there were opposing views. Unlike in ancient times, those in the minority did not suffer to have assorted limbs amputated as a consequence of losing an argument. In place of jaws and teeth and primitive weapons, only sharp words were employed. In many instances, these cut deeply enough.

Field Marshal MacCunn was conversing with Admiral Yirghiz when a comtech interrupted them. Yirghiz accepted the missive, perused it briefly, and then passed it on to MacCunn. The field marshal's face featured the protuberant, bony brows of a very early Cro-Magnon. It saddled him with an unfortunate countenance that was the source of many jokes among those within his command. Having risen from the ranks himself, he was delighted to so painlessly be of service to his troops.

"What's this about an alien task force entering Pitarian space?"

Yirghiz rose as general quarters sounded. "I haven't a clue, Hamish—but I have a feeling we're about to find out. I only hope that it's neutral, or if not, that it isn't materializing in response to a coordinated effort with the Pitar."

The bandy-legged MacCunn had to employ a longer stride to keep pace with the lanky admiral. "That would imply some sort of offensive gesture on the part of the Pitar, something totally out of character for them."

"I concur." Yirghiz nodded sharply. "Which doesn't mean we can afford to take the possibility lightly. Hence the automatic call to general quarters."

Long before the two senior officers reached the bridge at the center of the *Tamerlane*, the great warship and the rest of the blockading fleet on this side of the Dominion's sun were on full battle alert, ready to extend a polite, formal welcome to the as yet unrecognized newcomers, or to blow them out of the firmament, as the occasion demanded.

MacCunn took up his position alongside the admiral. Yirghiz was barking orders before his backside contacted the contoured command chair. "Incoming—identification!"

Captain Coulis was ready with a response. "Not ours. Not Pitar." A generally subdued murmur of relief sighed its way around the bridge at this announcement. "Thranx."

Both senior officers frowned. Their confusion had plenty of company among the rest of the bridge complement. "What are the bugs doing here?" MacCunn wondered aloud. "And with a task force, albeit a small one." He glanced in the captain's direction. "It is a small one?"

Coulis was studying a fully dimensional tridee replete with brightly hued embedded analyses. "One dreadnought. Not *Wellington*-class, taking into account that thranx design differs from ours. Nothing else appears to be bigger than destroyer-class. No cruisers, no smaller escorting craft."

"Odd configuration." Yirghiz frowned. "Too weak to participate in a serious fight, much more impressive than is required for a social call." He raised his voice as he again addressed Coulis. "Hail them, Captain, and find out what they're doing here. They're aware of the quarantine. See if you can find out what they want."

"Initial intership communications protocol is already being delimited, sir," the captain replied. At the moment her eyes were as busy as her fingers.

Answer and explanation arrived simultaneously mere moments later. Coulis swiveled around in her seat to address the two senior officers. Her expression effectively communicated her confusion.

"The vessels are indeed thranx, gentlemen. They are carrying a representative of the Grand Council of the Great Hive." Her gaze traveled from one senior officer to the other. "It wants to come aboard."

This was not the sort of decision either of the two men had expected to have to make when they had arisen at the start of the current shift. Yirghiz responded while MacCunn eloquently said nothing.

"This is your ship, Captain. Not being a strategic judgment, the decision whether or not to receive visitors is entirely yours."

"I'm a starship captain," Coulis replied. "This is a matter for diplomats."

Now MacCunn spoke up. "Not when a vessel is on combat station. No, it's your call, Captain."

Coulis rubbed at an uncooperative eyebrow. "No ship of the armada has seen any action for several weeks now. The next tactics are still in the process of being schematized. I see no reason to refuse such a request from a neutral power." She smiled laconically. "If it's secrets of military technology the thranx are after there are far easier ways to steal them."

"I've never met a thranx. Walked around tridee holos, but never encountered one in the flesh." Yirghiz was curious. "Let's see what they want here."

MacCunn grunted softly. "To try and ascertain who's winning, I would imagine. If that's the case, they'll need to use their imaginations."

Both men and everyone else on the *Tamerlane* and within the armada who obtained a good look at the thranx craft were suitably impressed. The KK-drive type vessels were sleek and well fitted out, their design and construction bespeaking a technology as advanced as anything humankind could devise. Nor just because the alien dreadnought massed almost as much as the *Wellington* or the *Tamerlane* could it be assumed that it was the most powerful ship in the thranx arsenal.

Insisting that any formalities be kept to a minimum, the insectoid emissary transferred to one of the flagship's locks via a small shuttle. There was some confusion resulting in a delay in the visitor being welcomed when it was discovered that he had a personal escort, but the matter was quickly resolved without rancor. As Coulis pointed out, it was natural to expect so high ranking an individual of any species to be accompanied by attendants. It was explained by the thranx that the emissary's two escorts were necessary to look after her health and not her security, and those on board the flagship could well believe it as soon as that worthy was helped from the shuttle's lock.

The thranx was very old. One of her ovipositors had been surgically removed, the consequence of a disease that was not mentioned. The other double-curled egg-laying appendage had lost so much of its natural spring that it lay nearly flat against her back. Instead of the familiar smooth blue-green, her exoskeleton was a rich, deep purple, the chitin worn rough and pebbly in places. The golden compound eyes did not shine as brightly as did those of her solicitous escorts, but the antennae were ever-moving and alert. The characteristically soft thranx voice was strong, spilling words and clicks and whistles without vacillation.

MacCunn and Yirghiz met her with translator in tow. That individual's presence was not required. The emissary spoke very good Terranglo. For his part, Yirghiz looked forward to trying out his stock of memorized Thranx phrases. He was terrible at grammar and could not figure out how to properly integrate the requisite gestures into the conversation, but he was a good whistler and an excellent mimic. Becoming truly fluent in the combination of Terranglo words and Thranx expressions that was evolving into a kind of mutual patois among the young of both species was beyond an old soldier like himself, but he had felt bound to try. He had also memorized a cache of stock AAnn phrases and could manage brief declarations in the single Pitar dialect. By contrast, the field marshal was a linguistic mute. But then, Yirghiz reminded himself with a hidden smile, MacCunn wasn't much of a conversationalist in his own tongue.

"Welcome aboard." Stepping forward, the admiral introduced himself and the field marshal before extending a hand palm down, fingers slightly spread and inclined upward. The elderly alien's antennae dipped forward to brush his fingertips.

"I am the Di-Eint Haajujurprox. From the Great Hive I bring you greetings and the taste of friendship."

"We are pleased to receive you." A delighted Yirghiz waved off the translator who was standing by, a young woman who was plainly relieved that her skills apparently would not be necessary. The bug's Terranglo was mellifluous and only slightly inflected. The insectoids had a much easier time with the simpler human tongue than humans did with the complex combination of words, clicks, whistles, and gestures that constituted High Thranx.

Alongside him, he observed MacCunn striving to appear inconspicuous as he inhaled repeatedly of the air in the lock. In the vicinity of the three thranx it had become suffused with the aromatic essence of a complex perfume. In respect of scent, age had not dimmed the emissary's personal bouquet.

"Won't you please walk with us?" Turning, Yirghiz led the way.

As they strolled toward the lift that would take them to a comfortable and private room he noted that unlike the images of thranx he had seen, the emissary never rose up on her four trulegs. She required the use of all six to ambulate adequately. Though wondering how old, in human terms, the visitor might be, he was too polite to ask. Among the thranx such a question might be regarded as normal and natural, or it might be considered intrusive. He did not know. Regardless, it had nothing to do with conventional diplomacy. But he was still curious.

They made small talk until they arrived at the senior officer's lounge. This was cleared, and the diplomatic party made itself comfortable. While the di-eint settled herself onto a makeshift couch of cushions placed end to end on the floor, her escorts remained standing. So did the four armed soldiers who had escorted MacCunn and Yirghiz. While their superiors conversed, the common soldiers eyed one another with unfettered interest.

"This is no place for a casual call," MacCunn began without further preamble. "Your government is aware of the quarantine that we have placed around the inhabited worlds of this system, and the conflict that is ongoing here." He started to cough and reached for a glass of water. When he had recovered sufficiently, he continued.

"We know that your ships are not simply 'passing through.' No one travels through space-plus without a definite destination in mind. So I think—we think—that it's safe to assume you came here to speak with us." He gestured absently, wishing he had Yirghiz's command of alien gesticulation. "We have to ask, Why here, when all previous diplomatic contact has taken place between your representatives and ours on Earth or Hivehom?"

"It was decided," the elderly di-eint replied evenly, "that since the matter to be discussed most directly involved the unfortunate situation here, it would be best to communicate directly with those of your kind who are most intimately involved." Her antennae dipped sharply forward. Somewhat startled, MacCunn drew back slightly. Yirghiz did not move.

"You know that we are outraged at what the Pitar did to your colony of Treetrunk. As sentient beings, their actions there horrified every hive. Ever since, there has been much discussion among my kind as to whether it would be appropriate for us to make our displeasure known in a more proactive fashion." Her finely shaped head continually shifted from one human to the other, even though the exceptional peripheral vision provided by her compound eyes meant that she could survey nearly the entire room without moving it at all. The cranial posturing was to assure the two senior humans that she was indeed focusing her attention on them.

Glancing in MacCunn's direction, Yirghiz saw no enlightenment there. Perhaps the field marshal was preoccupied with his persistent bowel problems, the admiral mused. That was not the case. MacCunn simply had nothing to say and was content to let his colleague take the lead in composing their response. It did not mean he was not paying attention.

"Could you be more specific as to what you mean when you say 'more proactive'?"

"I have come here on behalf of the Great Hive authorized to propose a formal military alliance between our peoples. We want to help you in your fight against these Pitar," the di-eint stated.

This time MacCunn was quick to respond. "Why?" he asked curtly. "So you were outraged by what they did on Treetrunk. All intelligent species were outraged. Only you are offering to help. Outrage is by itself an insufficient reason for actively engaging in interstellar warfare."

"Is it?" Many-lensed eyes shifted to face the field marshal. When he did not respond, the di-eint gestured acknowledgment. "Very well. It is as you say. There are other reasons. While a large faction finds the outrage sufficient for us to respond, they are not a majority. It was necessary to build an adequate consensus, corollary by corollary." She shifted her awkward position on the queue of cushions.

"As you know, we have been locked in an ongoing battle with the Empire of the AAnn since before your kind encountered ours. The AAnn are a devious, ruthless, expansionist race."

"We've had no trouble with the AAnn," Yirghiz felt compelled to point out.

"The AAnn are also very patient. They are evaluating your resources." The elderly alien leaned toward them. "They are especially interested in the present conflict. While they are too clever to aid the Pitar directly, they are delighted to watch them deplete your resources."

MacCunn frowned. "Why should they care who wins? As you say, they are completely neutral."

"On the face of it, they are. But the Pitar have nothing the AAnn want and pose no threat to their strategies. The Pitar are not colonizers. Humans are, very much so. As are the AAnn. As both spheres of influence continue to expand, they will inevitably begin to overlap. There will come a time when tenancy of a new world falls into dispute. If the Pitar succeed in severely weakening you, or are still tying down a large portion of your military strength, the AAnn will not hesitate to take advantage of the situation that results."

The field marshal was nodding slowly. This was an explanation he had heard before and could understand. "So by helping us against the Pitar you hope to ensure that our strength is not diminished, and that it will be available as a counterweight to future AAnn expansion."

She did not nod. Adoption of human gestures was a habitude for the young. But she did indicate her acknowledgment. "We also expect this alliance to operate in the opposite direction."

"Of course you do." As much was obvious to Yirghiz. "If your government is going to send its citizens to risk their lives on our behalf, it would be unreasonable not to expect the same from us. If the AAnn attack you, you'd want to be able to ask for our help."

"It'll never happen." MacCunn was darkly assured. "The world council will never vote to send ships and personnel to help defend—" He started to say what was in his mind, and hastily substituted something else. "—your kind."

With their fixed exoskeleton the thranx were incapable of smiling. Nor were the relevant inflections detectable even to the more linguistically adept Yirghiz. It did not matter. The di-eint's response contained sufficient inherent sarcasm.

"Bugs, you mean."

MacCunn replied calmly. "I didn't say that."

"You do not have to. It doesn't matter." The di-eint's antennae dipped and bobbed. "My government is prepared to leave the question of what degree of response your kind would provide should such a confrontation arise for future discussion. Our overriding concern is to assist you now."

"Before the Pitar can weaken us to the point where we might be unable to effectively resist the incursions of the AAnn."

"You may draw your own conclusions. The important thing is that you accept. And there is another reason."

Yirghiz was growing impatient to return to the bridge. "What else?"

"We happen to like you. Not all of my kind feel thusly, but a great many do. We do not like the Pitar. Not after what they have done, showing neither remorse nor repentance. But for an accident of biology it might have been a thranx world they despoiled. On a more informal level, I am compelled to say that *I* like you."

Yirghiz's instinct was to reply in kind, but he found he could not. However convivial it might be, the creature seated opposite him was still simply too . . . buggy. That was not a rational, scientific response, he knew, but he could not help it. Like so many he knew, he remained a prisoner of his racial history, of memories of thousands of years of competing with far smaller distant cousins of the thranx for food, for space, for very existence.

That would not prevent him, however, from accepting their help.

"It's not within my purview to agree to so momentous a proposition." He gestured in the field marshal's direction. "No one on this ship or in the armada has that power. Believe me, I personally would be glad to accept all and any additional assistance, regardless of its origin."

"Because you are going nowhere here," Haajujurprox told him.

MacCunn bridled. "We are making progress. With each engagement the Pitar lose ships and fighters. We're wearing them down."

"And they are wearing you down. We are quite capable of

monitoring human opinion. In a war of attrition conducted in the vastness of interstellar space, it is the well-emplaced defenders who usually win. With the forces at your command you cannot break through their defenses."

"Our land-based production plants and orbital assembly facilities are turning out newer and better ships and weapons." The field marshal's voice was tight.

"As are the Pitar, who have the advantage of bringing them to bear sooner and more easily than you can. It is not unreasonable to imagine that they might succeed in out-producing you. They have the resources of two planets as highly developed as Earth operating in close proximity to one another, whereas your subsidiary colony worlds are widely scattered. The raw resources of not one but two extensive asteroid belts are theirs to draw upon. Your position here becomes less, not more, tenable over time."

MacCunn swallowed hard. "Denigrating the efforts of the people you propose to help strikes me as a peculiar way to initiate an alliance."

"Truth is not denigration," the elderly thranx countered. "Mathematics is not prejudiced and does not take sides." Glancing down, she consulted a delicate device strapped to the forepart of one truhand. "By this time your world council should have reached a decision on our offer. Our arrival here, you see, was timed to coincide with the very secret debate that has been taking place within your government for several of your weeks."

MacCunn and Yirghiz exchanged a startled glance. The look was sufficient between friends to convey the awareness that neither man knew something relevant that he had neglected to tell the other.

As if choreographed, both senior officers' private readers vibrated for attention. Removing the instruments, the two men read in silence. Despite herself, Haajujurprox was impatient to receive more than visual reactions from the humans.

Sighing heavily, Yirghiz slipped his recorder back into its holster. "The actual communication was received before you set foot on this ship. It took the time we have spent talking to decode, recheck, and decode the recheck. If your skills in battle are as precise as the timing of your diplomacy, your help will be most welcome indeed."

The di-eint interpreted this promptly. "Then your government is agreed?"

MacCunn nodded briskly. "Any help you want to give us is hereby accepted. Details of a full alliance will continue to be discussed and debated. But in the interim, if you should happen to extirpate a Pitarian warship or two, the people of Earth and its colonies will be pleased not to look too deeply into questions of your motivation."

"Excellent." Haajujurprox started to rise, began to tremble, and slumped back toward the cushions. Her twin escorts rushed to assist the elderly di-eint.

Without realizing it, Yirghiz had started to do the same. It had been an instinctive gesture. Now he stood more slowly, watching as the two younger thranx assisted their elder in rising. One helped to support her while the other carefully removed the line of cushions from beneath the aged abdomen so that she would not have to step awkwardly over them.

Why had he started to go to her aid? The admiral found himself caught in a welter of unexpected emotions. Intelligent beyond doubt she was, but the emissary was still virtually a giant bug. He didn't like bugs. But he found that he was very much starting to like this one.

Not a bug, he told himself firmly. It's only the shape. Ignore the shape—or learn to see it differently.

MacCunn was speaking softly in his usual, clipped, formal tones. "We will work with the commanders of your vessels to include them in our general battle schematics. We certainly don't expect them to lead any thrusts, but their status as active reserves will be most welcome."

The di-eint rotated her head to a greater extreme than any human could manage in order to look back at the senior officer. "Don't you trust us, Field Marshal MacCunn? Or do you need to first see dead thranx bodies floating in space to be convinced of our earnestness in this matter?" When he started to reply, she raised a hand to forestall him. Yirghiz was quietly amazed to see him comply.

"No, do not try to explain yourself. Though I have not experienced them personally, I am well aware of human feelings toward my kind. You cannot help it. In this and many other ways you are still prisoners of your primitive past. Given time and effort, we hope to be able to effect changes in that."

Yirghiz stepped into the uncomfortable breach. "Blowing a few Pitarian warships out of existence would be an excellent way to begin."

Haajujurprox gesticulated acknowledgment, not pausing to wonder if any of the humans in the room understood the meaning of the gesture.

Flanking their superiors, the two thranx and four human soldiers formed up an escort. The meeting concluded, they found themselves eying each other very differently than they had been when it had first commenced. The thranx studied the flexible, flowing movements of their bipedal counterparts with bemused curiosity, while the human soldiers could not keep themselves from inhaling deeply and repeatedly. Of such small exchanges are great events fashioned.

MacCunn was constitutionally unable to keep himself from discussing strategy, even during what should have been a walk marked by casual conversation.

"Your task force will complement our ships nicely in sector twelve. We've been weaker there than I would like for nearly two months now."

"Task force?" Haajujurprox adjusted her valentine-shaped head to peer up at him.

"The one dreadnought you brought and the escorts that are accompanying it." MacCunn smiled, wondering if the venerable thranx knew the meaning and intent of the expression.

"My dear Field Marshal MacCunn, *cl!rrik,* that is no task force. That is our scouting force. Subsequent to the final approval by your full government of the terms of our mutual arrangement, a substantial portion of the Hive fleet will arrive here within days. Less what is required to maintain the adequate defense of Hivehom, Trix, Willow-Wane, and Calm Nursery, of course. While the AAnn wait in hopes of seeing you weakened, they would be more eager still to take advantage of any perceived frailty on our part."

MacCunn looked at Yirghiz, who was silent but visibly elated. "Then we can expect the assistance of a few more of your warships?"

"It is recognized that if the defense of Pitar is to be broken, any adjustment in the balance of forces must be significant. Otherwise the effort would be wasted."

The two senior officers indicated their agreement, reiterating that the blockading force would be grateful for any help, no matter how limited or unobtrusive.

Six days later two hundred and sixty-five thranx warships dropped out of space-plus around Pitar's sun.

20

The arrival of the unexpectedly impressive thranx forces was met with a unanimity of cheers and a spontaneous outpouring of warmth among the humans who crewed the ships charged with enforcing the quarantine around the defiant and venomous Dominion. The reaction on Earth and throughout the colonies was less homogenous. While delighted at the offer of assistance, a good deal of suspicion was voiced over the terms of the proposal.

The opposition to any formal agreement was led by the highly visible and equally vocal xenophobe faction. Dubious at having to deal on equal terms with giant bugs, the prospect of fighting alongside them and possibly at some point in the future for them drove the most extreme groups into paroxysms of fury. Consequent outbreaks of violence protesting the agreement, while distressing, were effectively contained by the world government. Despite vigorous attempts to do so, these could unfortunately not be concealed from an active and perceptive media. Agitated debate over the virtues and drawbacks of the understanding continued even as thranx warships prepared to go into battle alongside their human counterparts.

The reaction among the thranx was equally divisive, but deliberated with considerably more restraint. In the end the desires and self-serving rationales of both governments prevailed: Thranx warships would fight alongside those of the armada.

It was a moment in time fraught with significance when the order for the first combined attack was transmitted. Several dozen ships began to probe forward on a wide astronomical front, their movement and positioning coordinated by hastily forged closed communications. Throughout the armada tension ran higher than usual. No one knew how well human forces would operate alongside those of the insectoids.

Activity in normal space exposed ships and personnel to counterattack by Pitarian forces. It was impossible to conduct any kind of fight in space-plus, a realm of nonconforming physics where the customary definitions of matter and energy no longer held sway. But on low drive power, conventional weapons could wreak havoc in minutes. Ships could be damaged or destroyed, and thousands could lose their lives. Advancing to within accurate bombardment range of a target world in space-plus was of course impossible. The stress of emerging into a planet's gravitational field, even at a distance where its effects would be greatly reduced, would impact on the sensitive alignment of a ship's KK-drive field and tear it apart as soon as it emerged back into normal space.

So the commingled fleets advanced as rapidly as was feasible, knowing that the Pitar could not shift ships to meet them any faster than they were already traveling. Computation systems stood ready to orchestrate flights of explosives and high-energy weapons. All personnel were at battle stations and on full alert. Over the previous year many such confrontations had riven space in the vicinity of the twin asteroid belts and the innermost gas giant. Everyone hoped this battle would be different than those.

Detecting the incoming ships, the Pitar promptly allocated a force large enough to counter the incursion. As soon as far-ranging instrumentation descried this enemy activity, another human-thranx battle group began to move inward from its position on the far side of the Dominion's sun. As before, their location and movement was noted by the Pitar, and as previously, a sufficiency of warships was reassigned to intercept them.

Within an hour the entire armada, augmented by the substantial thranx force, was in motion, as were all available

Pitarian craft. It was very much like a gigantic chess game, one that involved hundreds of pieces of varying strength engaged in simultaneous motion on an interplanetary scale. Aboard the *Tamerlane* as aboard every ship in the armada, there was hope that the final and deciding battle might at last be at hand: that with the addition of the thranx force the blockaders might at last have enough strength to overwhelm and beat their way past the Pitarian defenders.

It was not to be.

Watching the constantly shifting readout within the flagship's main battle tridee, the lowliest ensign saw what was happening at the same time as general officers like Yirghiz and MacCunn. At first no one could believe it. The ship's battle instrumentation, which automatically compensated for far punier human senses, was quickly checked for error. Nothing was malfunctioning, and subsidiary instruments confirmed the accuracy of all primary modalities.

Pinpoints of light were rising from the vicinity of both the Twin Worlds. Ascending and racing outward along the appropriate vectors to support existing Pitarian defenders. They were prodigal in number, not staggeringly so but still disappointingly abundant. The Pitar had been holding a substantial number of perfectly good ships in reserve, not employing them even for routine patrol or to help rotate ships and crews. Designed to furnish an entirely unsuspected line of defense for the Twin Worlds, their masters were now forced to use them in order to counter the unexpectedly augmented human attack.

MacCunn, for one, did not have to wait for the official report from remote sensors. The moving pinpoints were difficult to count, but he could estimate.

The offensive was called off before any ships could engage. There was no point in risking personnel and material to fight to yet another draw. The efficacy of Pitarian ships, weapons, and tactics had already been amply demonstrated. No one wished to risk thousands of lives to secure a reiteration of what was already well known.

No one died in the aborted sortie, but the sense of disappointment that spread throughout the armada was crushing. Expecting a decisive battle, the ships had instead withdrawn without either side having loosed a single missile or fired so much as a ranging shot. The thranx had broken the status quo, and the Pitar had promptly reestablished it. The thranx commander, a di-eint himself, was apologetic. They would try harder next time. But no more thranx vessels could be expected to participate than those that had already arrived. The rest of the thranx fleet was obliged to remain on home station to defend their respective worlds.

The government of Earth and its colonies tried to minimize the aftermath. No ships had been lost in the most recent engagement, and not a single soldier had died. Furthermore, the clandestine strength of the Pitar had been exposed. They had been forced to reveal the extent of their reserves. As a military argument it was a good one, but it carried little weight with the discontented people of Earth and associated worlds.

Besides, what proof was there that the Pitar were not concealing still additional martial capacity? That the next assault, however greatly enhanced, would not be met by a similar counteraction? What if the Pitar had yet to divulge their full strength? These were questions a cautious military could not answer. The reaction on Earth and elsewhere, once more led by the xenophobes, was not salutary.

To break the deadlock around the Twin Worlds of the Pitarian Dominion a radical improvement in weaponry or change in tactics was obviously required. But what?

The one development no one expected was that both would occur simultaneously and as a consequence of the same research, or that it would be the thranx who first hit upon the singular idea.

In addition to the cultural and diplomatic exchanges that had permeated relations between human and thranx since the time of first contact, there was a quiet but continuous exchange of scientific information. Discovering that the human interstellar KK-drive was more efficient than their own, the thranx promptly adopted and incorporated into their own vessels specific aspects of its design. Human engineers and researchers also benefited from the results of thousands of years of thranx research. Largely ignored and overlooked by their respective governments, as well as by the fanatics on both sides, the scientists went about their work in stolid, systematic fashion. Which is to say they mutually engaged in the monotonous, boring, dull, everyday work that constitutes the vast bulk of what ordinary people think of as science.

Space-minus communications delivered information and accepted cautious propositions. Arcane theories were debated and hypotheses scrutinized. Good things arose from these communications, though nothing very dramatic.

Until a small group of thranx physicists decided to broach an idea to a visiting party of human colleagues.

The engineers were on Hivehom to explain certain aspects of KK-drive manufacture to their thranx counterparts. They were practical men and women who were far more interested in application than theory. As such, they were bemused by the physicists' insistence; for that matter, so were their thranx counterparts.

It was left to a senior member of the local research group to make the presentation. Humans and thranx alike had gathered to hear him in the casual surroundings of an underground esplanade. Organized water spilled in a systematic, tranquil manner from the ceiling, suffusing the air with the music of its falling while saturating the circumscribed atmosphere of the sizable chamber with additional moisture. The thranx delighted in its feel. Wearing as little as mutual modesty would allow, their human visitors tolerated the incredible humidity as best they were able, having long since learned that working with the thranx on one of their worlds meant sweating not just while at work, but every minute of every day.

Couvinpasdar was aware of all the eyes on him, compound and single-lensed alike. He could not interpret many of the multitudinous human facial expressions but would not have been wrong in supposing that they were the fleshy equivalent of the progressive gestures of skepticism being propounded by his fellow thranx. While humans and hive members chatted in the increasingly convenient and maturing language of Symbo-speech, the young physicist set up the small image generator he had brought with him. When he was ready, he was forced to gesture and call for attention, so indifferent to his proposed presentation were the members of his audience.

"I extend gratefulness to all who have taken time from their busy schedules to grant me a few moments worthy of their contemplation, especially our visiting human friends, whom I know find the controlled climate here in the inner levels of the hive less than homelike." Perspiration pouring down their bodies, the watching, slightly impatient bipeds could only agree.

Activating the projector that was attuned to his voice patterns, Couvinpasdar walked around and occasionally through the images it generated as he spoke, pointing out specific details and occasionally using a truhand to manipulate them. Some of his audience granted him their full attention, while that of others wandered. Around them, unaware that an important demonstration of combat physics was being presented in their midst, thranx strolled and clicked and whistled in pairs or small groups. To one of the humans who also happened to be something of a historian, reflecting later on the demonstration, it was as if Robert Oppenheimer had exposed the design and schematics of the first atomic bomb on a busy day in New York's Central Park. Few of the busy, preoccupied thranx gave the unusual gathering more than a passing glance. Those who did look ignored the shifting, shimmering projection in favor of scrutinizing the loose-limbed, gangly bipeds.

"We have found that your kind are very good at conceptualizing basic scientific breakthroughs," Couvinpasdar was saying. One of the attendant humans murmured something, and a couple of her companions responded with soft coughing noises—human laughter, the young physicist knew. He did not let it distract him. "Thranx are very good at finding improvements in existing engineering and other practical applications that humans often overlook." No laughter this time.

"My research group has been studying the problem of how it

might be possible to break the defenses that surround the Pitar. Very early in our discussions we came to the conclusion that this could not be done with existing weapons, not as long as the Pitar match ship for ship. Furthermore, any vessel mounting a radical and potentially advantageous new weapon would immediately be set upon by the Pitar in all their strength. Therefore it was decided that any new weapon must also incorporate into its scheme and make use of a corresponding shift in strategy." The projection mutated.

Floating before the assembled audience was one of the smallest ships any of them had ever seen. It was, in fact, smaller than the lifeboats that were carried about most ships. But it was neither lifeboat nor repair vessel nor intership shuttle. There was the KK-drive field projection fan, severely shrunken and modified, and behind it—absurdly close behind it—the main body of the vessel. A single tiny weapons blister on a standard body-girdling belt ran around the median of the ship. Its diminutive size rendered it virtually inoffensive. Atop the craft was a structure that at first glance resembled a lifeboat launcher. In the context of the ship's ridiculously small size it struck several of the onlookers as a structural extravagance.

Speaking in a mixture of Low Thranx, Terranglo, and Symbospeech, Couvinpasdar elaborated on the design. "We call this a stingship. As you can see, it is quite an unpretentious design. It is designed to carry a crew of two: one human and one thranx." He indicated the locations on the schematic. "One here, and the other here, on opposite sides of the vessel. They are intended to complement, not back up, one another. To carry out its intended mission with maximum efficiency, the stingship is designed to be flown by two pilots operating in tandem."

"Doing what, *currukk*?" a thranx member of the audience inquired. "The vessel is too small to do any real damage. Even a small Pitarian or AAnn warship would easily blast it out of the sky." The questioner gestured at the center of the model. "It is not even large enough to generate its own defensive screen."

"The stingship relies on agility for its defense," Couvinpasdar replied.

"With a drive attenuated to that size," one of the humans pointed out, "the vessel is not capable of interstellar travel."

"It is not intended to be," the physicist explained. "Stingships are meant to be carried, in sizable numbers, in the holds of larger craft. Dreadnought-class ships, or preferably, a new class of vessels specially built for the purpose."

"How did you work out the physics of a KK-drive that size?" another of the humans wanted to know.

"Engineering on the subatomic level is an art among my colleagues," Couvinpasdar informed her. "However, the proposed stingship propulsion system is still not the smallest drive we have contemplated. This is."

So saying he ran his fingers through the projection. The stingship model gave way to something appreciably smaller. If it was another diminutive ship, several members of the audience felt, it would function well only as a joke.

"By the Final Tunnel," the senior thranx scientist in the gathering clicked, "what is *that* supposed to be?"

"Maybe it's a KK-drive powered coffin," one of the humans commented drily, "for commending bodies to space who want to say their final farewells to their surviving comrades in a great big hurry." This time the laughter, both human and thranx, was more general.

Couvinpasdar gestured polite acknowledgment of the amusement, but his tone did not change. "The KK-drive unit you see here is only theoretically possible. Something of this reduced size has never been brooded before, much less built." His blue-green, hard-shelled fingers shuffled within the projection. "This is not a ship. Fitted behind the miniature drive is a sizable thermonuclear device. As you can see, the drive-driven explosive fits into the launcher on top of the stingship. Because of size considerations, and to preserve the exceptional maneuverability of the two-person vessel, only one such device is carried by each craft."

Laughter had given way to contemplative quiet. "So the stingship, hypothetically avoiding the attention of an enemy's weapons systems, penetrates its defenses as far as possible before releasing or firing this drive-driven missile. What's to prevent the enemy from simply blowing it out of the void?"

"This is not a normal missile," the young thranx physicist reminded his questioner. "It is powered not by conventional propulsion systems, but by a KK drive. Furthermore, it is being launched from a craft that is itself KK-drive driven. Some shells may indeed be intercepted and destroyed." Subdued light glinted off enthusiastic compound eyes. "But imagine the effect of several thousand such weapons deployed simultaneously across a wide sphere of conflict. It would be impossible for an enemy to detect, far less predict and intercept, the course of every single incoming munition.

One of the thranx who had not yet spoken now ventured a question. "The defense screens generated by Pitarian ships are very good. At distance, they can disperse even the energy released by a fusion explosion."

Couvinpasdar efficiently adjusted the projection. Ship models vanished, to be replaced by more intimate schematics decorated with fancies of mathematics. "That is so, but the thermonuclear device that rides behind the drive is only part of the effectiveness of the system. Once the SCCAM shell detects a target, at a safe distance from its launching stingship so as not to compromise that vessel's drive field, its own field warps into deliberate and irrevocable overdrive. This means it will be attracted to the nearest gravity well of size. In this instance, that would be the corresponding drive field of the target vessel." His eyes roved his now very solemn and attentive audience from which all suggestion of humor had fled.

"The computations have been crunched many times, and the consequences are inescapable. No defensive screen known can resist the effect of a KK drive on overload. Impacting on the active field of an enemy vessel, the resultant sudden and excessive gravitational distortion would rend both asunder. At the very least its drive would be permanently disabled, rendering the ship unable to move and effectively helpless."

One of the humans had an objection. "Then all an enemy vessel has to do to avoid such a hazardous interaction is shut down its drive whenever closing stingships or these SCCAM shells are detected. Without a substantial gravity well to attract it, at combat distances the shells are likely to speed right on past."

Couvinpasdar gestured to indicate that this objection too had been anticipated. "Except that the shell's sensors have already locked in on the coordinates and course of the target. A ship's defensive screens are powered by its KK drive. Turn off the drive to eliminate the attracting gravity well, and you also lose your screens. With screens down, a ship is then open and vulnerable to the effects of the thermonuclear device carried by the SCCAM shell." He watched his audience for reaction. "By either means or both, the enemy is completely destroyed or is rendered incapable of further maneuvering."

A long, thoughtful pause followed before another of the thranx spoke up. "The system is not perfect. Their proposed exceptional maneuverability notwithstanding, some of these unscreened stingships will still encounter enemy fire that they cannot evade. Ships and pilots will be hit."

"Two crew per ship. A far more acceptable ratio than if even a single cruiser is lost."

The human woman who had first spoken had set aside her sarcasm. "Why one human and one thranx pilot? Why not two humans or two thranx?"

"Because research has shown that our minds and bodies work in different ways. Because under the duress of combat, studies prove that humans do certain things well and thranx other things better. Because we complement one another."

The assembled scientists fell to arguing. Some debated with quiet intensity while others clustered around Couvinpasdar, bombarding him with questions that arrived as fast as if they were propelled by downsized KK drives of their own. The discussion consumed the remainder of the day and ran on into and through the night, the majority of the group forgetting or disdaining to eat. By morning everyone was exhausted. But out of acrimony and skepticism and doubt had come hope.

Following the designs and delimitations of Couvinpasdar's research group, a single stingship was fabricated. Out at the testing station beyond a moon of Hivehom's largest gas giant, it was activated. It did not succumb to the peculiar distortions of space-plus, nor did it tear itself to pieces and kill its two pilots. Others were built, the inaugural design tightened and refined in the process.

The first symbiotically cached concussive armed missile was built. True to the predictions of Couvinpasdar and his associates, when its absurdly tiny drive system was sent into deliberate overload, the shell promptly threw itself at a drone target vessel programmed to avoid and escape. The drone did not. When their drive fields intersected, both ship and shell vanished in an entirely satisfactory and supernally bright dissolution of energy-encumbered particles. It was a very gratifying demonstration.

Couvinpasdar and his colleagues accepted the honors and commendations bestowed upon them by both thranx and human authorities with quiet grace—and in traditional thranx fashion, promptly returned to their work. Though they had earned and were entitled to a rest, they replied with an old thranx metaphor to the effect that "no burrow was ever finished."

Eight years after humankind had taken pleasure in its first contact with the imposing Pitar and three years following the destruction of the colony of Treetrunk, the commingled human-thranx armada once more threw its combined strength against the defenses surrounding the Twin Worlds of the Pitarian Dominion. But this time the probe by hundreds of capital warships was augmented by a prodigious swarm of tiny stingships each armed with a single self-propelled SCCAM shell.

Caught in the annihilation sphere of hundreds of explosive devices, or swept by devastating beams of coherent energy, dozens of stingships and their pilots evanesced out of existence, many before they even had a chance to launch their weapons. Dozens more accomplished their runs and were destroyed before they could escape.

But Pitarian warships found themselves riven and ruptured from the aftereffects of their own overloaded drives, while others switched off their fields and screens only to be annihilated by precision-targeted thermonuclear devices. On the opposite side of the sun from the Twin Worlds, the hitherto impenetrable defensive sphere protecting the Dominion began to implode under the unexpected new kind of assault. In the end it collapsed like a balloon. Once a single hole had been punctured in the curvature, the rest of the orb simply caved in.

MacCunn was not there to exhort his troops. The field marshal had died six months before, a victim of his failed digestive system, when the outcome of the conflict was as much in doubt as it had been when the first assault had been launched against the Twin Worlds. His friend and colleague Admiral Hyargas Yirghiz was present at the final Pitarian collapse, however. Standing before the main battle tridee on the bridge of the damaged but still very battle-worthy *Tamerlane*, he watched in silent satisfaction as the surviving stingships returned to their mothercraft and the main body of the armada advanced to within orbital bombardment range of both worlds.

After three years of struggle there was no wish among the attackers to annihilate the population. Different degrees of punishment to be applied as circumstances dictated had been worked out by the world council of humankind and the Grand Council of the thranx. All depended on how the Pitar reacted to their defeat.

They reacted as if they had not been defeated. From the surfaces of both planets, ground-based missiles fired from hardened launchers streaked upward toward the assembled invaders. A few did damage, but most were easily knocked down or brushed aside. One by one, their flight paths were tracked, traced, and the launching facilities destroyed. Small red flowers erupted on the surface of both the Twin Worlds, blossoms of nuclear death.

And still the Pitar fought on.

It was finally deemed necessary to land troops, an eventuality the senior officers had hoped to avoid. Unrelenting

Pitarian hostility left them with no choice. The thranx participated in this exercise only as observers. Their alliance with humankind did not extend to providing support for ground action. Thranx enough had died crewing ships of the armada, as well as aboard the tiny, seemingly insignificant but ultimately lethal stingships that had at last altered the course of battle.

To dispassionate observers the concluding consequences were inconceivable. The Pitar would not surrender. Every community was armed. Those who capitulated did so only as a convenience of deception, turning on and slaughtering their captors the instant the humans' guard was down. Even Pitarian progeny knew how to pick up and fire a small weapon or rush a pod of human soldiers with explosives strapped to their bodies.

Scientists wished to preserve at least a remnant of Pitarian civilization in hopes of being able to study and perhaps understand their rabid xenophobia. It proved impossible. Whenever cornered and weaponless, the Pitar always managed to find a way to kill themselves, if not their enemies. Remembering the atrocity of Treetrunk, individual human soldiers were not inclined to go out of their way to ensure the survival of any Pitar.

Still, through the use of stun guns, soporific gas, and other nonlethal weapons, a small number were captured alive. They refused to be studied. Noncooperative and virulent to the last, they turned on their captors when possible, committed suicide when they could not, or retreated into a kind of voluntary madness until their minds and bodies finally expired of natural causes.

In the end, three habitable but unpopulated worlds remained as a consequence of the conflict—one human, two Pitarian. They are not often visited.

The research teams that followed the departure of the armada gleaned what clues they could from the ruins of Pitarian civilization. What they found was not so much that the Pitar had been incontrovertible xenophobes as they had been irredeemable narcissists. Unable to countenance the ongoing existence of any intelligent life-form but their own, they had deliberately set out to steal as much knowledge as they could from humankind before turning on Earth and its colonies. Hivehom and the thranx would have been next, or possibly the inoffensive and blandly expansionist Quillp. But the Pitar had a problem.

Every other sentient species was capable of outbreeding them. Unlike humans or thranx, Pitarian females ovulated only once a year. It helped to explain why no children were present on any of the ships that visited Earth or its colony worlds, why none participated in any of the infrequent cultural exchange programs. The occasional Pitarian progeny was precious.

The stolen reproductive organs of the several thousand human females on Treetrunk who had been surgically eviscerated were found—floating in carefully maintained tank batteries, rank upon rank of disembodied uteruses, ovaries, and fallopian tubes. The eggs of human females were removed, their DNA modified; they were then inseminated with Pitarian sperm and were replaced—returned to their natural cavities to follow the "normal" progression of plenteous human pregnancy. Once sufficiently matured, each embryo was then removed and implanted in a suitable Pitarian female for the sole purpose of giving birth.

Surrogate mothership of Pitarian offspring by living human females, even if it had been proposed to and accepted by qualified women, was a thought no Pitar could countenance. So they attempted to thieve the organs and eggs they needed in hopes of enlarging the population of the Twin Worlds to the point where they could successfully challenge the more prolific species that infested an otherwise unpolluted galaxy. The complete destruction of Treetrunk had been carried out to mask their real intentions.

How awful for a noble Pitar to have to live in a cosmos swarming with lesser humans and thranx, Quillp and AAnn, Unop-Patha and other debased species. But having confined themselves to their two perfect worlds, they could not begin to cleanse their portion of the galaxy until they had significantly increased their numerical strength. It was decided that a naïve, biologically similar humankind would unknowingly provide the means. And might have, had not a single sullen and solitary human succeeded in escaping the holocaust with proof of what had taken place.

The armada was disbanded, its constituent vessels returning to Earth or to their respective colony worlds. The vast majority of surviving stingships were decommissioned—but not all. Mindful of the expanding empire of the AAnn, who had watched the conflict with the Pitar with pitiless, impenitent interest, an active fleet and its buttressing reserve was maintained. The thranx returned to their own interests.

Following an initial outpouring of human gratitude for the insectoids' assistance in defeating the Pitar, there came a gradual return to normalcy, to the business of living lives and devoting time to more insular concerns. Colonies continued to expand, and potential colonies continued to develop. Worlds such as Wolophon III and Amropolus that technically fell within the human sphere of exploration but were too redolent of greenhouse effect for human comfort were conceded to the busy thranx, while humankind's chitinous friends willingly turned over to the more cold-tolerant bipeds information on planets they found too frigid to conveniently accommodate their kind. Given an extensive technological effort, each species *could* colonize the other's preferred worlds, of course, but the mutual trade-off in climatological comfort zones made infinitely more sense. Interstellar distances being what they were, there was no real perception of one species intruding on the space of another.

The AAnn watched these developments unhappily. Unable to challenge the maturing human-thranx axis directly, they pondered less confrontational means of impeding the resolution of a deeper, stronger alliance. There were many ways of doing this, at which the insidiously artful AAnn were masters. Their advantage lay in the fact that a great many humans and thranx remained ultimately suspicious of one another, and of any expansion of intimate contact.

With a little luck, and much shrewd manipulation of opportune circumstances, sagacious AAnn nobles and their skillful xenologists felt it might even be possible to bring both transient allies into open conflict with one another.

The AAnn set to work.

Please turn the page for a sneak preview of the next Pip and Flinx novel by

Alan Dean Foster

REUNION

1

When bad people are chasing you, life is dangerous. When good people are chasing you, life is awkward. But when you are chasing yourself, the most simple facts of existence become disturbing, destabilizing, and a source of unending waking confusion.

So it was with Flinx, who in searching for the history of himself, found that he was once again treading upon the hallowed, mystic soil of the spherical blue-white womb among the stars that had given birth to his whole species. Only, the soil he was treading presently was being treated by those around him with something other than veneration, and a means of sourcing the information he hoped to uncover was still to be found.

Tacrica was a beautiful place in which to be discouraged. Sensitive to his frustration, Pip had been acting fidgety for days. An iridescent flutter of pleated pink-and-blue wings and lethal, diamond-backed body, she would rise from his shoulder to dart aimlessly about his head and neck before settling restlessly back down into her customary position of repose. As active as she was colorful, the mature female minidrag was the only thing he was presently wearing.

His nudity did not excite comment because every one of the other sun and water worshipers strolling or lying about on the seashore was similarly unclothed. In the human beach culture of 554 A.A., the superfluity of wearing clothing into the sea or along its edge had long been recognized. Protective sprays blocked harmful UV rays without damaging the skin, and frivolous, transitory painted highlights decorated bodies both attractive and past their prime. It was these often elaborate anatomical decorations that were the focus of admiring attention, and not the commonplace nakedness that framed them.

Flinx flaunted no such artificial enhancements, unless one counted the Alaspinian minidrag coiled around his neck and left shoulder. Such contemporary cultural accoutrements were as alien to him as the primeval grains of sand beneath his feet. Culturally as well as historically, he was an utter and complete stranger here. Nor was he comfortable among the throngs of people. With its still unsettled steppes and unexplored reaches, Moth, where he had grown up, was far more familiar to him. He was more at home in the jungles of Alaspin, or among the blind Sumacrea of Longtunnel, or even in the aggressive world-girdling rain forest of Midworld. Anyplace but here. Anywhere but Earth.

Yet it was to Earth he had finally come for a second time, in search of himself. All roads led to Terra, it was said, and it was as true for him as for anyone else. Beyond Earth, the United Church had placed a moral imperative lock, an elaborate Edict, on all information about the Meliorares, the society of renegade eugenicists responsible for whatever bastard mutation he had become. Travels and adventures elsewhere had left him with hints as to their doings, with fragmentary bits and pieces of knowledge that tantalized without satisfying. If he was ever going to unravel the ultimate secrets of his heritage, it was here.

Even so, he had been reluctant to come. Not because he was fearful of what he might find: He had long since matured beyond such fears. But because it was dangerous. Not only did *he* want to learn all the details of his origins: so did others. Because of contacts he had been compelled to make, the United Church was now aware of him as an individual instead of merely as an overlooked statistic in the scientific record. As high-ranking an official as thranx Counselor Second Druvenmaquez had taken a personal interest in the red-haired, bright-eyed young man Flinx had become. The novice beachgoer smiled to himself. He had left the irascible, elderly thranx on Midworld, slipping away quietly when the science counselor had been occupied elsewhere. When he eventually discovered that the singular young human had taken surreptitious flight, the venerable thranx would be irked. He would have to be satisfied with what little he had already learned, because neither his people nor anyone else would be able to track Flinx's ship, the *Teacher*, through space-plus.

Ever cautious, Flinx had decided for the moment to hew to the hoary principle that the best place to hide was in plain sight. What better place to do that than on one of the Commonwealth's twin world centers of government and religion, where he had come looking for information years ago? It was where he needed to be anyway, if he was ever going to find out the truth about himself. In addition to his burgeoning curiosity, there had come upon him in the past year a new sense of urgency. With the onset of full adulthood looming over him, he could feel himself changing, in slow and sometimes not-so-subtle ways. Each month, it seemed, brought a new revelation. He could not define all the changes, could not quarantine and assess every one of them, but their periodic nebulosity rendered them no less real. Something was happening to him, inside him. The self he had known since infancy was becoming something else.

He was scared. With no one to talk to, no one to confide in save a highly empathetic but nonsapient flying snake, he could look only to himself for answers—answers he had always wished for but had never been able to acquire. It was for those reasons he had taken the risk of coming back to Earth. If he was going to find what he needed to know, it lay buried somewhere deep within the immense volume of sheer accumulated knowledge that was one of the homeworld's greatest treasures.

But if he was *home*, as every human who came to Earth was supposed to be, then why did he feel so much like an alien? It bothered him now even more than it had when last he had visited here some five years ago.

He tried to wean himself from the troubling chain of thought. Belaboring the accumulated neuroses of twenty years would solve nothing. He was here on a fact-finding mission; nothing more, nothing less. It was important to focus his attention and efforts, not only in hopes of securing the information he sought, but in order to avoid the attention of the authorities. With the exception of the thranx Druvenmaquez and his underlings, who were specifically looking for him, what other agencies and individuals might also be interested in one Philip Lynx he did not know. It did not matter. Until he left the homeworld, a little healthy paranoia would help to preserve him—but not if he allowed his thoughts to float aimlessly, adrift in a distraught sea of incomplete memories and internal conflicts.

Of course, he might well secure answers to all the questions that tormented him by the simple expedient of turning himself in. Druvenmaquez or a specialist in some other relevant bureau would gladly take the plunge into the secrets of him. But once committed to such research, he would not be allowed to leave whenever it might please him. Guinea pigs had no bill of rights. Revealing himself might also expose him to the scrutiny of those he wished to avoid—the great trading houses, other private concerns, the possible remnants of certain heretical and outlawed societies, and others. Becoming a potentially profitable lab subject carried with it dangers of its own—a long, healthy, and happy future not necessarily being among them.

Somehow he had to discover himself *by* himself, without alerting to his presence the very authorities who might help alleviate his seemingly illimitable anxieties. And he had to do it quickly, before the changes he was experiencing threatened to overwhelm him.

For one thing, the unpredictable, skull-pounding headaches he had suffered from since childhood—the ones that caused blinding flashes of light behind his eyes—were growing worse, in intensity if not frequency. When and if it occurred, would he be able to tell the difference between a common headache and a cerebral hemorrhage? Would he be able to deal with the physical as well as the mental consequences of the changes he was undergoing? He needed answers to all the old questions about himself, as well as to the new ones, and he needed them soon.

Of all the billions of humans on all the settled worlds scattered across the vast length and breadth of the Commonwealth, no one could claim that "nobody understands me" with the depth of veracity of a tall young redhead named Phillip Lynx, who was called Flinx.

Before setting his small transfer craft down at the Nazca shuttleport north of Tacrica, he had spent much time in free space planning his approach to the grand library that was Earth. First he had tried accessing the Shell, the free and omnipresent information network that spanned the globe, from one of the numerous orbiting stations that circled the planet. Unsurprisingly, the small segment he was able to access from orbit had been devoid of all but the most fundamental, freely available birth information on the subject of himself—save for one small historical reference to the destruction of the outlawed Meliorare Society in 530, three years before his birth. That information was already known to him. For what he wanted, for data that was no doubt restricted, banned, or even under Church Edict, he would have to probe much deeper.

That meant accessing in person one of the intelligence hubs that sustained the Shell. The Commonwealth Church and Science hub on Bali would have been ideal, but presenting himself at a highly visible and tightly secured site that offered only restricted access to the general public would have been asking for trouble—especially since he had entered its corridors once before, seeking information then only on the specifics of his birth. Ignorant of how widely and well his current physical description might have been disseminated to local authorities, it behooved him while conducting his research on Terra to keep as low a profile as possible. That meant avoiding the most famous and closely monitored centers of research.

Names and faces from his past congealed in the mirror that was his memory. Did a padre named Namoto still roam the depths of Genealogy Sector on Bali? Was Counselor Second Joshua Jiwe still in charge of security there? And where might a certain lissome thranx named Sylzenzuzex be working these days? On the other side of the vast ocean that lapped against his feet, which humans called the Pacific, remembrances lay like driftwood on a beach, waiting to be reexamined. He forced all such thoughts from his mind. He could not afford to present himself at the entrance to Church science headquarters for a second time in five years. Like it or not, whatever research he chose to conduct would have to be done from afar.

Roaming the Shell from the comparative anonymity of the orbiting station, he had reduced the number of suitable hubs he might safely visit to three. From centers in the Terran provinces of Kalahari, Kandy, and Cuzco, he chose the Shell hub at Surire, on the western slope of the mountain range called Andes. On-site access to the physical core was naturally off-limits to all but qualified personnel. But as with many such impressive, meaningful facilities, tours of its outer, less sensitive areas were offered to the public. They were deemed educational.

Wanting ardently to be educated, Flinx had taken one such tour. As expected, internal security, to which the tour guide casually alluded, was conspicuous. To penetrate both the facility and the knowledge it hopefully contained, he would need help. In order to secure it, he for one of the few times in his life prepared to use his talent not simply to receive, but to project. To perceive, and to then act upon those perceptions. Previously, he had done so only to defend himself against those intending to do him harm.

This time it made him feel, well, dirty.